I0819433

THE ILIAD

SIGNATURE EDITIONS

THE ILIAD

HOMER

This 2026 edition published by Union Square & Co., LLC

A Note on the Text: This translation was originally published in 1898 and reflects the attitudes of its time. The publisher's decision to present it as it was first published is not intended as endorsement of any offensive cultural representations or language.

ISBN 978-1-4549-6131-4
ISBN 978-1-4549-6132-1 (e-book)

Union Square & Co. books may be purchased in bulk for business, educational, or promotional use. For more information, please contact your local bookseller or the Hachette Book Group's Special Markets department at special.markets@hbgusa.com.

Printed in India

2 4 6 8 10 9 7 5 3 1

unionsquareandco.com

CONTENTS

PREFACE

THE HEADMASTER OF ONE OF OUR FOREMOST PUBLIC SCHOOLS told me not long since that he had been asked what canons he thought it most essential to observe in translating from English into Latin. His answer was that in the first place the Latin must be idiomatic, in the second it must flow, and in the third it must keep as near as it could to the English from which it was being translated.

I said, "Then you hold that if either the Latin or the English must perforce give place, it is the English that should yield rather than the Latin?"

This, he replied, was his opinion; and surely the very sound canons above given apply to all translation. The genius of the language into which a translation is being made is the first thing to be considered; if the original was readable, the translation must be so also, or however good it may be as a construe, it is not a translation.

It follows that a translation should depart hardly at all from the modes of speech current in the translator's own times, inasmuch as nothing is readable, for long, which affects any other diction than that of the age in which it is written. We know the charm of the Elizabethan translations, but he who would attempt one that shall vie with these must eschew all Elizabethanisms that are not good Victorianisms also.

For the charm of the Elizabethans does not lie in their Elizabethanisms; these are but as the mosses and lichens which Time will grow upon our Victorian literature as surely as he has grown them upon the Elizabethan—upon such of it, at least, as has not been jerry-built. Shakespeare tells us that it is Time's glory to stamp the seal of time on aged things. No doubt; but he will have no hands stamp it save his own; he will rot an artificial ruin, but he will not glorify it; if he is to hallow any work it must be frankly secular when he deigns to take it in hand—by this I mean honestly after the manner of its own age and country. The Elizabethans probably knew this too well to know that they knew it, but whether they knew it or no they did not lard a crib with Chaucerisms and think that they were translating. They aimed fearlessly and without taint of affectation at making a dead author living to a generation other than his own. To do this they transfused their blood into his cold veins, and quickened him with their own livingness.

Then the life is theirs not his? In part no doubt it is so; but if they have loved him well enough, his life will have entered into them and possessed them. They will have given him of their life, and he will have paid them in their own coin. If, however, the mouth of the ox who treads out the corn may not be muzzled, and if there is to be a certain give and take between a dead author and his translator, it follows that a translator should be allowed greater liberty when the work he is translating belongs to an age and country widely remote from his own. For a poem's prosperity is like a jest's—it is in the ear of him that hears it. It takes two people to say a thing—a sayee as well as a sayer—and by parity of reasoning a poem's original audience and environment are integral parts of the poem itself. Poem and audience are as ego and nonego; they blend into one another. Change either, and some corresponding change, spiritual rather than literal, will be necessary in the other, if the original harmony between them is to be preserved.

Happily in the cases both of the *Iliad* and the *Odyssey* we can see clearly enough that the audiences did not differ so widely from ourselves as we might expect after an interval of some three thousand years. But they differ, especially in the case of the *Iliad*, and the difference necessitates a greater amount of freedom on the part of a translator than would be tolerable if it did not exist.

Freedom of another kind is further involved in the initial liberty of rendering in prose a work that was composed in verse. Prose differs from verse much as singing from speaking or dancing from walking, and what is right in the one is often wrong in the other. Prose, for example, does not permit that iteration of epithet and title, sometimes due merely to the requirements of meter, and sometimes otiose, which abounds in the *Iliad* without in any way disfiguring it. We look, indeed, for the iteration and enjoy it. We are never weary of being told that Juno is white-armed, Minerva gray-eyed, and Agamemnon king of men; but had Homer written in prose he would not have told us these things so often. Therefore, though frequently allowing common form epithets and titles to recur, I have not less frequently suppressed them.

Lest, however, the reader should imagine that I have departed from the letter of the *Iliad* more than I have, I will give the first fifty lines or so of the best prose translation that has yet been made—I mean that of Messrs. Leaf, Lang, and Myers, to which throughout my work I have been greatly indebted. Often have they saved me from error, and rarely have I found occasion to differ from them as to the meaning of a passage. I do not believe that I have translated a single paragraph without reference to them, but this said, a comparison of their opening paragraphs with my own will show the kind of way in which I differ from them as to the manner in which Homer should be translated.

Their translation (here, by Dr. Leaf) opens thus:

> Sing, goddess, the wrath of Achilles Peleus's son, the ruinous wrath that brought on the Achaians woes innumerable, and hurled down into Hades many strong souls of heroes, and gave their bodies to be a prey to dogs and all winged fowls; and so the counsel of Zeus wrought out its accomplishment

from the day when strife first parted Atreides king of men and noble Achilles.

Who then among the gods set the twain at strife and variance? Even the son of Leto and of Zeus; for he in anger at the king sent a sore plague upon the host, that the folk began to perish, because Atreides had done dishonour to Chryses the priest. For he had come to the Achaians' fleet ships to win his daughter's freedom, and brought a ransom beyond telling; and bare in his hands the fillet of Apollo the Far-darter upon a golden staff; and made his prayer unto all the Achaians, and most of all to the two sons of Atreus, orderers of the host: "Ye sons of Atreus and all ye well-greaved Achaians, now may the gods that dwell in the mansions of Olympus grant you to lay waste the city of Priam, and to fare happily homeward; only set ye my dear child free, and accept the ransom in reverence to the son of Zeus, far-darting Apollo."

Then all the other Achaians cried assent, to reverence the priest and accept his goodly ransom; yet the thing pleased not the heart of Agamemnon son of Atreus, but he roughly sent him away, and laid stern charge upon him, saying, "Let me not find thee, old man, amid the hollow ships, whether tarrying now or returning again hereafter, lest the staff and fillet of the god avail thee naught. And her will I not set free; nay, ere that shall old age come on her in our house, in Argos, far from her native land, where she shall ply the loom and serve my couch. But depart, provoke me not, that thou mayest the rather go in peace."

So said he, and the old man was afraid and obeyed his word, and fared silently along the shore of the loud-sounding sea. Then went that aged man apart and prayed aloud to King Apollo, whom Leto of the fair locks bare, "Hear me, god of the silver bow, that standest over Chryse and holy Killa, and rulest Tenedos with might, O Smintheus! If ever I built a temple gracious in thine eyes, or if ever I burnt to thee fat flesh of thighs of bulls or goats, fulfil

> thou this my desire; let the Danaans pay by thine arrows for my tears."
>
> So spake he in prayer, and Phoebus Apollo heard him, and came down from the peaks of Olympus wroth at heart, bearing on his shoulders his bow and covered quiver. And the arrows clanged upon his shoulders in his wrath, as the god moved; and he descended like to night. Then he sate him aloof from the ships, and let an arrow fly; and there was heard a dread clanging of the silver bow. First did he assail the mules and fleet dogs, but afterward, aiming at the men his piercing dart, he smote; and the pyres of the dead burnt continually in multitude.

I have given the foregoing extract with less compunction, by reason of the reflection, ever present with me, that not a few readers—nor these the least cultured—will prefer Dr. Leaf's translation to my own. Throughout my work I have taken the same kind of liberties as those that the reader will readily detect if he compares Dr. Leaf's rendering with mine. But I do not believe that I have anywhere taken greater ones. The difference between us in the prayer of Chryses, where Dr. Leaf translates "If ever I built a temple," etc., while I render "If ever I decked your temple with garlands," etc., is not a case in point, for it is due to my preferring Liddell and Scott's translation. I very readily admit that Dr. Leaf has in the main kept more closely to the words of Homer, but I believe him to have lost more of the spirit of the original through his abandonment (no doubt deliberate) of all attempt at stately, and at the same time easy, musical, flow of language, than he has gained in adherence to the letter—to which, after all, neither he nor any man can adhere.

These last words may suggest that I claim graces which Dr. Leaf has not attained. I can make no such claim. All I claim is to have done my best towards making the less sanguinary parts of the *Iliad* interesting to English readers. The more sanguinary parts cannot be made interesting; indeed I doubt whether they can ever have been so, or even been intended to be so, to a highly cultivated audience. They had to be written, and they were written; but it is clear that Homer often wrote them with impatience, and that actual warfare was as distasteful to him as it was foreign to his experience. Happily there is much less fighting in the *Iliad* than people generally think.

One word more and I have done. I have burdened my translation with as few notes[1] as possible, intending to reserve what I have to say about the *Iliad* generally for another work to be undertaken when my complete translation of the *Odyssey* has been printed. Lastly, the reception of my recent book, *The Authoress of the Odyssey*, has convinced me that the general reader much prefers the Latinized names of gods and heroes to those which it has of late years been attempted to popularize: I have no hesitation, therefore, in adhering to the nomenclature to which Pope, Mr. Gladstone, and Lord Derby have long since familiarized the public.[2]

SAMUEL BUTLER
August 8, 1898

1 Butler's sparse and not very helpful notes have been omitted.

2 The names of gods and goddesses have been changed back to the Greek.

PRINCIPAL PERSONAGES OF *THE ILIAD*, THEIR PARENTAGE, AND POSITION

GODS AND GODDESSES

ZEUS (Jupiter, Jove), son of Cronus (Saturn); king of the gods and ruler of the sky, arbiter of human destiny.

POSEIDON (Neptune), son of Cronus; king of the sea; favors the Greeks.

HADES, son of Cronus; ruler of the underworld of the dead.

HERA (Juno), daughter of Cronus and wife of Zeus; queen of the gods; favors the Greeks.

ATHENE (Minerva), daughter of Zeus; favors the Greeks.

APOLLO, son of Zeus and Leto; favors the Trojans.

ARTEMIS (Diana), daughter of Zeus and Leto; favors the Trojans.

APHRODITE (Venus), daughter of Zeus and Dione; favors the Trojans.

ARES (Mars), son of Zeus; favors the Trojans.

HEPHAESTUS (Vulcan), son of Zeus and Hera; favors the Greeks.

HERMES (Mercury), son of Zeus; favors the Trojans.

IRIS, messenger of the gods.

PAEËON, physician to the gods.

THETIS, a sea nymph, wedded to a mortal, Peleus; mother of Achilles.

GOD OF THE RIVER SCAMANDER, also called Xanthus; favors the Trojans.

PRINCIPAL PERSONAGES OF *THE ILIAD*

GREEKS, CALLED BY HOMER ACHAEANS, DANAANS, OR ARGIVES

AGAMEMNON, son of Atreus; king of Argos and Mycenae; leader of the host.

MENELAUS, son of Atreus and husband of Helen; king of Sparta, also called Lacedaemon.

ACHILLES, son of Peleus and the sea nymph Thetis, grandson of Aeacus, son of Zeus; chief of the Myrmidons from Phthia and Hellas.

NESTOR, son of Neleus; aged king of Pylus and Dorium; father of Antilochus and Thrasymedes.

ODYSSEUS (Ulysses), son of Laertes and husband of Penelope; king of Ithaca and leader of the Cephallenians.

AJAX, son of Telamon; ruler of Salamis.

AJAX, son of Oïleus; ruler of Locris.

DIOMED, son of Tydeus and grandson of Oeneus; king of Middle Argos, Tiryns, and Aegina.

IDOMENEUS, son of Deucalion and grandson of Minos, king of Crete.

TLEPOLEMUS, son of Heracles; from Rhodes.

PATROCLUS, son of Menoetius; comrade and squire of Achilles.

PHOENIX, son of Amyntor; foster son of Achilles's father and old friend of Achilles; ruler of the Dolopians in Phthia.

STHENELUS, son of Capaneus; comrade of Diomed.

MERIONES, son of Molus; comrade and squire of Idomeneus

ANTILOCHUS, son of Nestor.

TEUCER, illegitimate son of Telamon, half brother of the first Ajax; a bowman.

CALCHAS, son of Thestor; seer and interpreter of omens.

MACHAON, son of the healer Asclepius; physician to the Greeks.

THERSITES, ugliest of the Greek soldiers; an endless talker.

ASCALAPHUS, leader of the Miniae; son of Ares.

TALTHYBIUS AND EURYBATES, Greek heralds.

TROJANS

PRIAM, son of Laomedon and descendant of Tros, the founder of Troy, and of Dardanus, son of Zeus; king of Troy.
PARIS, also called Alexander, son of Priam; seducer of Helen.
HECTOR, son of Priam; commander of the Trojan army.
HELENUS, son of Priam; soothsayer for the Trojans.
DEÏPHOBUS AND LYCAON, sons of Priam.
ANTENOR, aged counselor to Priam and the Trojans.
SARPEDON, son of Zeus and Laodamia, grandson of Bellerophon; leader of the Lycians.
GLAUCUS, son of Hippolochus and grandson of Bellerophon; comrade and squire of Sarpedon.
AENEAS, son of Anchises and the goddess Aphrodite; leader of the Dardanians.
RHESUS, son of Eoneus; king of Thrace.
PANDARUS, son of Lycaon; chief of Telea, near Mount Ida.
POLYDAMAS, son of Panthoüs; Trojan warrior and councilor.
ARCHELOCHUS, LAODOCUS, AND ACAMAS, sons of Antenor.
DOLON, son of Eumedes; scout for the Trojans.
IDAEUS, Trojan herald.

WOMEN IN TROY

HECUBA, wife of Priam; queen of Troy.
HELEN, daughter of Tyndareus and wife of the Greek king Menelaus; brought by Paris to Troy.
ANDROMACHE, daughter of Aëtion, king of Cilicia; wife of Hector and mother of his little son, Astyanax.
LAODICE, daughter of Priam and Hecuba; wife of Helicaon, son of Antenor.
CASSANDRA, daughter of Priam and Hecuba.
THEANO, daughter of Cisseus and wife of Antenor; priestess of Athene.

SCENE OF THE ACTION

The plain before Troy, through which flows the river Scamander, also called Xanthus.

The camp of the Greeks around their black ships, which lie drawn up in a long row on the edge of the seashore.

The city of Troy, also called Ilium, on a height above the plain, with its citadel, called Pergamum.

The seat of the gods on Mount Olympus in northern Thessaly.

BOOK I

Agamemnon is compelled to restore the captive girl Chryseis to her father, but in retaliation takes from Achilles the lovely Briseis. Achilles, enraged, vows he will fight no more for Agamemnon and through his mother, the sea nymph Thetis, secures the aid of Zeus for the Trojans. This provokes the wrath of the goddess Hera.

Sing, O Goddess, the anger of Achilles, son of Peleus, that brought countless ills upon the Achaeans. Many a brave soul did it send hurrying down to Hades, and many a hero did it yield a prey to dogs and vultures, for so were the counsels of Zeus fulfilled from the day on which the son of Atreus, king of men, and great Achilles first fell out with one another.

And which of the gods was it that set them on to quarrel? It was the son of Zeus and Leto; for he was angry with the king and sent a pestilence upon the host to plague the people, because the son of Atreus had dishonored Chryses, his priest. Now Chryses had come to the ships of the Achaeans to free his daughter and had brought with him a great ransom. Moreover, he bore in his hand the scepter of Apollo wreathed with a suppliant's wreath, and he besought the Achaeans, but most of all, the two sons of Atreus, who were their chiefs.

"Sons of Atreus," he cried, "and all other Achaeans, may the gods who dwell in Olympus grant you to sack the city of Priam and to reach your homes in safety; but free my daughter and accept a ransom for her, in reverence to Apollo, son of Zeus."

On this the rest of the Achaeans with one voice were for respecting the priest and taking the ransom that he offered; but not so Agamemnon, who spoke fiercely to him and sent him roughly away. "Old man," said he, "let me not find you tarrying about our ships, nor yet coming hereafter. Your scepter of the god and your wreath shall profit you nothing. I will not free her. She shall grow old in my house at Argos far from her own home, busying herself with her loom and visiting my couch. So go, and do not provoke me or it shall be the worse for you."

The old man feared him and obeyed. Not a word he spoke, but went by the shore of the sounding sea and prayed apart to King Apollo whom lovely Leto had borne. "Hear me," he cried, "O god of the silver bow; that protectest Chryse and holy Cilla and rulest Tenedos with thy might, hear me, O thou of Sminthe! If I have ever decked your temple with garlands, or burned your thighbones in fat of bulls or goats, grant my prayer and let your arrows avenge these my tears upon the Danaans."

Thus did he pray, and Apollo heard his prayer. He came down furious from the summits of Olympus, with his bow and his quiver upon his shoulder, and the arrows rattled on his back with the rage that trembled within him. He sat himself down away from the ships with a face as dark as night, and his silver bow rang death as he shot his arrow in the midst of them. First he smote their mules and their hounds, but presently he aimed his shafts at the people themselves, and all day long the pyres of the dead were burning.

For nine whole days he shot his arrows among the people, but upon the tenth day Achilles called them in assembly—moved thereto by Hera, who saw the Achaeans in their death throes and had compassion upon them. Then, when they were got together, he rose and spoke among them.

"Son of Atreus," said he, "I deem that we should now turn roving home if we would escape destruction, for we are being cut down by war and pestilence at once. Let us ask some priest or prophet, or some reader of dreams (for dreams, too, are of Zeus) who can tell us why Phoebus Apollo is so angry, and say whether it is for some vow that we have broken, or hecatomb that we have not offered, and whether he will accept the savor of lambs and goats without blemish, so as to take away the plague from us."

With these words he sat down, and Calchas, son of Thestor, wisest of augurs, who knew things past present and to come, rose to speak. He it was who had guided the Achaeans with their fleet to Ilium, through the prophesyings with which Phoebus Apollo had inspired him. With all sincerity and goodwill he addressed them thus:

"Achilles, loved of heaven, you bid me tell you about the anger of King Apollo; I will therefore do so; but consider first and swear that you will stand by me heartily in word and deed, for I know that I shall offend one who rules the Argives with might, and to whom all the Achaeans are in subjection. A plain man cannot stand against the anger of a king who, if he swallow his displeasure now, will yet nurse revenge till he has wreaked it. Consider, therefore, whether or no you will protect me."

And Achilles answered: "Fear not, but speak as it is borne in upon you from heaven, for by Apollo, Calchas, to whom you pray, and whose oracles you reveal to us, not a Danaan at our ships shall lay his hand upon you while I yet live to look upon the face of the earth—no, not though you name Agamemnon himself, who is by far the foremost of the Achaeans."

Thereon the seer spoke boldly. "The god," he said, "is angry neither about vow nor hecatomb, but for his priest's sake, whom Agamemnon has dishonored, in that he would not free his daughter nor take a ransom for her. Therefore has he sent these evils upon us and will yet send others. He will not deliver the Danaans from this pestilence till Agamemnon has restored the girl without fee or ransom to her father and has sent a holy hecatomb to Chryse. Thus we may perhaps appease him."

With these words he sat down, and Agamemnon rose in anger. His heart was black with rage, and his eyes flashed fire as he scowled on Calchas and said: "Seer of evil, you never yet prophesied smooth things concerning me, but have ever loved to foretell that which was evil. You have brought me neither comfort nor performance; and now you come seeing among the Danaans, and saying that Apollo has plagued us because I would not take a ransom for this girl, the daughter of Chryses. I have set my heart on keeping her in my own house, for I love her better even than my own wife, Clytemnestra, whose peer she is alike in form and feature, in understanding and accomplishments. Still I will give her up if I must, for I would have the people live, not die; but you must find me a prize instead, or I alone among the Argives shall be without one. This is not well; for you behold, all of you, that my prize is to go elsewhither."

And Achilles answered: "Most noble son of Atreus, covetous beyond all mankind, how shall the Achaeans find you another prize? We have no common store from which to take one. Those we took from the cities have been awarded; we cannot disallow the awards that have been made already. Give this girl, therefore, to the god, and if ever Zeus grants us to sack the city of Troy we will requite you three and fourfold."

Then Agamemnon said: "Achilles, valiant though you be, you shall not thus outwit me. You shall not overreach and you shall not persuade me. Are you to keep your own prize, while I sit tamely under my loss and give up the girl at your bidding? Let the Achaeans find me a prize in fair exchange to my liking, or I will come and take your own, or that of Ajax or of Odysseus; and he to whomsoever I may come shall rue my coming. But of this we will take thought hereafter; for the present, let us draw a ship into the sea, and find a crew for her expressly; let us put a hecatomb on board, and let us send Chryseis also. Further, let some chief man among us be in command, either Ajax, or Idomeneus, or yourself, son of Peleus, mighty warrior that you are, that we may offer sacrifice and appease the anger of the god."

Achilles scowled at him and answered: "You are steeped in insolence and lust of gain. With what heart can any of the Achaeans do your bidding, either on foray or in open fighting? I came not warring here for any ill the Trojans had done me. I have no quarrel with them. They have not raided my cattle or my horses, or cut down my harvests on the rich plains of Phthia; for between me and them there is a great space, both mountain and sounding sea. We have followed you, Sir Insolence! for your pleasure, not ours—to gain satisfaction from the Trojans for your shameless self and for Menelaus. You forget this, and threaten to rob me of the prize for which I have toiled, and which the sons of the Achaeans have given me. Never when the Achaeans sack any rich city of the Trojans do I receive so good a prize as you do, though it is my hands that do the better part of the fighting. When the sharing comes, your share is far the largest, and I, forsooth, must go back to my ships, take what I can get and be thankful, when my labor of fighting is done. Now, therefore, I shall go back to Phthia; it will be much better for me to return home with my ships, for I will not stay here dishonored to gather gold and substance for you."

And Agamemnon answered: "Fly if you will, I shall make you no prayers to stay you. I have others here who will do me honor, and above all Zeus, the lord of counsel. There is no king here so hateful to me as you are, for you are ever quarrelsome and ill-affected. What though you be brave? Was it not heaven that made you so? Go home, then, with your ships and comrades to lord it over the Myrmidons. I care neither for you nor for your anger; and thus will I do: since Phoebus Apollo is taking Chryseis from me, I shall send her with my ship and my followers, but I shall come to your tent and take your own prize Briseis, that you may learn how much stronger I am than you are, and that another may fear to set himself up as equal or comparable with me."

The son of Peleus was furious, and his heart within his shaggy breast was divided whether to draw his sword, push the others aside, and kill the son of Atreus, or to restrain himself and check his anger. While he was thus in two minds, and was drawing his mighty sword from its scabbard, Athene came down from heaven (for Hera had sent her in the love she bore to them both), and seized the son of Peleus by his yellow hair, visible to him alone, for of the others no man could see her. Achilles turned in amaze, and by the fire that flashed from her eyes at once knew that she was Athene. "Why are you here," said he, "daughter of aegis-bearing Zeus? To see the pride of Agamemnon, son of Atreus? Let me tell you—and it shall surely be—he shall pay for this insolence with his life."

And Athene said: "I come from heaven, if you will hear me, to bid you stay your anger. Hera has sent me, who cares for both of you alike. Cease, then, this brawling, and do not draw your sword. Rail at him if you will, and your railing will not be vain, for I tell you—and it shall surely be—that you shall hereafter receive gifts three times as splendid by reason of this present insult. Hold, therefore, and obey."

"Goddess," answered Achilles, "however angry a man may be, he must do as you two command him. This will be best, for the gods ever hear the prayers of him who has obeyed them."

He stayed his hand on the silver hilt of his sword, and thrust it back into the scabbard as Athene bade him. Then she went back to Olympus among the other gods, and to the house of aegis-bearing Zeus.

But the son of Peleus again began railing at the son of Atreus, for he was still in a rage. "Winebibber," he cried, "with the face of a dog and the heart of a hind, you never dare to go out with the host in fight, nor yet with our chosen men in ambuscade. You shun this as you do death itself. You had rather go round and rob his prizes from any man who contradicts you. You devour your people, for you are king over a feeble folk; otherwise, son of Atreus, henceforward you would insult no man. Therefore I say, and swear it with a great oath—nay, by this my scepter, which shall sprout neither leaf nor shoot, nor bud anew from the day on which it left its parent stem upon the mountains—for the ax stripped it of leaf and bark, and now the sons of the Achaeans bear it as judges and guardians of the decrees of heaven—so surely and solemnly do I swear that hereafter they shall look fondly for Achilles and shall not find him. In the day of your distress, when your men fall dying by the murderous hand of Hector, you shall not know how to help them and shall rend your heart with rage for the hour when you offered insult to the bravest of the Achaeans."

With this the son of Peleus dashed his gold-bestudded scepter on the ground and took his seat, while the son of Atreus was beginning fiercely from his place upon the other side. Then uprose smooth-tongued Nestor, the facile speaker of the Pylians, and the words fell from his lips sweeter than honey. Two generations of men born and bred in Pylos had passed away under his rule, and he was now reigning over the third. With all sincerity and goodwill, therefore, he addressed them thus:

"Of a truth," he said, "a great sorrow has befallen the Achaean land. Surely Priam with his sons would rejoice, and the Trojans be glad at heart if they could hear this quarrel between you two, who are so excellent in fight and counsel. I am older than either of you; therefore be guided by me. Moreover, I have been the familiar friend of men even greater than you are, and they did not disregard my counsels. Never again can I behold such men as Pirithoüs and Dryas, shepherd of his people, or as Caeneus, Exadius, godlike Polyphemus, and Theseus, son of Aegeus, peer of the immortals. These were the mightiest men ever born upon this earth—mightiest were they, and when they fought the fiercest tribes of mountain savages they utterly overthrew them. I came from distant Pylos and went about among them, for they would have me come, and I fought as it was in me to do. Not a man now living could withstand them, but they heard my words, and were persuaded by them. So be it also with yourselves, for this is the more excellent way. Therefore, Agamemnon, though you be strong, take not this girl away, for the sons of the Achaeans have already given her to Achilles; and you, Achilles, strive not further with the king, for no man who by the grace of Zeus wields a scepter has like honor with Agamemnon. You are strong and have a goddess for your mother, but Agamemnon is stronger than you, for he has more people under him. Son of Atreus, check your anger, I implore you; end this quarrel with Achilles, who in the day of battle is a tower of strength to the Achaeans."

And Agamemnon answered: "Sir, all that you have said is true, but this fellow must needs become our lord and master: he must be lord of all, king of all, and captain of all, and this shall hardly be. Granted that the gods have made him a great warrior, have they also given him the right to speak with railing?"

Achilles interrupted him. "I should be a mean coward," he cried, "were I to give in to you in all things. Order other people about, not me, for I shall obey no longer. Furthermore I say—and lay my saying to your heart—I shall fight neither you nor any man about this girl, for those that take were those also that gave. But of all else that is at my ship you shall carry away nothing by force. Try, that others may see; if you do, my spear shall be reddened with your blood."

When they had quarreled thus angrily, they rose, and broke up the assembly at the ships of the Achaeans. The son of Peleus went back to his tents and ships with the son of Menoetius and his company, while Agamemnon drew a vessel into the water and chose a crew of twenty oarsmen. He escorted Chryseis on board and sent moreover a hecatomb for the god. And Odysseus went as captain.

These, then, went on board and sailed their ways over the sea. But the son of Atreus bade the people purify themselves; so they purified themselves and cast their filth into the sea. Then they offered hecatombs of bulls and goats without blemish on the seashore, and the smoke with the savor of their sacrifice rose curling up towards heaven.

Thus did they busy themselves throughout the host. But Agamemnon did not forget the threat that he had made Achilles and called his trusty messengers and squires, Talthybius and Eurybates. "Go," said he, "to the tent of Achilles, son of Peleus. Take Briseis by the hand and bring her hither; if he will not give her I shall come with others and take her—which will press him harder."

He charged them straightly further and dismissed them, whereon they went their way sorrowfully by the seaside, till they came to the tents and ships of the Myrmidons. They found Achilles sitting by his tent and his ships, and ill-pleased he was when he beheld them. They stood fearfully and reverently before him, and never a word did they speak, but he knew them and said: "Welcome, heralds, messengers of gods and men; draw near; my quarrel is not with you but with Agamemnon who has sent you for the girl Briseis. Therefore, Patroclus, bring her and give her to them, but let them be witnesses by the blessed gods, by mortal men, and by the fierceness of Agamemnon's anger, that if ever again there be need of me to save the people from ruin, they shall seek and they shall not find. Agamemnon is mad with rage and knows not how to look before and after that the Achaeans may fight by their ships in safety."

Patroclus did as his dear comrade had bidden him. He brought Briseis from the tent and gave her over to the heralds, who took her with them to the ships of the Achaeans—and the woman was loath to go. Then Achilles went all alone by the side of the hoar sea, weeping and looking out upon the boundless waste of waters. He raised his hands in prayer to his immortal mother. "Mother," he cried, "you bore me doomed to live but for a little season. Surely Zeus, who thunders from Olympus, might have made that little glorious. It is not so. Agamemnon, son of Atreus, has done me dishonor, and has robbed me of my prize by force."

As he spoke he wept aloud, and his mother heard him where she was sitting in the depths of the sea hard by the old man, her father. Forthwith she rose as it were a gray mist out of the waves, sat down before him as he stood weeping, caressed him with her hand, and said, "My son, why are you weeping? What is it that grieves you? Keep it not from me, but tell me, that we may know it together."

Achilles drew a deep sigh and said: "You know it; why tell you what you know well already? We went to Thebe, the strong city of Eëtion, sacked it, and brought hither the spoil. The sons of the Achaeans shared it duly among themselves, and chose lovely Chryseis as the meed of Agamemnon; but Chryses, priest of Apollo, came to the ships of the Achaeans to free his daughter, and brought with him a great ransom. Moreover, he bore in his hand the scepter of Apollo, wreathed with a suppliant's wreath, and he besought the Achaeans, but most of all the two sons of Atreus who were their chiefs.

"On this the rest of the Achaeans with one voice were for respecting the priest and taking the ransom that he offered; but not so Agamemnon, who spoke fiercely to him and sent him roughly away. So he went back in anger, and Apollo, who loved him dearly, heard his prayer. Then the god sent a deadly dart upon the Argives, and the people died thick on one another, for the arrows went everywhither among the wide host of the Achaeans. At last a seer in the fullness of his knowledge declared to us the oracles of Apollo, and I was myself first to say that we should appease him. Whereon the son of Atreus rose in anger, and threatened that which he has since done. The Achaeans are now taking the girl in a ship to Chryse, and sending gifts of sacrifice to the god; but the heralds have just taken from my tent the daughter of Briseus, whom the Achaeans had awarded to myself.

"Help your brave son, therefore, if you are able. Go to Olympus, and if you have ever done him service in word or deed, implore the aid of Zeus. Ofttimes in my father's house have I heard you glory in that you alone of the immortals saved the son of Cronus from ruin, when the others, with Hera, Poseidon, and Pallas Athene would have put him in bonds. It was you, goddess, who delivered him by calling to Olympus the hundred-handed monster whom gods call Briareus, but men Aegaeon, for he is stronger even than his father. When, therefore, he took his seat all-glorious beside the son of Cronus, the other gods were afraid, and did not bind him. Go, then, to him, remind him of all this, clasp his knees, and bid him give succor to the Trojans. Let the Achaeans be hemmed in at the sterns of their ships, and perish on the seashore, that they may reap what joy they may of their king, and that Agamemnon may rue his blindness in offering insult to the foremost of the Achaeans."

Thetis wept and answered: "My son, woe is me that I should have borne or suckled you. Would indeed that you had lived your span free from all sorrow at your ships, for it is all too brief; alas, that you should be at once short of life and long of sorrow above your peers. Woe, therefore, was the hour in which I bore you. Nevertheless I will go to the snowy heights of Olympus, and tell this tale to Zeus, if he will hear our prayer. Meanwhile stay where you are with your ships, nurse your anger against the Achaeans, and hold aloof from fight. For Zeus went yesterday to Oceanus to a feast among the Ethiopians, and the other gods went with him. He will return to Olympus twelve days hence. I will then go to his mansion paved with bronze and will beseech him, nor do I doubt that I shall be able to persuade him."

On this she left him, still furious at the loss of her that had been taken from him. Meanwhile Odysseus reached Chryse with the hecatomb. When they had come inside the harbor they furled the sails and laid them in the ship's hold. They slackened the forestays, lowered the mast into its place, and rowed the ship to the place where they would have her lie. There they cast out their mooring stones and made fast the hawsers. They then got out upon the seashore and landed the hecatomb for Apollo; Chryseis also left the ship, and Odysseus led her to the altar to deliver her into the hands of her father. "Chryses," said he, "King Agamemnon has sent me to bring you back your child, and to offer sacrifice to Apollo on behalf of the Danaans, that we may propitiate the god, who has now brought much sorrow upon the Argives."

So saying he gave the girl over to her father, who received her gladly, and they ranged the holy hecatomb all orderly round the altar of the god. They washed their hands and took up the barley meal to sprinkle over the victims, while Chryses lifted up his hands and prayed aloud on their behalf. "Hear me," he cried, "O god of the silver bow, that protectest Chryse and holy Cilla, and rulest Tenedos with thy might! Even as thou didst hear me aforetime when I prayed, and didst press hardly upon the Achaeans, so hear me yet again, and stay this fearful pestilence from the Danaans."

Thus did he pray, and Apollo heard his prayer. When they had done praying and sprinkling the barley meal, they drew back the heads of the victims and killed and flayed them. They cut out the thighbones, wrapped them round in two layers of fat, set some pieces of raw meat on the top of them, and then Chryses laid them on the wood fire and poured wine over them, while the young men stood near him with five-pronged spits in their hands. When the thighbones were burned and they had tasted the inward meats, they cut the rest up small, put the pieces upon the spits, roasted them till they were done, and drew them off: then, when they had finished their work and the feast was ready, they ate it, and every man had his full share, so that all were satisfied. As soon as they had had enough to eat and drink, pages filled the mixing bowl with wine and water and handed it round, after giving every man his drink offering.

Thus all day long the young men worshiped the god with song, hymning him and chanting the joyous paean, and the god took pleasure in their voices; but when the sun went down and it came on dark, they laid themselves down to sleep by the stern cables of the ship, and when the child of morning, rosy-fingered Dawn, appeared they again set sail for the host of the Achaeans. Apollo sent them a fair wind, so they raised their mast and hoisted their white sails aloft. As the sail bellied with the wind the ship flew through the deep blue water, and the foam hissed against her bows as she sped onward. When they reached the wide-stretching host of the Achaeans, they drew the vessel ashore, high and dry upon the sands, set her strong props beneath her, and went their ways to their own tents and ships.

But Achilles abode at his ships and nursed his anger. He went not to the honorable assembly, and sallied not forth to fight, but gnawed at his own heart, pining for battle and the war cry.

Now after twelve days the immortal gods came back in a body to Olympus, and Zeus led the way. Thetis was not unmindful of the charge her son had laid upon her, so she rose from under the sea and went through great heaven with early morning to Olympus, where she found the mighty son of Cronus sitting all alone upon its topmost ridges. She sat herself down before him, and with her left hand seized his knees, while with her right she caught him under the chin, and besought him, saying:

"Father Zeus, if I ever did you service in word or deed among the immortals, hear my prayer, and do honor to my son, whose life is to be cut short so early. King Agamemnon has dishonored him by taking his prize and keeping her. Honor him then yourself, Olympian lord of counsel, and grant victory to the Trojans, till the Achaeans give my son his due and load him with riches in requital."

Zeus sat for a while silent, and without a word, but Thetis still kept firm hold of his knees, and besought him a second time. "Incline your head," said she, "and promise me surely, or else deny me—for you have nothing to fear—that I may learn how greatly you disdain me."

At this Zeus was much troubled and answered: "I shall have trouble if you set me quarreling with Hera, for she will provoke me with her taunting speeches; even now she is always railing at me before the other gods and accusing me of giving aid to the Trojans. Go back now, lest she should find out. I will consider the matter, and will bring it about as you wish. See, I incline my head that you may believe me. This is the most solemn token that I can give to any god. I never recall my word, or deceive, or fail to do what I say, when I have nodded my head."

As he spoke, the son of Cronus bowed his dark brows, and the ambrosial locks swayed on his immortal head, till vast Olympus reeled.

When the pair had thus laid their plans, they parted—Zeus to his own house, while the goddess quitted the splendor of Olympus, and plunged into the depths of the sea. The gods rose from their seats, before the coming of their sire. Not one of them dared to remain sitting, but all stood up as he came among them. There, then, he took his seat. But Hera, when she saw him, knew that he and the old merman's daughter, silver-footed Thetis, had been hatching mischief, so she at once began to upbraid him. "Trickster," she cried, "which of the gods have you been taking into your counsels now? You are always settling matters in secret behind my back, and have never yet told me, if you could help it, one word of your intentions."

"Hera," replied the sire of gods and men, "you must not expect to be informed of all my counsels. You are my wife, but you would find it hard to understand them. When it is proper for you to hear, there is no one, god or man, who will be told sooner, but when I mean to keep a matter to myself, you must not pry nor ask questions."

"Dread son of Cronus," answered Hera, "what are you talking about? I? Pry and ask questions? Never. I let you have your own way in everything. Still, I have a strong misgiving that the old merman's daughter Thetis has been talking you over, for she was with you and had hold of your knees this selfsame morning. I believe, therefore, that you have been promising her to give glory to Achilles, and to kill much people at the ships of the Achaeans."

"Wife," said Zeus, "I can do nothing but you suspect me and find it out. You will take nothing by it, for I shall only dislike you the more, and it will go harder with you. Granted that it is as you say; I mean to have it so. Sit down and hold your tongue as I bid you, for if I once begin to lay my hands about you, though all heaven were on your side it would profit you nothing."

On this Hera was frightened, so she curbed her stubborn will and sat down in silence. But the heavenly beings were disquieted throughout the house of Zeus, till the cunning workman Hephaestus began to try and pacify his mother Hera. "It will be intolerable," said he, "if you two fall to wrangling and setting heaven in an uproar about a pack of mortals. If such ill counsels are to prevail, we shall have no pleasure at our banquet. Let me then advise my mother—and she must herself know that it will be better—to make friends with my dear father Zeus, lest he again scold her and disturb our feast. If the Olympian Thunderer wants to hurl us all from our seats, he can do so, for he is far the strongest, so give him fair words, and he will then soon be in a good humor with us."

As he spoke, he took a double cup of nectar and placed it in his mother's hand. "Cheer up, my dear mother," said he, "and make the best of it. I love you dearly, and should be very sorry to see you get a thrashing; however grieved I might be, I could not help you, for there is no standing against Zeus. Once before when I was trying to help you, he caught me by the foot and flung me from the heavenly threshold. All day long from morn till eve, was I falling, till at sunset I came to ground in the island of Lemnos, and there I lay, with very little life left in me, till the Sintians came and tended me."

Hera smiled at this, and as she smiled she took the cup from her son's hands. Then Hephaestus drew sweet nectar from the mixing bowl, and served it round among the gods, going from left to right; and the blessed gods laughed out a loud applause as they saw him bustling about the heavenly mansion.

Thus through the livelong day to the going down of the sun they feasted, and everyone had his full share, so that all were satisfied. Apollo struck his lyre, and the Muses lifted up their sweet voices, calling and answering one another. But when the sun's glorious light had faded, they went home to bed, each in his own abode, which lame Hephaestus with his consummate skill had fashioned for them. So Zeus, the Olympian lord of thunder, hied him to the bed in which he always slept; and when he had got on to it he went to sleep, with Hera of the golden throne by his side.

BOOK II

Zeus, keeping his promise, tricks Agamemnon with a false dream into imagining he can capture Troy at once. Agamemnon craftily tests the spirit of his men by telling them that Zeus has bidden him give up the siege. Athene, sent by Hera, inspires Odysseus to oppose the plan, and with Nestor he incites the host to continue the struggle. Both armies muster for battle. Their chiefs and forces are counted.

Now the other gods and the armed Warriors on the Plain slept soundly, but Zeus was wakeful, for he was thinking how to do honor to Achilles and destroy much people at the ships of the Achaeans. In the end he deemed it would be best to send a lying dream to King Agamemnon. So he called one to him and said to it: "Lying Dream, go to the ships of the Achaeans, into the tent of Agamemnon, and say to him word for word as I now bid you. Tell him to get the Achaeans instantly under arms, for he shall take Troy. There are no longer divided counsels among the gods. Hera has brought them to her own mind, and woe betides the Trojans."

The dream went when it had heard its message, and soon reached the ships of the Achaeans. It sought Agamemnon, son of Atreus, and found him in his tent, wrapped in a profound slumber. It hovered over his head in the likeness of Nestor, son of Neleus, whom Agamemnon honored above all his councilors, and said:

"You are sleeping, son of Atreus; one who has the welfare of his host and so much other care upon his shoulders should dock his sleep. Hear me at once, for I come as a messenger from Zeus, who, though he be not near, yet takes thought for you and pities you. He bids you get the Achaeans instantly under arms, for you shall take Troy. There are no longer divided counsels among the gods; Hera has brought them over to her own mind, and woe betides the Trojans at the hands of Zeus. Remember this, and when you wake see that it does not escape you."

The dream then left him, and he thought of things that were surely not to be accomplished. He thought that on that same day he was to take the city of Priam, but he little knew what was in the mind of Zeus, who had many another hard-fought fight in store alike for Danaans and Trojans. Then presently he woke, with the divine message still ringing in his ears; so he sat upright, and put on his soft shirt so fair and new, and over this his heavy cloak. He bound his sandals on to his comely feet, and slung his silver-studded sword about his shoulders; then he took the imperishable staff of his father and sallied forth to the ships of the Achaeans.

The goddess Dawn now wended her way to vast Olympus that she might herald day to Zeus and to the other immortals, and Agamemnon sent the criers round to call the people in assembly; so they called them and the people gathered thereon. But first he summoned a meeting of the elders at the ship of Nestor, king of Pylos, and when they were assembled he laid a cunning counsel before them.

"My friends," said he, "I have had a dream from heaven in the dead of night, and its face and figure resembled none but Nestor's. It hovered over my head and said: 'You are sleeping, son of Atreus; one who has the welfare of his host and so much other care upon his shoulders should dock his sleep. Hear me at once, for I am a messenger from Zeus, who, though he be not near, yet takes thought for you and pities you. He bids you get the Achaeans instantly under arms, for you shall take Troy. There are no longer divided counsels among the gods; Hera has brought them over to her own mind, and woe betides the Trojans at the hands of Zeus. Remember this.' The dream then vanished and I awoke. Let us now, therefore, arm the sons of the Achaeans. But it will be well that I should first sound them, and to this end I will tell them to fly with their ships; but do you others go about among the host and prevent their doing so."

He then sat down, and Nestor, the prince of Pylos, with all sincerity and goodwill addressed them thus: "My friends," said he, "princes and councilors of the Argives, if any other man of the Achaeans had told us of this dream we should have declared it false, and would have had nothing to do with it. But he who has seen it is the foremost man among us; we must therefore set about getting the people under arms."

With this he led the way from the assembly, and the other sceptered kings rose with him in obedience to the word of Agamemnon; but the people pressed forward to hear. They swarmed like bees that sally from some hollow cave and flit in countless throng among the spring flowers, bunched in knots and clusters; even so did the mighty multitude pour from ships and tents to the assembly, and range themselves upon the wide-watered shore, while among them ran Wildfire Rumor, messenger of Zeus, urging them ever to the fore. Thus they gathered in a pell-mell of mad confusion, and the earth groaned under the tramp of men as the people sought their places. Nine heralds went crying about among them to stay their tumult and bid them listen to the kings, till at last they were got into their several places and ceased their clamor. Then King Agamemnon rose, holding his scepter. This was the work of Hephaestus, who gave it to Zeus, the son of Cronus. Zeus gave it to Hermes, slayer of Argus, guide and guardian. King Hermes gave it to Pelops, the mighty charioteer, and Pelops to Atreus, shepherd of his people. Atreus, when he died, left it to Thyestes, rich in flocks, and Thyestes in his turn left it to be borne by Agamemnon, that he might be lord of all Argos and of the isles. Leaning, then, on his scepter, he addressed the Argives.

"My friends," he said, "heroes, servants of Ares, the hand of heaven has been laid heavily upon me. Cruel Zeus gave me his solemn promise that I should sack the city of Priam before returning, but he has played me false, and is now bidding me go ingloriously back to Argos with the loss of much people. Such is the will of Zeus, who has laid many a proud city in the dust, as he will yet lay others, for his power is above all. It will be a sorry tale hereafter that an Achaean host, at once so great and valiant, battled in vain against men fewer in number than themselves; but as yet the end is not in sight. Think that the Achaeans and Trojans have sworn to a solemn covenant, and that they have each been numbered—the Trojans by the roll of their householders, and we by companies of ten; think further that each of our companies desired to have a Trojan householder to pour out their wine; we are so greatly more in number that full many a company would have to go without its cupbearer. But they have in the town many allies from other places, and it is these that hinder me from being able to sack the rich city of Ilium. Nine of Zeus's years are gone. The timbers of our ships have rotted; their tackling is sound no longer. Our wives and little ones at home look anxiously for our coming, but the work that we came hither to do has not been done. Now, therefore, let us all do as I say: let us sail back to our own land, for we shall not take Troy."

With these words he moved the hearts of the multitude, so many of them as knew not the cunning counsel of Agamemnon. They surged to and fro like the waves of the Icarian Sea, when the east and south winds break from heaven's clouds to lash them; or as when the west wind sweeps over a field of corn and the ears bow beneath the blast, even so were they swayed as they flew with loud cries towards the ships, and the dust from under their feet rose heavenward. They cheered each other on to draw the ships into the sea; they cleared the channels in front of them; they began taking away the stays from underneath them, and the welkin rang with their glad cries, so eager were they to return.

Then surely the Argives would have returned after a fashion that was not fated. But Hera said to Athene, "Alas, daughter of aegis-bearing Zeus, unweariable, shall the Argives fly home to their own land over the broad sea, and leave Priam and the Trojans the glory of still keeping Helen, for whose sake so many of the Achaeans have died at Troy, far from their homes? Go about at once among the host, and speak fairly to them, man by man, that they draw not their ships into the sea."

Athene was not slack to do her bidding. Down she darted from the topmost summits of Olympus, and in a moment she was at the ships of the Achaeans. There she found Odysseus, peer of Zeus in counsel, standing alone. He had not as yet laid a hand upon his ship, for he was grieved and sorry; so she went close up to him and said, "Odysseus, noble son of Laertes, are you going to fling yourselves into your ships, and be off home to your own land in this way? Will you leave Priam and the Trojans the glory of still keeping Helen, for whose sake so many of the Achaeans have died at Troy, far from their homes? Go about at once among the host, and speak fairly to them, man by man, that they draw not their ships into the sea."

Odysseus knew the voice as that of the goddess: he flung his cloak from him and set off to run. His servant Eurybates, a man of Ithaca, who waited on him, took charge of the cloak, whereon Odysseus went straight up to Agamemnon and received from him his ancestral, imperishable staff. With this he went about among the ships of the Achaeans.

Whenever he met a king or chieftain, he stood by him and spoke him fairly. "Sir," said he, "this flight is cowardly and unworthy. Stand to your post, and bid your people also keep their places. You do not yet know the full mind of Agamemnon; he was sounding us, and ere long will visit the Achaeans with his displeasure. We were not all of us at the council to hear what he then said. See to it lest he be angry and do us a mischief; for the pride of kings is great, and the hand of Zeus is with them."

But when he came across any common man who was making a noise, he struck him with his staff and rebuked him, saying: "Sirrah, hold your peace, and listen to better men than yourself. You are a coward and no soldier; you are nobody either in fight or council; we cannot all be kings; it is not well that there should be many masters; one man must be supreme—one king to whom the son of scheming Cronus has given the scepter of sovereignty over you all."

Thus masterfully did he go about among the host, and the people hurried back to the council from their tents and ships with a sound as the thunder of surf when it comes crashing down upon the shore, and all the sea is in an uproar.

The rest now took their seats and kept to their own several places, but Thersites still went on wagging his unbridled tongue—a man of many words, and those unseemly; a monger of sedition, a railer against all who were in authority, who cared not what he said, so that he might set the Achaeans in a laugh. He was the ugliest man of all those that came before Troy—bandy-legged, lame of one foot, with his two shoulders rounded and hunched over his chest. His head ran up to a point, but there was little hair on the top of it. Achilles and Odysseus hated him worst of all, for it was with them that he was most wont to wrangle. Now, however, with a shrill squeaky voice he began heaping his abuse on Agamemnon. The Achaeans were angry and disgusted, yet nonetheless he kept on brawling and bawling at the son of Atreus.

"Agamemnon," he cried, "what ails you now, and what more do you want? Your tents are filled with bronze and with fair women, for whenever we take a town we give you the pick of them. Would you have yet more gold, which some Trojan is to give you as a ransom for his son, when I or another Achaean has taken him prisoner? Or is it some young girl to hide away and lie with? It is not well that you, the ruler of the Achaeans, should bring them into such misery. Weakling cowards, women rather than men, let us sail home, and leave this fellow here at Troy to stew in his own meeds of honor, and discover whether we were of any service to him or no. Achilles is a much better man than he is, and see how he has treated him—robbing him of his prize and keeping it himself. Achilles takes it meekly and shows no fight; if he did, son of Atreus, you would never again insult him."

Thus railed Thersites, but Odysseus at once went up to him and rebuked him sternly. "Check your glib tongue, Thersites," said he, "and babble not a word further. Chide not with princes when you have none to back you. There is no viler creature come before Troy with the sons of Atreus. Drop this chatter about kings, and neither revile them nor keep harping about going home. We do not yet know how things are going to be, nor whether the Achaeans are to return with good success or evil. How dare you gibe at Agamemnon because the Danaans have awarded him so many prizes? I tell you, therefore—and it shall surely be—that if I again catch you talking such nonsense, I will either forfeit my own head and be no more called father of Telemachus, or I will take you, strip you stark naked, and whip you out of the assembly till you go blubbering back to the ships."

On this he beat him with his staff about the back and shoulders till he dropped and fell a-weeping. The golden scepter raised a bloody weal on his back, so he sat down frightened and in pain, looking foolish as he wiped the tears from his eyes. The people were sorry for him, yet they laughed heartily, and one would turn to his neighbor, saying: "Odysseus has done many a good thing ere now in fight and council, but he never did the Argives a better turn than when he stopped this fellow's mouth from prating further. He will give the kings no more of his insolence."

Thus said the people. Then Odysseus rose, scepter in hand, and Athene in the likeness of a herald bade the people be still, that those who were far off might hear him and consider his counsel. He therefore with all sincerity and goodwill addressed them thus:

"King Agamemnon, the Achaeans are for making you a byword among all mankind. They forget the promise they made you when they set out from Argos, that you should not return till you had sacked the town of Troy, and, like children or widowed women, they murmur and would set off homeward. True it is that they have had toil enough to be disheartened. A man chafes at having to stay away from his wife even for a single month, when he is on shipboard, at the mercy of wind and sea, but it is now nine long years that we have been kept here. I cannot, therefore, blame the Achaeans if they turn restive. Still we shall be shamed if we go home empty after so long a stay—therefore, my friends, be patient yet a little longer that we may learn whether the prophesyings of Calchas were false or true.

"All who have not since perished must remember as though it were yesterday or the day before, how the ships of the Achaeans were detained in Aulis when we were on our way hither to make war on Priam and the Trojans. We were ranged round about a fountain offering hecatombs to the gods upon their holy altars, and there was a fine plane tree from beneath which there welled a stream of pure water. Then we saw a prodigy; for Zeus sent a fearful serpent out of the ground, with blood-red stains upon its back, and it darted from under the altar on to the plane tree. Now there was a brood of young sparrows, quite small, upon the topmost bough, peeping out from under the leaves, eight in all, and their mother that hatched them made nine. The serpent ate the poor cheeping things, while the old bird flew about lamenting her little ones; but the serpent threw his coils about her and caught her by the wing as she was screaming. Then, when he had eaten both the sparrow and her young, the god who had sent him made him become a sign; for the son of scheming Cronus turned him into stone, and we stood there wondering at that which had come to pass. Seeing, then, that such a fearful portent had broken in upon our hecatombs, Calchas forthwith declared to us the oracles of heaven. 'Why, Achaeans,' said he, 'are you thus speechless? Zeus has sent us this sign, long in coming, and long ere it be fulfilled, though its fame shall last forever. As the serpent ate the eight fledglings and the sparrow that hatched them, which makes nine, so shall we fight nine years at Troy, but in the tenth shall take the town.' This was what he said, and now it is all coming true. Stay here, therefore, all of you, till we take the city of Priam."

On this the Argives raised a shout till the ships rang again with the uproar. Nestor, knight of Gerene, then addressed them. "Shame on you," he cried, "to stay talking here like children when you should fight like men. Where are our covenants now, and where the oaths that we have taken? Shall our counsels be flung into the fire, with our drink offerings and the right hands of fellowship wherein we have put our trust? We waste our time in words, and for all our talking here shall be no further forward. Stand, therefore, son of Atreus, by your own steadfast purpose. Lead the Argives on to battle, and leave this handful of men to rot, who scheme, and scheme in vain, to get back to Argos ere they have learned whether Zeus be true or a liar. For the mighty son of Cronus surely promised that we should succeed, when we Argives set sail to bring death and destruction upon the Trojans. He showed us favorable signs by flashing his lightning on our right hands. Therefore let none make haste to go till he has first lain with the wife of some Trojan and avenged the toil and sorrow that he has suffered for the sake of Helen. Nevertheless, if any man is in such haste to be at home again, let him lay his hand to his ship that he may meet his doom in the sight of all. But, O king, consider and give ear to my counsel, for the word that I say may not be neglected lightly. Divide your men, Agamemnon, into their several tribes and clans, that clans and tribes may stand by and help one another. If you do this, and if the Achaeans obey you, you will find out who, both chiefs and peoples, are brave, and who are cowards; for they will vie one against the other. Thus you shall also learn whether it is through the counsel of heaven or the cowardice of man that you shall fail to take the town."

And Agamemnon answered: "Nestor, you have again outdone the sons of the Achaeans in counsel. Would, by Father Zeus, Athene, and Apollo, that I had among them ten more such councilors, for the city of King Priam would then soon fall beneath our hands, and we should sack it. But the son of Cronus afflicts me with bootless wrangling and strife. Achilles and I are quarreling about this girl, in which matter I was the first to offend; if we can be of one mind again, the Trojans will not stave off destruction for a day. Now, therefore, get your morning meal, that our hosts may join in fight. Whet well your spears, see well to the ordering of your shields, give good feeds to your horses, and look your chariots carefully over, that we may do battle the livelong day; for we shall have no rest, not for a moment, till night falls to part us.

The bands that bear your shields shall be wet with the sweat upon your shoulders, your hands shall weary upon your spears, your horses shall steam in front of your chariots, and if I see any man shirking the fight, or trying to keep out of it at the ships, there shall be no help for him, but he shall be a prey to dogs and vultures."

Thus he spoke, and the Achaeans roared applause. As when the waves run high before the blast of the south wind and break on some lofty headland, dashing against it and buffeting it without ceasing as the storms from every quarter drive them, even so did the Achaeans rise and hurry in all directions to their ships. There they lighted their fires at their tents and got dinner, offering sacrifice every man to one or other of the gods, and praying each one of them that he might live to come out of the fight. Agamemnon, king of men, sacrificed a fat five-year-old bull to the mighty son of Cronus, and invited the princes and elders of his host. First he asked Nestor and King Idomeneus, then the two Ajaxes and the son of Tydeus, and sixthly, Odysseus, peer of gods in counsel; but Menelaus came of his own accord, for he knew how busy his brother then was. They stood round the bull with the barley meal in their hands, and Agamemnon prayed, saying: "Zeus, most glorious, supreme, that dwellest in heaven, and ridest upon the storm cloud, grant that the sun may not go down nor the night fall till the palace of Priam is laid low, and its gates are consumed with fire. Grant that my sword may pierce the shirt of Hector about his heart, and that full many of his comrades may bite the dust as they fall dying round him."

Thus he prayed, but the son of Cronus would not fulfill his prayer. He accepted the sacrifice, yet nonetheless increased their toil continually. When they had done praying and sprinkling the barley meal upon the victim, they drew back its head, killed it, and then flayed it. They cut out the thighbones, wrapped them round in two layers of fat, and set pieces of raw meat on the top of them. These they burned upon the split logs of firewood, but they spitted the inward meats and held them in the flames to cook. When the thighbones were burned, and they had tasted the inward meats, they cut the rest up small, put the pieces upon spits, roasted them till they were done, and drew them off; then, when they had finished their work and the feast was ready, they ate it, and every man had his full share, so that all were satisfied. As soon as they had had enough to eat and drink, Nestor, knight of Gerene, began to speak. "King Agamemnon," said he, "let us not stay talking here, nor be slack in the work that heaven has put into our hands. Let the heralds summon the people to gather at their several ships. We will then go about among the host, that we may begin fighting at once."

Thus did he speak, and Agamemnon heeded his words. He at once sent the criers round to call the people in assembly. So they called them, and the people gathered thereon. The chiefs about the son of Atreus chose their men and marshaled them, while Athene went among them holding her priceless aegis that knows neither age nor death. From it there waved a hundred tassels of pure gold, all deftly woven, and each one of them worth a hundred oxen. With this she darted furiously everywhere among the hosts of the Achaeans, urging them forward, and putting courage into the heart of each, so that he might fight and do battle without ceasing. Thus war became sweeter in their eyes even than returning home in their ships. As when some great forest fire is raging upon a mountain top and its light is seen afar, even so as they marched the gleam of their armor flashed up into the firmament of heaven.

They were like great flocks of geese, or cranes, or swans on the plain about the waters of Cayster, that wing their way hither and thither, glorying in the pride of flight, and crying as they settle till the fen is alive with their screaming. Even thus did their tribes pour from ships and tents on to the plain of the Scamander, and the ground rang as brass under the feet of men and horses. They stood as thick upon the flower-bespangled field as leaves that bloom in summer.

As countless swarms of flies buzz around a herdsman's homestead in the time of spring when the pails are drenched with milk, even so did the Achaeans swarm on to the plain to charge the Trojans and destroy them.

The chiefs disposed their men this way and that before the fight began, drafting them out as easily as goatherds draft their flocks when they have got mixed while feeding; and among them went King Agamemnon, with a head and face like Zeus, the lord of thunder, a waist like Ares, and a chest like that of Poseidon. As some great bull that lords it over the herds upon the plain, even so did Zeus make the son of Atreus stand peerless among the multitude of heroes.

And now, O Muses, dwellers in the mansions of Olympus, tell me—for you are goddesses and are in all places so that you see all things, while we know nothing but by report—who were the chiefs and princes of the Danaans? As for the common soldiers, they were so many that I could not name every single one of them though I had ten tongues, and though my voice failed not and my heart were of bronze within me, unless you, O Olympian Muses, daughters of aegis-bearing Zeus, were to recount them to me. Nevertheless, I will tell the captains of the ships and all the fleet together.

Peneleos, Leïtus, Arcesilaus, Prothoënor, and Clonius were captains of the Boeotians. These were they that dwelt in Hyria and rocky Aulis, and who held Schoenus, Scolus, and the highlands of Eteonus, with Thespeia, Graia, and the fair city of Mycalessus. They also held Harma, Eilesium, and Erythrae; and they had Eleon, Hyle, and Peteon; Ocalea and the strong fortress of Medeon; Copae, Eutresis, and Thisbe, the haunt of doves; Coronea, and the pastures of Haliartus; Plataea and Glisas; the fortress of Thebes the less; holy Onchestus with its famous grove of Neptune; Arne rich in vineyards; Midea, sacred Nisa, and Anthedon upon the sea. From these there came fifty ships, and in each there were a hundred and twenty young men of the Boeotians.

Ascalaphus and Ialmenus, sons of Ares, led the people that dwelt in Aspledon and Orchomenus, the realm of Minyas. Astyoche, a noble maiden, bore them in the house of Actor, son of Azeus; for she had gone with Ares secretly into an upper chamber, and he had lain with her. With these there came thirty ships.

The Phoceans were led by Schedius and Epistrophus, sons of mighty Iphitus, the son of Naubolus. These were they that held Cyparissus, rocky Pytho, holy Crisa, Daulis, and Panopeus; they also that dwelt in Anemorea and Hyampolis, and about the waters of the river Cephissus, and Lilaea by the springs of the Cephissus; with their chieftains came forty ships, and they marshaled the forces of the Phoceans, which were stationed next to the Boeotians, on their left.

Ajax, the fleet son of Oïleus, commanded the Locrians. He was not so great, nor nearly so great, as Ajax, the son of Telamon. He was a little man, and his breastplate was made of linen, but in use of the spear he excelled all the Hellenes and the Achaeans. These dwelt in Cynus, Opoüs, Calliarus, Bessa, Scarphe, fair Augeae, Tarphe, and Thronium about the river Boagrius. With him there came forty ships of the Locrians who dwell beyond Euboea.

The fierce Abantes held Euboea with its cities, Chalcis, Eretria, Histiaea, rich in vines, Cerinthus upon the sea, and the rock-perched town of Dium; with them were also the men of Carystus and Styra; Elephenor of the race of Ares was in command of these; he was son of Chalcodon, and chief over all the Abantes. With him they came, fleet of foot and wearing their hair long behind, brave warriors, who would ever strive to tear open the corslets of their foes with their long ashen spears. Of these there came fifty ships.

And they that held the strong city of Athens, the people of great Erechtheus, who was born of the soil itself, but Zeus's daughter, Athene, fostered him, and established him at Athens in her own rich sanctuary. There, year by year, the Athenian youths worship him with sacrifices of bulls and rams. These were commanded by Menestheus, son of Peteos. No man living could equal him in the marshaling of chariots and foot soldiers. Nestor could alone rival him, for he was older. With him there came fifty ships.

Ajax brought twelve ships from Salamis and stationed them alongside those of the Athenians.

The men of Argos, again, and those who held the walls of Tiryns, with Hermione, and Asine upon the gulf; Troezene,

Eïonae, and the vineyard lands of Epidaurus; the Achaean youths, moreover, who came from Aegina, and Mases; these were led by Diomed of the loud battle cry, and Sthenelus, son of famed Capaneus. With them in command was Euryalus, son of king Mecisteus, son of Talaus; but Diomed was chief over them all. With these there came eighty ships.

Those who held the strong city of Mycenae, rich Corinth and Cleonae; Orneae, Araethyrea, and Sicyon, where Adrastus reigned of old; Hyperesia, high Gonoëssa, and Pellene; Aegium and all the coastland round about Helice. These sent a hundred ships under the command of King Agamemnon, son of Atreus. His force was far both finest and most numerous, and in their midst was the king himself, all glorious in his armor of gleaming bronze—foremost among the heroes, for he was the greatest king, and had most men under him.

And those that dwelt in Lacedaemon, lying low among the hills, Pharis, Sparta, with Messe, the haunt of doves; Bryseae, Augeae, Amyclae, and Helos upon the sea; Laas, moreover, and Oetylus. These were led by Menelaus of the loud battle cry, brother to Agamemnon, and of them there were sixty ships, drawn up apart from the others. Among them went Menelaus himself, strong in zeal, urging his men to fight; for he longed to avenge the toil and sorrow that he had suffered for the sake of Helen.

The men of Pylos and Arene, and Thryum where is the ford of the river Alpheus; strong Aipy, Cyparisseis, and Amphigenea; Pteleum, Helos, and Dorium, where the Muses met Thamyris, and stilled his minstrelsy forever. He was returning from Oechalia, where Eurytus lived and reigned, and boasted that he would surpass even the Muses, daughters of aegis-bearing Zeus, if they should sing against him; whereon they were angry, and maimed him. They robbed him of his divine power of song, and thenceforth he could strike the lyre no more. These were commanded by Nestor, knight of Gerene, and with him there came ninety ships.

And those that held Arcadia, under the high mountain of Cyllene, near the tomb of Aepytus, where the people fight hand to hand; the men of Pheneus also, and Orchomenus, rich in flocks; of Rhipae, Stratie, and bleak Enispe; of Tegea and fair Mantinea; of Stymphelus and Parrhasia; of these King Agapenor, son of Ancaeus, was commander, and they had sixty ships. Many Arcadians, good soldiers, came in each one of them, but Agamemnon found them the ships in which to cross the sea, for they were not a people that occupied their business upon the waters.

The men, moreover, of Buprasium and of Elis, so much of it as is enclosed between Hyrmine, Myrsinus upon the seashore, the rock Olene and Alesium. These had four leaders, and each of them had ten ships, with many Epeans on board. Their captains were Amphimachus and Thalpius—the one, son of Cteatus, and the other, of Eurytus—both of the race of Actor. The two others were Diores, son of Amarynces, and Polyxenus, son of King Agasthenes, son of Augeas.

And those of Dulichium with the sacred Echinean islands, who dwelt beyond the sea off Elis. These were led by Meges, peer of Ares, and the son of valiant Phyleus, dear to Zeus, who quarreled with his father, and went to settle in Dulichium. With him there came forty ships.

Odysseus led the brave Cephallenians, who held Ithaca, Neritum with its forests, Crocylea, rugged Aegilips, Samos and Zacynthus, with the mainland also that was over against the islands. These were led by Odysseus, peer of Zeus in counsel, and with him there came twelve ships.

Thoas, son of Andraemon, commanded the Aetolians, who dwelt in Pleuron, Olenus, Pylene, Chalcis by the sea, and rocky Calydon, for the great king Oeneus had now no sons living, and was himself dead, as was also golden-haired Meleager, who had been set over the Aetolians to be their king. And with Thoas there came forty ships.

The famous spearsman Idomeneus led the Cretans, who held Cnossus, and the well-walled city of Gortys; Lyctus also, Miletus and Lycastus that lies upon the chalk; the populous towns of Phaestus and Rhytium, with the other peoples that dwelt in the hundred cities of Crete. All these were led by Idomeneus, and by

Meriones, peer of murderous Ares. And with these there came eighty ships.

Tlepolemus, son of Heracles, a man both brave and large of stature, brought nine ships of lordly warriors from Rhodes. These dwelt in Rhodes which is divided among the three cities of Lindus, Ielysus, and Cameirus, that lies upon the chalk. These were commanded by Tlepolemus, son of Heracles by Astyochea, whom he had carried off from Ephyra, on the river Selleis, after sacking many cities of valiant warriors. When Tlepolemus grew up, he killed his father's uncle Licymnius, who had been a famous warrior in his time, but was then grown old. On this he built himself a fleet, gathered a great following, and fled beyond the sea, for he was menaced by the other sons and grandsons of Heracles. After a voyage, during which he suffered great hardship, he came to Rhodes, where the people divided into three communities, according to their tribes, and were dearly loved by Zeus, the lord of gods and men; wherefore the son of Cronus showered down great riches upon them.

And Nireus brought three ships from Syme—Nireus, who was the handsomest man that came up under Ilium of all the Danaans after the son of Peleus—but he was a man of no substance, and had but a small following.

And those that held Nisyrus, Crapathus, and Casus, with Cos, the city of Eurypylus, and the Calydnian islands, these were commanded by Pheidippus and Antiphus, two sons of King Thessalus, the son of Heracles. And with them there came thirty ships.

Those again who held Pelasgic Argos, Alos, Alope, and Trachis; and those of Phthia and Hellas, the land of fair women, who were called Myrmidons, Hellenes, and Achaeans; these had fifty ships, over which Achilles was in command. But they now took no part in the war, inasmuch as there was no one to marshal them; for Achilles stayed by his ships, furious about the loss of the girl Briseis, whom he had taken from Lyrnessus at his own great peril, when he had sacked Lyrnessus and Thebe, and had overthrown Mynes and Epistrophus, sons of king Evenor, son of Selepus. For her sake Achilles was still grieving, but ere long he was again to join them.

And those that held Phylace and the flowery meadows of Pyrasus, sanctuary of Demeter; Iton, mother of sheep; Antrum upon the sea, and Pteleum that lies upon the grasslands. Of these brave Protesilaus had been captain while he was yet alive, but he was now lying under the earth. He had left a wife behind him in Phylace to tear her cheeks in sorrow, and his house was only half finished, for he was slain by a Dardanian warrior while leaping foremost of the Achaeans upon the soil of Troy. Still, though his people mourned their chieftain, they were not without a leader, for Podarces, of the race of Ares, marshaled them; he was son of Iphiclus, rich in sheep, who was the son of Phylacus, and he was own brother to Protesilaus, only younger, Protesilaus being at once the elder and the more valiant. So the people were not without a leader, though they mourned him whom they had lost. With him there came forty ships.

And those that held Pherae by the Boebean lake, with Boebe, Glaphyrae, and the populous city of Iolcus, these with their eleven ships were led by Eumelus, son of Admetus, whom Alcestis bore to him, loveliest of the daughters of Pelias.

And those that held Methone and Thaumacia, with Meliboea and rugged Olizon, these were led by the skillful archer Philoctetes, and they had seven ships, each with fifty oarsmen all of them good archers; but Philoctetes was lying in great pain in the Island of Lemnos, where the sons of the Achaeans left him, for he had been bitten by a poisonous water snake. There he lay sick and sorry, and full soon did the Argives come to miss him. But his people, though they felt his loss, were not leaderless, for Medon, the bastard son of Oïleus by Rhene, set them in array.

Those, again, of Tricca and the stony region of Ithome, and they that held Oechalia, the city of Oechalian Eurytus, these were commanded by the two sons of Asclepius, skilled in the art of healing, Podalirius and Machaon. And with them there came thirty ships.

The men, moreover, of Ormenius, and by the fountain of Hypereia, with those that held Asterius, and the white crests of Titanus, these were led by Eurypylus, the son of Euaemon, and with them there came forty ships.

Those that held Argissa and Gyrtone, Orthe, Elone, and the white city of Oloösson, of these brave Polypoetes was leader. He was son of Pirithoüs, who was son of Zeus himself, for Hippodameia bore him to Pirithoüs on the day when he took his revenge on the shaggy mountain savages, and drove them from Mount Pelion to the Aithices. But Polypoetes was not sole in command, for with him was Leonteus, of the race of Ares, who was son of Coronus, the son of Caeneus. And with these there came forty ships.

Guneus brought two and twenty ships from Cyphus, and he was followed by the Enienes and the valiant Peraebi, who dwelt about wintry Dodona, and held the lands round the lovely river Titaresius, which sends its waters into the Peneus. They do not mingle with the silver eddies of the Peneus, but flow on the top of them like oil; for the Titaresius is a branch of dread Orcus and of the river Styx.

Of the Magnetes, Prothoüs, son of Tenthredon, was commander. They were they that dwelt about the river Peneus and Mount Pelion. Prothoüs, fleet of foot, was their leader, and with him there came forty ships.

Such were the chiefs and princes of the Danaans. Who, then, O Muse, was the foremost, whether man or horse, among those that followed after the sons of Atreus?

Of the horses, those of the son of Pheres were by far the finest. They were driven by Eumelus, and were as fleet as birds. They were of the same age and color, and perfectly matched in height. Apollo, of the silver bow, had bred them in Perea—both of them mares, and terrible as Ares in battle. Of the men, Ajax, son of Telamon, was much the foremost so long as Achilles's anger lasted, for Achilles excelled him greatly and he had also better horses; but Achilles was now holding aloof at his ships by reason of his quarrel with Agamemnon, and his people passed their time upon the seashore, throwing discs or aiming with spears at a mark, and in archery. Their horses stood each by his own chariot, champing lotus and wild celery. The chariots were housed under cover, but their owners, for lack of leadership, wandered hither and thither about the host and went not forth to fight.

Thus marched the host like a consuming fire, and the earth groaned beneath them as when the lord of thunder is angry and lashes the land about Typhoeus among the Arimi, where they say Typhoeus lies. Even so did the earth groan beneath them as they sped over the plain.

And now Iris, fleet as the wind, was sent by Zeus to tell the bad news among the Trojans. They were gathered in assembly, old and young, at Priam's gates, and Iris came close up to Priam, speaking with the voice of Priam's son Polites, who, being fleet of foot, was stationed as watchman for the Trojans on the tomb of old Aesyetes, to look out for any sally of the Achaeans. In his likeness Iris spoke, saying: "Old man, you talk idly, as in time of peace, while war is at hand. I have been in many a battle, but never yet saw such a host as is now advancing. They are crossing the plain to attack the city as thick as leaves or as the sands of the sea. Hector, I charge you above all others, do as I say. There are many allies dispersed about the city of Priam from distant places and speaking divers tongues. Therefore, let each chief give orders to his own people, setting them severally in array and leading them forth to battle."

Thus she spoke, but Hector knew that it was the goddess, and at once broke up the assembly. The men flew to arms; all the gates were opened, and the people thronged through them, horse and foot, with the tramp as of a great multitude.

Now there is a high mound before the city, rising by itself upon the plain. Men call it Batieia, but the gods know that it is the tomb of lithe Myrine. Here the Trojans and their allies divided their forces.

Priam's son, great Hector of the gleaming helmet, commanded the Trojans, and with him were arrayed by far the greater number and most valiant of those who were longing for the fray.

The Dardanians were led by brave Aeneas, whom Aphrodite bore to Anchises, when she, goddess though she was, had lain with him upon the mountain slopes of Ida. He was not alone, for with him were the two sons of Antenor, Archilochus and Acamas, both skilled in all the arts of war.

They that dwelt in Zelea under the lowest spurs of Mount Ida, men of substance, who drink the limpid waters of the Aesepus, and are of Trojan blood—these were led by Pandarus, son of Lycaon, whom Apollo had taught to use the bow.

They that held Adresteia and the land of Apaesus, with Pityeia, and the high mountain of Tereia—these were led by Adrestus and Amphius, whose breastplate was of linen. These were the sons of Merops of Percote, who excelled in all kinds of divination. He told them not to take part in the war, but they gave him no heed, for fate lured them to destruction.

They that dwelt about Percote and Practius, with Sestos, Abydos, and Arisbe—these were led by Asius, son of Hyrtacus, a brave commander—Asius, the son of Hyrtacus, whom his powerful dark bay steeds, of the breed that comes from the river Selleïs, had brought from Arisbe.

Hippothoüs led the tribes of Pelasgian spearsmen, who dwelt in fertile Larisa—Hippothoüs, and Pylaeus of the race of Ares, two sons of the Pelasgian Lethus, son of Teutamus.

Acamas and the warrior Peiroüs commanded the Thracians and those that came from beyond the mighty stream of the Hellespont.

Euphemus, son of Troezenus, the son of Ceos, was captain of the Ciconian spearsmen.

Pyraechmes led the Paeonian archers from distant Amydon, by the broad waters of the river Axius, the fairest that flow upon the earth.

The Paphlagonians were commanded by stouthearted Pylaemenes from Enetae, where the mules run wild in herds. These were they that held Cytorus and the country round Sesamus, with the cities by the river Parthenius, Cromna, Aegialus, and lofty Erithini.

Odius and Epistrophus were captains over the Halizoni from distant Alybe, where there are mines of silver.

Chromis, and Ennomus, the augur, led the Mysians, but his skill in augury availed not to save him from destruction, for he fell by the hand of the fleet descendant of Aeacus in the river, where he slew others also of the Trojans.

Phorcys, again, and noble Ascanius led the Phrygians from the far country of Ascania, and both were eager for the fray.

Mesthles and Antiphus commanded the Meonians, sons of Talaemenes, born to him of the Gygaean lake. These led the Meonians, who dwelt under Mount Tmolus.

Nastes led the Carians, men of a strange speech. These held Miletus and the wooded mountain of Phthires, with the water of the river Maeander and the lofty crests of Mount Mycale. These were commanded by Nastes and Amphimachus, the brave sons of Nomion. He came into the fight with gold about him, like a girl; fool that he was, his gold was of no avail to save him, for he fell in the river by the hand of the fleet descendant of Aeacus, and Achilles bore away his gold.

Sarpedon and Glaucus led the Lycians from their distant land, by the eddying waters of the Xanthus.

BOOK III

Paris challenges Menelaus to single combat, to decide the war and the fate of Helen and her treasure. Priam and Agamemnon solemnize the agreement with oaths and sacrifices to Zeus. Helen mounts the Trojan battlements to watch the duel, and when Menelaus is getting the upper hand, Aphrodite rescues Paris, wafting him back to Troy in a cloud. Agamemnon demands that the Trojans keep their oath and surrender Helen.

WHEN THE COMPANIES WERE THUS ARRAYED, EACH UNDER ITS own captain, the Trojans advanced as a flight of wild fowl or cranes that scream overhead when rain and winter drive them over the flowing waters of Oceanus to bring death and destruction on the Pygmies, and they wrangle in the air as they fly; but the Achaeans marched silently, in high heart, and minded to stand by one another.

As when the south wind spreads a curtain of mist upon the mountain tops, bad for shepherds but better than night for thieves, and a man can see no further than he can throw a stone, even so rose the dust from under their feet as they made all speed over the plain.

When they were close up with one another, Paris came forward as champion on the Trojan side. On his shoulders he bore the skin of a panther, his bow, and his sword, and he brandished two spears shod with bronze as a challenge to the bravest of the Achaeans to meet him in single fight. Menelaus saw him thus stride out before the ranks, and was glad as a hungry lion that lights on the carcass of some goat or horned stag and devours it there and then, though dogs and youths set upon him. Even thus was Menelaus glad when his eyes caught sight of Paris, for he deemed that now he should be revenged. He sprang, therefore, from his chariot, clad in his suit of armor.

Paris quailed as he saw Menelaus come forward, and shrank in fear of his life under cover of his men. As one who starts back affrighted, trembling and pale, when he comes suddenly upon a serpent in some mountain glade, even so did Paris plunge into the throng of Trojan warriors, terror-stricken at the sight of the son of Atreus.

Then Hector upbraided him. "Paris," said he, "evil-hearted Paris, fair to see, but woman-mad and false of tongue, would that you had never been born, or that you had died unwed. Better so, than live to be disgraced and looked askance at. Will not the Achaeans mock at us and say that we have sent one to champion us who is fair to see but who has neither wit nor courage? Did you not, such as you are, get your following together and sail beyond the seas? Did you not from a far country carry off a lovely woman wedded among a people of warriors—to bring sorrow upon your father, your city, and your whole country, but joy to your enemies, and hangdog shamefacedness to yourself? And now can you not dare face Menelaus and learn what manner of man he is whose wife you have stolen? Where indeed would be your lyre and your love tricks, your comely locks and your fair favor, when you were lying in the dust before him? The Trojans are a weak-kneed people, or ere this you would have had a shirt of stones for the wrongs you have done them."

And Paris answered: "Hector, your rebuke is just. You are hard as the ax which a shipwright wields at his work, and cleaves the timber to his liking. As the ax in his hand, so keen is the edge of your scorn. Still, taunt me not with the gifts that golden Aphrodite has given me; they are precious; let not a man disdain them, for the gods give them where they are minded, and none can have them for the asking. If you would have me do battle with Menelaus, bid the Trojans and Achaeans take their seats, while he and I fight in their midst for Helen and all her wealth. Let him who shall be victorious and prove to be the better man take the woman and all she has, to bear them to his home, but let the rest swear to a solemn covenant of peace whereby you Trojans shall stay here in Troy, while the others go home to Argos and the land of the Achaeans."

When Hector heard this he was glad and went about among the Trojan ranks, holding his spear by the middle to keep them back, and they all sat down at his bidding: but the Achaeans still aimed at him with stones and arrows, till Agamemnon shouted to them, saying, "Hold, Argives, shoot not, sons of the Achaeans. Hector desires to speak."

They ceased taking aim and were still, whereon Hector spoke. "Hear from my mouth," said he, "Trojans and Achaeans, the saying of Paris, through whom this quarrel has come about. He bids the Trojans and Achaeans lay their armor upon the ground, while he and Menelaus fight in the midst of you for Helen and all her wealth. Let him who shall be victorious and prove to be the better man take the woman and all she has, to bear them to his own home, but let the rest swear to a solemn covenant of peace."

Thus he spoke, and they all held their peace till Menelaus of the loud battle cry addressed them. "And now," he said, "hear me too, for it is I who am the most aggrieved. I deem that the parting of Achaeans and Trojans is at hand, as well it may be, seeing how much you have suffered for my quarrel with Paris and the wrong he did me. Let him who shall die, die, and let the others fight no more. Bring, then, two lambs, a white ram and a black ewe, for Earth and Sun, and we will bring a third for Zeus. Moreover, you shall bid Priam come, that he may swear to the covenant himself; for his sons are high-handed and ill to trust, and the oaths of Zeus must not be transgressed or taken in vain. Young men's minds are light as air, but when an old man comes he looks before and after, deeming that which shall be fairest upon both sides."

The Trojans and Achaeans were glad when they heard this, for they thought that they should now have rest. They backed their chariots toward the ranks, got out of them, and put off their armor, laying it down upon the ground; and the hosts were near to one another with a little space between them. Hector sent two messengers to the city to bring the lambs and to bid Priam come, while Agamemnon told Talthybius to fetch the other lamb from the ships, and he did as Agamemnon had said.

Meanwhile Iris went to Helen in the form of her sister-in-law, wife of the son of Antenor, for Helicaon, son of Antenor, had married Laodice, the fairest of Priam's daughters. She found her in her own room, working at a great web of purple linen, on which she was embroidering the battles between Trojans and Achaeans, that Ares had made them fight for her sake. Iris then came close up to her and said: "Come hither, child, and see the strange doings of the Trojans and Achaeans; till now they have been warring upon the plain, mad with lust of battle, but now they have left off fighting, and are leaning upon their shields, sitting still with their spears planted beside them. Paris and Menelaus are going to fight about yourself, and you are to be the wife of him who is the victor."

Thus spoke the goddess, and Helen's heart yearned after her former husband, her city, and her parents. She threw a white mantle over her head, and hurried from her room, weeping as she went, not alone, but attended by two of her handmaids, Aethra, daughter of Pittheus, and Clymene. And straightaway they were at the Scaean gates.

The two sages, Ucalegon and Antenor, elders of the people, were seated by the Scaean gates, with Priam, Panthoüs, Thymoetes, Lampus, Clytius, and Hiketaon of the race of Ares. These were too old to fight, but they were fluent orators, and sat on the tower like cicadas that chirrup delicately from the boughs of some high tree in a wood. When they saw Helen coming towards the tower, they said softly to one another: "Small wonder that

Trojans and Achaeans should endure so much and so long, for the sake of a woman so marvelously and divinely lovely. Still, fair though she be, let them take her and go, or she will breed sorrow for us and for our children after us."

But Priam bade her draw nigh. "My child," said he, "take your seat in front of me that you may see your former husband, your kinsmen, and your friends. I lay no blame upon you, it is the gods, not you, who are to blame. It is they that have brought about this terrible war with the Achaeans. Tell me, then, who is yonder huge hero so great and goodly? I have seen men taller by a head, but none so comely and so royal. Surely he must be a king."

"Sir," answered Helen, "father of my husband, dear and reverend in my eyes, would that I had chosen death rather than to have come here with your son, far from my bridal chamber, my friends, my darling daughter, and all the companions of my girlhood. But it was not to be, and my lot is one of tears and sorrow. As for your question, the hero of whom you ask is Agamemnon, son of Atreus, a good king and a brave soldier, brother-in-law as surely as that he lives, to my abhorred and miserable self."

The old man marveled at him, and said: "Happy son of Atreus, child of good fortune. I see that the Achaeans are subject to you in great multitudes. When I was in Phrygia I saw much horsemen, the people of Otreus and of Mygdon, who were camping upon the banks of the river Sangarius. I was their ally, and with them when the Amazons, peers of men, came up against them, but even they were not so many as the Achaeans."

The old man next looked upon Odysseus. 'Tell me," he said, "who is that other, shorter by a head than Agamemnon, but broader across the chest and shoulders? His armor is laid upon the ground, and he stalks in front of the ranks as it were some great woolly ram ordering his ewes."

And Helen answered: "He is Odysseus, a man of great craft, son of Laertes. He was born in rugged Ithaca, and excels in all manner of stratagems and subtle cunning."

On this Antenor said: "Madam, you have spoken truly. Odysseus once came here as envoy about yourself, and Menelaus with him. I received them in my own house, and therefore know both of them by sight and conversation. When they stood up in presence of the assembled Trojans, Menelaus was the broader-shouldered, but when both were seated Odysseus had the more royal presence. After a time they delivered their message, and the speech of Menelaus ran trippingly on the tongue. He did not say much, for he was a man of few words, but he spoke very clearly and to the point, though he was the younger man of the two. Odysseus, on the other hand, when he rose to speak was at first silent and kept his eyes fixed upon the ground. There was no play nor graceful movement of his scepter; he kept it straight and stiff like a man unpracticed in oratory—one might have taken him for a mere churl or simpleton; but when he raised his voice, and the words came driving from his deep chest like winter snow before the wind, then there was none to touch him, and no man thought further of what he looked like."

Priam then caught sight of Ajax and asked, "Who is that great and goodly warrior whose head and broad shoulders tower above the rest of the Argives?"

"That," answered Helen, "is huge Ajax, bulwark of the Achaeans, and on the other side of him, among the Cretans, stands Idomeneus looking like a god, and with the captains of the Cretans round him. Often did Menelaus receive him as a guest in our house when he came visiting us from Crete. I see, moreover, many other Achaeans whose names I could tell you, but there are two whom I can nowhere find, Castor, breaker of horses, and Pollux, the mighty boxer; they are children of my mother, and own brothers to myself. Either they have not left Lacedaemon, or else, though they have brought their ships, they will not show themselves in battle for the shame and disgrace that I have brought upon them."

She knew not that both these heroes were already lying under the earth in their own land of Lacedaemon.

Meanwhile the heralds were bringing the holy oath offerings through the city—two lambs and a goatskin of wine, the gift of earth; and Idaeus brought the mixing bowl and the cups of gold.

He went up to Priam and said, "Son of Laomedon, the princes of the Trojans and Achaeans bid you come down on to the plain and swear to a solemn covenant. Paris and Menelaus are to fight for Helen in single combat, that she and all her wealth may go with him who is the victor. We are to swear to a solemn covenant of peace whereby we others shall dwell here in Troy, while the Achaeans return to Argos and the land of the Achaeans."

The old man trembled as he heard, but bade his followers yoke the horses, and they made all haste to do so. He mounted the chariot, gathered the reins in his hand, and Antenor took his seat beside him; they then drove through the Scaean gates on to the plain. When they reached the ranks of the Trojans and Achaeans they left the chariot and with measured pace advanced into the space between the hosts.

Agamemnon and Odysseus both rose to meet them. The attendants brought on the oath offerings and mixed the wine in the mixing bowls; they poured water over the hands of the chieftains, and the son of Atreus drew the dagger that hung by his sword, and cut wool from the lambs' heads; this the menservants gave about among the Trojan and Achaean princes, and the son of Atreus lifted up his hands in prayer. "Father Zeus," he cried, "that rulest in Ida, most glorious in power, and thou O Sun, that seest and givest ear to all things, Earth and Rivers, and ye who in the realms below chastise the soul of him that has broken his oath, witness these rites and guard them, that they be not vain. If Paris kills Menelaus, let him keep Helen and all her wealth, while we sail home with our ships; but if Menelaus kills Paris, let the Trojans give back Helen and all that she has; let them moreover pay such fine to the Achaeans as shall be agreed upon, in testimony among those that shall be born hereafter. And if Priam and his sons refuse such fine when Paris has fallen, then will I stay here and fight on till I have got satisfaction."

As he spoke he drew his knife across the throats of the victims, and laid them down gasping and dying upon the ground, for the knife had reft them of their strength. Then they poured wine from the mixing bowl into the cups, and prayed to the everlasting gods, saying, Trojans and Achaeans among one another, "Zeus, most great and glorious, and ye other everlasting gods, grant that the brains of them who shall first sin against their oaths—of them and their children—may be shed upon the ground even as this wine, and let their wives become the slaves of strangers."

Thus they prayed, but not as yet would Zeus grant them their prayer. Then Priam, descendant of Dardanus, spoke, saying: "Hear me, Trojans and Achaeans, I will now go back to the wind-beaten city of Ilium. I dare not with my own eyes witness this fight between my son and Menelaus, for Zeus and the other immortals alone know which shall fall."

On this he laid the two lambs on his chariot and took his seat. He gathered the reins in his hand, and Antenor sat beside him; the two then went back to Ilium. Hector and Odysseus measured the ground and cast lots from a helmet of bronze to see which should take aim first. Meanwhile the two hosts lifted up their hands and prayed, saying, "Father Zeus, that rulest from Ida, most glorious in power, grant that he who first brought about this war between us may die and enter the house of Hades, while we others remain at peace and abide by our oaths."

Great Hector now turned his head aside while he shook the helmet, and the lot of Paris flew out first. The others then took their several stations, each by his horses and the place where his arms were lying, while Paris, husband of lovely Helen, put on his goodly armor. First he greaved his legs with greaves of good make and fitted with ankle-clasps of silver; after this he donned the cuirass of his brother Lycaon, and fitted it to his own body. He hung his silver-studded sword of bronze about his shoulders, and then his mighty shield. On his comely head he set his helmet, well-wrought, with a crest of horsehair that nodded menacingly above it, and he grasped a redoubtable spear that suited his hands. In like fashion Menelaus also put on his armor.

When they had thus armed, each amid his own people, they strode fierce of aspect into the open space, and both Trojans and Achaeans were struck with awe as they beheld them. They stood near one another on the measured ground, brandishing their spears, and each furious against the other. Paris aimed first, and struck the round shield of the son of Atreus, but the spear did not pierce it, for the shield turned its point. Menelaus next took aim, praying to Father Zeus as he did so. "King Zeus," he said, "grant me revenge on Paris who has wronged me. Subdue him under my hand that in ages yet to come a man may shrink from doing ill deeds in the house of his host."

He poised his spear as he spoke and hurled it at the shield of Paris. Through shield and cuirass it went and tore the shirt by his flank, but Paris swerved aside, and thus saved his life. Then the son of Atreus drew his sword, and drove at the projecting part of his helmet, but the sword fell shivered in three or four pieces from his hand, and he cried, looking towards heaven, "Father Zeus, of all gods thou art the most despiteful; I made sure of my revenge, but the sword has broken in my hand, my spear has been hurled in vain, and I have not killed him."

With this he flew at Paris, caught him by the horsehair plume of his helmet, and began dragging him towards the Achaeans. The strap of the helmet that went under his chin was choking him, and Menelaus would have dragged him off to his own great glory had not Zeus's daughter Aphrodite been quick to mark and to break the strap of oxhide, so that the empty helmet came away in his hand. This he flung to his comrades among the Achaeans, and was again springing upon Paris to run him through with a spear, but Aphrodite snatched him up in a moment (as a god can do), hid him under a cloud of darkness, and conveyed him to his own bedchamber.

Then she went to call Helen, and found her on a high tower with the Trojan women crowding round her. She took the form of an old woman who used to dress wool for her when she was still in Lacedaemon, and of whom she was very fond. Thus disguised she plucked her by her perfumed robe, and said: "Come hither; Paris says you are to go to the house; he is on his bed in his own room, radiant with beauty and dressed in gorgeous apparel. No one would think he had just come from fighting, but rather that he was going to a dance, or had done dancing and was sitting down."

With these words she moved the heart of Helen to anger. When she marked the beautiful neck of the goddess, her lovely bosom, and sparkling eyes, she marveled at her and said: "Goddess, why do you thus beguile me? Are you going to send me afield still further to some man whom you have taken up in Phrygia or fair Meonia? Menelaus has just vanquished Paris, and is to take my hateful self back with him. You are come here to betray me. Go sit with Paris yourself; henceforth be goddess no longer; never let your feet carry you back to Olympus; worry about him and look after him till he make you his wife, or, for the matter of that, his slave—but me? I shall not go; I can garnish his bed no longer. I should be a byword among all the women of Troy. Besides, I have trouble on my mind."

Aphrodite was very angry, and said: "Bold hussy, do not provoke me; if you do, I shall leave you to your fate and hate you as much as I have loved you. I will stir up fierce hatred between Trojans and Achaeans, and you shall come to a bad end."

At this Helen was frightened. She wrapped her mantle about her and went in silence, following the goddess and unnoticed by the Trojan women.

When they came to the house of Paris the maidservants set about their work, but Helen went into her own room, and the laughter-loving goddess took a seat and set it for her facing Paris. On this Helen, daughter of aegis-bearing Zeus, sat down, and with eyes askance began to upbraid her husband.

"So you are come from the fight," said she; "would that you had fallen rather by the hand of that brave man who was my husband. You used to brag that you were a better man with your hands and spear than Menelaus; go, then, and challenge him again—but I should advise you not to do so, for if you are foolish enough to meet him in single combat, you will soon fall by his spear."

And Paris answered: "Wife, do not vex me with your reproaches. This time, with the help of Athene, Menelaus has vanquished me; another time I may myself be victor, for I too have gods that will stand by me. Come, let us lie down together and make friends. Never yet was I so passionately enamored of you as at this moment—not even when I first carried you off from Lacedaemon and sailed away with you—not even when I had converse with you upon the couch of love in the island of Cranaë was I so enthralled by my desire of you as now." On this he led her towards the bed, and his wife went with him.

Thus they laid themselves on the bed together; but the son of Atreus strode among the throng, looking everywhere for Paris, and no man, neither of the Trojans nor of the allies, could find him. If they had seen him they were in no mind to hide him, for they all of them hated him as they did death itself. Then Agamemnon, king of men, spoke, saying: "Hear me, Trojans, Dardanians, and allies. The victory has been with Menelaus. Therefore give back Helen with all her wealth, and pay such fine as shall be agreed upon, in testimony among them that shall be born hereafter."

Thus spoke the son of Atreus, and the Achaeans shouted in applause.

BOOK IV

On Olympus Zeus agrees that the Trojans should suffer for Paris's failure to fight his battle through. Athene goes down to the plain in disguise and persuades the Trojan Pandarus to shoot an arrow at the unsuspecting Menelaus, thereby breaking the solemn truce between the armies. Agamemnon, indignant, marshals his men for war.

Now the gods were sitting with Zeus in Council upon the Golden floor while Hebe went round pouring out nectar for them to drink, and as they pledged one another in their cups of gold they looked down upon the town of Troy. The son of Cronus then began to tease Hera, talking at her so as to provoke her. "Menelaus," said he, "has two good friends among the goddesses, Hera of Argos, and Athene of Alalcomene, but they only sit still and look on, while Aphrodite keeps ever by Paris's side to defend him in any danger. Indeed she has just rescued him when he made sure that it was all over with him—for the victory really did lie with Menelaus. We must consider what we shall do about all this; shall we set them fighting anew or make peace between them? If you will agree to this last Menelaus can take back Helen and the city of Priam may remain still inhabited."

Athene and Hera muttered their discontent as they sat side by side hatching mischief for the Trojans. Athene scowled at her father, for she was in a furious passion with him, and said nothing, but Hera could not contain herself. "Dread son of Cronus," said she, "what, pray, is the meaning of all this? Is my trouble, then, to go for nothing, and the sweat that I have sweated, to say nothing of my horses, while getting the people together against Priam and his children? Do as you will, but we other gods shall not all of us approve your counsel."

Zeus was angry and answered: "My dear, what harm have Priam and his sons done you that you are so hotly bent on sacking the city of Ilium? Will nothing do for you but you must go within their walls and eat Priam raw, with his sons and all the other Trojans to boot? Have it your own way then; for I would not have this matter become a bone of contention between us. I say further, and lay my saying to your heart, if ever I want to sack a city belonging to friends of yours, you must not try to stop me; you will have to let me do it, for I am giving in to you sorely against my will. Of all inhabited cities under the sun and stars of heaven, there was none that I so much respected as Ilium with Priam and his whole people. Equitable feasts were never wanting about my altar, nor the savor of burning fat, which is the honor due to ourselves."

"My own three favorite cities," answered Hera, "are Argos, Sparta, and Mycenae. Sack them whenever you may be displeased with them. I shall not defend them and I shall not care. Even if I did, and tried to stay you, I should take nothing by it, for you are much stronger than I am, but I will not have my own work wasted. I too am a god and of the same race with yourself. I am Cronus's eldest daughter, and am honorable not on this ground only, but also because I am your wife and you are king over the gods. Let it be a case, then, of give-and-take between us, and the rest of the gods will follow our lead. Tell Athene to go and take part in the fight at once, and let her contrive that the Trojans shall be the first to break their oaths and set upon the Achaeans."

The sire of gods and men heeded her words and said to Athene, "Go at once into the Trojan and Achaean hosts, and contrive that the Trojans shall be the first to break their oaths and set upon the Achaeans."

This was what Athene was already eager to do, so down she darted from the topmost summits of Olympus. She shot through the sky as some brilliant meteor which the son of scheming Cronus has sent as a sign to mariners or to some great army, and a fiery train of light follows in its wake. The Trojans and Achaeans were struck with awe as they beheld, and one would turn to his neighbor, saying, "Either we shall again have war and din of combat, or Zeus, the lord of battle, will now make peace between us."

Thus did they converse. Then Athene took the form of Laodocus, son of Antenor, and went through the ranks of the Trojans to find Pandarus, the redoubtable son of Lycaon. She found him standing among the stalwart heroes who had followed him from the banks of the Aesopus, so she went close up to him and said: "Brave son of Lycaon, will you do as I tell you? If you dare send an arrow at Menelaus you will win honor and thanks from all the Trojans, and especially from prince Paris—he would be the first to requite you very handsomely if he could see Menelaus mount his funeral pyre, slain by an arrow from your hand. Take your aim then, and pray to Lycian Apollo, the famous archer; vow that when you get home to your strong city of Zelea you will offer a hecatomb of firstling lambs in his honor."

His fool's heart was persuaded, and he took his bow from its case. This bow was made from the horns of a wild ibex which he had killed as it was bounding from a rock; he had stalked it, and it had fallen as the arrow struck it to the heart. Its horns were sixteen palms long, and a worker in horn had made them into a bow, smoothing them well down, and giving them tips of gold. When Pandarus had strung his bow he laid it carefully on the ground, and his brave followers held their shields before him lest the Achaeans should set upon him before he had shot Menelaus. Then he opened the lid of his quiver and took out a winged arrow that had never yet been shot, fraught with the pangs of death.

He laid the arrow on the string and prayed to Lycian Apollo, the famous archer, vowing that when he got home to his strong city of Zelea he would offer a hecatomb of firstling lambs in his honor. He laid the notch of the arrow on the oxhide bowstring, and drew both notch and string to his breast till the arrowhead was near the bow; then when the bow was arched into a half circle, he let fly, and the bow twanged, and the string sang as the arrow flew gladly on over the heads of the throng.

But the blessed gods did not forget thee, O Menelaus, and Zeus's daughter, driver of the spoil, was the first to stand before thee and ward off the piercing arrow. She turned it from his skin as a mother whisks a fly from off her child when it is sleeping sweetly. She guided it to the part where the golden buckles of the belt that passed over his double cuirass were fastened, so the arrow struck the belt that went tightly round him. It went right through this and through the cuirass of cunning workmanship; it also pierced the belt beneath it, which he wore next his skin to keep out darts or arrows; it was this that served him in the best stead, nevertheless the arrow went through it and grazed the top of the skin, so that blood began flowing from the wound.

As when some woman of Meonia or Caria strains purple dye on to a piece of ivory that is to be the cheekpiece of a horse, and is to be laid up in a treasure house—many a knight is fain to bear it, but the king keeps it as an ornament of which both horse and driver may be proud—even so, O Menelaus, were your shapely thighs and your legs down to your fair ankles stained with blood.

When King Agamemnon saw the blood flowing from the wound he was afraid, and so was brave Menelaus himself till he saw that the barbs of the arrow and the thread that bound the arrowhead to the shaft were still outside the wound. Then he took heart, but Agamemnon heaved a deep sigh as he held Menelaus's hand in his own, and his comrades made moan in concert. "Dear brother," he cried, "I have been the death of you in pledging this covenant and letting you come forward as our champion. The Trojans have trampled on their oaths and have wounded you; nevertheless the oath, the blood of lambs, the drink offerings, and the right hands of fellowship in which we have put our trust shall not be vain. If he that rules Olympus fulfill it not here and now, he will yet fulfill it hereafter, and they shall pay dearly with their lives and with their wives and children. The day will surely come when mighty Ilium shall be laid low, with Priam and Priam's people, when the son of Cronus from his high throne shall overshadow them with his awful aegis in punishment of their present treachery. This shall surely be; but how, Menelaus, shall I mourn you, if it be your lot now to die? I should return to Argos as a byword, for the Achaeans will at once go home. We shall leave Priam and the Trojans the glory of still keeping Helen, and the earth will rot your bones as you lie here at Troy with your purpose not fulfilled. Then shall some braggart Trojan leap upon your tomb and say, 'Ever thus may Agamemnon wreak his vengeance. He brought his army in vain, he is gone home to his own land with empty ships, and has left Menelaus behind him.' Thus will one of them say, and may the earth then swallow me."

But Menelaus reassured him and said: "Take heart, and do not alarm the people; the arrow has not struck me in a mortal part, for my outer belt of burnished metal first stayed it, and under this my cuirass and the belt of mail which the bronze-smiths made me."

And Agamemnon answered: "I trust, dear Menelaus, that it may be even so, but the surgeon shall examine your wound and lay herbs upon it to relieve your pain."

He then said to Talthybius: "Talthybius, tell Machaon, son to the great physician Asclepius, to come and see Menelaus immediately. Some Trojan or Lycian archer has wounded him with an arrow to our dismay, and to his own great glory."

Talthybius did as he was told, and went about the host trying to find Machaon. Presently he found him standing amid the brave warriors who had followed him from Tricca; thereon he went up to him and said, "Son of Asclepius, King Agamemnon says you are to come and see Menelaus immediately. Some Trojan or Lycian archer has wounded him with an arrow to our dismay and to his own great glory."

Thus did he speak, and Machaon was moved to go. They passed through the spreading host of the Achaeans and went on till they came to the place where Menelaus had been wounded and was lying with the chieftains gathered in a circle round him. Machaon passed into the middle of the ring and at once drew the arrow from the belt, bending its barbs back through the force with which he pulled it out. He undid the burnished belt, and beneath this the cuirass and the belt of mail which the bronzesmiths had made; then, when he had seen the wound, he wiped away the blood and applied some soothing drugs which Chiron had given to Asclepius out of the goodwill he bore him.

While they were thus busy about Menelaus, the Trojans came forward against them, for they had put on their armor, and now renewed the fight.

You would not have then found Agamemnon asleep nor cowardly and unwilling to fight, but eager rather for the fray. He left his chariot rich with bronze and his panting steeds in charge of Eurymedon, son of Ptolemaeus, the son of Peiraeus, and bade him hold them in readiness against the time his limbs should weary of going about and giving orders to so many, for he went among the ranks on foot. When he saw men hasting to the front he stood by them and cheered them on. "Argives," said he, "slacken not one whit in your onset. Father Zeus will be no helper of liars. The Trojans have been the first to break their oaths and to attack us; therefore they shall be devoured of vultures. We shall take their city and carry off their wives and children in our ships."

But he angrily rebuked those whom he saw shirking and disinclined to fight. "Argives," he cried, "cowardly, miserable creatures, have you no shame to stand here like frightened fawns who, when they can no longer scud over the plain, huddle together but show no fight? You are as dazed and spiritless as deer. Would you wait till the Trojans reach the stems of our ships as they lie on the shore, to see whether the son of Cronus will hold his hand over you to protect you?"

Thus did he go about giving his orders among the ranks. Passing through the crowd, he came presently on the Cretans, arming round Idomeneus, who was at their head, fierce as a wild boar, while Meriones was bringing up the battalions that were in the rear. Agamemnon was glad when he saw him, and spoke him fairly. "Idomeneus," said he, "I treat you with greater distinction than I do any other of the Achaeans, whether in war or in other things, or at table. When their princes are mixing my choicest wine in the mixing bowls, they have each of them a fixed allowance, but your cup is kept always full like my own, that you may drink whenever you are minded. Go, therefore, into battle, and show yourself the man you have been always proud to be."

Idomeneus answered: "I will be a trusty comrade, as I promised you from the first I would be. Urge on the other Achaeans, that we may join battle at once, for the Trojans have trampled upon their covenants. Death and destruction shall be theirs, seeing they have been the first to break their oaths and to attack us."

The son of Atreus went on, glad at heart, till he came upon the two Ajaxes arming themselves amid a host of foot soldiers. As when a goatherd from some high post watches a storm drive over the deep before the west wind—black as pitch is the offing and a mighty whirlwind draws towards him, so that he is afraid and drives his flock into a cave—even thus did the ranks of stalwart youths move in a dark mass to battle under the Ajaxes, horrid with shield and spear. Glad was King Agamemnon when he saw them. "No need," he cried, "to give orders to such leaders of the Argives as you are, for of your own selves you spur your men on to fight with might and main. Would, by father Zeus, Athene, and Apollo that all were so minded as you are, for the city of Priam would then soon fall beneath our hands, and we should sack it."

With this he left them and went onward to Nestor, the facile speaker of the Pylians, who was marshaling his men and urging them on, in company with Pelagon, Alastor, Chromius, Haemon, and Bias, shepherd of his people. He placed his knights with their chariots and horses in the front rank, while the foot soldiers, brave men and many, whom he could trust, were in the rear. The cowards he drove into the middle, that they might fight whether they would or no. He gave his orders to the knights first, bidding them hold their horses well in hand, so as to avoid confusion. "Let no man," he said, "relying on his strength or horsemanship, get before the others and engage singly with the Trojans, nor yet let him lag behind, or you will weaken your attack; but let each when he meets an enemy's chariot throw his spear from his own; this will be much the best. This is how the men of old took towns and strongholds; in this wise were they minded."

Thus did the old man charge them, for he had been in many a fight, and King Agamemnon was glad. "I wish," he said to him, "that your limbs were as supple and your strength as sure as your judgment is; but age, the common enemy of mankind, has laid his hand upon you; would that it had fallen upon some other, and that you were still young."

And Nestor, knight of Gerene, answered: "Son of Atreus, I too would gladly be the man I was when I slew mighty Ereuthalion; but the gods will not give us everything at one and the same time. I was then young and now I am old; still I can go with my knights and give them that counsel which old men have a right to give. The wielding of the spear I leave to those who are younger and stronger than myself."

Agamemnon went his way rejoicing, and presently found Menestheus, son of Peteos, tarrying in his place, and with him were the Athenians loud of tongue in battle. Near him also tarried cunning Odysseus, with his sturdy Cephallenians round him; they had not yet heard the battle cry, for the ranks of Trojans and Achaeans had only just begun to move, so they were standing still, waiting for some other columns of the Achaeans to attack the Trojans and begin the fighting. When he saw this Agamemnon rebuked them and said: "Son of Peteos, and you other, steeped in cunning, heart of guile, why stand you here cowering and waiting on others? You two should be of all men foremost when there is hard fighting to be done, for you are ever foremost to accept my invitation when we counselors of the Achaeans are holding feast. You are glad enough then to take your fill of roast meats and to drink wine as long as you please, whereas now you would not care though you saw ten columns of Achaeans engage the enemy in front of you."

Odysseus glared at him and answered: "Son of Atreus, what are you talking about? How can you say that we are slack? When the Achaeans are in full fight with the Trojans you shall see, if you care to do so, that the father of Telemachus will join battle with the foremost of them. You are talking idly."

When Agamemnon saw that Odysseus was angry, he smiled pleasantly at him and withdrew his words. "Odysseus," said he, "noble son of Laertes, excellent in all good counsel, I have neither fault to find nor orders to give you, for I know your heart is right, and that you and I are of a mind. Enough; I will make you amends for what I have said, and if any ill has now been spoken may the gods bring it to nothing."

He then left them and went on to others. Presently he saw the son of Tydeus, noble Diomed, standing by his chariot and horses with Sthenelus, the son of Capaneus, beside him; whereon he began to upbraid him. "Son of Tydeus," he said, "why stand you cowering here upon the brink of battle? Tydeus did not shrink thus, but was ever ahead of his men when leading them on against the foe—so, at least, say they that saw him in battle, for I never set eyes upon him myself. They say that there was no man like him. He came once to Mycenae, not as an enemy but as a guest, in company with Polynices to recruit his forces, for they were levying war against the strong city of Thebes and prayed our people for a body of picked men to help them. The men of Mycenae were willing to let them have one, but Zeus dissuaded them by showing them unfavorable omens. Tydeus, therefore, and Polynices went their way. When they had got as far as the deep-meadowed and rush-grown banks of the Aesopus, the Achaeans sent Tydeus as their envoy, and he found the Cadmeans gathered in great numbers to a banquet in the house of Eteocles. Stranger though he was, he knew no fear on finding himself single-handed among so many, but challenged them to contests of all kinds, and in each one of them was at once victorious, so mightily did Athene help him. The Cadmeans were incensed at his success, and set a force of fifty youths with two captains—the godlike hero Maeon, son of Haemon, and Polyphontes, son of Autophonus—at their head, to lie in wait for him on his return journey; but Tydeus slew every man of them, save only Maeon, whom he let go in obedience to heaven's omens. Such was Tydeus of Aetolia. His son can talk more glibly, but he cannot fight as his father did."

Diomed made no answer, for he was shamed by the rebuke of Agamemnon; but the son of Capaneus took up his words and said: "Son of Atreus, tell no lies, for you can speak truth if you will. We boast ourselves as even better men than our fathers; we took seven-gated Thebes, though the wall was stronger and our men were fewer in number, for we trusted in the omens of the gods and in the help of Zeus, whereas they perished through their own sheer folly; hold not, then, our fathers in like honor with us."

Diomed looked sternly at him and said, "Hold your peace, my friend, as I bid you. It is not amiss that Agamemnon should urge the Achaeans forward, for the glory will be his if we take the city, and his the shame if we are vanquished. Therefore let us acquit ourselves with valor."

As he spoke he sprang from his chariot, and his armor rang so fiercely about his body that even a brave man might well have been scared to hear it.

As when some mighty wave that thunders on the beach when the west wind has lashed it into fury—it has reared its head afar and now comes crashing down on the shore; it bows its arching crest high over the jagged rocks and spews its salt foam in all directions—even so did the serried phalanxes of the Danaans march steadfastly to battle. The chiefs gave orders each to his own people, but the men said never a word; no man would think it, for huge as the host was, it seemed as though there was not a tongue among them, so silent were they in their obedience; and as they marched the armor about their bodies glistened in the sun. But the clamor of the Trojan ranks was as that of many thousand ewes that stand waiting to be milked in the yards of some rich flockmaster, and bleat incessantly in answer to the bleating of their lambs; for they had not one speech nor language, but their tongues were diverse, and they came from many different places. These were inspired of Ares, but the others by Athene—and with them came Panic, Rout, and Strife whose fury never tires, sister and friend of murderous Ares, who, from being at first but low in stature, grows till she uprears her head to heaven, though her feet are still on earth. She it was that went about among them and flung down discord to the waxing of sorrow with even hand between them.

When they were got together in one place shield clashed with shield and spear with spear in the rage of battle. The bossed shields beat one upon another, and there was a tramp as of a great multitude—death cry and shout of triumph of slain and slayers, and the earth ran red with blood. As torrents swollen with rain course madly down their deep channels till the angry floods meet in some gorge, and the shepherd on the hillside hears their roaring from afar—even such was the toil and uproar of the hosts as they joined in battle.

First Antilochus slew an armed warrior of the Trojans, Echepolus, son of Thalysius, fighting in the foremost ranks. He struck at the projecting part of his helmet and drove the spear into his brow; the point of bronze pierced the bone, and darkness veiled his eyes; headlong as a tower he fell amid the press of the fight, and as he dropped King Elephenor, son of Chalcodon and captain of the proud Abantes, began dragging him out of reach of the darts that were falling around him, in haste to strip him of his armor. But his purpose was not for long; Agenor saw him haling the body away, and smote him in the side with his bronze-shod spear—for as he stooped his side was left unprotected by his shield—and thus he perished. Then the fight between Trojans and Achaeans grew furious over his body, and they flew upon each other like wolves, man and man crushing one upon the other.

Forthwith Ajax, son of Telamon, slew the fair youth Simoëisius, son of Anthemion, whom his mother bore by the banks of the Simois, as she was coming down from Mount Ida, where she had been with her parents to see their flocks. Therefore he was named Simoëisius, but he did not live to pay his parents for his rearing, for he was cut off untimely by the spear of mighty Ajax, who struck him in the breast by the right nipple as he was coming on among the foremost fighters; the spear went right through his shoulder, and he fell as a poplar that has grown straight and tall in a meadow by some mere, and its top is thick with branches. Then the wheelwright lays his ax to its roots that he may fashion a felly for the wheel of some goodly chariot, and it lies seasoning by the waterside. In such wise did Ajax fell to earth Simoëisius, son of Anthemion. Thereon Antiphus of the gleaming corslet, son of Priam, hurled a spear at Ajax from amid the crowd and missed him, but he hit Leucus, the brave comrade of Odysseus, in the groin, as he was dragging the body of Simoëisius over to the other side; so he fell upon the body and loosed his hold upon it. Odysseus was furious when he saw Leucus slain, and strode in full armor through the front ranks till he was quite close; then he glared round about him and took aim, and the Trojans fell back as he did so. His dart was not sped in vain, for it struck Democoön, the bastard son of Priam, who had come to him from Abydos, where he had charge of his father's mares. Odysseus, infuriated by the death of his comrade, hit him with his spear on one temple, and the bronze point came through on the other side of his forehead. Thereon darkness veiled his eyes, and his armor rang rattling round him as he fell heavily to the ground. Hector and they that were in front then gave ground while the Argives raised a shout and drew off the dead, pressing further forward as they did so. But Apollo looked down from Pergamus and called aloud to the Trojans, for he was displeased. "Trojans," he cried, "rush on the foe, and do not let yourselves be thus beaten by the Argives. Their skins are not stone nor iron that when you hit them you do them no harm. Moreover, Achilles, the son of lovely Thetis, is not fighting, but is nursing his anger at the ships."

Thus spoke the mighty god, crying to them from the city, while Zeus's redoubtable daughter, the Trito-born, went about among the host of the Achaeans, and urged them forward whenever she beheld them slackening.

Then fate fell upon Diores, son of Amarynceus, for he was struck by a jagged stone near the ankle of his right leg. He that hurled it was Peiroüs, son of Imbrasus, captain of the Thracians, who had come from Aenus; the bones and both the tendons were crushed by the pitiless stone. He fell to the ground on his back, and in his death throes stretched out his hands towards his comrades. But Peiroüs, who had wounded him, sprang on him and thrust a spear into his belly, so that his bowels came gushing out upon the ground, and darkness veiled his eyes. As he was leaving the body, Thoas of Aetolia struck him in the chest near the nipple, and the point fixed itself in his lungs. Thoas came close up to him, pulled the spear out of his chest, and then drawing his sword, smote him in the middle of the belly so that he died. But he did not strip him of his armor, for his Thracian comrades, men who wear their hair in a tuft at the top of their heads, stood round the body and kept him off with their long spears for all his great stature and valor; so he was driven back. Thus the two corpses lay stretched on earth near to one another, the one captain of the Thracians and the other of the Epeans; and many another fell round them.

And now no man would have made light of the fighting if he could have gone about among it scatheless and unwounded, with Athene leading him by the hand, and protecting him from the storm of spears and arrows. For many Trojans and Achaeans on that day lay stretched side by side face downwards upon the earth.

BOOK V

Diomed, guided by Athene, performs great exploits. Wounded by Pandarus, he rallies and kills him and later wounds Aeneas, who is snatched from death by his mother Aphrodite and healed by Apollo. Diomed then attacks and wounds Aphrodite, driving her from the field. The Trojans are spurred on by the god Ares and their leader Hector, but Athene shows Diomed how to drive Ares out of the fight and back to Olympus.

THEN PALLAS ATHENE PUT VALOR INTO THE HEART OF Diomed, son of Tydeus, that he might excel all the other Argives, and cover himself with glory. She made a stream of fire flare from his shield and helmet like the star that shines most brilliantly in summer after its bath in the waters of Oceanus—even such a fire did she kindle upon his head and shoulders as she bade him speed into the thickest hurly-burly of the fight.

Now there was a certain rich and honorable man among the Trojans, priest of Hephaestus, and his name was Dares. He had two sons, Phegeus and Idaeus, both of them skilled in all the arts of war. These two came forward from the main body of Trojans, and set upon Diomed, he being on foot, while they fought from their chariot. When they were close up to one another, Phegeus took aim first, but his spear went over Diomed's left shoulder without hitting him. Diomed then threw, and his spear sped not in vain, for it hit Phegeus on the breast near the nipple, and he fell from his chariot. Idaeus did not dare to bestride his brother's body, but sprang from the chariot and took to flight, or he would have shared his brother's fate; whereon Hephaestus saved him by wrapping him in a cloud of darkness, that his old father might not be utterly overwhelmed with grief; but the son of Tydeus drove off with the horses, and bade his followers take them to the ships. The Trojans were scared when they saw the two sons of Dares, one of them in flight and the other lying dead by his chariot. Athene, therefore, took Ares by the hand and said: "Ares, Ares, bane of men, bloodstained stormer of cities, may we not now leave the Trojans and Achaeans to fight it out, and see to which of the two Zeus will vouchsafe the victory? Let us go away, and thus avoid his anger."

So saying, she drew Ares out of the battle, and set him down upon the steep banks of the Scamander. Upon this the Danaans drove the Trojans back, and each one of their chieftains killed his man. First King Agamemnon flung mighty Odius, captain of the Halizoni, from his chariot. The spear of Agamemnon caught him on the broad of his back, just as he was turning in flight. It struck him between the shoulders and went right through his chest, and his armor rang rattling round him as he fell heavily to the ground.

Then Idomeneus killed Phaesus, son of Borus, the Meonian, who had come from Tarne. Mighty Idomeneus speared him on the right shoulder as he was mounting his chariot, and the darkness of death enshrouded him as he fell heavily from the car.

The squires of Idomeneus spoiled him of his armor, while Menelaus, son of Atreus, killed Scamandrius, the son of Strophius, a mighty huntsman and keen lover of the chase. Artemis herself had taught him how to kill every kind of wild creature that is bred in mountain forests, but neither she nor his famed skill in archery could now save him, for the spear of Menelaus struck him in the back as he was flying. It struck him between the shoulders and went right through his chest, so that he fell headlong and his armor rang rattling round him.

Meriones then killed Phereclus, the son of Tecton, who was the son of Harmon, a man whose hand was skilled in all manner of cunning workmanship, for Pallas Athene had dearly loved him. He it was that made the ships for Paris, which were the beginning of all mischief, and brought evil alike both on the Trojans and on Paris himself; for he heeded not the decrees of heaven. Meriones overtook him as he was flying, and struck him on the right buttock. The point of the spear went through the bone into the bladder, and death came upon him as he cried aloud and fell forward on his knees.

Meges, moreover, slew Pedaeus, son of Antenor, who, though he was a bastard, had been brought up by Theano as one of her own children, for the love she bore her husband. The son of Phyleus got close up to him and drove a spear into the nape of his neck: it went under his tongue all among his teeth, so he bit the cold bronze, and fell dead in the dust.

And Eurypylus, son of Euaemon, killed Hypsenor, the son of noble Dolopion, who had been made priest of the river Scamander, and was honored among the people as though he were a god. Eurypylus gave him chase as he was flying before him, smote him with his sword upon the arm, and lopped his strong hand from off it. The bloody hand fell to the ground, and the shades of death, with fate that no man can withstand, came over his eyes.

Thus furiously did the battle rage between them. As for the son of Tydeus, you could not say whether he was more among the Achaeans or the Trojans. He rushed across the plain like a winter torrent that has burst its barrier in full flood; no dykes, no walls of fruitful vineyards can embank it when it is swollen with rain from heaven, but in a moment it comes tearing onward, and lays many a field waste that many a strong man's hand has reclaimed—even so were the dense phalanxes of the Trojans driven in rout by the son of Tydeus, and many though they were, they dared not abide his onslaught.

Now when the son of Lycaon saw him scouring the plain and driving the Trojans pell-mell before him, he aimed an arrow and hit the front part of his cuirass near the shoulder. The arrow went right through the metal and pierced the flesh, so that the cuirass was covered with blood. On this the son of Lycaon shouted in triumph: "Knights Trojans, come on! The bravest of the Achaeans is wounded, and he will not hold out much longer if King Apollo was indeed with me when I sped from Lycia hither."

Thus did he vaunt; but his arrow had not killed Diomed, who withdrew and made for the chariot and horses of Sthenelus, the son of Capaneus. "Dear son of Capaneus," said he, "come down from your chariot, and draw the arrow out of my shoulder."

Sthenelus sprang from his chariot, and drew the arrow from the wound, whereon the blood came spouting out through the hole that had been made in his shirt. Then Diomed prayed, saying: "Hear me, daughter of aegis-bearing Zeus, unweariable! If ever you loved my father well and stood by him in the thick of a fight, do the like now by me; grant me to come within a spear's throw of that man and kill him. He has been too quick for me and has wounded me; and now he is boasting that I shall not see the light of the sun much longer."

Thus he prayed, and Pallas Athene heard him; she made his limbs supple and quickened his hands and his feet. Then she went close up to him and said, "Fear not, Diomed, to do battle with the Trojans, for I have set in your heart the spirit of your knightly father Tydeus. Moreover, I have withdrawn the veil from your eyes, that you may know gods and men apart. If, then, any other god comes here and offers you battle, do not fight him; but should Zeus's daughter Aphrodite come, strike her with your spear and wound her."

When she had said this Athene went away, and the son of Tydeus again took his place among the foremost fighters, three times more fierce even than he had been before. He was like a lion that some mountain shepherd has wounded, but not killed, as he is springing over the wall of a sheep yard to attack the sheep. The shepherd has roused the brute to fury but cannot defend his flock, so he takes shelter under cover of the buildings, while the sheep, panic-stricken on being deserted, are smothered in heaps one on top of the other, and the angry lion leaps out over the sheep yard wall. Even thus did Diomed go furiously about among the Trojans.

He killed Astynoüs and Hypeiron, shepherd of his people, the one with a thrust of his spear, which struck him above the nipple, the other with a sword cut on the collar bone, that severed his shoulder from his neck and back. He let both of them lie, and went in pursuit of Abas and Polyidus, sons of the old reader of dreams, Eurydamas. They never came back for him to read them any more dreams, for mighty Diomed made an end of them. He then gave chase to Xanthus and Thoön, the two sons of Phaenops, both of them very dear to him, for he was now worn out with age, and begat no more sons to inherit his possessions. But Diomed took both their lives and left their father sorrowing bitterly, for he nevermore saw them come home from battle alive, and his kinsmen divided his wealth among themselves.

Then he came upon two sons of Priam, Echemmon and Chromius, as they were both in one chariot. He sprang upon them as a lion fastens on the neck of some cow or heifer when the herd is feeding in a coppice. For all their vain struggles he flung them both from their chariot and stripped the armor from their bodies. Then he gave their horses to his comrades to take them back to the ships.

When Aeneas saw him thus making havoc among the ranks, he went through the fight amid the rain of spears to see if he could find Pandarus. When he had found the brave son of Lycaon, he said: "Pandarus, where is now your bow, your winged arrows, and your renown as an archer, in respect of which no man here can rival you nor is there any in Lycia that can beat you? Lift then your hands to Zeus and send an arrow at this fellow who is going so masterfully about, and has done such deadly work among the Trojans. He has killed many a brave man—unless indeed he is some god who is angry with the Trojans about their sacrifices, and has set his hand against them in his displeasure."

And the son of Lycaon answered: "Aeneas, I take him for none other than the son of Tydeus. I know him by his shield, the visor of his helmet, and by his horses. It is possible that he may be a god, but if he is the man I say he is, he is not making all this havoc without heaven's help, but has some god by his side who is shrouded in a cloud of darkness, and who turned my arrow aside when it had hit him. I have taken aim at him already and hit him on the right shoulder; my arrow went through the breastpiece of his cuirass; and I made sure I should send him hurrying to the world below, but it seems that I have not killed him. There must be a god who is angry with me. Moreover, I have neither horse nor chariot. In my father's stables there are eleven excellent chariots, fresh from the builder, quite new, with cloths spread over them; and by each of them there stand a pair of horses, champing barley and rye. My old father Lycaon urged me again and again when I was at home and on the point of starting to take chariots and horses with me that I might lead the Trojans in battle, but I would not listen to him. It would have been much better if I had done so, but I was thinking about the horses, which had been used to eat their fill, and I was afraid that in such a great gathering of men they might be ill-fed, so I left them at home and came on foot to Ilium armed only with my bow and arrows. These it seems, are of no use, for I have already hit two chieftains, the sons of Atreus and of Tydeus, and though I drew blood surely enough, I have only made them still more furious. I did ill to take my bow down from its peg on the day I led my band of Trojans to Ilium in Hector's service, and if ever I get home again to set eyes on my native place, my wife, and the greatness of my house, may someone cut my head off then and there if I do not break the bow and set it on a hot fire—such pranks as it plays me."

Aeneas answered: "Say no more. Things will not mend till we two go against this man with chariot and horses and bring him to a trial of arms. Mount my chariot, and note how cleverly the horses of Tros can speed hither and thither over the plain in pursuit or flight. If Zeus again vouchsafes glory to the son of Tydeus they will carry us safely back to the city. Take hold, then, of the whip and reins while I stand upon the car to fight, or else do you wait this man's onset while I look after the horses."

"Aeneas," replied the son of Lycaon, "take the reins and drive. If we have to fly before the son of Tydeus the horses will go better for their own driver. If they miss the sound of your voice when they expect it they may be frightened, and refuse to take us out of the fight. The son of Tydeus will then kill both of us and take the horses. Therefore, drive them yourself and I will be ready for him with my spear."

They then mounted the chariot and drove full-speed towards the son of Tydeus. Sthenelus, son of Capaneus, saw them coming and said to Diomed: "Diomed, son of Tydeus, man after my own heart, I see two heroes speeding towards you, both of them men of might—the one a skillful archer, Pandarus, son of Lycaon, the other, Aeneas, whose sire is Anchises, while his mother is Aphrodite. Mount the chariot and let us retreat. Do not, I pray you, press so furiously forward, or you may get killed."

Diomed looked angrily at him and answered: "Talk not of flight, for I shall not listen to you: I am of a race that knows neither flight nor fear, and my limbs are as yet unwearied. I am in no mind to mount, but will go against them even as I am. Pallas Athene bids me be afraid of no man, and even though one of them escape, their steeds shall not take both back again. I say further, and lay my saying to your heart—if Athene sees fit to vouchsafe me the glory of killing both, stay your horses here and make the reins fast to the rim of the chariot; then be sure you spring upon Aeneas's horses and drive them from the Trojan to the Achaean ranks. They are of the stock that great Zeus gave to Tros in payment for his son Ganymede, and are the finest that live and move under the sun. King Anchises stole the blood by putting his mares to them without Laomedon's knowledge, and they bore him six foals. Four are still in his stables, but he gave the other two to Aeneas. We shall win great glory if we can take them."

Thus did they converse, but the other two had now driven close up to them, and the son of Lycaon spoke first. "Great and mighty son," said he, "of noble Tydeus, my arrow failed to lay you low, so I will now try with my spear."

He poised his spear as he spoke and hurled it from him. It struck the shield of the son of Tydeus; the bronze point pierced it and passed on till it reached the breastplate. Thereon the son of Lycaon shouted out and said, "You are hit clean through the belly; you will not stand out for long, and the glory of the fight is mine."

But Diomed all undismayed made answer, "You have missed, not hit, and before you two see the end of this matter one or other of you shall glut tough-shielded Ares with his blood."

With this he hurled his spear, and Athene guided it on to Pandarus's nose near the eye. It went crashing in among his white teeth. The bronze point cut through the root of his tongue, coming out under his chin, and his glistening armor rang rattling round him as he fell heavily to the ground. The horses started aside for fear, and he was reft of life and strength.

Aeneas sprang from his chariot armed with shield and spear, fearing lest the Achaeans should carry off the body. He bestrode it as a lion in the pride of strength, with shield and spear before him and a cry of battle on his lips—resolute to kill the first that should dare face him. But the son of Tydeus caught up a mighty stone, so huge and great that as men now are it would take two to lift it; nevertheless he bore it aloft with ease unaided, and with this he struck Aeneas on the groin where the hip turns in the joint that is called the "cup bone." The stone crushed this joint, and broke both the sinews, while its jagged edges tore away all the flesh. The hero fell on his knees, and propped himself with his hand resting on the ground till the darkness of night fell upon his eyes. And now Aeneas, king of men, would have perished then and there, had not his mother, Zeus's daughter Aphrodite, who had conceived him by Anchises when he was herding cattle, been quick to mark, and thrown her two white arms about the body of her dear son. She protected him by covering him with a fold of her own fair garment, lest some Danaan should drive a spear into his breast and kill him.

Thus, then, did she bear her dear son out of the fight. But the son of Capaneus was not unmindful of the orders that Diomed had given him. He made his own horses fast, away from the hurlyburly, by binding the reins to the rim of the chariot. Then he sprang upon Aeneas's horses and drove them from the Trojan to the Achaean ranks. When he had so done he gave them over to his chosen comrade Deipylus, whom he valued above all others as the one who was most like-minded with himself, to take them on to the ships. He then remounted his own chariot, seized the reins, and drove with all speed in search of the son of Tydeus.

Now the son of Tydeus was in pursuit of the Cyprian goddess, spear in hand, for he knew her to be feeble and not one of those goddesses that can lord it among men in battle like Athene, or Enyo, the waster of cities, and when at last after a long chase he caught her up, he flew at her and thrust his spear into the flesh of her delicate hand. The point tore through the ambrosial robe which the Graces had woven for her, and pierced the skin between her wrist and the palm of her hand, so that the immortal blood, or ichor, that flows in the veins of the blessed gods, came pouring from the wound; for the gods do not eat bread nor drink wine, hence they have no blood such as ours, and are immortal. Aphrodite screamed aloud, and let her son fall, but Phoebus Apollo caught him in his arms, and hid him in a cloud of darkness, lest some Danaan should drive a spear into his breast and kill him; and Diomed shouted out as he left her, "Daughter of Zeus, leave war and battle alone; can you not be contented with beguiling silly women? If you meddle with fighting you will get what will make you shudder at the very name of war."

The goddess went dazed and discomfited away, and Iris, fleet as the wind, drew her from the throng, in pain and with her fair skin all besmirched. She found fierce Ares waiting on the left of the battle, with his spear and his two fleet steeds resting on a cloud; whereon she fell on her knees before her brother and implored him to let her have his horses. "Dear brother," she cried, "save me, and give me your horses to take me to Olympus where the gods dwell. I am badly wounded by a mortal, the son of Tydeus, who would now fight even with father Zeus."

Thus she spoke, and Ares gave her his gold-bedizened steeds. She mounted the chariot sick and sorry at heart, while Iris sat beside her and took the reins in her hand. She lashed her horses on and they flew forward nothing loath, till in a trice they were at high Olympus, where the gods have their dwelling. There she stayed them, unloosed them from the chariot, and gave them their ambrosial forage; but Aphrodite flung herself on to the lap of her mother Dione, who threw her arms about her and caressed her, saying, "Which of the heavenly beings has been treating you in this way, as though you had been doing something wrong in the face of day?"

And laughter-loving Aphrodite answered: "Proud Diomed, the son of Tydeus, wounded me because I was bearing my dear son Aeneas, whom I love best of all mankind, out of the fight. The war is no longer one between Trojans and Achaeans, for the Danaans have now taken to fighting with the immortals."

"Bear it, my child," replied Dione, "and make the best of it. We dwellers in Olympus have to put up with much at the hands of men, and we lay much suffering on one another. Ares had to suffer when Otus and Ephialtes, children of Aloeus, bound him in cruel bonds, so that he lay thirteen months imprisoned in a vessel of bronze. Ares would have then perished had not fair Eëriboea, stepmother to the sons of Aloeus, told Hermes, who stole him away when he was already well-nigh worn out by the severity of his bondage. Hera again suffered when the mighty son of Amphitryon wounded her on the right breast with a three-barbed arrow, and nothing could assuage her pain. So, also, did huge Hades, when this same man, the son of aegis-bearing Zeus, hit him with an arrow even at the gates of hell and hurt him badly. Thereon Hades went to the house of Zeus on great Olympus, angry and full of pain; and the arrow in his brawny shoulder caused him great anguish till Paeëon healed him by spreading soothing herbs on the wound, for Hades was not of mortal mold. Daring, headstrong, evildoer who recked not of his sin in shooting the gods that dwell in Olympus. And now Athene has egged this son of Tydeus on against yourself, fool that he is for not reflecting that no man who fights with gods will live long or hear his children prattling about his knees when he returns from battle. Let, then, the son of Tydeus see that he does not have to fight with one who is stronger than you are. Then shall his brave wife, Aegialeia, daughter of Adrestus, rouse her whole house from sleep, wailing for the loss of her wedded lord, Diomed, the bravest of the Achaeans."

So saying, she wiped the ichor from the wrist of her daughter with both hands, whereon the pain left her, and her hand was healed. But Athene and Hera, who were looking on, began to taunt Zeus with their mocking talk, and Athene was first to speak. "Father Zeus," said she, "do not be angry with me, but I think the Cyprian must have been persuading some one of the Achaean women to go with the Trojans of whom she is so very fond, and while caressing one or other of them she must have torn her delicate hand with the gold pin of the woman's brooch."

The sire of gods and men smiled, and called golden Aphrodite to his side. "My child," said he, "it has not been given you to be a warrior. Attend, henceforth, to your own delightful matrimonial duties, and leave all this fighting to Ares and to Athene."

Thus did they converse. But Diomed sprang upon Aeneas, though he knew him to be in the very arms of Apollo. Not one whit did he fear the mighty god, so set was he on killing Aeneas and stripping him of his armor. Thrice did he spring forward with might and main to slay him, and thrice did Apollo beat back his gleaming shield. When he was coming on for the fourth time, as though he were a god, Apollo shouted to him with an awful voice and said, "Take heed, son of Tydeus, and draw off. Think not to match yourself against gods, for men that walk the earth cannot hold their own with the immortals."

The son of Tydeus then gave way for a little space, to avoid the anger of the god, while Apollo took Aeneas out of the crowd and set him in sacred Pergamus, where his temple stood. There, within the mighty sanctuary, Latona and Artemis healed him and made him glorious to behold, while Apollo of the silver bow fashioned a wraith in the likeness of Aeneas, and armed as he was. Round this the Trojans and Achaeans hacked at the bucklers about one another's breasts, hewing each other's round shields and light hide-covered targets. Then Phoebus Apollo said to Ares, "Ares, Ares, bane of men, bloodstained stormer of cities, can you not go to this man, the son of Tydeus, who would now fight even with father Zeus, and draw him out of the battle? He first went up to the Cyprian and wounded her in the hand near her wrist, and afterwards sprang upon me too, as though he were a god."

He then took his seat on the top of Pergamus, while murderous Ares went about among the ranks of the Trojans, cheering them on, in the likeness of fleet Acamas, chief of the Thracians. "Sons of Priam," said he, "how long will you let your people be thus slaughtered by the Achaeans? Would you wait till they are at the walls of Troy? Aeneas, the son of Anchises, has fallen, he whom we held in as high honor as Hector himself. Help me, then, to rescue our brave comrade from the stress of the fight."

With these words he put heart and soul into them all. Then Sarpedon rebuked Hector very sternly. "Hector," said he, "where is your prowess now? You used to say that though you had neither people nor allies you could hold the town alone with your brothers and brothers-in-law. I see not one of them here; they cower as hounds before a lion; it is we, your allies, who bear the brunt of the battle. I have come from afar, even from Lycia and the banks of the river Xanthus, where I have left my wife, my infant son, and much wealth to tempt whoever is needy. Nevertheless, I head my Lycian soldiers and stand my ground against any who would fight me though I have nothing here for the Achaeans to plunder, while you look on, without even bidding your men stand firm in defense of their wives. See that you fall not into the hands of your foes as men caught in the meshes of a net, and they sack your fair city forthwith. Keep this before your mind night and day, and beseech the captains of your allies to hold on without flinching, and thus put away their reproaches from you."

So spoke Sarpedon, and Hector smarted under his words. He sprang from his chariot clad in his suit of armor, and went about among the host brandishing his two spears, exhorting the men to fight and raising the terrible cry of battle. Then they rallied and again faced the Achaeans, but the Argives stood compact and firm, and were not driven back. As the breezes sport with the chaff upon some goodly threshing floor when men are winnowing—while yellow Demeter blows with the wind to sift the chaff from the grain, and the chaff heaps grow whiter and whiter—even so did the Achaeans whiten in the dust which the horses' hoofs raised to the firmament of heaven, as their drivers turned them back to battle, and they bore down with might upon the foe. Fierce Ares, to help the Trojans, covered them in a veil of darkness and went about everywhere among them, inasmuch as Phoebus Apollo had told him that when he saw Pallas Athene leave the fray he was to put courage into the hearts of the Trojans—for it was she who was helping the Danaans. Then Apollo sent Aeneas forth from his rich sanctuary, and filled his heart with valor, whereon he took his place among his comrades, who were overjoyed at seeing him alive, sound, and of a good courage; but they could not ask him how it had all happened, for they were too busy with the turmoil raised by Ares and by Strife, who raged insatiably in their midst.

The two Ajaxes, Odysseus, and Diomed cheered the Danaans on, fearless of the fury and onset of the Trojans. They stood as still as clouds which the son of Cronus has spread upon the mountain tops when there is no air and fierce Boreas sleeps with the other boisterous winds whose shrill blasts scatter the clouds in all directions—even so did the Danaans stand firm and unflinching against the Trojans. The son of Atreus went about among them and exhorted them. "My friends," said he, "quit yourselves like brave men, and shun dishonor in one another's eyes amid the stress of battle. They that shun dishonor more often live than get killed, but they that fly save neither life nor name."

As he spoke he hurled his spear and hit one of those who were in the front rank, the comrade of Aeneas, Deicoön, son of Pergasus, whom the Trojans held in no less honor than the sons of Priam, for he was ever quick to place himself among the foremost. The spear of King Agamemnon struck his shield and went right through it, for the shield stayed it not. It drove through his belt into the lower part of his belly, and his armor rang rattling round him as he fell heavily to the ground.

Then Aeneas killed two champions of the Danaans, Crethon and Orsilochus. Their father was a rich man who lived in the strong city of Phere and was descended from the river Alpheus, whose broad stream flows through the land of the Pylians. The river begat Orsilochus, who ruled over much people and was father to Diocles, who in his turn begat twin sons, Crethon and Orsilochus, well skilled in all the arts of war. These, when they grew up, went to Ilium with the Argive fleet in the cause of Menelaus and Agamemnon, sons of Atreus, and there they both of them fell. As two lions whom their dam has reared in the depths of some mountain forest to plunder homesteads and carry sheep and cattle till they get killed by the hand of man, so were these two vanquished by Aeneas, and fell like high pine trees to the ground.

Brave Menelaus pitied them in their fall, and made his way to the front, clad in gleaming bronze and brandishing his spear, for Ares egged him on to do so with intent that he should be killed by Aeneas; but Antilochus, the son of Nestor, saw him and sprang forward, fearing that the king might come to harm and thus bring all their labor to nothing; when, therefore, Aeneas and Menelaus were setting their hands and spears against one another eager to do battle, Antilochus placed himself by the side of Menelaus. Aeneas, bold though he was, drew back on seeing the two heroes side by side in front of him, so they drew the bodies of Credion and Orsilochus to the ranks of the Achaeans and committed the two poor fellows into the hands of their comrades. They then turned back and fought in the front ranks.

They killed Pylaemenes, peer of Ares, leader of the Paphlagonian warriors. Menelaus struck him on the collarbone, as he was standing on his chariot, while Antilochus hit his charioteer and squire Mydon, the son of Atymnius, who was turning his horses in flight. He hit him with a stone upon the elbow, and the reins, enriched with white ivory, fell from his hands into the dust.

Antilochus rushed towards him and struck him on the temples with his sword, whereon he fell head first from the chariot to the ground. There he stood for a while with his head and shoulders buried deep in the dust—for he had fallen on sandy soil—till his horses kicked him and laid him flat on the ground, as Antilochus lashed them and drove them off to the host of the Achaeans.

But Hector marked them from across the ranks, and with a loud cry rushed towards them, followed by the strong battalions of the Trojans. Ares and dread Enyo led them on, she fraught with ruthless turmoil of battle, while Ares wielded a monstrous spear, and went about, now in front of Hector and now behind him.

Diomed shook with passion as he saw them. As a man crossing a wide plain is dismayed to find himself on the brink of some great river rolling swiftly to the sea—he sees its boiling waters and starts back in fear—even so did the son of Tydeus give ground. Then he said to his men: "My friends, how can we wonder that Hector wields the spear so well? Some god is ever by his side to protect him, and now Ares is with him in the likeness of mortal man. Keep your faces therefore towards the Trojans, but give ground backwards, for we dare not fight with gods."

As he spoke the Trojans drew close up, and Hector killed two men, both in one chariot, Menesthes and Anchialus, heroes well-versed in war. Ajax, son of Telamon, pitied them in their fall; he came close up and hurled his spear, hitting Amphius, the son of Selagus, a man of great wealth who lived in Paesus and owned much corn-growing land, but his lot had led him to come to the aid of Priam and his sons. Ajax struck him in the belt; the spear pierced the lower part of his belly, and he fell heavily to the ground. Then Ajax ran towards him to strip him of his armor, but the Trojans rained spears upon him, many of which fell upon his shield. He planted his heel upon the body and drew out his spear, but the darts pressed so heavily upon him that he could not strip the goodly armor from his shoulders. The Trojan chieftains, moreover, many and valiant, came about him with their spears, so that he dared not stay; great, brave, and valiant though he was, they drove him from them and he was beaten back.

Thus, then, did the battle rage between them. Presently the strong hand of fate impelled Tlepolemus, the son of Heracles, a man both brave and of great stature, to fight Sarpedon; so the two, son and grandson of great Zeus, drew near to one another, and Tlepolemus spoke first. "Sarpedon," said he, "councilor of the Lycians, why should you come skulking here—you who are a man of peace? They lie who call you son of aegis-bearing Zeus, for you are little like those who were of old his children. Far other was Heracles, my own brave and lion-hearted father, who came here for the horses of Laomedon, and though he had six ships only, and few men to follow him, sacked the city of Ilium and made a wilderness of her highways. You are a coward, and your people are falling from you. For all your strength, and all your coming from Lycia, you will be no help to the Trojans but will pass the gates of Hades vanquished by my hand."

And Sarpedon, captain of the Lycians, answered: "Tlepolemus, your father overthrew Ilium by reason of Laomedon's folly in refusing payment to one who had served him well. He would not give your father the horses which he had come so far to fetch. As for yourself, you shall meet death by my spear. You shall yield glory to myself, and your soul to Hades of the noble steeds."

Thus spoke Sarpedon and Tlepolemus upraised his spear. They threw at the same moment, and Sarpedon struck his foe in the middle of his throat; the spear went right through, and the darkness of death fell upon his eyes. Tlepolemus's spear struck Sarpedon on the left thigh with such force that it tore through the flesh and grazed the bone, but his father as yet warded off destruction from him.

His comrades bore Sarpedon out of the fight, in great pain by the weight of the spear that was dragging from his wound. They were in such haste and stress as they bore him that no one thought of drawing the spear from his thigh so as to let him walk uprightly. Meanwhile the Achaeans carried off the body of Tlepolemus, whereon Odysseus was moved to pity, and panted for the fray as he beheld them. He doubted whether to pursue the son of Zeus or to make slaughter of the Lycian rank and file. It was not decreed, however, that he should slay the son of Zeus. Athene, therefore, turned him against the main body of the Lycians. He killed Coeranus, Alastor, Chromius, Alcandrus, Halius, Noëmon, and Prytanis, and would have slain yet more, had not great Hector marked him, and sped to the front of the fight clad in his suit of mail, filling the Danaans with terror. Sarpedon was glad when he saw him coming, and besought him, saying: "Son of Priam, let me not lie here to fall into the hands of the Danaans. Help me, and since I may not return home to gladden the hearts of my wife and of my infant son, let me die within the walls of your city."

Hector made him no answer, but rushed onward to fall at once upon the Achaeans and kill many among them. His comrades then bore Sarpedon away and laid him beneath Zeus's spreading oak tree. Pelagon his friend and comrade drew the spear out of his thigh, but Sarpedon fainted and a mist came over his eyes. Presently he came to himself again, for the breath of the north wind as it played upon him gave him new life, and brought him out of the deep swoon into which he had fallen.

Meanwhile the Argives were neither driven towards their ships by Ares and Hector, nor yet did they attack them; when they knew that Ares was with the Trojans they retreated, but kept their faces still turned towards the foe. Who, then, was first and who last to be slain by Ares and Hector? They were valiant Teuthras, and Orestes, the renowned charioteer, Trechus, the Aetolian warrior, Oenomaus, Helenus, the son of Oenops, and Oresbius of the gleaming girdle, who was possessed of great wealth, and dwelt by the Cephisian lake with the other Boeotians who lived near him, owners of a fertile country.

Now when the goddess Hera saw the Argives thus falling, she said to Athene, "Alas, daughter of aegis-bearing Zeus, unweariable, the promise we made Menelaus that he should not return till he had sacked the city of Ilium will be of none effect if we let Ares rage thus furiously. Let us go into the fray at once."

Athene did not gainsay her. Thereon the august goddess, daughter of great Cronus, began to harness her gold-bedizened steeds. Hebe with all speed fitted on the eight-spoked wheels of bronze that were on either side of the iron axletree. The fellies of the wheels were of gold, imperishable, and over these there was a tire of bronze, wondrous to behold. The naves of the wheels were silver, turning round the axle upon either side. The car itself was made with plaited bands of gold and silver, and it had a double top rail running all round it. From the body of the car there went a pole of silver, on to the end of which she bound the golden yoke, with the bands of gold that were to go under the necks of the horses. Then Hera put her steeds under the yoke, eager for battle and the war cry.

Meanwhile Athene flung her richly embroidered vesture, made with her own hands, on to her father's threshold, and donned the shirt of Zeus, arming herself for battle. She threw her tasseled aegis about her shoulders, wreathed round with Rout as with a fringe, and on it were Strife, and Strength, and Panic whose blood runs cold; moreover there was the head of the dread monster Gorgon, grim and awful to behold, portent of aegis-bearing Zeus. On her head she set her helmet of gold, with four plumes, and coming to a peak both in front and behind—decked with the emblems of a hundred cities. Then she stepped into her flaming chariot and grasped the spear, so stout and sturdy and strong, with which she quells the ranks of heroes who have displeased her. Hera lashed the horses on, and the gates of heaven bellowed as they flew open of their own accord—gates over which the Hours preside, in whose hands are Heaven and Olympus, either to open the dense cloud that hides them, or to close it. Through these the goddesses drove their obedient steeds, and found the son of Cronus sitting all alone on the topmost ridges of Olympus. There Hera stayed her horses, and spoke to Zeus, the son of Cronus, lord of all. "Father Zeus," said she, "are you not angry with Ares for these high doings? See how great and goodly a host of the Achaeans he has destroyed to my great grief, and without either right or reason, while the Cyprian and Apollo are enjoying it all at their ease and setting this unrighteous madman on to do further mischief. I hope, Father Zeus, that you will not be angry if I hit Ares hard, and chase him out of the battle."

And Zeus answered, "Set Athene on to him, for she punishes him more often than anyone else does."

Hera did as he had said. She lashed her horses, and they flew forward nothing loath midway betwixt earth and sky. As far as a man can see when he looks out upon the sea from some high beacon, so far can the loud-neighing horses of the gods spring at a single bound. When they reached Troy and the place where its two flowing streams, Simois and Scamander, meet, there Hera stayed down and took them from the chariot. She hid them in a thick cloud, and Simois made ambrosia spring up for them to eat; the two goddesses then went on, flying like turtledoves in their eagerness to help the Argives. When they came to the part where the bravest and most in number were gathered about mighty Diomed, fighting like lions or wild boars of great strength and endurance, there Hera stood still and raised a shout like that of brazen-voiced Stentor, whose cry was as loud as that of fifty men together. "Argives," she cried; "shame on you, cowardly creatures, brave in semblance only! As long as Achilles was fighting his spear was so deadly that the Trojans dared not show themselves outside the Dardanian gates, but now they sally far from the city and fight even at your ships."

With these words she put heart and soul into them all, while Athene sprang to the side of the son of Tydeus whom she found near his chariot and horses, cooling the wound that Pandarus had given him. For the sweat caused by the band that bore the weight of his shield irritated the hurt: his arm was weary with pain, and he was lifting up the strap to wipe away the blood. The goddess laid her hand on the yoke of his horses, and said: "The son of Tydeus is not such another as his father. Tydeus was a little man, but he could fight, and rushed madly into the fray even when I told him not to do so. When he went all unattended as envoy to the city of Thebes among the Cadmeans, I bade him feast in their houses and be at peace; but with that high spirit which was ever present with him, he challenged the youth of the Cadmeans, and at once beat them in all that he attempted, so mightily did I help him. I stand by you too to protect you, and I bid you be instant in fighting the Trojans; but either you are tired out, or you are afraid and out of heart, and in that case I say that you are no true son of Tydeus, the son of Oeneus."

Diomed answered, "I know you, goddess, daughter of aegis-bearing Zeus, and will hide nothing from you. I am not afraid nor out of heart, nor is there any slackness in me. I am only following your own instructions; you told me not to fight any of the blessed gods, but if Zeus's daughter Aphrodite came into battle I was to wound her with my spear. Therefore I am retreating, and bidding the other Argives gather in this place, for I know that Ares is now lording it in the field."

"Diomed, son of Tydeus," replied Athene, "man after my own heart, fear neither Ares nor any other of the immortals, for I will befriend you. Nay, drive straight at Ares, and smite him in close combat. Fear not this raging madman, villain incarnate, first on one side and then on the other. But now he was holding talk with Hera and myself, saying he would help the Argives and attack the Trojans. Nevertheless, he is with the Trojans, and has forgotten the Argives."

With this she caught hold of Sthenelus and lifted him off the chariot on to the ground. In a second he was on the ground, whereupon the goddess mounted the car and placed herself by the side of Diomed. The oaken axle groaned aloud under the burden of the awful goddess and the hero; Pallas Athene took the whip and reins, and drove straight at Ares. He was in the act of stripping huge Periphas, son of Ochesius and bravest of the Aetolians. Bloody Ares was stripping him of his armor, and Athene donned the helmet of Hades, that he might not see her; when, therefore, he saw Diomed, he made straight for him and let Periphas lie where he had fallen. As soon as they were at close quarters he let fly with his bronze spear over the reins and yoke, thinking to take Diomed's life, but Athene caught the spear in her hand and made it fly harmlessly over the chariot. Diomed then threw, and Pallas Athene drove the spear into the pit of Ares's stomach where his under-girdle went round him. There Diomed wounded him, tearing his fair flesh and then drawing his spear out again. Ares roared as loudly as nine or ten thousand men in the thick of a fight, and the Achaeans and Trojans were struck with panic, so terrible was the cry he raised.

As a dark cloud in the sky when it comes on to blow after heat, even so did Diomed, son of Tydeus, see Ares ascend into the broad heavens. With all speed he reached high Olympus, home of the gods, and in great pain sat down beside Zeus, the son of Cronus. He showed Zeus the immortal blood that was flowing from his wound, and spoke piteously, saying: "Father Zeus, are you not angered by such doings? We gods are continually suffering in the most cruel manner at one another's hands while helping mortals; and we all owe you a grudge for having begotten that mad termagant of a daughter, who is always committing outrage of some kind. We other gods must all do as you bid us, but her you neither scold nor punish; you encourage her because the pestilent creature is your daughter. See how she has been inciting proud Diomed to vent his rage on the immortal gods. First he went up to the Cyprian and wounded her in the hand near her wrist, and then he sprang upon me too as though he were a god. Had I not run for it I must either have lain there for long enough in torments among the ghastly corpses, or have been beaten alive with spears till I had no more strength left in me."

Zeus looked angrily at him and said: "Do not come whining here, Sir Facing-both-ways. I hate you worst of all the gods in Olympus, for you are ever fighting and making mischief. You have the intolerable and stubborn spirit of your mother Hera: it is all I can do to manage her, and it is her doing that you are now in this plight: still, I cannot let you remain longer in such great pain; you are my own offspring, and it was by me that your mother conceived you. If, however, you had been the son of any other god, you are so destructive that by this time you should have been lying lower than the Titans."

He then bade Paeëon heal him, whereon Paeëon spread pain-killing herbs upon his wound and cured him, for he was not of mortal mold. As the juice of the fig tree curdles milk, and thickens it in a moment though it is liquid, even so instantly did Paeëon cure fierce Ares. Then Hebe washed him and clothed him in goodly raiment, and he took his seat by his father Zeus all glorious to behold.

But Hera of Argos and Athene of Alalcomene, now that they had put a stop to the murderous doings of Ares, went back again to the house of Zeus.

BOOK VI

The tide of war surges back and forth across the plain. The Trojan Glaucus challenges Diomed, only to discover that old ties of friendship prevent their fighting one another. Hector, seeing his side hard-pressed, goes back to Troy to order special sacrifices to Athene. Finding Paris with Helen, he scornfully rebukes him. To his own wife, Andromache, and his baby son he bids farewell. The two brothers then return together to the fray.

THE FIGHT BETWEEN TROJANS AND ACHAEANS WAS NOW LEFT to rage as it would, and the tide of war surged hither and thither over the plain as they aimed their bronze-shod spears at one another between the streams of Simois and Xanthus.

First, Ajax, son of Telamon, tower of strength to the Achaeans, broke a phalanx of the Trojans, and came to the assistance of his comrades by killing Acamas, son of Eussorus, the best man among the Thracians, being both brave and of great stature. The spear struck the projecting peak of his helmet; its bronze point then went through his forehead into the brain, and darkness veiled his eyes.

Then Diomed killed Axylus, son of Teuthranus, a rich man who lived in the strong city of Arisbe, and was beloved by all men;

for he had a house by the roadside, and entertained everyone who passed; howbeit not one of his guests stood before him to save his life, and Diomed killed both him and his squire Calesius, who was then his charioteer—so the pair passed beneath the earth.

Euryalus killed Dresus and Opheltius, and then went in pursuit of Aesepus and Pedasus, whom the naiad nymph Abarbarea had borne to noble Bucolion. Bucolion was eldest son to Laomedon, but he was a bastard. While tending his sheep he had converse with the nymph, and she conceived twin sons. These the son of Mecisteus now slew, and he stripped the armor from their shoulders. Polypoetes then killed Astyalus, Ulysses Pidytes of Percote, and Teucer Aretaon. Ablerus fell by the spear of Nestor's son Antilochus, and Agamemnon, king of men, killed Elatus who dwelt in Pedasus by the banks of the river Satnioeis. Leĭtus killed Phylacus as he was flying, and Eurypylus slew Melanthus.

Then Menelaus of the loud war cry took Adrestus alive, for his horses ran into a tamarisk bush, as they were flying wildly over the plain, and broke the pole from the car; they went on towards the city along with the others in full flight, but Adrestus rolled out, and fell in the dust flat on his face by the wheel of his chariot. Menelaus came up to him spear in hand, but Adrestus caught him by the knees begging for his life. "Take me alive," he cried, "son of Atreus, and you shall have a full ransom for me! My father is rich and has much treasure of gold, bronze, and wrought iron laid by in his house. From this store he will give you a large ransom should he hear of my being alive and at the ships of the Achaeans."

Thus did he plead, and Menelaus was for yielding and giving him to a squire to take to the ships of the Achaeans, but Agamemnon came running up to him and rebuked him. "My good Menelaus," said he, "this is no time for giving quarter. Has, then, your house fared so well at the hands of the Trojans? Let us not spare a single one of them—not even the child unborn and in its mother's womb; let not a man of them be left alive, but let all in Ilium perish, unheeded and forgotten."

Thus did he speak, and his brother was persuaded by him, for his words were just. Menelaus, therefore, thrust Adrestus from him, whereon King Agamemnon struck him in the flank, and he fell. Then the son of Atreus planted his foot upon his breast to draw his spear from the body.

Meanwhile Nestor shouted to the Argives, saying: "My friends, Danaan warriors, servants of Ares, let no man lag that he may spoil the dead, and bring back much booty to the ships. Let us kill as many as we can; the bodies will lie upon the plain, and you can despoil them later at your leisure."

With these words he put heart and soul into them all. And now the Trojans would have been routed and driven back into Ilium had not Priam's son Helenus, wisest of augurs, said to Hector and Aeneas: "Hector and Aeneas, you two are the mainstays of the Trojans and Lycians, for you are foremost at all times, alike in fight and counsel. Hold your ground here, and go about among the host to rally them in front of the gates, or they will fling themselves into the arms of their wives, to the great joy of our foes. Then, when you have put heart into all our companies, we will stand firm here and fight the Danaans however hard they press us, for there is nothing else to be done. Meanwhile do you, Hector, go to the city and tell our mother what is happening. Tell her to bid the matrons gather at the temple of Athene in the acropolis; let her then take her key and open the doors of the sacred building; there, upon the knees of Athene, let her lay the largest, fairest robe she has in her house—the one she sets most store by; let her, moreover, promise to sacrifice twelve yearling heifers that have never yet felt the goad, in the temple of the goddess, if she will take pity on the town, with the wives and little ones of the Trojans, and keep the son of Tydeus from falling on the goodly city of Ilium; for he fights with fury and fills men's souls with panic. I hold him mightiest of them all. We did not fear even their great champion Achilles, son of a goddess though he be, as we do this man. His rage is beyond all bounds, and there is none can vie with him in prowess."

Hector did as his brother bade him. He sprang from his chariot, and went about everywhere among the host, brandishing his spears, urging the men on to fight, and raising the dread cry of battle. Thereon they rallied and again faced the Achaeans, who gave ground and ceased their murderous onset, for they deemed that some one of the immortals had come down from starry heaven to help the Trojans, so strangely had they rallied. And Hector shouted to the Trojans, "Trojans and allies, be men, my friends, and fight with might and main, while I go to Ilium and tell the old men of our council and our wives to pray to the gods and vow hecatombs in their honor."

With this he went his way, and the black rim of hide that went round his shield beat against his neck and his ankles.

Then Glaucus, son of Hippolochus, and the son of Tydeus went into the open space between the hosts to fight in single combat. When they were close up to one another Diomed of the loud war cry was the first to speak. "Who, my good sir," said he, "who are you among men? I have never seen you in battle until now, but you are daring beyond all others if you abide my onset. Woe to those fathers whose sons face my might. If, however, you are one of the immortals and have come down from heaven, I will not fight you; for even valiant Lycurgus, son of Dryas, did not live long when he took to fighting with the gods. He it was that drove the nursing women who were in charge of frenzied Dionysus through the land of Nysa, and they flung their thyrsi on the ground as murderous Lycurgus beat them with his ox-goad. Dionysus himself plunged terror-stricken into the sea, and Thetis took him to her bosom to comfort him, for he was scared by the fury with which the man reviled him. Thereon the gods who live at ease were angry with Lycurgus and the son of Cronus struck him blind, nor did he live much longer after he had become hateful to the immortals. Therefore I will not fight with the blessed gods; but if you are of them that eat the fruit of the ground, draw near and meet your doom."

And the son of Hippolochus answered: "Mighty son of Tydeus, why ask me of my lineage? Men come and go as leaves year by year upon the trees. Those of autumn the wind sheds upon the ground, but when spring returns the forest buds forth with fresh ones. Even so is it with the generations of mankind, the new spring up as the old are passing away. If, then, you would learn my descent, it is one that is well known to many. There is a city in the heart of Argos, pastureland of horses, called Ephyra, where Sisyphus lived, who was the craftiest of all mankind. He was the son of Aeolus, and had a son named Glaucus, who was father to Bellerophon, whom heaven endowed with the most surpassing comeliness and beauty. But Proetus devised his ruin, and being stronger than he, drove him from the land of the Argives over which Zeus had made him ruler. For Antea, wife of Proetus, lusted after him, and would have had him lie with her in secret; but Bellerophon was an honorable man and would not, so she told lies about him to Proetus. 'Proetus,' said she, 'kill Bellerophon or die, for he would have had converse with me against my will.' The king was angered, but shrank from killing Bellerophon, so he sent him to Lycia with lying letters of introduction, written on a folded tablet, and containing much ill against the bearer. He bade Bellerophon show these letters to his father-in-law, to the end that he might thus perish. Bellerophon, therefore, went to Lycia, and the gods convoyed him safely.

"When he reached the river Xanthus, which is in Lycia, the king received him with all goodwill, feasted him nine days, and killed nine heifers in his honor, but when rosy-fingered morning appeared upon the tenth day, he questioned him and desired to see the letter from his son-in-law Proetus. When he had received the wicked letter he first commanded Bellerophon to kill that savage monster, the Chimaera, who was not a human being, but a goddess, for she had the head of a lion and the tail of a serpent, while her body was that of a goat, and she breathed forth flames of fire; but Bellerophon slew her, for he was guided by signs from heaven. He next fought the far-famed Solymi, and this, he said, was the hardest of all his battles. Thirdly, he killed the Amazons, women who were the peers of men, and as he was returning thence the king devised yet another plan for his destruction; he picked the bravest warriors in all Lycia and placed them in ambuscade, but not a man ever came back, for Bellerophon killed every one of them. Then the king knew that he must be the valiant offspring of a god, so he kept him in Lycia, gave him his daughter in marriage, and made him of equal honor in the kingdom with himself; and the Lycians gave him a piece of land, the best in all the country, fair with vineyards and tilled fields, to have and to hold.

"The king's daughter bore Bellerophon three children, Isander, Hippolochus, and Laodameia. Zeus, the lord of counsel, lay with Laodameia, and she bore him noble Sarpedon; but when Bellerophon came to be hated by all the gods, he wandered all desolate and dismayed upon the Alean plain, gnawing at his own heart, and shunning the path of man. Ares, insatiate of battle, killed his son Isander while he was fighting the Solymi; his daughter was killed by Artemis of the golden reins, for she was angered with her; but Hippolochus was father to myself, and when he sent me to Troy he urged me again and again to fight ever among the foremost and outvie my peers, so as not to shame the blood of my fathers who were the noblest in Ephyra and in all Lycia. This, then, is the descent I claim."

Thus did he speak, and the heart of Diomed was glad. He planted his spear in the ground, and spoke to him with friendly words. "Then," he said, "you are an old friend of my father's house. Great Oeneus once entertained Bellerophon for twenty days, and the two exchanged presents. Oeneus gave a belt rich with purple, and Bellerophon a double cup, which I left at home when I set out for Troy. I do not remember Tydeus, for he was taken from us while I was yet a child, when the army of the Achaeans was cut to pieces before Thebes. Henceforth, however, I must be your host in middle Argos, and you mine in Lycia, if I should ever go there; let us avoid one another's spears even during a general engagement. There are many noble Trojans and allies whom I can kill, if I overtake them and heaven delivers them into my hand; so again with yourself, there are many Achaeans whose lives you may take if you can; we two, then, will exchange armor, that all present may know of the old ties that subsist between us."

With these words they sprang from their chariots, grasped one another's hands, and plighted friendship. But the son of Cronus made Glaucus take leave of his wits, for he exchanged golden armor for bronze, the worth of a hundred head of cattle for the worth of nine.

Now when Hector reached the Scaean gates and the oak tree, the wives and daughters of the Trojans came running towards him to ask after their sons, brothers, kinsmen, and husbands; he told them to set about praying to the gods, and many were made sorrowful as they heard him.

Presently he reached the splendid palace of King Priam, adorned with colonnades of hewn stone. In it there were fifty bedchambers—all of hewn stone—built near one another, where the sons of Priam slept, each with his wedded wife. Opposite these, on the other side the courtyard, there were twelve upper rooms also of hewn stone for Priam's daughters, built near one another, where his sons-in-law slept with their wives. When Hector got there, his fond mother came up to him with Laodice, the fairest of her daughters. She took his hand within her own and said: "My son, why have you left the battle to come hither? Are the Achaeans, woe betide them, pressing you hard about the city that you have thought fit to come and uplift your hands to Zeus from the citadel? Wait till I can bring you wine that you may make offering to Zeus and to the other immortals, and may then drink and be refreshed. Wine gives a man fresh strength when he is wearied, as you now are with fighting on behalf of your kinsmen."

And Hector answered, "Honored mother, bring no wine, lest you unman me and I forget my strength. I dare not make a drink offering to Zeus with unwashed hands. One who is bespattered with blood and filth may not pray to the son of Cronus. Get the matrons together, and go with offerings to the temple of Athene, driver of the spoil; there, upon the knees of Athene, lay the largest and fairest robe you have in your house—the one you set most store by. Promise, moreover, to sacrifice twelve yearling heifers that have never yet felt the goad, in the temple of the goddess, if she will take pity on the town, with the wives and little ones of the Trojans, and keep the son of Tydeus from off the goodly city of Ilium, for he fights with fury, and fills men's souls with panic. Go, then, to the temple of Athene, while I seek Paris and exhort him, if he will hear my words. Would that the earth might open her jaws and swallow him, for Zeus bred him to be the bane of the Trojans, and of Priam and Priam's sons. Could I but see him go down into the house of Hades, my heart would forget its heaviness."

His mother went into the house and called her waiting-women who gathered the matrons throughout the city. She then went down into her fragrant storeroom, where her embroidered robes were kept, the work of Sidonian women, whom Paris had brought over from Sidon when he sailed the seas upon that voyage during which he carried off noble Helen. Hecuba took out the largest robe and the one that was most beautifully enriched with embroidery, as an offering to Athene: it glittered like a star and lay at the very bottom of the chest. With this she went on her way and many matrons with her.

When they reached the temple of Athene, lovely Theano, daughter of Cisseus and wife of Antenor, opened the doors, for the Trojans had made her priestess of Athene. The women lifted up their hands to the goddess with a loud cry, and Theano took the robe to lay it upon the knees of Athene, praying the while to the daughter of great Zeus. "Holy Athene," she cried, "protectress of our city, mighty goddess, break the spear of Diomed and lay him low before the Scaean gates. Do this, and we will sacrifice twelve heifers that have never yet known the goad, in your temple, if you will have pity upon the town, with the wives and little ones of the Trojans." Thus she prayed, but Pallas Athene granted not her prayer.

While they were thus praying to the daughter of great Zeus, Hector went to the fair house of Paris, which he had had built for him by the foremost builders in the land. They had built him his house, storehouse, and courtyard near those of Priam and Hector on the acropolis. Here Hector entered, with a spear eleven cubits long in his hand; the bronze point gleamed in front of him, and was fastened to the shaft of the spear by a ring of gold. He found Paris within the house, busied about his armor, his shield and cuirass, and handling his curved bow; there, too, sat Argive Helen with her women, setting them their several tasks; and as Hector saw him he rebuked him with words of scorn. "Sir," said he, "you do ill to nurse this rancor. The people perish fighting round this our town. You would yourself chide one whom you saw shirking his part in the combat. Up then, or ere long the city will be in a blaze."

And Paris answered: "Hector, your rebuke is just; listen therefore, and believe me when I tell you that I am not here so much through rancor or ill will towards the Trojans, as from a desire to indulge my grief. My wife was even now gently urging me to battle, and I hold it better that I should go, for victory is ever fickle. Wait, then, while I put on my armor, or go first and I will follow. I shall be sure to overtake you."

Hector made no answer, but Helen tried to soothe him. "Brother," said she, "to my abhorred and sinful self, would that a whirlwind had caught me up on the day my mother brought me forth and had borne me to some mountain or to the waves of the roaring sea that should have swept me away ere this mischief had come about. But, since the gods have devised these evils, would, at any rate, that I had been wife to a better man—to one who could smart under dishonor and men's evil speeches. This fellow was never yet to be depended upon, nor never will be, and he will surely reap what he has sown. Still, brother, come in and rest upon this seat, for it is you who bear the brunt of that toil that has been caused by my hateful self and by the sin of Paris—both of whom Zeus has doomed to be a theme of song among those that shall be born hereafter."

And Hector answered: "Bid me not be seated, Helen, for all the goodwill you bear me. I cannot stay. I am in haste to help the Trojans, who miss me greatly when I am not among them; but urge your husband, and of his own self also let him make haste to overtake me before I am out of the city. I must go home to see my household, my wife, and my little son, for I know not whether I shall ever again return to them, or whether the gods will cause me to fall by the hands of the Achaeans."

Then Hector left her, and forthwith was at his own house. He did not find Andromache, for she was on the wall with her child and one of her maids, weeping bitterly. Seeing, then, that she was not within, he stood on the threshold of the women's rooms and said: "Women, tell me, and tell me true, where did Andromache go when she left the house? Was it to my sisters or to my brothers' wives? Or is she at the temple of Athene where the other women are propitiating the awful goddess?"

His good housekeeper answered: "Hector, since you bid me tell you truly, she did not go to your sisters nor to your brothers' wives, nor yet to the temple of Athene, where the other women are propitiating the awful goddess, but she is on the high wall of Ilium, for she had heard the Trojans were being hard pressed, and that the Achaeans were in great force: therefore she went to the wall in frenzied haste, and the nurse went with her carrying the child."

Hector hurried from the house when she had done speaking, and went down the streets by the same way that he had come. When he had gone through the city and had reached the Scaean gates through which he would go out on to the plain, his wife came running towards him, Andromache, daughter of great Eëtion who ruled in Thebe under the wooded slopes of Mount Placus, and was king of the Cilicians. His daughter had married Hector, and now came to meet him with a nurse who carried his little child in her bosom—a mere babe, Hector's darling son, and lovely as a star. Hector had named him Scamandrius, but the people called him Astyanax ["king of the city"] for his father stood alone as chief guardian of Ilium.

Hector smiled as he looked upon the boy, but he did not speak, and Andromache stood by him weeping and taking his hand in her own. "Dear husband," said she, "your valor will bring you to destruction. Think on your infant son, and on my hapless self who ere long shall be your widow—for the Achaeans will set upon you in a body and kill you. It would be better for me, should I lose you, to lie dead and buried, for I shall have nothing left to comfort me when you are gone, save only sorrow. I have neither father nor mother now. Achilles slew my father when he sacked Thebe, the goodly city of the Cilicians. He slew him, but did not for very shame despoil him. When he had burned him in his wondrous armor, he raised a barrow over his ashes and the mountain nymphs, daughters of aegis-bearing Zeus, planted a grove of elms about his tomb. I had seven brothers in my father's house, but on the same day they all went within the house of Hades. Achilles killed them as they were with their sheep and cattle. My mother—her who had been queen of all the land under Mount Placus—he brought hither with the spoil, and freed her for a great sum, but the archer-queen Artemis took her in the house of your father. Nay—Hector—you who to me are father, mother, brother, and dear husband—have mercy upon me; stay here upon this wall; make not your child fatherless, and your wife a widow; as for the host, place them near the fig tree, where the city can be best scaled, and the wall is weakest. Thrice have the bravest of them come thither and assailed it, under the two Ajaxes, Idomeneus, the sons of Atreus, and the brave son of Tydeus, either of their own bidding, or because some soothsayer had told them."

And Hector answered: "Wife, I too have thought upon all this, but with what face should I look upon the Trojans, men or women, if I shirked battle like a coward? I cannot do so: I know nothing save to fight bravely in the forefront of the Trojan host and win renown alike for my father and myself. Well do I know that the day will surely come when mighty Ilium shall be destroyed with Priam and Priam's people, but I grieve for none of these—not even for Hecuba, nor King Priam, nor for my brothers many and brave who may fall in the dust before their foes—for none of these do I grieve as for yourself when the day shall come on which some one of the Achaeans shall rob you forever of your freedom, and bear you weeping away. It may be that you will have to ply the loom in Argos at the bidding of a mistress, or to fetch water from the springs Messeïs or Hypereia, treated brutally by some cruel taskmaster; then will one say who sees you weeping,

'She was wife to Hector, the bravest warrior among the Trojans during the war before Ilium.' On this your tears will break forth anew for him who would have put away the day of captivity from you. May I lie dead under the barrow that is heaped over my body ere I hear your cry as they carry you into bondage."

He stretched his arms towards his child, but the boy cried and nestled in his nurse's bosom, scared at the sight of his father's armor, and at the horsehair plume that nodded fiercely from his helmet. His father and mother laughed to see him, but Hector took the helmet from his head and laid it all gleaming upon the ground. Then he took his darling child, kissed him, and dandled him in his arms, praying over him the while to Zeus and to all the gods. "Zeus," he cried, "grant that this my child may be even as myself, chief among the Trojans; let him be not less excellent in strength, and let him rule Ilium with his might. Then may one say of him as he comes from battle, 'The son is far better than the father.' May he bring back the bloodstained spoils of him whom he has laid low, and let his mother's heart be glad."

With this he laid the child again in the arms of his wife, who took him to her own soft bosom, smiling through her tears. As her husband watched her his heart yearned towards her and he caressed her fondly, saying: "My own wife, do not take these things too bitterly to heart. No one can hurry me down to Hades before my time, but if a man's hour is come, be he brave or be he coward, there is no escape for him when he has once been born. Go, then, within the house, and busy yourself with your daily duties, your loom, your distaff, and the ordering of your servants; for war is man's matter, and mine above all others of them that have been born in Ilium."

He took his plumed helmet from the ground, and his wife went back again to her house, weeping bitterly and often looking back towards him. When she reached her home she found her maidens within, and bade them all join in her lament; so they mourned Hector in his own house though he was yet alive, for they deemed that they should never see him return safe from battle, and from the furious hands of the Achaeans.

Paris did not remain long in his house. He donned his goodly armor overlaid with bronze, and hasted through the city as fast as his feet could take him. As a horse, stabled and full-fed, breaks loose and gallops gloriously over the plain to the place where he is wont to bathe in the fair-flowing river—he holds his head high, and his mane streams upon his shoulders as he exults in his strength and flies like the wind to the haunts and feeding ground of the mares—even so went forth Paris from high Pergamus, gleaming like sunlight in his armor, and he laughed aloud as he sped swiftly on his way. Forthwith he came upon his brother Hector, who was then turning away from the place where he had held converse with his wife, and he was himself the first to speak. "Sir," said he, "I fear that I have kept you waiting when you are in haste, and have not come as quickly as you bade me."

"My good brother," answered Hector, "you fight bravely, and no man with any justice can make light of your doings in battle. But you are careless and willfully remiss. It grieves me to the heart to hear the ill that the Trojans speak about you, for they have suffered much on your account. Let us be going, and we will make things right hereafter, should Zeus vouchsafe us to set the cup of our deliverance before the ever-living gods of heaven in our own homes, when we have chased the Achaeans from Troy."

BOOK VII

Paris and Hector raise such havoc that Athene and Apollo decide to stop the bloodshed, while Hector and Ajax meet in single combat. The fall of night stops the duel. A truce is agreed upon to allow both sides to bury their dead, and the Greeks use this respite also to build a wall in front of their ships. In Troy, old Antenor proposes that Helen be returned to Menelaus in accordance with the covenant, but Paris refuses.

WITH THESE WORDS HECTOR PASSED THROUGH THE GATES, and his brother Paris with him, both eager for the fray. As when heaven sends a breeze to sailors who have long looked for one in vain and have labored at their oars till they are faint with toil, even so welcome was the sight of these two heroes to the Trojans.

Thereon Paris killed Menesthius, the son of Areïthoüs. He lived in Arne and was son of Areïthoüs, the Mace-man, and of Phylomedusa. Hector threw a spear at Eioneus and struck him dead with a wound in the neck under the bronze rim of his helmet. Glaucus, moreover, son of Hippolochus, captain of the Lycians, in hard hand-to-hand fight smote Iphinoüs, son of Dexius, on the shoulder, as he was springing on to his chariot behind his fleet mares; so he fell to earth from the car, and there was no life left in him.

When, therefore, Athene saw these men making havoc of the Argives, she darted down to Ilium from the summits of Olympus, and Apollo, who was looking on from Pergamus, went out to meet her; for he wanted the Trojans to be victorious. The pair met by the oak tree, and King Apollo, son of Zeus, was first to speak. "What would you have," said he, "daughter of great Zeus, that your proud spirit has sent you hither from Olympus? Have you no pity upon the Trojans, and would you incline the scales of victory in favor of the Danaans? Let me persuade you—for it will be better thus—stay the combat for today, but let them renew the fight hereafter till they compass the doom of Ilium, since you goddesses have made up your minds to destroy the city."

And Athene answered, "So be it, Far-darter; it was in this mind that I came down from Olympus to the Trojans and Achaeans. Tell me, then, how do you propose to end this present fighting?"

Apollo, son of Zeus, replied, "Let us incite great Hector to challenge some one of the Danaans in single combat; on this the Achaeans will be shamed into finding a man who will fight him."

Athene assented, and Helenus, son of Priam, divined the counsel of the gods. He therefore went up to Hector and said: "Hector, son of Priam, peer of gods in counsel, I am your brother, let me then persuade you. Bid the other Trojans and Achaeans all of them take their seats, and challenge the best man among the Achaeans to meet you in single combat. I have heard the voice of the ever-living gods, and the hour of your doom is not yet come."

Hector was glad when he heard this saying, and went in among the Trojans, grasping his spear by the middle to hold them back, and they all sat down. Agamemnon also bade the Achaeans be seated. But Athene and Apollo, in the likeness of vultures, perched on father Zeus's high oak tree, proud of their men; and the ranks sat close-ranged together, bristling with shield and helmet and spear. As when the rising west wind furs the face of the sea and the waters grow dark beneath it, so sat the companies of Trojans and Achaeans upon the plain. And Hector spoke thus:

"Hear me, Trojans and Achaeans, that I may speak even as I am minded. Zeus on his high throne has brought our oaths and covenants to nothing, and foreshadows ill for both of us, till you either take the towers of Troy, or are yourselves vanquished at your ships. The princes of the Achaeans are here present in the midst of you. Let him, then, that will fight me stand forward as your champion against Hector. Thus I say, and may Zeus be witness between us. If your champion slay me, let him strip me of my armor and take it to your ships, but let him send my body home that the Trojans and their wives may give me my dues of fire when I am dead. In like manner if Apollo vouchsafe me glory and I slay your champion, I will strip him of his armor and take it to the city of Ilium, where I will hang it in the temple of Apollo, but I will give up his body, that the Achaeans may bury him at their ships, and build him a mound by the wide waters of the Hellespont. Then will one say hereafter as he sails his ship over the sea, 'This is the monument of one who died long since—a champion who was slain by mighty Hector.' Thus will one say, and my fame shall not be lost."

Thus did he speak, but they all held their peace, ashamed to decline the challenge, yet fearing to accept it, till at last Menelaus rose and rebuked them, for he was angry. "Alas," he cried, "vain braggarts, women forsooth, not men, double-dyed indeed will be the stain upon us if no man of the Danaans will now face Hector! May you be turned every man of you into earth and water as you sit spiritless and inglorious in your places. I will myself go out against this man, but the upshot of the fight will be from on high in the hands of the immortal gods."

With these words he put on his armor; and then, O Menelaus, your life would have come to an end at the hands of Hector, for he was far the better man, had not the princes of the Achaeans sprung upon you and checked you. King Agamemnon caught him by the right hand and said: "Menelaus, you are mad; a truce to this folly. Be patient in spite of passion, do not think of fighting a man so much stronger than yourself as Hector, son of Priam, who is feared by many another as well as you. Even Achilles, who is far more doughty than you are, shrank from meeting him in battle. Sit down among your own people, and the Achaeans will send some other champion to fight Hector. Fearless and fond of battle though he be, I ween his knees will bend gladly under him if he comes out alive from the hurly-burly of this fight."

With these words of reasonable counsel he persuaded his brother, whereon his squires gladly stripped the armor from off his shoulders. Then Nestor rose and spoke. "Of a truth," said he, "the Achaean land is fallen upon evil times. The old knight Peleus, counselor and orator among the Myrmidons, loved when I was in his house to question me concerning the race and lineage of all the Argives. How would it not grieve him could he hear of them as now quailing before Hector? Many a time would he lift his hands in prayer that his soul might leave his body and go down within the house of Hades. Would, by father Zeus, Athene, and Apollo, that I were still young and strong as when the Pylians and Arcadians were gathered in fight by the rapid river Celadon under the walls of Pheia, and round about the waters of the river Iardanus. The godlike hero Ereuthalion stood forward as their champion, with the armor of King Areïthoüs upon his shoulders—Areïthoüs whom men and women had surnamed 'the Mace-man,' because he fought neither with bow nor spear, but broke the battalions of the foe with his iron mace. Lycurgus killed him, not in fair fight, but by entrapping him in a narrow way where his mace served him in no stead; for Lycurgus was too quick for him and speared him through the middle, so he fell to earth on his back. Lycurgus then spoiled him of the armor which Ares had given him, and bore it in battle thenceforward; but when he grew old and stayed at home, he gave it to his faithful squire Ereuthalion, who in this same armor challenged the foremost men among us. The others quaked and quailed, but my high spirit bade me fight him though none other would venture. I was the youngest man of them all, but when I fought him Athene vouchsafed me victory. He was the biggest and strongest man that ever I killed, and covered much ground as he lay sprawling upon the earth. Would that I were still young and strong as I then was, for the son of Priam would then soon find one who would face him. But you, foremost among the whole host though you be, have none of you any stomach for fighting Hector."

Thus did the old man rebuke them, and forthwith nine men started to their feet. Foremost of all uprose King Agamemnon, and after him brave Diomed, the son of Tydeus. Next were the two Ajaxes, men clothed in valor as with a garment, and then Idomeneus, and Meriones his brother in arms. After these, Eurypylus, son of Euaemon, Thoas, the son of Andraemon, and Odysseus also rose. Then Nestor, knight of Gerene, again spoke, saying: "Cast lots among you to see who shall be chosen. If he come alive out of this fight he will have done good service alike to his own soul and to the Achaeans."

Thus he spoke, and when each of them had marked his lot, and had thrown it into the helmet of Agamemnon, son of Atreus, the people lifted their hands in prayer, and thus would one of them say as he looked into the vault of heaven, "Father Zeus, grant that the lot fall on Ajax, or on the son of Tydeus, or upon the king of rich Mycene himself."

As they were speaking, Nestor, knight of Gerene, shook the helmet, and from it there fell the very lot which they wanted—the lot of Ajax. The herald bore it about and showed it to all the chieftains of the Achaeans, going from left to right; but they none of them owned it. When, however, in due course he reached the man who had written upon it and had put it into the helmet, brave Ajax held out his hand, and the herald gave him the lot. When Ajax saw his mark he knew it and was glad; he threw it to the ground and said: "My friends, the lot is mine, and I rejoice, for I shall vanquish Hector. I will put on my armor; meanwhile, pray to King Zeus in silence among yourselves that the Trojans may not hear you—or aloud if you will, for we fear no man. None shall overcome me, neither by force nor cunning, for I was born and bred in Salamis, and can hold my own in all things."

With this they fell praying to King Zeus, the son of Cronus, and thus would one of them say as he looked into the vault of heaven, "Father Zeus that rulest from Ida, most glorious in power, vouchsafe victory to Ajax, and let him win great glory: but if you wish well to Hector also and would protect him, grant to each of them equal fame and prowess."

Thus they prayed, and Ajax armed himself in his suit of gleaming bronze. When he was in full array he sprang forward as monstrous Ares when he takes part among men whom Zeus has set fighting with one another—even so did huge Ajax, bulwark of the Achaeans, spring forward with a grim smile on his face as he brandished his long spear and strode onward. The Argives were elated as they beheld him, but the Trojans trembled in every limb, and the heart even of Hector beat quickly, but he could not now retreat and withdraw into the ranks behind him, for he had been the challenger. Ajax came up bearing his shield in front of him like a wall—a shield of bronze with seven folds of oxhide—the work of Tychius, who lived in Hyle and was by far the best worker in leather. He had made it with the hides of seven full-fed bulls, and over these he had set an eighth layer of bronze. Holding his shield before him, Ajax, son of Telamon, came close up to Hector and menaced him, saying: "Hector, you shall now learn, man to man, what kind of champions the Danaans have among them even besides lion-hearted Achilles, cleaver of the ranks of men. He now abides at the ships in anger with Agamemnon, shepherd of his people, but there are many of us who are well able to face you; therefore begin the fight."

And Hector answered: "Noble Ajax, son of Telamon, captain of the host, treat me not as though I were some puny boy or woman that cannot fight. I have been long used to the blood and butcheries of battle. I am quick to turn my leathern shield either to right or left, for this I deem the main thing in battle. I can charge among the chariots and horsemen, and in hand-to-hand fighting can delight the heart of Ares; howbeit I would not take such a man as you are off his guard—but I will smite you openly if I can."

He poised his spear as he spoke, and hurled it from him. It struck the sevenfold shield in its outermost layer—the eighth, which was of bronze—and went through six of the layers, but in the seventh hide it stayed. Then Ajax threw in his turn and struck the round shield of the son of Priam. The terrible spear went through his gleaming shield and pressed onward through his cuirass of cunning workmanship; it pierced the shirt against his side, but he swerved and thus saved his life. They then each of them drew out the spear from his shield and fell on one another like savage lions or wild boars of great strength and endurance. The son of Priam struck the middle of Ajax's shield, but the bronze did not break, and the point of his dart was turned. Ajax then sprang forward and pierced the shield of Hector; the spear went through it and staggered him as he was springing forward to attack. It gashed his neck and the blood came pouring from the wound, but even so Hector did not cease fighting. He gave ground, and with his brawny hand seized a stone, rugged and huge, that was lying upon the plain; with this he struck the shield of Ajax on the boss that was in its middle, so that the bronze rang again. But Ajax in turn caught up a far larger stone, swung it aloft, and hurled it with prodigious force. This millstone of a rock broke Hector's shield inwards and threw him down on his back with the shield crushing him under it, but Apollo raised him at once. Thereon they would have hacked at one another in close combat with their swords, had not heralds, messengers of gods and men, come forward, one from the Trojans and the other from the Achaeans—Talthybius and Idaeus, both of them honorable men; these parted them with their staves, and the good herald Idaeus said: "My sons, fight no longer, you are both of you valiant, and both are dear to Zeus; we know this; but night is now falling, and the behests of night may not be well gainsaid."

Ajax, son of Telamon, answered: "Idaeus, bid Hector say so, for it was he that challenged our princes. Let him speak first and I will accept his saying."

Then Hector said: "Ajax, heaven has vouchsafed you stature and strength, and judgment; and in wielding the spear you excel all others of the Achaeans. Let us for this day cease fighting; hereafter we will fight anew till heaven decide between us, and give victory to one or to the other; night is now falling, and the behests of night may not be well gainsaid. Gladden, then, the hearts of the Achaeans at your ships, and more especially those of your own followers and clansmen, while I, in the great city of King Priam, bring comfort to the Trojans and their women, who vie with one another in their prayers on my behalf. Let us, moreover, exchange presents, that it may be said among Achaeans and Trojans, 'They fought with might and main, but were reconciled and parted in friendship.' "

On this he gave Ajax a silver-studded sword with its sheath and leathern baldric, and in return Ajax gave him a girdle dyed with purple. Thus they parted, the one going to the host of the Achaeans, and the other to that of the Trojans, who rejoiced when they saw their hero come to them safe and unharmed from the strong hands of mighty Ajax. They led him, therefore, to the city as one that had been saved beyond their hopes. On the other side the Achaeans brought Ajax elated with victory to Agamemnon.

When they reached the quarters of the son of Atreus, Agamemnon sacrificed for them a five-year-old bull in honor of Zeus, the son of Cronus. They flayed the carcass, made it ready, and divided it into joints. These they cut carefully up into smaller pieces, putting them on the spits, roasting them sufficiently, and then drawing them off. When they had done all this and had prepared the feast, they ate it, and every man had his full and equal share, so that all were satisfied, and King Agamemnon gave Ajax some slices cut lengthways down the loin, as a mark of special honor. As soon as they had had enough to eat and drink, old Nestor, whose counsel was ever truest, began to speak; with all sincerity and goodwill, therefore, he addressed them thus:

"Son of Atreus, and other chieftains, inasmuch as many of the Achaeans are now dead, whose blood Ares has shed by the banks of the Scamander, and their souls have gone down to the house of Hades, it will be well when morning comes that we should cease fighting; we will then wheel our dead together with oxen and mules and burn them not far from the ships, that when we sail hence we may take the bones of our comrades home to their children. Hard by the funeral pyre we will build a barrow that shall be raised from the plain for all in common; near this let us set about building a high wall, to shelter ourselves and our ships, and let it have well-made gates that there may be a way through them for our chariots. Close outside we will dig a deep trench all round it to keep off both horse and foot, that the Trojan chieftains may not bear hard upon us."

Thus he spoke, and the princes shouted in applause. Meanwhile the Trojans held a council, angry and full of discord, on the acropolis by the gates of King Priam's palace; and wise Antenor spoke. "Hear me," he said, "Trojans, Dardanians, and allies, that I may speak even as I am minded. Let us give up Argive Helen and her wealth to the sons of Atreus, for we are now fighting in violation of our solemn covenants, and shall not prosper till we have done as I say."

He then sat down and Paris, husband of lovely Helen, rose to speak. "Antenor," said he, "your words are not to my liking; you can find a better saying than this if you will. If, however, you have spoken in good earnest, then indeed has heaven robbed you of your reason. I will speak plainly, and hereby notify to the Trojans that I will not give up the woman; but the wealth that I brought home with her from Argos I will restore, and will add yet further of my own."

On this, when Paris had spoken and taken his seat, Priam of the race of Dardanus, peer of gods in counsel, rose and with all sincerity and goodwill addressed them thus: "Hear me, Trojans, Dardanians, and allies, that I may speak even as I am minded. Get your suppers now as hitherto throughout the city, but keep your watches and be wakeful. At daybreak let Idaeus go to the ships, and tell Agamemnon and Menelaus, sons of Atreus, the saying of Paris through whom this quarrel has come about; and let him also be instant with them that they now cease fighting till we burn our dead; hereafter we will fight anew, till heaven decide between us and give victory to one or to the other."

Thus did he speak, and they did even as he had said. They took supper in their companies and at daybreak Idaeus went his way to the ships. He found the Danaans, servants of Ares, in council at the stern of Agamemnon's ship, and took his place in the midst of them. "Son of Atreus," he said, "and princes of the Achaean host, Priam and the other noble Trojans have sent me to tell you the saying of Paris through whom this quarrel has come about, if so be that you may find it acceptable. All the treasure he took with him in his ships to Troy—would that he had sooner perished—he will restore, and will add yet further of his own, but he will not give up the wedded wife of Menelaus, though the Trojans would have him do so. Priam bade me inquire further if you will cease fighting till we burn our dead. Hereafter we will fight anew, till heaven decide between us and give victory to one or to the other."

They all held their peace, but presently Diomed of the loud war cry spoke, saying, "Let there be no taking, neither treasure, nor yet Helen, for even a child may see that the doom of the Trojans is at hand."

The sons of the Achaeans shouted applause at the words that Diomed had spoken, and thereon King Agamemnon said to Idaeus: "Idaeus, you have heard the answer the Achaeans make you—and I with them. But as concerning the dead, I give you leave to burn them, for when men are once dead there should be no grudging them the rites of fire. Let Zeus, the mighty husband of Hera, be witness to this covenant."

As he spoke he upheld his scepter in the sight of all the gods, and Idaeus went back to the strong city of Ilium. The Trojans and Dardanians were gathered in council waiting his return; when he came, he stood in their midst and delivered his message. As soon as they heard it they set about their twofold labor, some to gather the corpses, and others to bring in wood. The Argives on their part also hastened from their ships, some to gather the corpses, and others to bring in wood.

The sun was beginning to beat upon the fields, fresh risen into the vault of heaven from the slow still currents of deep Oceanus, when the two armies met. They could hardly recognize their dead, but they washed the clotted gore from off them, shed tears over them, and lifted them upon their wagons. Priam had forbidden the Trojans to wail aloud, so they heaped their dead sadly and silently upon the pyre, and having burned them went back to the city of Ilium. The Achaeans in like manner heaped their dead sadly and silently on the pyre, and having burned them went back to their ships.

Now in the twilight when it was not yet dawn, chosen bands of the Achaeans were gathered round the pyre and built one barrow that was raised in common for all, and hard by this they built a high wall to shelter themselves and their ships. They gave it strong gates that there might be a way through them for their chariots, and close outside it they dug a trench deep and wide, and they planted it within with stakes.

Thus did the Achaeans toil, and the gods, seated by the side of Zeus, the lord of lightning, marveled at their great work; but Poseidon, lord of the earthquake, spoke, saying, "Father Zeus, what mortal in the whole world will again take the gods into his counsel? See you not how the Achaeans have built a wall about their ships and driven a trench all round it, without offering hecatombs to the gods? The fame of this wall will reach as far as dawn itself, and men will no longer think anything of the one which Phoebus Apollo and myself built with so much labor for Laomedon."

Zeus was displeased and answered: "What, O shaker of the earth, are you talking about? A god less powerful than yourself might be alarmed at what they are doing, but your fame reaches as far as dawn itself. Surely when the Achaeans have gone home with their ships, you can shatter their wall and fling it into the sea; you can cover the beach with sand again, and the great wall of the Achaeans will then be utterly effaced."

Thus did they converse, and by sunset the work of the Achaeans was completed; they then slaughtered oxen at their tents and got their supper. Many ships had come with wine from Lemnos, sent by Euneüs, the son of Jason, born to him by Hypsipyle. The son of Jason freighted them with ten thousand measures of wine, which he sent specially to the sons of Atreus, Agamemnon and Menelaus. From this supply the Achaeans bought their wine, some with bronze, some with iron, some with hides, some with whole heifers, and some again with captives. They spread a goodly banquet and feasted the whole night through, as also did the Trojans and their allies in the city. But all the time Zeus boded them ill and roared with his portentous thunder. Pale fear got hold upon them, and they spilled the wine from their cups on to the ground, nor did any dare drink till he had made offerings to the most mighty son of Cronus. Then they laid themselves down to rest and enjoyed the boon of sleep.

BOOK VIII

In the morning, Zeus forbids further interference by the gods and goes down to Mount Ida to watch events. The advantage now goes to the Trojans. Nestor and Diomed drive together against Hector, but recoil as Zeus hurls flaming thunderbolts at them. Hera and Athene, who have started down from Olympus to aid the Greeks, are ordered back by Zeus. The Greeks are forced to retire behind their new wall and the Trojans bivouac confidently on the plain.

Now when morning, clad in her robe of saffron, had begun to suffuse light over the earth, Zeus called the gods in council on the topmost crest of serrated Olympus. Then he spoke and all the other gods gave ear. "Hear me," said he, "gods and goddesses, that I may speak even as I am minded. Let none of you, neither goddess nor god, try to cross me, but obey me every one of you that I may bring this matter to an end. If I see anyone acting apart and helping either Trojans or Danaans, he shall be beaten inordinately ere he come back again to Olympus; or I will hurl him down into dark Tartarus far into the deepest pit under the earth, where the gates are iron and the floor bronze, as far beneath Hades as heaven is high above the earth, that you may learn how much the mightiest I am among you. Try me and find out for yourselves. Hang me a golden chain from heaven, and lay hold of it all of you, gods and goddesses together—tug as you will, you will not drag Zeus, the supreme counselor, from heaven to earth; but were I to pull at it myself I should draw you up with earth and sea into the bargain, then would I bind the chain about some pinnacle of Olympus and leave you all dangling in the mid-firmament. So far am I above all others either of gods or men."

They were frightened and all of them held their peace, for he had spoken masterfully; but at last Athene answered: "Father, son of Cronus, king of kings, we all know that your might is not to be gainsaid, but we are also sorry for the Danaan warriors, who are perishing and coming to a bad end. We will, however, since you so bid us, refrain from actual fighting, but we will make serviceable suggestions to the Argives that they may not all of them perish in your displeasure."

Zeus smiled at her and answered, "Take heart, my child, Trito-born; I am not really in earnest, and I wish to be kind to you."

With this he yoked his fleet horses, with hoofs of bronze and manes of glittering gold. He girded himself also with gold about the body, seized his gold whip, and took his seat in his chariot. Thereon he lashed his horses and they flew forward nothing loath, midway twixt earth and starry heaven. After a while he reached many-fountained Ida, mother of wild beasts, and Gargarus, where are his grove and fragrant altar. There the father of gods and men stayed his horses, took them from the chariot, and hid them in a thick cloud. Then he took his seat all glorious upon the topmost crests, looking down upon the city of Troy and the ships of the Achaeans.

The Achaeans took their morning meal hastily at the ships, and afterwards put on their armor. The Trojans on the other hand likewise armed themselves throughout the city, fewer in numbers but nevertheless eager perforce to do battle for their wives and children. All the gates were flung wide open, and horse and foot sallied forth with the tramp as of a great multitude.

When they were got together in one place, shield clashed with shield, and spear with spear, in the conflict of mail-clad men.

Mighty was the din as the bossed shields pressed hard on one another—death cry and shout of triumph of slain and slayers, and the earth ran red with blood.

Now so long as the day waxed and it was still morning their weapons beat against one another, and the people fell, but when the sun had reached mid-heaven, the sire of all balanced his golden scales and put two fates of death within them, one for the Trojans and the other for the Achaeans. He took the balance by the middle, and when he lifted it up the day of the Achaeans sank. The death-fraught scale of the Achaeans settled down upon the ground, while that of the Trojans rose heavenwards. Then he thundered aloud from Ida, and sent the glare of his lightning upon the Achaeans; when they saw this, pale fear fell upon them and they were sore afraid.

Idomeneus dared not stay nor yet Agamemnon, nor did the two Ajaxes, servants of Ares, hold their ground. Nestor, knight of Gerene, alone stood firm, bulwark of the Achaeans, not of his own will, but one of his horses was disabled. Paris, husband of lovely Helen, had hit it with an arrow just on the top of its head where the mane begins to grow away from the skull, a very deadly place. The horse bounded in his anguish as the arrow pierced his brain, and his struggles threw the others into confusion. The old man instantly began cutting the traces with his sword, but Hector's fleet horses bore down upon him through the rout with their bold charioteer, even Hector himself, and the old man would have perished there and then had not Diomed been quick to mark, and with a loud cry called Odysseus to help him.

"Odysseus," he cried, "noble son of Laertes, where are you flying to, with your back turned like a coward? See that you are not struck with a spear between the shoulders. Stay here and help me to defend Nestor from this man's furious onset."

Odysseus would not give ear, but sped onward to the ships of the Achaeans, and the son of Tydeus, flinging himself alone into the thick of the fight, took his stand before the horses of the son of Neleus. "Sir," said he, "these young warriors are pressing you hard, your force is spent, and age is heavy upon you, your squire is naught, and your horses are slow to move. Mount my chariot and see what the horses of Tros can do—how cleverly they can scud hither and thither over the plain either in flight or in pursuit. I took them from the hero Aeneas. Let our squires attend to your own steeds, but let us drive mine straight at the Trojans, that Hector may learn how furiously I too can wield my spear."

Nestor, knight of Gerene, hearkened to his words. Thereon the doughty squires, Sthenelus and kind-hearted Eurymedon, saw to Nestor's horses, while the two both mounted Diomed's chariot. Nestor took the reins in his hands and lashed the horses on. They were soon close up with Hector, and the son of Tydeus aimed a spear at him as he was charging full speed towards them. He missed him, but struck his charioteer and squire Eniopeus, son of noble Thebaeus, in the breast by the nipple while the reins were in his hands, so that he died there and then, and the horses swerved as he fell headlong from the chariot. Hector was greatly grieved at the loss of his charioteer, but let him lie for all his sorrow, while he went in quest of another driver; nor did his steeds have to go long without one, for he presently found brave Archeptolemus, the son of Iphitus, and made him get up behind the horses, giving the reins into his hand.

All had then been lost and no help for it, for they would have been penned up in Ilium like sheep, had not the sire of gods and men been quick to mark, and hurled a fiery flaming thunderbolt which fell just in front of Diomed's horses with a flare of burning brimstone. The horses were frightened and tried to back beneath the car, while the reins dropped from Nestor's hands. Then he was afraid and said to Diomed: "Son of Tydeus, turn your horses in flight. See you not that the hand of Zeus is against you? Today he vouchsafes victory to Hector; tomorrow, if it so please him, he will again grant it to ourselves. No man, however brave, may thwart the purpose of Zeus, for he is far stronger than any."

Diomed answered: "All that you have said is true; there is a grief however which pierces me to the very heart, for Hector will talk among the Trojans and say, 'The son of Tydeus fled before me to the ships.' This is the vaunt he will make, and may earth then swallow me."

"Son of Tydeus," replied Nestor, "what mean you?' Though Hector say that you are a coward the Trojans and Dardanians will not believe him, nor yet the wives of the mighty warriors whom you have laid low."

So saying he turned the horses back through the thick of the battle, and with a cry that rent the air the Trojans and Hector rained their darts after them. Hector shouted to him and said: "Son of Tydeus, the Danaans have done you honor hitherto as regards your place at table, the meals they give you, and the filling of your cup with wine. Henceforth they will despise you, for you are become no better than a woman. Be off, girl and coward that you are, you shall not scale our walls through any flinching on my part; neither shall you carry off our wives in your ships, for I shall kill you with my own hand."

The son of Tydeus was in two minds whether or no to turn his horses round again and fight him. Thrice did he doubt, and thrice did Zeus thunder from the heights of Ida in token to the Trojans that he would turn the battle in their favor. Hector then shouted to them and said: "Trojans, Lycians, and Dardanians, lovers of close fighting, be men, my friends, and fight with might and with main. I see that Zeus is minded to vouchsafe victory and great glory to myself, while he will deal destruction upon the Danaans. Fools, for having thought of building this weak and worthless wall. It shall not stay my fury; my horses will spring lightly over their trench, and when I am at their ships forget not to bring me fire that I may burn them, while I slaughter the Argives who will be all dazed and bewildered by the smoke."

Then he cried to his horses: "Xanthus and Podargus, and you Aethon and goodly Lampus, pay me for your keep now and for all the honey-sweet corn with which Andromache, daughter of great Eëtion, has fed you, and for the way in which she has mixed wine and water for you to drink whenever you would, before doing so even for me who am her own husband. Haste in pursuit, that we may take the shield of Nestor, the fame of which ascends to heaven, for it is of solid gold, arm-rods and all, and that we may strip from the shoulders of Diomed the cuirass which Hephaestus made him. Could we take these two things, the Achaeans would set sail in their ships this selfsame night."

Thus did he vaunt, but Queen Hera made high Olympus quake as she shook with rage upon her throne. Then said she to the mighty god Poseidon: "What now, wide-ruling lord of the earthquake? Can you find no compassion in your heart for the dying Danaans, who bring you many a welcome offering to Helice and to Aegae? Wish them well then. If all of us who are with the Danaans were to drive the Trojans back and keep Zeus from helping them, he would have to sit there sulking alone on Ida."

King Poseidon was greatly troubled and answered, "Hera, rash of tongue, what are you talking about? We other gods must not set ourselves against Zeus, for he is far stronger than we are."

Thus did they converse; but the whole space enclosed by the ditch, from the ships even to the wall, was filled with horses and warriors, who were pent up there by Hector, son of Priam, now that the hand of Zeus was with him. He would even have set fire to the ships and burned them had not Queen Hera put it into the mind of Agamemnon to bestir himself and to encourage the Achaeans. To this end he went round the ships and tents carrying a great purple cloak, and took his stand by the huge black hull of Odysseus's ship, which was middlemost of all. It was from this place that his voice would carry farthest, on the one hand towards the tents of Ajax, son of Telamon, and on the other towards those of Achilles—for these two heroes, well-assured of their own strength, had valorously drawn up their ships at the two ends of the line. From this spot then, with a voice that could be heard afar, he shouted to the Danaans, saying: "Argives, shame on you cowardly creatures, brave in semblance only! Where are now our vaunts that we should prove victorious—the vaunts we made so vaingloriously in Lemnos, when we ate the flesh of horned cattle and filled our mixing bowls to the brim? You vowed that you would each of you stand against a hundred or two hundred men, and now you prove no match even for one—for Hector, who will be ere long setting our ships in a blaze. Father Zeus, did you ever so ruin a great king and rob him so utterly of his greatness? Yet, when to my sorrow I was coming hither, I never let my ship pass your altars without offering the fat and thighbones of heifers upon every one of them, so eager was I to sack the city of Troy. Vouchsafe me then this prayer—suffer us to escape at any rate with our lives, and let not the Achaeans be so utterly vanquished by the Trojans."

Thus did he pray, and father Zeus pitying his tears vouchsafed him that his people should live, not die. Forthwith he sent them an eagle, most unfailingly portentous of all birds, with a young fawn in its talons; the eagle dropped the fawn by the altar on which the Achaeans sacrificed to Zeus the lord of omens. When, therefore, the people saw that the bird had come from Zeus, they sprang more fiercely upon the Trojans and fought more boldly.

There was no man of all the many Danaans who could then boast that he had driven his horses over the trench and gone forth to fight sooner than the son of Tydeus; long before anyone else could do so he slew an armed warrior of the Trojans, Agelaus, the son of Phradmon. He had turned his horses in flight, but the spear struck him in the back midway between his shoulders and went right through his chest, and his armor rang rattling round him as he fell forward from his chariot.

After him came Agamemnon and Menelaus, sons of Atreus, the two Ajaxes clothed in valor as with a garment, Idomeneus and his companion in arms, Meriones, peer of murderous Ares, and Eurypylus, the brave son of Euaemon. Ninth came Teucer with his bow, and took his place under cover of the shield of Ajax, son of Telamon. When Ajax lifted his shield Teucer would peer round, and when he had hit anyone in the throng, the man would fall dead; then Teucer would hie back to Ajax as a child to its mother, and again duck down under his shield.

Which of the Trojans did brave Teucer first kill? Orsilochus, and then Ormenus and Ophelestes, Daetor, Chromius, and godlike Lycophontes, Amopaon, son of Polyaemon, and Melanippus.

All these in turn did he lay low upon the earth, and King Agamemnon was glad when he saw him making havoc of the Trojans with his mighty bow. He went up to him and said: "Teucer, man after my own heart, son of Telamon, captain among the host, shoot on, and be at once the saving of the Danaans and the glory of your father Telamon, who brought you up and took care of you in his own house when you were a child, bastard though you were. Cover him with glory though he is far off. I will promise and I will assuredly perform; if aegis-bearing Zeus and Athene grant me to sack the city of Ilium, you shall have the next best meed of honor after my own—a tripod, or two horses with their chariot, or a woman who shall go up into your bed."

And Teucer answered: "Most noble son of Atreus, you need not urge me. From the moment we began to drive them back to Ilium, I have never ceased so far as in me lies to look out for men whom I can shoot and kill; I have shot eight barbed shafts, and all of them have been buried in the flesh of warlike youths, but this mad dog I cannot hit."

As he spoke he aimed another arrow straight at Hector, for he was bent on hitting him. Nevertheless he missed him, and the arrow hit Priam's brave son Gorgythion in the breast. His mother, fair Castianeira, lovely as a goddess, had been married from Aesyme, and now he bowed his head as a garden poppy in full bloom when it is weighed down by showers in spring—even thus heavily bowed his head beneath the weight of his helmet.

Again he aimed at Hector, for he was longing to hit him, and again his arrow missed, for Apollo turned it aside; but he hit Hector's brave charioteer Archeptolemus in the breast, by the nipple, as he was driving furiously into the fight. The horses swerved aside as he fell headlong from the chariot, and there was no life left in him. Hector was greatly grieved at the loss of his charioteer, but for all his sorrow he let him lie where he fell, and bade his brother Cebriones, who was hard by, take the reins. Cebriones did as he had said. Hector thereon with a loud cry sprang from his chariot to the ground and seizing a great stone made straight for Teucer with intent to kill him. Teucer had just taken an arrow from his quiver and had laid it upon the bowstring, but Hector struck him with the jagged stone as he was taking aim and drawing the string to his shoulder. He hit him just where the collarbone divides the neck from the chest, a very deadly place, and broke the sinew of his arm so that his wrist was powerless, and the bow dropped from his hand as he fell forward on his knees. Ajax saw that his brother had fallen, and running towards him bestrode him and sheltered him with his shield. Meanwhile his two trusty squires, Mecisteus, son of Echius, and Alastor, came up and bore him to the ships groaning in his great pain.

Zeus now again put heart into the Trojans, and they drove the Achaeans to their deep trench with Hector in all his glory at their head. As a hound grips a wild boar or lion in flank or buttock when he gives him chase, and watches warily for his wheeling, even so did Hector follow close upon the Achaeans, ever killing the hindmost as they rushed panic-stricken onwards. When they had fled through the set stakes and trench and many Achaeans had been laid low at the hands of the Trojans, they halted at their ships, calling upon one another and praying every man instantly as they lifted up their hands to the gods; but Hector wheeled his horses this way and that, his eyes glaring like those of Gorgo or murderous Ares.

Hera when she saw them had pity upon them, and at once said to Athene, "Alas, child of aegis-bearing Zeus, shall you and I take no more thought for the dying Danaans, though it be the last time we ever do so? See how they perish and come to a bad end before the onset of but a single man. Hector, the son of Priam, rages with intolerable fury, and has already done great mischief."

Athene answered: "Would, indeed, this fellow might die in his own land, and fall by the hands of the Achaeans; but my father Zeus is mad with spleen, ever foiling me, ever headstrong and unjust. He forgets how often I saved his son when he was worn out by the labors Eurystheus had laid on him. He would weep till his cry came up to heaven, and then Zeus would send me down to help him; if I had had the sense to foresee all this, when Eurystheus sent him to the house of Hades to fetch the hellhound from Erebus, he would never have come back alive out of the deep waters of the river Styx. And now Zeus hates me, while he lets Thetis have her way because she kissed his knees and took hold of his beard, when she was begging him to do honor to Achilles. I shall know what to do next time he begins calling me his gray-eyed darling. Get our horses ready, while I go within the house of aegis-bearing Zeus and put on my armor. We shall then find out whether Priam's son Hector will be glad to meet us in the highways of battle, or whether the Trojans will glut hounds and vultures with the fat of their flesh as they lie dead by the ships of the Achaeans."

Thus did she speak and white-armed Hera, daughter of great Cronus, obeyed her words; she set about harnessing her gold-bedizened steeds, while Athene, daughter of aegis-bearing Zeus, flung her richly embroidered vesture, made with her own hands, on to the threshold of her father, and donned the shirt of Zeus, arming herself for battle. Then she stepped into her flaming chariot, and grasped the spear so stout and sturdy and strong with which she quells the ranks of heroes who have displeased her. Hera lashed her horses, and the gates of heaven bellowed as they flew open of their own accord—gates over which the Hours preside, in whose hands are heaven and Olympus, either to open the dense cloud that hides them or to close it. Through these the goddesses drove their obedient steeds.

But father Zeus when he saw them from Ida was very angry, and sent winged Iris with a message to them. "Go," said he, "fleet Iris, turn them back and see that they do not come near me, for if we come to fighting there will be mischief. This is what I say and this is what I mean to do. I will lame their horses for them; I will hurl them from their chariot, and will break it in pieces. It will take them all ten years to heal the wounds my lightning shall inflict upon them; my gray-eyed daughter will then learn what quarreling with her father means. I am less surprised and angry with Hera, for whatever I say she always contradicts me."

With this Iris went her way, fleet as the wind, from the heights of Ida to the lofty summits of Olympus. She met the goddesses at the outer gates of its many valleys and gave them her message. "What," said she, "are you about? Are you mad? The son of Cronus forbids your going. This is what he says, and this is what he means to do: he will lame your horses for you, he will hurl you from your chariot, and will break it in pieces. It will take you all ten years to heal the wounds his lightning will inflict upon you, that you may learn, gray-eyed goddess, what quarreling with your father means. He is less hurt and angry with Hera, for whatever he says she always contradicts him—but you, bold hussy, will you really dare to raise your huge spear in defiance of Zeus?"

With this she left them, and Hera said to Athene, "Of a truth, child of aegis-bearing Zeus, I am not for fighting men's battles further in defiance of Zeus. Let them live or die as luck will have it, and let Zeus mete out his judgments upon the Trojans and Danaans according to his own pleasure."

She turned her steeds; the Hours presently unyoked them, made them fast to their ambrosial mangers, and leaned the chariot against the end wall of the courtyard. The two goddesses then sat down upon their golden thrones, amid the company of the other gods; but they were very angry.

Presently father Zeus drove his chariot to Olympus, and entered the assembly of gods. The mighty lord of the earthquake unyoked his horses for him, set the car upon its stand, and threw a cloth over it. Zeus then sat down upon his golden throne and Olympus reeled beneath him. Athene and Hera sat alone, apart from Zeus, and neither spoke nor asked him questions, but Zeus knew what they meant, and said, "Athene and Hera, why are you so angry? Are you fatigued with killing so many of your dear friends the Trojans? Be this as it may, such is the might of my hands that all the gods in Olympus cannot turn me. You were both of you trembling all over ere ever you saw the fight and its terrible doings. I tell you therefore—and it would have surely been—I should have struck you with lightning, and your chariots would never have brought you back again to Olympus."

Athene and Hera groaned in spirit as they sat side by side and brooded mischief for the Trojans. Athene sat silent without a word, for she was in a furious passion and bitterly incensed against her father; but Hera could not contain herself and said, "What, dread son of Cronus, are you talking about? We know how great your power is, nevertheless we have compassion upon the Danaan warriors who are perishing and coming to a bad end. We will, however, since you so bid us, refrain from actual fighting, but we will make serviceable suggestions to the Argives, that they may not all of them perish in your displeasure."

And Zeus answered: "Tomorrow morning, Hera, if you choose to do so, you will see the son of Cronus destroying large numbers of the Argives, for fierce Hector shall not cease fighting till he has roused the son of Peleus when they are fighting in dire straits at their ships' sterns about the body of Patroclus. Like it or no, this is how it is decreed. For aught I care, you may go to the lowest depths beneath earth and sea, where Iapetus and Cronus dwell in lone Tartarus with neither ray of light nor breath of wind to cheer them. You may go on and on till you get there, and I shall not care one whit for your displeasure; you are the greatest vixen living."

Hera made him no answer. The sun's glorious orb now sank into Oceanus and drew down night over the land. Sorry indeed were the Trojans when light failed them, but welcome and thrice prayed for did darkness fall upon the Achaeans.

Then Hector led the Trojans back from the ships, and held a council on the open space near the river, where there was a spot clear of corpses. They left their chariots and sat down on the ground to hear the speech he made them. He grasped a spear eleven cubits long, the bronze point of which gleamed in front of it, while the ring round the spearhead was of gold. Spear in hand he spoke.

"Hear me," said he, "Trojans, Dardanians, and allies. I deemed but now that I should destroy the ships and all the Achaeans with them ere I went back to Ilium, but darkness came on too soon. It was this alone that saved them and their ships upon the seashore. Now, therefore, let us obey the behests of night, and prepare our suppers. Take your horses out of their chariots and give them their feeds of corn; then make speed to bring sheep and cattle from the city; bring wine also and corn for your horses and gather much wood, that from dark till dawn we may burn watchfires whose flare may reach to heaven. For the Achaeans may try to fly beyond the sea by night, and they must not embark scatheless and unmolested; many a man among them must take a dart with him to nurse at home, hit with spear or arrow as he is leaping on board his ship, that others may fear to bring war and weeping upon the Trojans.

"Moreover, let the heralds tell it about the city that the growing youths and gray-bearded men are to camp upon its heaven-built walls. Let the women each of them light a great fire in her house, and let watch be safely kept lest the town be entered by surprise while the host is outside. See to it, brave Trojans, as I have said, and let this suffice for the moment; at daybreak I will instruct you further. I pray in hope to Zeus and to the gods that we may then drive those fate-sped hounds from our land, for 'tis the fates that have borne them and their ships hither. This night, therefore, let us keep watch, but with early morning let us put on our armor and rouse fierce war at the ships of the Achaeans; I shall then know whether brave Diomed, the son of Tydeus, will drive me back from the ships to the wall, or whether I shall myself slay him and carry off his bloodstained spoils. Tomorrow let him show his mettle, and abide my spear if he dare. I ween that at break of day, he shall be among the first to fall and many another of his comrades round him. Would that I were as sure of being immortal and never growing old, and of being worshiped like Athene and Apollo, as I am that this day will bring evil to the Argives."

Thus spoke Hector and the Trojans shouted applause. They took their sweating steeds from under the yoke and made them fast each by his own chariot. They made haste to bring sheep and cattle from the city, they brought wine also and corn from their houses and gathered much wood. They then offered unblemished hecatombs to the immortals, and the wind carried the sweet savor of sacrifice to heaven—but the blessed gods partook not thereof, for they bitterly hated Ilium with Priam and Priam's people. Thus high in hope they sat through the livelong night by the highways of war, and many a watchfire did they kindle. As when the stars shine clear, and the moon is bright—there is not a breath of air, not a peak nor a glade nor jutting headland but it stands out in the ineffable radiance that breaks from the serene of heaven; the stars can all of them be told and the heart of the shepherd is glad—even thus shone the watchfires of the Trojans before Ilium midway between the ships and the river Xanthus. A thousand campfires gleamed upon the plain, and in the glow of each there sat fifty men, while the horses, champing oats and corn beside their chariots, waited till dawn should come.

BOOK IX

In despair of ever capturing Troy, Agamemnon calls his chiefs together and proposes a return to Greece. Diomed and Nestor chide him for cowardice, and also for his injustice to Achilles, which has lost them the help of the bravest among them. Agamemnon admits his mistake and offers full reparation if Achilles will fight. Odysseus, Ajax, and Phoenix are dispatched as envoys, but Achilles rejects the offer.

THUS DID THE TROJANS WATCH. BUT PANIC, COMRADE OF bloodstained Rout, had taken fast hold of the Achaeans, and their princes were all of them in despair. As when the two winds that blow from Thrace—the north and the northwest—spring up of a sudden and rouse the fury of the main—in a moment the dark waves uprear their heads and scatter their sea-wrack in all directions—even thus troubled were the hearts of the Achaeans.

The son of Atreus in dismay bade the heralds call the people to a council man by man, but not to cry the matter aloud; he made haste also himself to call them, and they sat sorry at heart in their assembly. Agamemnon shed tears as it were a running stream or cataract on the side of some sheer cliff; and thus, with many a heavy sigh he spoke to the Achaeans. "My friends," said he, "princes and councilors of the Argives, the hand of heaven has been laid heavily upon me. Cruel Zeus gave me his solemn promise that I should sack the city of Troy before returning, but he has played me false, and is now bidding me go ingloriously back to Argos with the loss of much people. Such is the will of Zeus, who has laid many a proud city in the dust as he will yet lay others, for his power is above all. Now, therefore, let us all do as I say and sail back to our own country, for we shall not take Troy."

Thus he spoke, and the sons of the Achaeans for a long while sat sorrowful there, but they all held their peace, till at last Diomed of the loud battle cry made answer, saying: "Son of Atreus, I will chide your folly, as is my right in council. Be not then aggrieved that I should do so. In the first place you attacked me before all the Danaans and said that I was a coward and no soldier. The Argives young and old know that you did so. But the son of scheming Cronus endowed you by halves only. He gave you honor as the chief ruler over us, but valor, which is the highest both right and might, he did not give you. Sir, think you that the sons of the Achaeans are indeed as unwarlike and cowardly as you say they are? If your own mind is set upon going home—go—the way is open to you: the many ships that followed you from Mycene stand ranged upon the seashore; but the rest of us will stay here till we have sacked Troy. Nay, though these too should turn homeward with their ships, Sthenelus and myself will still fight on till we reach the goal of Ilium, for heaven was with us when we came."

The sons of the Achaeans shouted applause at the words of Diomed, and presently Nestor rose to speak. "Son of Tydeus," said he, "in war your prowess is beyond question, and in counsel you excel all who are of your own years; no one of the Achaeans can make light of what you say nor gainsay it, but you have not yet come to the end of the whole matter. You are still young—you might be the youngest of my own children—still you have spoken wisely and have counseled the chief of the Achaeans not without discretion. Nevertheless, I am older than you and I will tell you everything. Therefore let no man, not even King Agamemnon, disregard my saying, for he that foments civil discord is a clanless, hearthless outlaw.

"Now, however, let us obey the behests of night and get our suppers, but let the sentinels every man of them camp by the trench that is without the wall. I am giving these instructions to the young men. When they have been attended to, do you, son of Atreus, give your orders, for you are the most royal among us all. Prepare a feast for your councilors; it is right and reasonable that you should do so. There is abundance of wine in your tents, which the ships of the Achaeans bring from Thrace daily. You have everything at your disposal wherewith to entertain guests, and you have many subjects. When many are got together, you can be guided by him whose counsel is wisest—and sorely do we need shrewd and prudent counsel, for the foe has lit his watchfires hard by our ships. Who can be other than dismayed? This night will either be the ruin of our host, or save it."

Thus did he speak, and they did even as he had said. The sentinels went out in their armor under command of Nestor's son Thrasymedes, a captain of the host, and of the bold warriors Ascalaphus and Ialmenus. There were also Meriones, Aphareus and Deipyrus, and the son of Creion, noble Lycomedes. There were seven captains of the sentinels, and with each there went a hundred youths armed with long spears. They took their places midway between the trench and the wall, and when they had done so they lit their fires and got every man his supper.

The son of Atreus then bade many councilors of the Achaeans to his quarters and prepared a great feast in their honor. They laid their hands on the good things that were before them, and as soon as they had had enough to eat and drink, old Nestor, whose counsel was ever truest, was the first to lay his mind before them. He, therefore, with all sincerity and goodwill addressed them thus:

"With yourself, most noble son of Atreus, king of men, Agamemnon, will I both begin my speech and end it, for you are king over much people. Zeus, moreover, has vouchsafed you to wield the scepter and to uphold righteousness, that you may take thought for your people under you. Therefore, it behooves you above all others both to speak and to give ear, and to carry out the counsel of another who shall have been minded to speak wisely. All turns on you and on your commands, therefore I will say what I think will be best. No man will be of a truer mind than that which has been mine from the hour when you, sir, angered Achilles by taking the girl Briseis from his tent against my judgment. I urged you not to do so, but you yielded to your own pride, and dishonored a hero whom heaven itself had honored—for you still hold the prize that had been awarded to him. Now, however, let us think how we may appease him, both with presents and fair speeches that may conciliate him."

And King Agamemnon answered: "Sir, you have reproved my folly justly. I was wrong. I own it. One whom heaven befriends is in himself a host, and Zeus has shown that he befriends this man by destroying much people of the Achaeans. I was blinded with passion and yielded to my worser mind; therefore I will make amends, and will give him great gifts by way of atonement. I will tell them in the presence of you all. I will give him seven tripods that have never yet been on the fire, and ten talents of gold. I will give him twenty iron cauldrons and twelve strong horses that have won races and carried off prizes. Rich, indeed, both in land and gold is he that has as many prizes as my horses have won me. I will give him seven excellent workwomen, Lesbians, whom I chose for myself when he took Lesbos—all of surpassing beauty. I will give him these, and with them her whom I erewhile took from him, the daughter of Briseus; and I swear a great oath that I never went up into her couch, nor have been with her after the manner of men and women.

"All these things will I give him now down, and if hereafter the gods vouchsafe me to sack the city of Priam, let him come when we Achaeans are dividing the spoil, and load his ship with gold and bronze to his liking. Furthermore let him take twenty Trojan women, the loveliest after Helen herself. Then, when we reach Achaean Argos, wealthiest of all lands, he shall be my son-in-law and I will show him like honor with my own dear son Orestes, who is being nurtured in all abundance. I have three daughters, Chrysothemis, Laodice, and Iphianassa: let him take the one of his choice, freely and without gifts of wooing, to the house of Peleus. I will add such dower to boot as no man ever yet gave his daughter, and will give him seven well-established cities, Cardamyle, Enope, and Hire, where there is grass; holy Pherae and the rich meadows of Anthea; Aepea also, and the vine-clad slopes of Pedasus, all near the sea, and on the borders of sandy Pylos. The men that dwell there are rich in cattle and sheep; they will honor him with gifts as though he were a god, and be obedient to his comfortable ordinances. All this will I do if he will now forgo his anger. Let him then yield—it is only Hades who is utterly ruthless and unyielding—and hence he is of all gods the one most hateful to mankind. Moreover, I am older and more royal than himself. Therefore, let him now obey me."

Then Nestor answered: "Most noble son of Atreus, king of men, Agamemnon. The gifts you offer are no small ones; let us then send chosen messengers, who may go to the tent of Achilles, son of Peleus, without delay. Let those go whom I shall name. Let Phoenix, dear to Zeus, lead the way; let Ajax and Odysseus follow, and let the heralds Odius and Eurybates go with them. Now bring water for our hands, and bid all keep silence while we pray to Zeus, the son of Cronus, if so be that he may have mercy upon us."

Thus did he speak, and his saying pleased them well. Menservants poured water over the hands of the guests, while pages filled the mixing bowls with wine and water, and handed it round after giving every man his drink offering; then, when they had made their offerings, and had drunk each as much as he was minded, the envoys set out from the tent of Agamemnon, son of Atreus; and Nestor, looking first to one and then to another, but most especially at Odysseus, was insistent with them that they should prevail with the noble son of Peleus.

They went their way by the shore of the sounding sea, and prayed earnestly to earth-encircling Poseidon that the high spirit of the son of Aeacus might incline favorably towards them. When they reached the ships and tents of the Myrmidons, they found

Achilles playing on a lyre, fair, of cunning workmanship, and its cross-bar was of silver. It was part of the spoils which he had taken when he sacked the city of Eëtion, and he was now diverting himself with it and singing the feats of heroes. He was alone with Patroclus, who sat opposite to him and said nothing, waiting till he should cease singing. Odysseus and Ajax now came in—Odysseus leading the way—and stood before him. Achilles sprang from his seat with the lyre still in his hand, and Patroclus, when he saw the strangers, rose also. Achilles then greeted them, saying, "All hail and welcome! You must come upon some great matter, you, who for all my anger are still dearest to me of the Achaeans."

With this he led them forward, and bade them sit on seats covered with purple rugs; then he said to Patroclus, who was close by him, "Son of Menoetius, set a larger bowl upon the table, mix less water with the wine, and give every man his cup, for these are very dear friends, who are now under my roof."

Patroclus did as his comrade bade him; he set the chopping block in front of the fire, and on it he laid the loin of a sheep, the loin also of a goat, and the chine of a fat hog. Automedon held the meat while Achilles chopped it; he then sliced the pieces and put them on spits while the son of Menoetius made the fire burn high. When the flame had died down, he spread the embers, laid the spits on top of them, lifting them up and setting them upon the spit-racks; and he sprinkled them with salt. When the meat was roasted, he set it on platters, and handed bread round the table in fair baskets, while Achilles dealt them their portions. Then Achilles took his seat facing Odysseus against the opposite wall, and bade his comrade Patroclus offer sacrifice to the gods. So he cast the offerings into the fire, and they laid their hands upon the good things that were before them. As soon as they had had enough to eat and drink, Ajax made a sign to Phoenix, and when he saw this, Odysseus filled his cup with wine and pledged Achilles.

"Hail," said he, "Achilles, we have had no scant of good cheer, neither in the tent of Agamemnon, nor yet here; there has been plenty to eat and drink, but our thought turns upon no such matter. Sir, we are in the face of great disaster, and without your help know not whether we shall save our fleet or lose it. The Trojans and their allies have camped hard by our ships and by the wall; they have lit watchfires throughout their host and deem that nothing can now prevent them from falling on our fleet. Zeus, moreover, has sent his lightnings on their right. Hector, in all his glory, rages like a maniac. Confident that Zeus is with him he fears neither god nor man, but is gone raving mad, and prays for the approach of day. He vows that he will hew the high sterns of our ships in pieces, set fire to their hulls, and make havoc of the Achaeans while they are dazed and smothered in smoke. I much fear that heaven will make good his boasting, and it will prove our lot to perish at Troy far from our home in Argos. Up, then, and late though it be, save the sons of the Achaeans who faint before the fury of the Trojans. You will repent bitterly hereafter if you do not, for when the harm is done there will be no curing it; consider ere it be too late, and save the Danaans from destruction.

"My good friend, when your father Peleus sent you from Phthia to Agamemnon, did he not charge you saying, 'Son, Athene and Hera will make you strong if they choose, but check your high temper, for the better part is in goodwill. Eschew vain quarreling, and the Achaeans old and young will respect you more for doing so.' These were his words, but you have forgotten them. Even now, however, be appeased, and put away your anger from you. Agamemnon will make you great amends if you will forgive him. Listen, and I will tell you what he has said in his tent that he will give you. He will give you seven tripods that have never yet been on the fire, and ten talents of gold, twenty iron cauldrons, and twelve strong horses that have won races and carried off prizes. Rich indeed both in land and gold is he who has as many prizes as these horses have won for Agamemnon. Moreover, he will give you seven excellent workwomen, Lesbians, whom he chose for himself, when you took Lesbos—all of surpassing beauty. He will give you these, and with them her whom he ere while took from you, the daughter of Briseus, and he will swear a great oath, he has never gone up into her couch nor been with her after the manner of men and women. All these things will he give you now down, and if hereafter the gods vouchsafe him to sack the city of Priam, you can come when we Achaeans are dividing the spoil, and load your ship with gold and bronze to your liking. You can take twenty Trojan women, the loveliest after Helen herself.

"Then, when we reach Achaean Argos, wealthiest of all lands, you shall be his son-in-law, and he will show you like honor with his own dear son Orestes, who is being nurtured in all abundance. Agamemnon has three daughters, Chrysothemis, Laodice, and Iphianassa: you may take the one of your choice, freely and without gifts of wooing, to the house of Peleus. He will add such dower to boot as no man ever yet gave his daughter, and will give you seven well-established cities, Cardamyle, Enope, and Hire where there is grass; holy Pherae and the rich meadows of Anthea; Aepea also, and the vine-clad slopes of Pedasus, all near the sea, and on the borders of sandy Pylos. The men that dwell there are rich in cattle and sheep; they will honor you with gifts as though you were a god, and be obedient to your comfortable ordinances. All this will he do if you will forgo your anger.

"Moreover, though you hate both him and his gifts with all your heart, yet pity the rest of the Achaeans who are being harassed in all their host; they will honor you as a god, and you will earn great glory at their hands. You might even kill Hector; he will come within your reach, for he is infatuated, and declares that not a Danaan whom the ships have brought can hold his own against him."

Achilles answered: "Odysseus, noble son of Laertes, I should give you formal notice plainly and in all fixity of purpose that there be no more of this cajoling, from whatsoever quarter it may come. Him do I hate even as the gates of hell who says one thing while he hides another in his heart; therefore I will say what I mean. I will be appeased neither by Agamemnon, son of Atreus, nor by any other of the Danaans, for I see that I have no thanks for all my fighting. He that fights fares no better than he that does not. Coward and hero are held in equal honor, and death deals like measure to him who works and him who is idle. I have taken nothing by all my hardships—with my life ever in my hand. As a bird when she has found a morsel takes it to her nestlings and herself fares hardly, even so many a long night have I been wakeful, and many a bloody battle have I waged by day against those who were fighting for their women. With my ships I have taken twelve cities, and eleven round about Troy have I stormed with my men by land. I took great store of wealth from every one of them, but I gave all up to Agamemnon, son of Atreus. He stayed where he was by his ships, yet of what came to him he gave little, and kept much himself.

"Nevertheless, he did distribute some meeds of honor among the chieftains and kings, and these have them still; from me alone of the Achaeans did he take the woman in whom I delighted—let him keep her and sleep with her. Why, pray, must the Argives needs fight the Trojans? What made the son of Atreus gather the host and bring them? Was it not for the sake of Helen? Are the sons of Atreus the only men in the world who love their wives? Any man of common right feeling will love and cherish her who is his own, as I this woman, with my whole heart, though she was but a fruitling of my spear. Agamemnon has taken her from me; he has played me false; I know him; let him tempt me no further, for he shall not move me. Let him look to you, Odysseus, and to the other princes to save his ships from burning. He has done much without me already. He has built a wall, he has dug a trench deep and wide all round it, and he has planted it within with stakes; but even so he stays not the murderous might of Hector. So long as I fought among the Achaeans Hector suffered not the battle to range far from the city walls. He would come to the Scaean gates and to the oak tree, but no further. Once he stayed to meet me—and hardly did he escape my onset.

"Now, however, since I am in no mood to fight him, I will tomorrow offer sacrifice to Zeus and to all the gods; I will draw my ships into the water and then victual them duly; tomorrow morning, if you care to look, you will see my ships on the Hellespont, and my men rowing out to sea with might and main. If great Poseidon vouchsafes me a fair passage, in three days I shall be in

Phthia. I have much there that I left behind me when I came here to my sorrow, and I shall bring back still further store of gold, of red copper, of fair women, and of iron, my share of the spoils that we have taken; but one prize, he who gave has insolently taken away. Tell him all as I now bid you, and tell him in public that the Achaeans may hate him and beware of him should he think that he can yet dupe others—for his effrontery never fails him.

"As for me, hound that he is, he dares not look me in the face. I will take no counsel with him, and will undertake nothing in common with him. He has wronged me and deceived me enough, he shall not cozen me further; let him go his own way, for Zeus has robbed him of his reason. I loathe his presents and for himself care not one straw. He may offer me ten or even twenty times what he has now done, nay—not though it be all that he has in the world, both now or ever shall have. He may promise me the wealth of Orchomenus or of Egyptian Thebes, which is the richest city in the whole world, for it has a hundred gates through each of which two hundred men may drive at once with their chariots and horses. He may offer me gifts as the sands of the sea or the dust of the plain in multitude, but even so he shall not move me till I have been revenged in full for the bitter wrong he has done me. I will not marry his daughter; she may be fair as Aphrodite, and skillful as Athene, but I will have none of her: let another take her, who may be a good match for her and who rules a larger kingdom. If the gods spare me to return home, Peleus will find me a wife; there are Achaean women in Hellas and Phthia, daughters of kings that have cities under them; of these I can take whom I will and marry her. Many a time was I minded when at home in Phthia to woo and wed a woman who would make me a suitable wife, and to enjoy the riches of my old father Peleus. My life is more to me than all the wealth of Ilium while it was yet at peace before the Achaeans went there, or than all the treasure that lies on the stone floor of Apollo's temple beneath the cliffs of Pytho. Cattle and sheep are to be had for harrying, and a man may buy both tripods and horses if he wants them, but when his life has once left him it can neither be bought nor harried back again.

"My mother Thetis tells me that there are two ways in which I may meet my end. If I stay here and fight, I shall not return alive but my name will live forever: whereas if I go home my name will die, but it will be long ere death shall take me. To the rest of you, then, I say, 'Go home, for you will not take Ilium.' Zeus has held his hand over her to protect her, and her people have taken heart. Go, therefore, as in duty bound, and tell the princes of the Achaeans the message that I have sent them. Tell them to find some other plan for the saving of their ships and people, for so long as my displeasure lasts the one that they have now hit upon may not be. As for Phoenix, let him sleep here that he may sail with me in the morning if he so will. But I will not take him by force."

They all held their peace, dismayed at the sternness with which he had denied them, till presently the old knight Phoenix in his great fear for the ships of the Achaeans, burst into tears and said: "Noble Achilles, if you are now minded to return, and in the fierceness of your anger will do nothing to save the ships from burning, how, my son, can I remain here without you? Your father Peleus bade me go with you when he sent you as a mere lad from Phthia to Agamemnon. You knew nothing neither of war nor of the arts whereby men make their mark in council, and he sent me with you to train you in all excellence of speech and action. Therefore, my son, I will not stay here without you—no, not though heaven itself vouchsafe to strip my years from off me, and make me young as I was when I first left Hellas, the land of fair women. I was then flying the anger of my father Amyntor, son of Ormenus, who was furious with me in the matter of his concubine, of whom he was enamored to the wronging of his wife my mother. My mother, therefore, prayed me without ceasing to lie with the woman myself, that so she might hate my father, and in the course of time I yielded.

"But my father soon came to know, and cursed me bitterly, calling the dread Erinyes to witness. He prayed that no son of mine might ever sit upon my knees—and the gods, Zeus of the world below and awful Proserpine, fulfilled his curse. I took counsel to kill him, but some god stayed my rashness and bade me think on men's evil tongues and how I should be branded as the murderer of my father. Nevertheless, I could not bear to stay in my father's house with him so bitter against me. My cousins and clansmen came about me, and pressed me sorely to remain. Many a sheep and many an ox did they slaughter, and many a fat hog did they set down to roast before the fire; many a jar, too, did they broach of my father's wine. Nine whole nights did they set a guard over me taking it in turns to watch, and they kept a fire always burning, both in the cloister of the outer court and in the inner court at the doors of the room wherein I lay. But when the darkness of the tenth night came, I broke through the closed doors of my room, and climbed the wall of the outer court after passing quickly and unperceived through the men on guard and the womenservants. I then fled through Hellas till I came to fertile Phthia, mother of sheep, and to King Peleus, who made me welcome and treated me as a father treats an only son who will be heir to all his wealth. He made me rich and set me over much people, establishing me on the borders of Phthia where I was chief ruler over the Dolopians.

"It was I, Achilles, who had the making of you; I loved you with all my heart: for you would eat neither at home nor when you had gone out elsewhere, till I had first set you upon my knees, cut up the dainty morsel that you were to eat, and held the wine cup to your lips. Many a time have you slobbered your wine in baby helplessness over my shirt. I had infinite trouble with you, but I knew that heaven had vouchsafed me no offspring of my own, and I made a son of you, Achilles, that in my hour of need you might protect me.

"Now, therefore, I say battle with your pride and beat it; cherish not your anger forever; the might and majesty of heaven are more than ours, but even heaven may be appeased; and if a man has sinned he prays the gods, and reconciles them to himself by his piteous cries and by frankincense, with drink offerings and the savor of burnt sacrifice. For prayers are as daughters to great Zeus; halt, wrinkled, with eyes askance, they follow in the footsteps of sin, who, being fierce and fleet of foot, leaves them far behind him, and ever baneful to mankind outstrips them even to the ends of the world; but, nevertheless, the prayers come hobbling and healing after. If a man has pity upon these daughters of Zeus when they draw near him, they will bless him and hear him too when he is praying; but if he deny them and will not listen to them, they go to Zeus, the son of Cronus, and pray that he may presently fall into sin—to his rueing bitterly hereafter.

"Therefore, Achilles, give these daughters of Zeus due reverence, and bow before them as all good men will bow. Were not the son of Atreus offering you gifts and promising others later—if he were still furious and implacable—I am not he that would bid you throw off your anger and help the Achaeans, no matter how great their need; but he is giving much now, and more hereafter. He has sent his captains to urge his suit, and has chosen those who of all the Argives are most acceptable to you; make not then their words and their coming to be of none effect. Your anger has been righteous so far. We have heard in song how heroes of old time quarreled when they were roused to fury, but still they could be won by gifts, and fair words could soothe them.

"I have an old story in my mind—a very old one—but you are all friends and I will tell it. The Curetes and the Aetolians were fighting and killing one another round Calydon—the Aetolians defending the city and the Curetes trying to destroy it. For Artemis of the golden throne was angry and did them hurt because Oeneus had not offered her his harvest first fruits. The other gods had all been feasted with hecatombs, but to the daughter of great Zeus alone he had made no sacrifice. He had forgotten her, or somehow or other it had escaped him, and this was a grievous sin. Thereon the archer goddess in her displeasure sent a prodigious creature against him—a savage wild boar with great white tusks that did much harm to his orchard lands, uprooting apple trees in full bloom and throwing them to the ground. But Meleager, son of Oeneus, got huntsmen and hounds from many cities and killed it—for it was so monstrous that not a few were needed, and many a man did it stretch upon his funeral pyre. On this the goddess set the Curetes and the Aetolians fighting furiously about the head and skin of the boar.

"So long as Meleager was in the field things went badly with the Curetes, and for all their numbers they could not hold their ground under the city walls; but in the course of time Meleager was angered as even a wise man will sometimes be. He was incensed with his mother Althaea, and therefore stayed at home with his wedded wife, fair Cleopatra, who was daughter of Marpessa, daughter of Euenus, and of Ides, the strongest man then living. He it was who took his bow and faced King Apollo himself for fair Marpessa's sake; her father and mother then named her Alcyone, because her mother had mourned with the plaintive strains of the halcyon-bird when Phoebus Apollo had carried her off. Meleager, then, stayed at home with Cleopatra, nursing the anger which he felt by reason of his mother's curses. His mother, grieving for the death of her brother, prayed the gods and beat the earth with her hands, calling upon Hades and on awful Proserpine. She went down upon her knees and her bosom was wet with tears as she prayed that they would kill her son—and Erinys that walks in darkness and knows no ruth heard her from Erebus.

"Then was heard the din of battle about the gates of Calydon, and the dull thump of the battering against their walls. Thereon the elders of the Aetolians besought Meleager. They sent the chiefest of their priests, and begged him to come out and help them, promising him a great reward. They bade him choose fifty plough-gates, the most fertile in the plain of Calydon, the one-half vineyard and the other open ploughland. The old warrior Oeneus implored him, standing at the threshold of his room and beating the doors in supplication. His sisters and his mother herself besought him sore, but he the more refused them. Those of his comrades who were nearest and dearest to him also prayed him, but they could not move him till the foe was battering at the very doors of his chamber, and the Curetes had scaled the walls and were setting fire to the city. Then at last his sorrowing wife detailed the horrors that befall those whose city is taken. She reminded him how the men are slain, and the city is given over to the flames, while the women and children are carried into captivity. When he heard all this, his heart was touched, and he donned his armor to go forth. Thus of his own inward motion he saved the city of the Aetolians, but they now gave him nothing of those rich rewards that they had offered earlier, and though he saved the city he took nothing by it. Be not then, my son, thus minded; let not heaven lure you into any such course. When the ships are burning it will be a harder matter to save them. Take the gifts, and go, for the Achaeans will then honor you as a god; whereas if you fight without taking them, you may beat the battle back, but you will not be held in like honor."

And Achilles answered: "Phoenix, old friend and father, I have no need of such honor. I have honor from Zeus himself, which will abide with me at my ships while I have breath in my body, and my limbs are strong. I say further—and lay my saying to your heart—vex me no more with this weeping and lamentation, all in the cause of the son of Atreus. Love him so well, and you may lose the love I bear you. You ought to help me rather in troubling those that trouble me. Be king as much as I am, and share like honor with myself. The others shall take my answer. Stay here yourself and sleep comfortably in your bed; at daybreak we will consider whether to remain or go."

On this he nodded quietly to Patroclus as a sign that he was to prepare a bed for Phoenix, and that the others should take their leave. Ajax, son of Telamon, then said: "Odysseus, noble son of Laertes, let us be gone, for I see that our journey is vain. We must now take our answer, unwelcome though it be, to the Danaans who are waiting to receive it. Achilles is savage and remorseless. He is cruel, and cares nothing for the love his comrades lavished upon him more than on all the others. He is implacable—and yet if a man's brother or son has been slain he will accept a fine by way of amends from him that killed him, and the wrongdoer having paid in full remains in peace among his own people; but as for you, Achilles, the gods have put a wicked unforgiving spirit in your heart, and this, all about one single girl, whereas we now offer you the seven best we have, and much else into the bargain. Be then of a more gracious mind, respect the hospitality of your own roof. We are with you as messengers from the host of the Danaans, and would fain be held nearest and dearest to yourself of all the Achaeans."

"Ajax," replied Achilles, "noble son of Telamon, you have spoken much to my liking, but my blood boils when I think it all over, and remember how the son of Atreus treated me with contumely as though I were some vile tramp, and that too in the presence of the Argives. Go, then, and deliver your message. Say that I will have no concern with fighting till Hector, son of noble Priam, reaches the tents of the Myrmidons in his murderous course, and flings fire upon their ships. For all his lust of battle, I take it he will be held in check when he is at my own tent and ship."

On this they took every man his double cup, made their drink offerings, and went back to the ships, Odysseus leading the way. But Patroclus told his men and the maidservants to make ready a comfortable bed for Phoenix; they therefore did so with sheepskins, a rug, and a sheet of fine linen. The old man then laid himself down and waited till morning came. But Achilles slept in an inner room, and beside him the daughter of Phorbas, lovely Diomedè, whom he had carried off from Lesbos. Patroclus lay on the other side of the room, and with him fair Iphis whom Achilles had given him when he took Scyros the city of Enyeüs.

When the envoys reached the tents of the son of Atreus, the Achaeans rose, pledged them in cups of gold, and began to question them. King Agamemnon was the first to do so. "Tell me, Odysseus," said he, "will he save the ships from burning, or did he refuse, and is he still furious?"

Odysseus answered: "Most noble son of Atreus, king of men, Agamemnon, Achilles will not be calmed, but is more fiercely angry than ever, and spurns both you and your gifts. He bids you take counsel with the Achaeans to save the ships and host as you best may; as for himself, he said that at daybreak he should draw his ships into the water. He said further that he should advise everyone to sail home likewise, for that you will not reach the goal of Ilium. 'Zeus,' he said, 'has laid his hand over the city to protect it, and the people have taken heart.' This is what he said, and the others who were with me can tell you the same story—Ajax and the two heralds, men, both of them, who may be trusted. The old man Phoenix stayed where he was to sleep, for so Achilles would have it, that he might go home with him in the morning if he so would; but he will not take him by force."

They all held their peace, sitting for a long time silent and dejected, by reason of the sternness with which Achilles had refused them, till presently Diomed said: "Most noble son of Atreus, king of men, Agamemnon, you ought not to have sued the son of Peleus nor offered him gifts. He is proud enough as it is, and you have encouraged him in his pride still further. Let him stay or go as he will. He will fight later when he is in the humor, and heaven puts it in his mind to do so. Now, therefore, let us all do as I say. We have eaten and drunk our fill, let us then take our rest, for in rest there is both strength and stay. But when fair rosy-fingered morn appears, forthwith bring out your host and your horsemen in front of the ships, urging them on, and yourself fighting among the foremost."

Thus he spoke, and the other chieftains approved his words. They then made their drink offerings and went every man to his own tent, where they lay down to rest and enjoyed the boon of sleep.

BOOK X

Later in the night, Agamemnon summons the Greek chiefs again. Diomed and Odysseus are sent out to spy on the enemy's camp. From the Trojan side Hector sends Dolon to spy on the Greeks. Diomed and Odysseus capture Dolon, learn from him the disposition of the Trojan forces, and kill him. They then surprise and kill Rhesus, the Thracian king, and drive his fine horses back to their ships.

Now the other princes of the Achaeans slept soundly the whole night through, but Agamemnon, son of Atreus, was troubled, so that he could get no rest. As when fair Hera's lord flashes his lightning in token of great rain or hail or snow when the snowflakes whiten the ground, or again as a sign that he will open the wide jaws of hungry war, even so did Agamemnon heave many a heavy sigh, for his soul trembled within him. When he looked upon the plain of Troy he marveled at the many watchfires burning in front of Ilium, and at the sound of pipes and flutes and of the hum of men, but when presently he turned towards the ships and hosts of the Achaeans, he tore his hair by handfuls before Zeus on high, and groaned aloud for the very disquietness of his soul. In the end he deemed it best to go at once to Nestor, son of Neleus, and see if between them they could find any way of saving the Achaeans from destruction. He therefore rose, put on his shirt, bound his sandals about his comely feet, flung the skin of a huge tawny lion over his shoulders—a skin that reached his feet—and took his spear in his hand.

Neither could Menelaus sleep, for he too boded ill for the Argives who for his sake had sailed from far over the seas to fight the Trojans. He covered his broad back with the skin of a spotted panther, put a casque of bronze upon his head, and took his spear in his brawny hand. Then he went to rouse his brother, who was by far the most powerful of the Achaens, and was honored by the people as though he were a god. He found him by the stern of his ship already putting his goodly array about his shoulders, and right glad was he that his brother had come.

Menelaus spoke first. "Why," said he, "my dear brother, are you thus arming? Are you going to send any of our comrades to exploit the Trojans? I greatly fear that no one will do you this service, and spy upon the enemy alone in the dead of night. It will be a deed of great daring."

And King Agamemnon answered: "Menelaus, we both of us need shrewd counsel to save the Argives and our ships, for Zeus has changed his mind, and inclines towards Hector's sacrifices rather than ours. I never saw nor heard tell of any man as having wrought such ruin in one day as Hector has now wrought against the sons of the Achaeans—and that too of his own unaided self, for he is son neither to god nor goddess. The Argives will rue it long and deeply. Run, therefore, with all speed by the line of the ships and call Ajax and Idomeneus. Meanwhile I will go to Nestor, and bid him rise and go about among the companies of our sentinels to give them their instructions. They will listen to him sooner than to any man, for his own son, and Meriones, brother in arms to Idomeneus, are captains over them. It was to them more particularly that we gave this charge."

Menelaus replied: "How do I take your meaning? Am I to stay with them and wait your coming, or shall I return here as soon as I have given your orders?" "Wait," answered King Agamemnon, "for there are so many paths about the camp that we might miss one another. Call every man on your way, and bid him be stirring. Name him by his lineage and by his father's name, give each all titular observance, and stand not too much upon your own dignity. We must take our full share of toil, for at our birth Zeus laid this heavy burden upon us."

With these instructions he sent his brother on his way, and went on to Nestor, shepherd of his people. He found him sleeping in his tent hard by his own ship. His goodly armor lay beside him—his shield, his two spears, and his helmet; beside him also lay the gleaming girdle with which the old man girded himself when he armed to lead his people into battle—for his age stayed him not. He raised himself on his elbow and looked up at Agamemnon. "Who is it," said he, "that goes thus about the host and the ships alone and in the dead of night, when men are sleeping? Are you looking for one of your mules or for some comrade? Do not stand there and say nothing, but speak. What is your business?"

And Agamemnon answered: "Nestor, son of Neleus, honor to the Achaean name, it is I, Agamemnon, son of Atreus, on whom Zeus has laid labor and sorrow so long as there is breath in my body and my limbs carry me. I am thus abroad because sleep sits not upon my eyelids, but my heart is big with war and with the jeopardy of the Achaeans. I am in great fear for the Danaans. I am at sea, and without sure counsel; my heart beats as though it would leap out of my body, and my limbs fail me. If then you can do anything—for you too cannot sleep—let us go the round of the watch, and see whether they are drowsy with toil and sleeping to the neglect of their duty. The enemy is encamped hard by, and we know not but he may attack us by night."

Nestor replied: "Most noble son of Atreus, king of men, Agamemnon, Zeus will not do all for Hector that Hector thinks he will. He will have troubles yet in plenty if Achilles will lay aside his anger. I will go with you, and we will rouse others, either the son of Tydeus, or Odysseus, or fleet Ajax and the valiant son of Phyleus. Someone had also better go and call Ajax and King Idomeneus, for their ships are not near at hand but the farthest of all. I cannot however refrain from blaming Menelaus, much as I love him and respect him—and I will say so plainly, even at the risk of offending you—for sleeping and leaving all this trouble to yourself. He ought to be going about imploring aid from all the princes of the Achaeans, for we are in extreme danger."

And Agamemnon answered: "Sir, you may sometimes blame him justly, for he is often remiss and unwilling to exert himself—not indeed from sloth, nor yet heedlessness, but because he looks to me and expects me to take the lead. On this occasion, however, he was awake before I was, and came to me of his own accord. I have already sent him to call the very men whom you have named. And now let us be going. We shall find them with the watch outside the gates, for it was there I said that we would meet them."

"In that case," answered Nestor, "the Argives will not blame him nor disobey his orders when he urges them to fight or gives them instructions."

With this he put on his shirt, and bound his sandals about his comely feet. He buckled on his purple coat, of two thicknesses, large, and of a rough shaggy texture, grasped his redoubtable bronze-shod spear, and wended his way along the line of the Achaean ships. First he called loudly to Odysseus, peer of gods in counsel, and woke him, for he was soon roused by the sound of the battle cry. He came outside his tent and said: "Why do you go thus alone about the host, and along the line of the ships in the stillness of the night? What is it that you find so urgent?" And Nestor, knight of Gerene, answered: "Odysseus, noble son of Laertes, take it not amiss, for the Achaeans are in great straits. Come with me and let us wake some other, who may advise well with us whether we shall fight or fly."

On this Odysseus went at once into his tent, put his shield about his shoulders and came out with them. First they went to Diomed, son of Tydeus, and found him outside his tent clad in his armor with his comrades sleeping round him and using their shields as pillows; as for their spears, they stood upright on the spikes of their butts that were driven into the ground, and the burnished bronze flashed afar like the lightning of father Zeus.

The hero was sleeping upon the skins of an ox, with a piece of fine carpet under his head. Nestor went up to him and stirred him with his heel to rouse him, upbraiding him and urging him to bestir himself. "Wake up," he exclaimed, "son of Tydeus. How can you sleep on in this way? Can you not see that the Trojans are encamped on the brow of the plain hard by our ships with but a little space between us and them?"

On these words Diomed leaped up instantly and said, "Old man, your heart is of iron; you rest not one moment from your labors. Are there no younger men among the Achaeans who could go about to rouse the princes? There is no tiring you."

And Nestor, knight of Gerene, made answer: "My son, all that you have said is true. I have good sons, and also much people who might call the chieftains, but the Achaeans are in the gravest danger. Life and death are balanced as it were on the edge of a razor. Go then, for you are younger than I, and of your courtesy rouse Ajax and the fleet son of Phyleus."

Diomed threw the skin of a great tawny lion about his shoulders—a skin that reached his feet—and grasped his spear. When he had roused the heroes, he brought them back with him; they then went the round of those who were on guard, and found the captains not sleeping at their posts but wakeful and sitting with their arms about them. As sheep dogs that watch their flocks when they are yarded, and hear a wild beast coming through the mountain forest towards them—forthwith there is a hue and cry of dogs and men, and slumber is broken—even so was sleep chased from the eyes of the Achaeans as they kept the watches of the wicked night, for they turned constantly towards the plain whenever they heard any stir among the Trojans. The old man was glad and bade them be of good cheer. "Watch on, my children," said he, "and let not sleep get hold upon you, lest our enemies triumph over us."

With this he passed the trench, and with him the other chiefs of the Achaeans who had been called to the council. Meriones and the brave son of Nestor went also, for the princes bade them. When they were beyond the trench that was dug round the wall they held their meeting on the open ground where there was a space clear of corpses, for it was here that when night fell Hector had turned back from his onslaught on the Argives. They sat down, therefore, and held debate with one another.

Nestor spoke first. "My friends," said he, "is there any man bold enough to venture among the Trojans, and cut off some straggler, or bring us news of what the enemy mean to do—whether they will stay here by the ships away from the city, or whether, now that they have worsted the Achaeans, they will retire within their walls. If he could learn all this and come back safely here, his fame would be high as heaven in the mouths of all men, and he would be rewarded richly; for the chiefs from all our ships would each of them give him a black ewe with her lamb—which is a present of surpassing value—and he would be asked as a guest to all feasts and clan gatherings."

They all held their peace, but Diomed of the loud war cry spoke saying: "Nestor, gladly will I visit the host of the Trojans over against us, but if another will go with me I shall do so in greater confidence and comfort. When two men are together, one of them may see some opportunity which the other has not caught sight of; if a man is alone he is less full of resources, and his wit is weaker."

On this several offered to go with Diomed. The two Ajaxes, servants of Ares, Meriones, and the son of Nestor all wanted to go, so did Menelaus, son of Atreus; Odysseus also wished to go among the host of the Trojans, for he was ever full of daring, and thereon Agamemnon, king of men, spoke thus: "Diomed," said he, "son of Tydeus, man after my own heart, choose your comrade for yourself—take the best man of those that have offered, for many would now go with you. Do not through delicacy reject the better man, and take the worst out of respect for his lineage, because he is of more royal blood."

He said this because he feared for Menelaus. Diomed answered: "If you bid me take the man of my own choice, how in that case can I fail to think of Odysseus, than whom there is no man more eager to face all kinds of danger—and Pallas Athene loves him well? If he were to go with me we should pass safely through fire itself, for he is quick to see and understand."

"Son of Tydeus," replied Odysseus, "say neither good nor ill about me, for you are among Argives who know me well. Let us be going, for the night wanes and dawn is at hand. The stars have gone forward, two-thirds of the night are already spent, and the third is alone left us."

They then put on their armor. Brave Thrasymedes provided the son of Tydeus with a sword and a shield (for he had left his own at his ship) and on his head he set a helmet of bull's hide without either peak or crest; it is called a skullcap and is a common headgear. Meriones found a bow and quiver for Odysseus, and on his head he set a leathern helmet that was lined with a strong plaiting of leathern thongs, while on the outside it was thickly studded with boar's teeth, well and skillfully set into it; next the head there was an inner lining of felt. This helmet had been stolen by Autolycus out of Eleon when he broke into the house of Amyntor, son of Ormenus. He gave it to Amphidamas of Cythera to take to Scandea, and Amphidamas gave it as a guest-gift to Molus, who gave it to his son Meriones; and now it was set upon the head of Odysseus.

When the pair had armed, they set out, and left the other chieftains behind them. Pallas Athene sent them a heron by the wayside upon their right hands; they could not see it for the darkness, but they heard its cry. Odysseus was glad when he heard it and prayed to Athene: "Hear me," he cried, "daughter of aegis-bearing Zeus, you who spy out all my ways and who are with me in all my hardships! Befriend me in this mine hour, and grant that we may return to the ships covered with glory after having achieved some mighty exploit that shall bring sorrow to the Trojans."

Then Diomed of the loud war cry also prayed: "Hear me too," said he, "daughter of Zeus, unweariable; be with me even as you were with my noble father Tydeus when he went to Thebes as envoy sent by the Achaeans. He left the Achaeans by the banks of the river Aesopus, and went to the city bearing a message of peace to the Cadmeians. On his return thence, with your help, goddess, he did great deeds of daring, for you were his ready helper. Even so guide me and guard me now, and in return I will offer you in sacrifice a broad-browed heifer of a year old, unbroken, and never yet brought by man under the yoke. I will gild her horns and will offer her up to you in sacrifice."

Thus they prayed, and Pallas Athene heard their prayer. When they had done praying to the daughter of great Zeus, they went their way like two lions prowling by night amid the armor and bloodstained bodies of them that had fallen.

Neither again did Hector let the Trojans sleep; for he too called the princes and councilors of the Trojans that he might set his counsel before them. "Is there one," said he, "who for a great reward will do me the service of which I will tell you? He shall be well paid if he will. I will give him a chariot and a couple of horses, the fleetest that can be found at the ships of the Achaeans, if he will dare this thing; and he will win infinite honor to boot. He must go to the ships and find out whether they are still guarded as heretofore, or whether now that we have beaten them the Achaeans design to fly, and through sheer exhaustion are neglecting to keep their watches."

They all held their peace; but there was among the Trojans a certain man named Dolon, son of Eumedes, the famous herald—a man rich in gold and bronze. He was ill-favored, but a good runner, and was an only son among five sisters. He it was that now addressed the Trojans. "I, Hector," said he, "will go to the ships and will exploit them. But first hold up your scepter and swear that you will give me the chariot, bedight with bronze, and the horses that now carry the noble son of Peleus. I will make you a good scout, and will not fail you. I will go through the host from one end to the other till I come to the ship of Agamemnon, where I take it the princes of the Achaeans are now consulting whether they shall fight or fly."

When he had done speaking Hector held up his scepter, and swore him his oath, saying, "May Zeus, the thundering husband of Hera, bear witness that no other Trojan but yourself shall mount those steeds, and that you shall have your will with them forever."

The oath he swore was bootless, but it made Dolon more keen on going. He hung his bow over his shoulder, and as an overall he wore the skin of a gray wolf, while on his head he set a cap of ferret skin. Then he took a pointed javelin, and left the camp for the ships, but he was not to return with any news for Hector. When he had left the horses and the troops behind him, he made all speed on his way, but Odysseus perceived his coming and said to Diomed: "Diomed, here is someone from the camp. I am not sure whether he is a spy, or whether it is some thief who would plunder the bodies of the dead; let him get a little past us, we can then spring upon him and take him. If, however, he is too quick for us, go after him with your spear and hem him in towards the ships away from the Trojan camp, to prevent his getting back to the town."

With this they turned out of their way and lay down among the corpses. Dolon suspected nothing and soon passed them, but when he had got about as far as the distance by which a mule-ploughed furrow exceeds one that has been ploughed by oxen (for mules can plough fallow land quicker than oxen) they ran after him, and when he heard their footsteps he stood still, for he made sure they were friends from the Trojan camp come by Hector's order to bid him return. When, however, they were only a spear's cast, or less, away from him, he saw that they were enemies and ran away as fast as his legs could take him. The others gave chase at once, and as a couple of well-trained hounds press forward after a doe or hare that runs screaming in front of them, even so did the son of Tydeus and Odysseus pursue Dolon and cut him off from his own people. But when he had fled so far towards the ships that he would soon have fallen in with the outposts, Athene infused fresh strength into the son of Tydeus for fear some other of the Achaeans might have the glory of being first to hit him, and he might himself be only second. He therefore sprang forward with his spear and said, "Stand, or I shall throw my spear, and in that case I shall soon make an end of you."

He threw as he spoke, but missed his aim on purpose. The dart flew over the man's right shoulder, and then stuck in the ground. He stood stock still, trembling and in great fear; his teeth chattered, and he turned pale with fear. The two came breathless up to him and seized his hands, whereon he began to weep and said: 'Take me alive; I will ransom myself. We have great store of gold, bronze, and wrought iron, and from this my father will satisfy you with a very large ransom, should he hear of my being alive at the ships of the Achaeans."

"Fear not," replied Odysseus, "let no thought of death be in your mind; but tell me, and tell me true, why are you thus going about alone in the dead of night away from your camp and towards the ships, while other men are sleeping? Is it to plunder the bodies of the slain, or did Hector send you to spy out what was going on at the ships? Or did you come here of your own mere notion?"

Dolon answered, his limbs trembling beneath him: "Hector, with his vain flattering promises, lured me from my better judgment. He said he would give me the horses of the noble son of Peleus and his bronze bedizened chariot; he bade me go through the darkness of the flying night, get close to the enemy, and find out whether the ships are still guarded as heretofore, or whether, now that we have beaten them, the Achaeans design to fly, and through sheer exhaustion are neglecting to keep their watches."

Odysseus smiled at him and answered: "You had indeed set your heart upon a great reward, but the horses of the descendant of Aeacus are hardly to be kept in hand or driven by any other mortal man than Achilles himself, whose mother was an immortal. But tell me, and tell me true, where did you leave Hector when you started? Where lies his armor and his horses? How, too, are the watches and sleeping ground of the Trojans ordered? What are their plans? Will they stay here by the ships and away from the city or, now that they have worsted the Achaeans, will they retire within their walls?"

And Dolon answered: "I will tell you truly all. Hector and the other councilors are now holding conference by the monument of great Ilus, away from the general tumult; as for the guards about which you ask me, there is no chosen watch to keep guard over the host. The Trojans have their watchfires, for they are bound to have them. They, therefore, are awake and keep each other to their duty as sentinels; but the allies who have come from other places are asleep and leave it to the Trojans to keep guard, for their wives and children are not here."

Odysseus then said: "Now tell me, are they sleeping among the Trojan troops, or do they lie apart? Explain this that I may understand it."

"I will tell you truly all," replied Dolon. 'To the seaward lie the Carians, the Paeonian bowmen, the Leleges, the Cauconians, and the noble Pelasgi. The Lysians and proud Mysians, with the Phrygians and Meonians, have their place on the side towards Thymbra; but why ask about all this? If you want to find your way into the host of the Trojans, there are the Thracians, who have lately come here and lie apart from the others at the far end of the camp; and they have Rhesus, son of Eïoneus, for their king. His horses are the finest and strongest that I have ever seen; they are whiter than snow and fleeter than any wind that blows. His chariot is bedight with silver and gold, and he has brought his marvelous golden armor, of the rarest workmanship—too splendid for any mortal man to carry, and meet only for the gods. Now, therefore, take me to the ships or bind me securely here, until you come back and have proved my words whether they be false or true."

Diomed looked sternly at him and answered: "Think not, Dolon, for all the good information you have given us, that you shall escape now you are in our hands, for if we ransom you or let you go, you will come some second time to the ships of the Achaeans either as a spy or as an open enemy, but if I kill you and make an end of you, you will give no more trouble."

On this Dolon would have caught him by the beard to beseech him further, but Diomed struck him in the middle of his neck with his sword and cut through both sinews so that his head fell rolling in the dust while he was yet speaking. They took the ferret-skin cap from his head, and also the wolf skin, the bow, and his long spear. Odysseus hung them up aloft in honor of Athene, the goddess of plunder, and prayed saying, "Accept these, goddess, for we give them to you in preference to all the gods in Olympus: therefore speed us still further towards the horses and sleeping ground of the Thracians."

With these words he took up the spoils and set them upon a tamarisk tree, and they marked the place by pulling up reeds and gathering boughs of tamarisk that they might not miss it as they came back through the flying hours of darkness. The two then went onwards amid the fallen armor and the blood, and came presently to the company of Thracian soldiers, who were sleeping, tired out with their day's toil. Their goodly armor was lying on the ground beside them all orderly in three rows, and each man had his yoke of horses beside him. Rhesus was sleeping in the middle, and hard by him his horses were made fast to the topmost rim of his chariot. Odysseus from some way off saw him and said: "This, Diomed, is the man, and these are the horses about which Dolon, whom we killed, told us. Do your very utmost; dally not about your armor, but loose the horses at once—or else kill the men yourself, while I see to the horses."

Thereon Athene put courage into the heart of Diomed, and he smote them right and left. They made a hideous groaning as they were being hacked about, and the earth was red with their blood. As a lion springs furiously upon a flock of sheep or goats when he finds them without their shepherd, so did the son of Tydeus set upon the Thracian soldiers till he had killed twelve. As he killed them Odysseus came and drew them aside by their feet one by one, that the horses might go forward freely without being frightened as they passed over the dead bodies, for they were not yet used to them. When the son of Tydeus came to the king, he killed him too (which made thirteen), as he was breathing hard, for by the counsel of Athene an evil dream, the seed of Oeneus, hovered that night over his head. Meanwhile Odysseus untied the horses, made them fast one to another and drove them off, striking them with his bow, for he had forgotten to take the whip from the chariot. Then he whistled as a sign to Diomed.

But Diomed stayed where he was, thinking what other daring deed he might accomplish. He was doubting whether to take the chariot in which the king's armor was lying, and draw it out by the pole, or to lift the armor out and carry it off; or whether again, he should not kill some more Thracians. While he was thus hesitating Athene came up to him and said, "Get back, Diomed, to the ships, or you may be driven thither, should some other god rouse the Trojans."

Diomed knew that it was the goddess, and at once sprang upon the horses. Odysseus beat them with his bow and they flew onward to the ships of the Achaeans.

But Apollo kept no blind lookout when he saw Athene with the son of Tydeus. He was angry with her, and coming to the host of the Trojans he roused Hippocoön, a counselor of the Thracians and a noble kinsman of Rhesus. He started up out of his sleep and saw that the horses were no longer in their place, and that the men were gasping in their death agony; on this he groaned aloud, and called upon his friend by name. Then the whole Trojan camp was in an uproar as the people kept hurrying together, and they marveled at the deeds of the heroes who had now got away towards the ships.

When they reached the place where they had killed Hector's scout, Odysseus stayed his horses, and the son of Tydeus, leaping to the ground, placed the bloodstained spoils in the hands of Odysseus and remounted: then he lashed the horses onwards, and they flew forward nothing loath towards the ships, as though of their own free will. Nestor was first to hear the tramp of their feet. "My friends," said he, "princes and counselors of the Argives, shall I guess right or wrong?—but I must say what I think: there is a sound in my ears as of the tramp of horses. I hope it may be Diomed and Odysseus driving in horses from the Trojans, but I much fear that the bravest of the Argives may have come to some harm at their hands."

He had hardly done speaking when the two men came in and dismounted, whereon the others shook hands right gladly with them and congratulated them. Nestor, knight of Gerene, was first to question them. "Tell me," said he, "renowned Odysseus, how did you two come by these horses? Did you steal in among the

Trojan forces, or did some god meet you and give them to you? They are like sunbeams. I am well conversant with the Trojans, for old warrior though I am I never hold back by the ships, but I never yet saw or heard of such horses as these are. Surely some god must have met you and given them to you, for you are both of you dear to Zeus, and to Zeus's daughter Athene."

And Odysseus answered, "Nestor, son of Neleus, honor to the Achaean name, heaven, if it so will, can give us even better horses than these, for the gods are far mightier than we are. These horses, however, about which you ask me, are freshly come from Thrace. Diomed killed their king with the twelve bravest of his companions. Hard by the ships we took a thirteenth man—a scout whom Hector and the other Trojans had sent as a spy upon our ships."

He laughed as he spoke and drove the horses over the ditch, while the other Achaeans followed him gladly. When they reached the strongly built quarters of the son of Tydeus, they tied the horses with thongs of leather to the manger, where the steeds of Diomed stood eating their sweet corn, but Odysseus hung the bloodstained spoils of Dolon at the stern of his ship, that they might prepare a sacred offering to Athene. As for themselves, they went into the sea and washed the sweat from their bodies, and from their necks and thighs. When the sea water had taken all the sweat from off them, and had refreshed them, they went into the baths and washed themselves. After they had so done and had anointed themselves with oil, they sat down to table, and drawing from a full mixing bowl, made a drink offering of wine to Athene.

BOOK XI

In the morning when the battle is resumed, Agamemnon is wounded and retires to the ships. Hector, encouraged by Zeus, leads the Trojans forward. Diomed attacks and stuns Hector, but is himself wounded by Paris and leaves the field. Odysseus and the physician Machaon are also wounded. Ajax tries to guard the Greek retreat while Nestor suggests to Achilles's friend Patroclus that he fight in Achilles's armor to deceive the Trojans.

AND NOW AS DAWN ROSE FROM HER COUCH BESIDE TITHONUS, harbinger of light alike to mortals and immortals, Zeus sent fierce Discord with the ensign of war in her hands to the ships of the Achaeans. She took her stand by the huge black hull of Odysseus's ship which was middlemost of all, so that her voice might carry farthest on either side, on the one hand towards the tents of Ajax, son of Telamon, and on the other towards those of Achilles—for these two heroes, well-assured of their own strength, had valorously drawn up their ships at the two ends of the line. There she took her stand, and raised a cry both loud and shrill that filled the Achaeans with courage, giving them heart to fight resolutely and with all their might, so that they had rather stay there and do battle than go home in their ships.

The son of Atreus shouted aloud and bade the Argives gird themselves for battle while he put on his armor. First he girded his goodly greaves about his legs, making them fast with ankle-clasps of silver; and about his chest he set the breastplate which Cinyras had once given him as a guest-gift. It had been noised abroad as far as Cyprus that the Achaeans were about to sail for Troy, and therefore he gave it to the king. It had ten courses of dark cyanus, twelve of gold, and ten of tin. There were serpents of cyanus that reared themselves up towards the neck, three upon either side, like the rainbows which the son of Cronus has set in heaven as a sign to mortal men. About his shoulders he threw his sword, studded with bosses of gold; and the scabbard was of silver with a chain of gold wherewith to hang it. He took moreover the richly dight shield that covered his body when he was in battle—fair to see, with ten circles of bronze running all round it. On the body of the shield there were twenty bosses of white tin, with another of dark cyanus in the middle: this last was made to show a Gorgon's head, fierce and grim, with Rout and Panic on either side. The band for the arm to go through was of silver, on which there was a writhing snake of cyanus with three heads that sprang from a single neck, and went in and out among one another. On his head Agamemnon set a helmet, with a peak before and behind, and four plumes of horsehair that nodded menacingly above it. Then he grasped two redoubtable bronze-shod spears, and the gleam of his armor shot from him as a flame into the firmament, while Hera and Athene thundered in honor of the king of rich Mycenae.

Every man now left his horses in charge of his charioteer to hold them in readiness by the trench, while he went into battle on foot clad in full armor, and a mighty uproar rose on high into the dawning. The chiefs were armed and at the trench before the horses got there, but these came up presently. The son of Cronus sent a portent of evil sound about their host, and the dew fell red with blood, for he was about to send many a brave man hurrying down to Hades.

The Trojans, on the other side upon the rising slope of the plain, were gathered round great Hector, noble Polydamas, Aeneas who was honored by the Trojans like an immortal, and the three sons of Antenor, Polybus, Agenor, and young Acamas, beauteous as a god. Hector's round shield showed in the front rank, and as some baneful star that shines for a moment through a rent in the clouds and is again hidden beneath them; even so was Hector now seen in the front ranks and now again in the hindermost, and his bronze armor gleamed like the lightning of aegis-bearing Zeus.

And now as a band of reapers mow swathes of wheat or barley upon a rich man's land, and the sheaves fall thick before them, even so did the Trojans and Achaeans fall upon one another; they were in no mood for yielding but fought like wolves, and neither side got the better of the other. Discord was glad as she beheld them, for she was the only god that went among them; the others were not there, but stayed quietly each in his own home among the dells and valleys of Olympus. All of them blamed the son of Cronos for wanting to give victory to the Trojans, but father Zeus heeded them not: he held aloof from all, and sat apart in his all-glorious majesty, looking down upon the city of the Trojans, the ships of the Achaeans, the gleam of bronze, and alike upon the slayers and on the slain.

Now so long as the day waxed and it was still morning, their darts rained thick on one another and the people perished, but as the hour drew nigh when a woodman working in some mountain forest will get his midday meal—for he has felled till his hands are weary; he is tired out, and must now have food—then the Danaans with a cry that rang through all their ranks, broke the battalions of the enemy. Agamemnon led them on, and slew first Bienor, a leader of his people, and afterwards his comrade and charioteer Oïleus, who sprang from his chariot and was coming full towards him; but Agamemnon struck him on the forehead with his spear; his bronze vizor was of no avail against the weapon, which pierced both bronze and bone, so that his brains were battered in and he was killed in full fight.

Agamemnon stripped their shirts from off them and left them with their breasts all bare to lie where they had fallen. He then went on to kill Isus and Antiphus, two sons of Priam, the one a bastard, the other born in wedlock; they were in the same chariot—the bastard driving, while noble Antiphus fought beside him. Achilles had once taken both of them prisoners in the glades of Ida, and had bound them with fresh withes as they were shepherding, but he had taken a ransom for them; now, however, Agamemnon, son of Atreus, smote Isus in the chest above the nipple with his spear, while he struck Antiphus hard by the ear and threw him from his chariot. Forthwith he stripped their goodly armor from off them and recognized them, for he had already seen them at the ships when Achilles brought them in from Ida. As a lion fastens on the fawns of a hind and crushes them in his great jaws, robbing them of their tender life while he is on his way back to his lair—the hind can do nothing for them even though she be close by, for she is in an agony of fear, and flies through the thick forest, sweating, and at her utmost speed before the mighty monster—so, no man of the Trojans could help Isus and Antiphus, for they were themselves flying in panic before the Argives.

Then King Agamemnon took the two sons of Antimachus, Pisander and brave Hippolochus. It was Antimachus who had been foremost in preventing Helen's being restored to Menelaus, for he was largely bribed by Paris; and now Agamemnon took his two sons, both in the same chariot, trying to bring their horses to a stand—for they had lost hold of the reins and the horses were mad with fear. The son of Atreus sprang upon them like a lion, and the pair besought him from their chariot. "Take us alive," they cried, "son of Atreus, and you shall receive a great ransom for us. Our father Antimachus has great store of gold, bronze, and wrought iron, and from this he will satisfy you with a very large ransom should he hear of our being alive at the ships of the Achaeans."

With such piteous words and tears did they beseech the king, but they heard no pitiful answer in return. "If," said Agamemnon, "you are sons of Antimachus, who once at a council of Trojans proposed that Menelaus and Odysseus, who had come to you as envoys, should be killed and not suffered to return, you shall now pay for the foul iniquity of your father."

As he spoke he felled Pisander from his chariot to the earth, smiting him on the chest with his spear, so that he lay face uppermost upon the ground. Hippolochus fled, but him too did Agamemnon smite. He cut off his hands and his head—which he sent rolling in among the crowd as though it were a ball. There he let them both lie, and wherever the ranks were thickest thither he flew, while the other Achaeans followed. Foot soldiers drove the foot soldiers of the foe in rout before them, and slew them. Horsemen did the like by horsemen, and the thundering tramp of the horses raised a cloud of dust from off the plain. King Agamemnon followed after, ever slaying them and cheering on the Achaeans. As when some mighty forest is all ablaze—the eddying gusts whirl fire in all directions till the thickets shrivel and are consumed before the blast of the flame—even so fell the heads of the flying Trojans before Agamemnon, son of Atreus, and many a noble pair of steeds drew an empty chariot along the highways of war, for lack of drivers who were lying on the plain, more useful now to vultures than to their wives.

Zeus drew Hector away from the darts and dust, with the carnage and din of battle; but the son of Atreus sped onwards, calling out lustily to the Danaans. They flew on by the tomb of old Ilus, son of Dardanus, in the middle of the plain, and past the place of the wild fig tree making always for the city—the son of Atreus still shouting, and with hands all bedrabbled in gore; but when they had reached the Scaean gates and the oak tree, there they halted and waited for the others to come up. Meanwhile the Trojans kept on flying over the middle of the plain like a herd of cows maddened with fright when a lion has attacked them in the dead of night—he springs on one of them, seizes her neck in the grip of his strong teeth, and then laps up her blood and gorges himself upon her entrails—even so did King Agamemnon, son of Atreus, pursue the foe, ever slaughtering the hindmost as they fled pell-mell before him. Many a man was flung headlong from his chariot by the hand of the son of Atreus, for he wielded his spear with fury.

But when he was just about to reach the high wall and the city, the father of gods and men came down from heaven and took his seat, thunderbolt in hand, upon the crest of many-fountained Ida. He then told Iris of the golden wings to carry a message for him. "Go," said he, "fleet Iris, and speak thus to Hector—say that so long as he sees Agamemnon heading his men and making havoc of the Trojan ranks, he is to keep aloof and bid the others bear the brunt of the battle, but when Agamemnon is wounded either by spear or arrow, and takes to his chariot, then will I vouchsafe him strength to slay till he reach the ships and night falls at the going down of the sun."

Iris hearkened and obeyed. Down she went to strong Ilium from the crests of Ida, and found Hector, son of Priam, standing by his chariot and horses. Then she said: "Hector, son of Priam, peer of gods in counsel, father Zeus has sent me to bear you this message—so long as you see Agamemnon heading his men and making havoc of the Trojan ranks, you are to keep aloof and bid the others bear the brunt of the battle, but when Agamemnon is wounded either by spear or arrow, and takes to his chariot, then will Zeus vouchsafe you strength to slay till you reach the ships, and till night falls at the going down of the sun."

When she had thus spoken Iris left him, and Hector sprang full-armed from his chariot to the ground, brandishing his spear as he went about everywhere among the host, cheering his men on to fight, and stirring the dread strife of battle. The Trojans then wheeled round, and again met the Achaeans, while the Argives on their part strengthened their battalions. The battle was now in array and they stood face to face with one another, Agamemnon ever pressing forward in his eagerness to be ahead of all others.

Tell me now, ye Muses that dwell in the mansions of Olympus, who, whether of the Trojans or of their allies, was first to face Agamemnon? It was Iphidamas, son of Antenor, a man both brave and of great stature, who was brought up in fertile Thrace, the mother of sheep. Cisses, his mother's father, brought him up in his own house when he was a child—Cisses, father to fair

Theano. When he reached manhood, Cisses would have kept him there, and was for giving him his daughter in marriage, but as soon as he had married he set out to fight the Achaeans with twelve ships that followed him: these he had left at Percote and had come on by land to Ilium. He it was that now met Agamemnon, son of Atreus. When they were close up with one another, the son of Atreus missed his aim, and Iphidamas hit him on the girdle below the cuirass and then flung himself upon him, trusting to his strength of arm. The girdle, however, was not pierced, nor nearly so, for the point of the spear struck against the silver and was turned aside as though it had been lead. King Agamemnon caught it from his hand, and drew it towards him with the fury of a lion. He then drew his sword and killed Iphidamas by striking him on the neck. So there the poor fellow lay, sleeping a sleep as it were of bronze, killed in the defense of his fellow citizens, far from his wedded wife, of whom he had had no joy though he had given much for her: he had given a hundred head of cattle down, and had promised later on to give a thousand sheep and goats mixed, from the countless flocks of which he was possessed. Agamemnon, son of Atreus, then despoiled him, and carried off his armor into the host of the Achaeans.

When noble Coön, Antenor's eldest son, saw this, sore indeed were his eyes at the sight of his fallen brother. Unseen by Agamemnon he got beside him, spear in hand, and wounded him in the middle of his arm below the elbow, the point of the spear going right through the arm. Agamemnon was convulsed with pain, but still not even for this did he leave off struggling and fighting, but grasped his spear that flew as fleet as the wind, and sprang upon Coön who was trying to drag off the body of his brother—his father's son—by the foot, and was crying for help to all the bravest of his comrades; but Agamemnon struck him with a bronze-shod spear and killed him as he was dragging the dead body through the press of men under cover of his shield: he then cut off his head, standing over the body of Iphidamas. Thus did the sons of Antenor meet their fate at the hands of the son of Atreus, and go down into the house of Hades.

As long as the blood still welled warm from his wound, Agamemnon went about attacking the ranks of the enemy with spear and sword and with great handfuls of stone, but when the blood had ceased to flow and the wound grew dry, the pain became great. As the sharp pangs which the Eilithuiae, goddesses of childbirth, daughters of Hera and dispensers of cruel pain, send upon a woman when she is in labor—even so sharp were the pangs of the son of Atreus. He sprang on to his chariot, and bade his charioteer drive to the ships, for he was in great agony. With a loud clear voice he shouted to the Danaans, "My friends, princes and counselors of the Argives, defend the ships yourselves, for Zeus has not suffered me to fight the whole day through against the Trojans."

With this the charioteer turned his horses towards the ships, and they flew forward nothing loath. Their chests were white with foam and their bellies with dust, as they drew the wounded king out of the battle.

When Hector saw Agamemnon quit the field, he shouted to the Trojans and Lycians, saying: "Trojans, Lycians, and Dardanian warriors, be men, my friends, and acquit yourselves in battle bravely. Their best man has left them, and Zeus has vouchsafed me a great triumph; charge the foe with your chariots that you may win still greater glory."

With these words he put heart and soul into them all, and as a huntsman hounds his dogs on against a lion or wild boar, even so did Hector, peer of Ares, hound the proud Trojans on against the Achaeans. Full of hope, he plunged in among the foremost, and fell on the fight like some fierce tempest that swoops down upon the sea and lashes its deep blue waters into fury.

What, then, is the full tale of those whom Hector, son of Priam, killed in the hour of triumph which Zeus then vouchsafed him? First Asaeus, Autonoüs, and Opites; Dolops, son of Clytius, Opheltius, and Agelaus; Aesymnus, Orus, and Hipponoüs, steadfast in battle. These chieftains of the Achaeans did Hector slay, and then he fell upon the rank and file. As when the west wind hustles the clouds of the white south and beats them down with the fierceness of its fury—the waves of the sea roll high, and the spray is flung aloft in the rage of the wandering wind—even so thick were the heads of them that fell by the hand of Hector.

All had then been lost and no help for it, and the Achaeans would have fled pell-mell to their ships, had not Odysseus cried out to Diomed, "Son of Tydeus, what has happened to us that we thus forget our prowess? Come, my good fellow, stand by my side and help me, we shall be shamed forever if Hector takes the ships."

And Diomed answered, "Come what may, I will stand firm; but we shall have scant joy of it, for Zeus is minded to give victory to the Trojans rather than to us."

With these words he struck Thymbraeus from his chariot to the ground, smiting him in the left breast with his spear, while Odysseus killed Molion who was his squire. These they let lie, now that they had stopped their fighting; the two heroes then went on playing havoc with the foe, like two wild boars that turn in fury and rend the hounds that hunt them. Thus did they turn upon the Trojans and slay them, and the Achaeans were thankful to have breathing time in their flight from Hector.

They then took two princes with their chariot, the two sons of Merops of Percote, who excelled all others in the arts of divination. He had forbidden his sons to go to the war, but they would not obey him, for fate lured them to their fall. Diomed, son of Tydeus, slew them both and stripped them of their armor, while Odysseus killed Hippodamus and Hypeirochus.

And now the son of Cronus as he looked down from Ida ordained that neither side should have the advantage, and they kept on killing one another. The son of Tydeus speared Agastrophus, son of Paeon, in the hip joint with his spear. His chariot was not at hand for him to fly with, so blindly confident had he been. His squire was in charge of it at some distance and he was fighting on foot among the foremost until he lost his life. Hector soon marked the havoc Diomed and Odysseus were making, and bore down upon them with a loud cry, followed by the Trojan ranks. Brave Diomed was dismayed when he saw them, and said to Odysseus who was beside him: "Great Hector is bearing down upon us and we shall be undone; let us stand firm and wait his onset."

He poised his spear as he spoke and hurled it, nor did he miss his mark. He had aimed at Hector's head near the top of his helmet, but bronze was turned by bronze, and Hector was untouched, for the spear was stayed by the vizored helm made with three plates of metal, which Phoebus Apollo had given him. Hector sprang back with a great bound under cover of the ranks. He fell on his knees and propped himself with his brawny hand leaning on the ground, for darkness had fallen on his eyes. The son of Tydeus, having thrown his spear, dashed in among the foremost fighters to the place where he had seen it strike the ground. Meanwhile Hector recovered himself and springing back into his chariot mingled with the crowd, by which means he saved his life. But Diomed made at him with his spear and said: "Dog, you have again got away though death was close on your heels. Phoebus Apollo, to whom I ween you pray ere you go into battle, has again saved you; nevertheless I will meet you and make an end of you hereafter, if there is any god who will stand by me too and be my helper. For the present I must pursue those whom I can lay hands on."

As he spoke he began stripping the spoils from the son of Paeon, but Paris, husband of lovely Helen, aimed an arrow at him, leaning against a pillar of the monument which men had raised to Ilus, son of Dardanus, a ruler in days of old. Diomed had taken the cuirass from off the breast of Agastrophus, his heavy helmet also, and the shield from off his shoulders, when Paris drew his bow and let fly an arrow that sped not from his hand in vain, but pierced the flat of Diomed's right foot, going right through it and fixing itself in the ground. Thereon Paris with a hearty laugh sprang forward from his hiding place, and taunted him saying: "You are wounded—my arrow has not been shot in vain. Would that it had hit you in the belly and killed you, for thus the Trojans, who fear you as goats fear a lion, would have had a truce from evil."

Diomed all undaunted answered: "Archer, you who without your bow are nothing, slanderer and seducer, if you were to be tried in single combat fighting in full armor, your bow and your arrows would serve you in little stead. Vain is your boast in that you have scratched the sole of my foot. I care no more than if a girl or some silly boy had hit me. A worthless coward can inflict but a light wound. When I wound a man, though I but graze his skin, it is another matter, for my weapon will lay him low. His wife will tear her cheeks for grief and his children will be fatherless: there will he rot, reddening the earth with his blood, and vultures, not women, will gather round him."

Thus he spoke, but Odysseus came up and stood over him. Under this cover he sat down to draw the arrow from his foot, and sharp was the pain he suffered as he did so. Then he sprang on to his chariot and bade the charioteer drive him to the ships, for he was sick at heart.

Odysseus was now alone; not one of the Argives stood by him, for they were all panic-stricken. "Alas," said he to himself in his dismay, "what will become of me? It is ill if I turn and fly before these odds, but it will be worse if I am left alone and taken prisoner, for the son of Cronus has struck the rest of the Danaans with panic. But why talk to myself in this way? Well do I know that though cowards quit the field, a hero, whether he wound or be wounded, must stand firm and hold his own."

While he was thus in two minds, the ranks of the Trojans advanced and hemmed him in, and bitterly did they come to rue it. As hounds and lusty youths set upon a wild boar that sallies from his lair whetting his white tusks—they attack him from every side and can hear the gnashing of his jaws, but for all his fierceness they still hold their ground—even so furiously did the Trojans attack Odysseus. First he sprang spear in hand upon Deïopites and wounded him on the shoulder with a downward blow; then he killed Thoön and Ennomus. After these he struck Chersidamas in the loins under his shield as he had just sprung down from his chariot; so he fell in the dust and clutched the earth in the hollow of his hand. These he let lie, and went on to wound Charops, son of Hippasus, own brother to noble Socus. Socus, hero that he was, made all speed to help him, and when he was close to Odysseus, he said, "Far-famed Odysseus, insatiable of craft and toil, this day you shall either boast of having killed both the sons of Hippasus and stripped them of their armor, or you shall fall before my spear."

With these words he struck the shield of Odysseus. The spear went through the shield and passed on through his richly wrought cuirass, tearing the flesh from his side, but Pallas Athene did not suffer it to pierce the entrails of the hero. Odysseus knew that his hour was not yet come, but he gave ground and said to Socus: "Wretch, you shall now surely die. You have stayed me from fighting further with the Trojans, but you shall now fall by my spear, yielding glory to myself, and your soul to Hades of the noble steeds."

Socus had turned in flight, but as he did so, the spear struck him in the back midway between the shoulders and went right through his chest. He fell heavily to the ground and Odysseus vaunted over him, saying: "O Socus, son of Hippasus, tamer of horses, death has been too quick for you and you have not escaped him. Poor wretch, not even in death shall your father and mother close your eyes, but the ravening vultures shall enshroud you with the flapping of their dark wings and devour you. Whereas even though I fall the Achaeans will give me my due rites of burial."

So saying he drew Socus's heavy spear out of his flesh and from his shield, and the blood welled forth when the spear was withdrawn so that he was much dismayed. When the Trojans saw that Odysseus was bleeding they raised a great shout and came on in a body towards him. He therefore gave ground, and called his comrades to come and help him. Thrice did he cry as loudly as man can cry, and thrice did brave Menelaus hear him. He turned, therefore, to Ajax who was close beside him and said: "Ajax, noble son of Telamon, captain of your people, the cry of Odysseus rings in my ears, as though the Trojans had cut him off and were worsting him while he is single-handed. Let us make our way through the throng; it will be well that we defend him. I fear he may come to harm for all his valor if he be left without support, and the Danaans would miss him sorely."

He led the way and mighty Ajax went with him. The Trojans had gathered round Odysseus like ravenous mountain jackals round the carcass of some horned stag that has been hit with an arrow—the stag has fled at full speed so long as his blood was warm and his strength has lasted, but when the arrow has overcome him, the savage jackals devour him in the shady glades of the forest. Then heaven sends a fierce lion thither, whereon the jackals fly in terror and the lion robs them of their prey—even so did Trojans many and brave gather round crafty Odysseus, but the hero stood at bay and kept them off with his spear. Ajax then came up with his shield before him like a wall and stood hard by, whereon the Trojans fled in all directions. Menelaus took Odysseus by the hand, and led him out of the press while his squire brought up his chariot, but Ajax rushed furiously on the Trojans and killed Doryclus, a bastard son of Priam; then he wounded Pandocus, Lysandrus, Pyrasus, and Pylartes. As some swollen torrent comes rushing in full flood from the mountains on to the plain, big with the rain of heaven—many a dry oak and many a pine does it engulf, and much mud does it bring down and cast into the sea—even so did brave Ajax chase the foe furiously over the plain, slaying both men and horses.

Hector did not yet know what Ajax was doing, for he was fighting on the extreme left of the battle by the banks of the river Scamander, where the carnage was thickest and the war cry loudest round Nestor and brave Idomeneus. Among these Hector was making great slaughter with his spear and furious driving, and was destroying the ranks that were opposed to him. Still the Achaeans would have given no ground, had not Paris, husband of lovely Helen, stayed the prowess of Machaon, shepherd of his people, by wounding him in the right shoulder with a triple-barbed arrow. The Achaeans were in great fear that as the fight had turned against them the Trojans might take him prisoner, and Idomeneus said to Nestor: "Nestor, son of Neleus, honor to the Achaean name, mount your chariot at once. Take Machaon with you and drive your horses to the ships as fast as you can. A physician is worth more than several other men put together, for he can cut out arrows and spread healing herbs."

Nestor, knight of Gerene, did as Idomeneus had counseled. He at once mounted his chariot, and Machaon, son of the famed physician Asclepius, went with him. He lashed his horses and they flew onward nothing loath towards the ships, as though of their own free will.

Then Cebriones, seeing the Trojans in confusion, said to Hector from his place beside him: "Hector, here are we two fighting on the extreme wing of the battle, while the other Trojans are in pell-mell rout, they and their horses. Ajax, son of Telamon, is driving them before him. I know him by the breadth of his shield. Let us turn our chariot and horses thither, where horse and foot are fighting most desperately, and where the cry of battle is loudest."

With this he lashed his goodly steeds, and when they felt the whip they drew the chariot full speed among the Achaeans and Trojans, over the bodies and shields of those that had fallen: the axle was bespattered with blood, and the rail round the car was covered with splashes both from the horses' hoofs and from the tires of the wheels. Hector tore his way through and flung himself into the thick of the fight, and his presence threw the Danaans into confusion, for his spear was not long idle. Nevertheless, though he went among the ranks with sword and spear and throwing great stones, he avoided Ajax, son of Telamon, for Zeus would have been angry with him if he had fought a better man than himself.

Then father Zeus from his high throne struck fear into the heart of Ajax, so that he stood there dazed and threw his shield behind him—looking fearfully at the throng of his foes as though he were some wild beast, and turning hither and thither but crouching slowly backwards. As peasants with their hounds chase a lion from their stockyard, and watch by night to prevent his carrying off the pick of their herd—he makes his greedy spring, but in vain, for the darts from many a strong hand fall thick around him, with burning brands that scare him for all his fury, and when morning comes he slinks foiled and angry away—even so did Ajax, sorely against his will, retreat angrily before the Trojans, fearing for the ships of the Achaeans. Or as some lazy ass that has had many a cudgel broken about his back, when he gets into a field begins eating the corn—boys beat him but he is too many for them, and though they lay about with their sticks they cannot hurt him; still, when he has had his fill they at last drive him from the field—even so did the Trojans and their allies pursue great Ajax, ever smiting the middle of his shield with their darts. Now and again he would turn and show fight, keeping back the battalions of the Trojans, and then he would again retreat; but he prevented any of them from making his way to the ships. Single-handed he stood midway between the Trojans and Achaeans. The spears that sped from their hands stuck some of them in his mighty shield, while many, though thirsting for his blood, fell to the ground ere they could reach him to the wounding of his fair flesh.

Now when Eurypylus, the brave son of Euaemon, saw that Ajax was being overpowered by the rain of arrows, he went up to him and hurled his spear. He struck Apisaon, son of Phausius, in the liver below the midriff, and laid him low. Eurypylus sprang upon him, and stripped the armor from his shoulders; but when Paris saw him, he aimed an arrow at him which struck him in the right thigh. The arrow broke, but the point that was left in the wound dragged on the thigh. He drew back, therefore, under cover of his comrades to save his life, shouting as he did so to the Danaans: "My friends, princes and counselors of the Argives, rally to the defense of Ajax who is being overpowered, and I doubt whether he will come out of the fight alive. Hither, then, to the rescue of great Ajax, son of Telamon."

Even so did he cry when he was wounded; thereon the others came near, and gathered round him, holding their shields upwards from their shoulders so as to give him cover. Ajax then made towards them, and turned round to stand at bay as soon as he had reached his men.

Thus then did they fight as it were a flaming fire. Meanwhile the mares of Neleus, all in a lather with sweat, were bearing Nestor out of the fight, and with him Machaon, shepherd of his people. Achilles saw and took note, for he was standing on the stem of his ship watching the hard stress and struggle of the fight. He called from the ship to his comrade Patroclus, who heard him in the tent and came out looking like Ares himself—here indeed was the beginning of the ill that presently befell him. "Why," said he, "Achilles, do you call me? What do you want with me?" And Achilles answered: "Noble son of Menoetius, man after my own heart, I take it that I shall now have the Achaeans praying at my knees, for they are in great straits. Go, Patroclus, and ask Nestor who it is that he is bearing away wounded from the field; from his back I should say it was Machaon, son of Asclepius, but I could not see his face for the horses went by me at full speed."

Patroclus did as his dear comrade had bidden him, and set off running by the ships and tents of the Achaeans.

When Nestor and Machaon had reached the tents of the son of Neleus, they dismounted, and an esquire, Eurymedon, took the horses from the chariot. The pair then stood in the breeze by the seaside to dry the sweat from their shirts, and when they had so done they came inside and took their seats. Fair Hecamedé, whom Nestor had had awarded to him from Tenedos when Achilles took it, mixed them a mess. She was daughter of wise Arsinoüs, and the Achaeans had given her to Nestor because he excelled all of them in counsel. First she set for them a fair and well-made table that had feet of cyanus. On it there was a vessel of bronze and an onion to give relish to the drink, with honey and cakes of barley meal. There was also a cup of rare workmanship which the old man had brought with him from home, studded with bosses of gold; it had four handles, on each of which there were two golden doves feeding, and it had two feet to stand on. Anyone else would hardly have been able to lift it from the table when it was full, but Nestor could do so quite easily. In this the woman, as fair as a goddess, mixed them a mess with Pramnian wine. She grated goat's-milk cheese into it with a bronze grater, threw in a handful of white barley meal, and having thus prepared the mess she bade them drink it. When they had done so and had thus quenched their thirst, they fell talking with one another, and at this moment Patroclus appeared at the door.

When the old man saw him he sprang from his seat, seized his hand, led him into the tent, and bade him take his place among them; but Patroclus stood where he was and said, "Noble sir, I may not stay, you cannot persuade me to come in; he that sent me is not one to be trifled with, and he bade me ask who the wounded man was whom you were bearing away from the field. I can now see for myself that he is Machaon, shepherd of his people. I must go back and tell Achilles. You, sir, know what a terrible man he is, and how ready to blame even where no blame should lie."

And Nestor answered: "Why should Achilles care to know how many of the Achaeans may be wounded? He recks not of the dismay that reigns in our host; our most valiant chieftains lie disabled, brave Diomed, son of Tydeus, is wounded; so are Odysseus and Agamemnon; Eurypylus has been hit with an arrow in the thigh, and I have just been bringing this man from the field—he too wounded with an arrow. Nevertheless, Achilles, so valiant though he be, cares not and knows no ruth. Will he wait till the ships, do what we may, are in a blaze, and we perish one upon the other? As for me, I have no strength nor stay in me any longer; would that I were still young and strong as in the days when there was a fight between us and the men of Elis about some cattle raiding. I then killed Itymoneus, the valiant son of Hypeirochus, a dweller in Elis, as I was driving in the spoil; he was hit by a dart thrown by my hand while fighting in the front rank in defense of his cows, so he fell and the country people around him were in great fear. We drove off a vast quantity of booty from the plain, fifty herds of cattle and as many flocks of sheep; fifty droves also of pigs, and as many widespreading flocks of goats. Of horses, moreover, we seized a hundred and fifty, all of them mares, and many had foals running with them. All these did we drive by night to Pylus, the city of Neleus, taking them within the city; and the heart of Neleus was glad in that I had taken so much, though it was the first time I had ever been in the field. At daybreak the heralds went round crying that all in Elis to whom there was a debt owing should come, and the leading Pylians assembled to divide the spoils. There were many to whom the Epeans owed chattels, for we men of Pylus were few and had been oppressed with wrong. In former years Heracles had come, and had laid his hand heavy upon us, so that all our best men had perished. Neleus had had twelve sons, but I alone was left; the others had all been killed. The Epeans presuming upon all this had looked down upon us and had done us much evil. My father chose a herd of cattle and a great flock of sheep—three hundred in all—and he took their shepherds with him, for there was a great debt due to him in Elis, to wit four horses, winners of prizes. They and their chariots with them had gone to the games and were to run for a tripod, but King Augeas took them, and sent back their driver grieving for the loss of his horses. Neleus was angered by what he had both said and done, and took great value in return, but he divided the rest, that no man might have less than his full share.

"Thus did we order all things, and offer sacrifices to the gods throughout the city; but three days afterwards the Epeans came in a body, many in number, they and their chariots, in full array, and with them the two Moliones in their armor, though they were still lads and unused to fighting. Now there is a certain town, Thryoëssa, perched upon a rock on the river Alpheus, the border city of Pylos. This they would destroy, and pitched their camp about it, but when they had crossed their whole plain, Athene darted down by night from Olympus and bade us set ourselves in array; and she found willing soldiers in Pylos, for the men meant fighting. Neleus would not let me arm, and hid my horses, for he said that as yet I could know nothing about war. Nevertheless, Athene so ordered the fight that, all on foot as I was, I fought among our mounted forces and vied with the foremost of them. There is a river Minyeius that falls into the sea near Arene, and there they that were mounted (and I with them) waited till morning, when the companies of foot soldiers came up with us in force. Thence in full panoply and equipment we came towards noon to the sacred waters of the Alpheus, and there we offered victims to almighty Zeus, with a bull to Alpheus, another to Poseidon, and a herd-heifer to Athene. After this we took supper in our companies, and laid us down to rest each in his armor by the river.

"The Epeans were beleaguering the city and were determined to take it, but ere this might be there was a desperate fight in store for them. When the sun's rays began to fall upon the earth we joined battle, praying to Zeus and to Athene, and when the fight had begun, I was the first to kill my man and take his horses—to wit the warrior Mulius. He was son-in-law to Augeas, having married his eldest daughter, golden-haired Agamedé, who knew the virtues of every herb which grows upon the face of the earth. I speared him as he was coming towards me, and when he fell headlong in the dust, I sprang upon his chariot and took my place in the front ranks. The Epeans fled in all directions when they saw the captain of their horsemen (the best man they had) laid low, and I swept down on them like a whirlwind, taking fifty chariots—and in each of them two men bit the dust, slain by my spear. I should have even killed the two Moliones, sons of Actor, unless their real father, Poseidon, lord of the earthquake, had hidden them in a thick mist and borne them out of the fight. Thereon Zeus vouchsafed the Pylians a great victory, for we chased them far over the plain, killing the men and bringing in their armor, till we had brought our horses to Buprasium, rich in wheat, and to the Olenian rock, with the hill that is called Alision, at which point Athene turned the people back. There I slew the last man and left him; then the Achaeans drove their horses back from Buprasium to Pylos and gave thanks to Zeus among the gods, and among mortal men to Nestor.

"Such was I among my peers, as surely as ever was, but Achilles is for keeping all his valor for himself; bitterly will he rue it hereafter when the host is being cut to pieces. My good friend, did not Menoetius charge you thus, on the day when he sent you from Phthia to Agamemnon? Odysseus and I were in the house, inside, and heard all that he said to you; for we came to the fair house of Peleus while beating up recruits throughout all Achaea, and when we got there we found Menoetius and yourself, and

Achilles with you. The old knight Peleus was in the outer court, roasting the fat thighbones of a heifer to Zeus, the lord of thunder; and he held a gold chalice in his hand from which he poured drink offerings of wine over the burning sacrifice. You two were busy cutting up the heifer, and at that moment we stood at the gates, whereon Achilles sprang to his feet, led us by the hand into the house, placed us at table, and set before us such hospitable entertainment as guests expect. When we had satisfied ourselves with meat and drink, I said my say and urged both of you to join us. You were ready enough to do so, and the two old men charged you much and straitly. Old Peleus bade his son Achilles fight ever among the foremost and outvie his peers, while Menoetius, the son of Actor, spoke thus to you: 'My son,' said he, 'Achilles is of nobler birth than you are, but you are older than he, though he is far the better man of the two. Counsel him wisely, guide him in the right way, and he will follow you to his own profit.' Thus did your father charge you, but you have forgotten. Nevertheless, even now, say all this to Achilles if he will listen to you. Who knows but with heaven's help you may talk him over, for it is good to take a friend's advice. If, however, he is fearful about some oracle, or if his mother has told him something from Zeus, then let him send you, and let the rest of the Myrmidons follow with you, if perchance you may bring light and saving to the Danaans. And let him send you into battle clad in his own armor, that the Trojans may mistake you for him and leave off fighting. The sons of the Achaeans may thus have time to get their breath, for they are hard pressed and there is little breathing time in battle. You, who are fresh, might easily drive a tired enemy back to his walls and away from the tents and ships."

With these words he moved the heart of Patroclus, who set off running by the line of the ships to Achilles, descendant of Aeacus. When he had got as far as the ships of Odysseus, where was their place of assembly and court of justice, with their altars dedicated to the gods, Eurypylus, son of Euaemon, met him, wounded in the thigh with an arrow, and limping out of the fight. Sweat rained from his head and shoulders, and black blood welled from his cruel wound, but his mind did not wander. The son of Menoetius when he saw him had compassion upon him and spoke piteously, saying: "O unhappy princes and counselors of the Danaans, are you then doomed to feed the hounds of Troy with your fat, far from your friends and your native land? Say, noble Eurypylus, will the Achaeans be able to hold great Hector in check, or will they fall now before his spear?"

Wounded Eurypylus made answer: "Noble Patroclus, there is no hope left for the Achaeans but they will perish at their ships. All they that were princes among us are lying struck down and wounded at the hands of the Trojans, who are waxing stronger and stronger. But save me and take me to your ship. Cut out the arrow from my thigh, wash the black blood from off it with warm water, and lay upon it those gracious herbs which, so they say, have been shown you by Achilles, who was himself shown them by Chiron, most righteous of all the centaurs. For of the physicians Podalirius and Machaon, I hear that the one is lying wounded in his tent and is himself in need of healing, while the other is fighting the Trojans upon the plain."

"Hero Eurypylus," replied the brave son of Menoetius, "how may these things be? What can I do? I am on my way to bear a message to noble Achilles from Nestor of Gerene, bulwark of the Achaeans, but even so I will not be unmindful of your distress."

With this he clasped him round the middle and led him into the tent, and a servant, when he saw him, spread bullock skins on the ground for him to lie on. He laid him at full length and cut out the sharp arrow from his thigh; he washed the black blood from the wound with warm water; he then crushed a bitter herb, rubbing it between his hands, and spread it upon the wound. This was a virtuous herb which killed all pain, so the wound presently dried and the blood left off flowing.

BOOK XII

Led by Hector, the Trojans leave their horses and chariots and assail the Greek wall on foot. The two Ajaxes head the Greek defense. Hector, however, crashes through the gate and the Trojans behind him pour over the wall, while the Greeks flee in panic to their ships.

So the son of Menoetius was attending to the hurt of Eurypylus within the tent, but the Argives and Trojans still fought desperately, nor were the trench and the high wall above it to keep the Trojans in check longer. They had built it to protect their ships and had dug the trench all round it that it might safeguard both the ships and the rich spoils which they had taken, but they had not offered hecatombs to the gods. It had been built without the consent of the immortals, and therefore it did not last. So long as Hector lived and Achilles nursed his anger and so long as the city of Priam remained untaken, the great wall of the Achaeans stood firm; but when the bravest of the Trojans were no more, and many also of the Argives, though some were yet left alive—when, moreover, the city was sacked in the tenth year, and the Argives had gone back with their ships to their own country—then Poseidon and Apollo took counsel to destroy the wall, and they turned on to it the streams of all the rivers from Mount Ida into the sea, Rhesus, Heptaporus, Caresus, Rhodius, Grenicus, Aesopus, and goodly Scamander, with Simois, where many a shield and helm had fallen, and many a hero of the race of demigods had bitten the dust. Phoebus Apollo turned the mouths of all these rivers together and made them flow for nine days against the wall, while Zeus rained the whole time that he might wash it sooner into the sea. Poseidon himself, trident in hand, surveyed the work and threw into the sea all the foundations of beams and stones which the Achaeans had laid with so much toil. He made all level by the mighty stream of the Hellespont, and then when he had swept the wall away he spread a great beach of sand over the place where it had been. This done he turned the rivers back into their old courses.

This was what Poseidon and Apollo were to do in after time; but as yet battle and turmoil were still raging round the wall till its timbers rang under the blows that rained upon them. The Argives, cowed by the scourge of Zeus, were hemmed in at their ships in fear of Hector, the mighty minister of Rout, who as heretofore fought with the force and fury of a whirlwind. As a lion or wild boar turns fiercely on the dogs and men that attack him, while these form a solid wall and shower their javelins as they face him—his courage is all undaunted, but his high spirit will be the death of him. Many a time does he charge at his pursuers to scatter them, and they fall back as often as he does so—even so did Hector go about among the host exhorting his men and cheering them on to cross the trench.

But the horses dared not do so, and stood neighing upon its brink, for the width frightened them. They could neither jump it nor cross it, for it had overhanging banks all round upon either side, above which there were the sharp stakes that the sons of the Achaeans had planted so close and strong as a defense against all who would assail it. A horse, therefore, could not get into it and draw his chariot after him, but those who were on foot kept trying their very utmost. Then Polydamas went up to Hector and said: "Hector, and you other captains of the Trojans and allies, it is madness for us to try and drive our horses across the trench; it will be very hard to cross, for it is full of sharp stakes, and beyond these there is the wall. Our horses therefore cannot get down into it and would be of no use if they did; moreover, it is a narrow place and we should come to harm. If, indeed, great Zeus is minded to help the Trojans and in his anger will utterly destroy the Achaeans, I would myself gladly see them perish now and here far from Argos; but if they should rally and we are driven back from the ships pell-mell into the trench there will be not so much as a man get back to the city to tell the tale. Now, therefore, let us all do as I say: let our squires hold our horses by the trench, but let us follow Hector in a body on foot, clad in full armor, and if the day of their doom is at hand the Achaeans will not be able to withstand us."

Thus spoke Polydamas and his saying pleased Hector, who sprang in full armor to the ground, and all the other Trojans, when they saw him do so, also left their chariots. Each man then gave his horses over to his charioteer in charge to hold them ready for him at the trench. Then they formed themselves into companies, made themselves ready, and in five bodies followed their leaders. Those that went with Hector and Polydamas were the bravest and most in number, and the most determined to break through the wall and fight at the ships. Cebriones was also joined with them as third in command, for Hector had left his chariot in charge of a less valiant soldier. The next company was led by Paris, Alcathoüs, and Agenor; the third by Helenus and Deïphobus, two sons of Priam, and with them was the hero Asius—Asius, the son of Hyrtacus, whose great black horses of the breed that comes from the river Selleis had brought him from Arisbe. Aeneas, the valiant son of Anchises, led the fourth; he and the two sons of Antenor, Archelochus and Acamas, men well-versed in all the arts of war. Sarpedon was captain over the allies, and took with him Glaucus and Asteropaeus whom he deemed most valiant after himself—for he was far the best man of them all. These helped to array one another in their oxhide shields, and then charged straight at the Danaans, for they felt sure that they would not hold out longer and that they should themselves now fall upon the ships.

The rest of the Trojans and their allies now followed the counsel of Polydamas, but Asius, son of Hyrtacus, would not leave his horses and his esquire behind him; in his foolhardiness he took them on with him towards the ships, nor did he fail to come by his end in consequence. Nevermore was he to return to wind-beaten Ilium, exulting in his chariot and his horses. Ere he could do so, death of ill-omened name had overshadowed him and he had fallen by the spear of Idomeneus, the noble son of Deucalion. He had driven towards the left wing of the ships, by which way the Achaeans used to return with their chariots and horses from the plain. Hither he drove and found the gates with their doors opened wide and the great bar down—for the gatemen kept them open so as to let those of their comrades enter who might be flying towards the ships. Hither of set purpose did he direct his horses, and his men followed him with a loud cry, for they felt sure that the Achaeans would not hold out longer and that they should now fall upon the ships. Little did they know that at the gates they should find two of the bravest chieftains, proud sons of the fighting Lapithae—the one, Polypoetes, mighty son of Pirithoüs, and the other Leonteus, peer of murderous Ares.

These stood before the gates like two high oak trees upon the mountains that tower from their widespreading roots and year after year battle with wind and rain—even so did these two men await the onset of great Asius confidently and without flinching. The Trojans led by him and by Iamenus, Orestes, Adamas, the son of Asius, Thoön, and Oenomaus, raised a loud cry of battle and made straight for the wall, holding their shields of dry oxhide above their heads; for a while the two defenders remained inside and cheered the Achaeans on to stand firm in the defense of their ships. When, however, they saw that the Trojans were attacking the wall, while the Danaans were crying out for help and being routed, they rushed outside and fought in front of the gates like two wild boars upon the mountains that abide the attack of men and dogs, and charging on either side break down the wood all around them tearing it up by the roots, and one can hear the clattering of their tusks, till someone hits them and makes an end of them—even so did the gleaming bronze rattle about their breasts as the weapons fell upon them; for they fought with great fury, trusting to their own prowess and to those who were on the wall above them. These threw great stones at their assailants in defense of themselves, their tents, and their ships. The stones fell thick as the flakes of snow which some fierce blast drives from the dark clouds and showers down in sheets upon the earth—even so fell the weapons from the hands alike of Trojans and Achaeans.

Helmet and shield rang out as the great stones rained upon them, and Asius, the son of Hyrtacus, in his dismay cried aloud and smote his two thighs. "Father Zeus," he cried, "of a truth you too are altogether given to lying. I made sure the Argive heroes could not withstand us, whereas like slim-waisted wasps, or bees that have their nests in the rocks by the wayside—they leave not the holes wherein they have built undefended, but fight for their little ones against all who would take them—even so these men, though they be but two, will not be driven from the gates, but stand firm either to slay or be slain." He spoke, but moved not the mind of Zeus, whose counsel it then was to give glory to Hector. Meanwhile the rest of the Trojans were fighting about the other gates. I, however, am no god to be able to tell about all these things, for the battle raged everywhere about the stone wall as it were a fiery furnace. The Argives, discomfited though they were, were forced to defend their ships, and all the gods who were defending the Achaeans were vexed in spirit; but the Lapithae kept on fighting with might and main.

Thereon Polypoetes, mighty son of Pirithoüs, hit Damasus with a spear upon his cheek-pierced helmet. The helmet did not protect him, for the point of the spear went through it and broke the bone, so that the brain inside was scattered about, and he died fighting. He then slew Pylon and Ormenus. Leonteus, of the race of Ares, killed Hippomachus, the son of Antimachus, by striking him with his spear upon the girdle. He then drew his sword and sprang first upon Antiphates whom he killed in close combat, and who fell face upwards on the earth. After him he killed Menon, Iamenus, and Orestes, and laid them low one after the other.

While they were busy stripping the armor from these heroes, the youths who were led on by Polydamas and Hector (and these were the greater part and the most valiant of those that were trying to break through the wall and fire the ships) were still standing by the trench, uncertain what they should do; for they had seen a sign from heaven when they had essayed to cross it—a soaring eagle that flew skirting the left wing of their host, with a monstrous blood-red snake in its talons still alive and struggling to escape. The snake was still bent on revenge, wriggling and twisting itself backwards till it struck the bird that held it, on the neck and breast; whereon the bird being in pain, let it fall, dropping it into the middle of the host, and then flew down the wind with a sharp cry. The Trojans were struck with terror when they saw the snake, portent of aegis-bearing Zeus, writhing in the midst of them, and Polydamas went up to Hector and said:

"Hector, at our councils of war you are ever given to rebuke me, even when I speak wisely, as though it were not well, forsooth, that one of the people should cross your will either in the field or at the council board; you would have them support you always. Nevertheless, I will say what I think will be best; let us not now go on to fight the Danaans at their ships, for I know what will happen if this soaring eagle which skirted the left wing of our host with a monstrous blood-red snake in its talons (the snake being still alive) was really sent as an omen to the Trojans on their essaying to cross the trench. The eagle let go her hold; she did not succeed in taking it home to her little ones, and so will it be with ourselves. Even though by a mighty effort we break through the gates and wall of the Achaeans, and they give way before us, still we shall not return in good order by the way we came, but shall leave many a man behind us whom the Achaeans will do to death in defense of their ships. Thus would any seer who was expert in these matters, and was trusted by the people, read the portent."

Hector looked fiercely at him and said: "Polydamas, I like not of your reading. You can find a better saying than this if you will. If, however, you have spoken in good earnest, then indeed has heaven robbed you of your reason. You would have me pay no heed to the counsels of Zeus, nor to the promises he made me"—and he bowed his head in confirmation; "you bid me be ruled rather by the flight of wild fowl. What care I whether they fly towards dawn or dark, and whether they be on my right hand or on my left? Let us put our trust rather in the counsel of great Zeus, king of mortals and immortals. There is one omen, and one only—that a man should fight for his country. Why are you so fearful? Though we be all of us slain at the ships of the Argives you are not likely to be killed yourself, for you are not steadfast nor courageous. If you will not fight, or would talk others over from doing so, you shall fall forthwith before my spear."

With these words he led the way, and the others followed after with a cry that rent the air. Then Zeus, the lord of thunder, sent the blast of a mighty wind from the mountains of Ida that bore the dust down towards the ships. He thus lulled the Achaeans into security, and gave victory to Hector and to the Trojans, who, trusting to their own might and to the signs he had shown them, essayed to break through the great wall of the Achaeans. They tore down the breastworks from the walls and overthrew the battlements. They upheaved the buttresses, which the Achaeans had set in front of the wall in order to support it; when they had pulled these down they made sure of breaking through the wall, but the Danaans still showed no sign of giving ground; they still fenced the battlements with their shields of oxhide and hurled their missiles down upon the foe as soon as any came below the wall.

The two Ajaxes went about everywhere on the walls cheering on the Achaeans, giving fair words to some while they spoke sharply to anyone whom they saw to be remiss. "My friends," they cried, "Argives one and all—good, bad, and indifferent, for there was never fight yet in which all were of equal prowess—there is now work enough, as you very well know, for all of you. See that you none of you turn in flight towards the ships, daunted by the shouting of the foe, but press forward and keep one another in heart, if it may so be that Olympian Zeus, the lord of lightning, will vouchsafe us to repel our foes, and drive them back towards the city."

Thus did the two go about shouting and cheering the Achaeans on. As the flakes that fall thick upon a winter's day, when Zeus is minded to snow and to display these his arrows to mankind—he lulls the wind to rest, and snows hour after hour till he has buried the tops of the high mountains, the headlands that jut into the sea, the grassy plains, and the tilled fields of men; the snow lies deep upon the forelands and havens of the gray sea, but the waves as they come rolling in stay it that it can come no further, though all else is wrapped as with a mantle, so heavy are the heavens with snow—even thus thickly did the stones fall on one side and on the other, some thrown at the Trojans, and some by the Trojans at the Achaeans; and the whole wall was in an uproar.

Still the Trojans and brave Hector would not yet have broken down the gates and the great bar, had not Zeus turned his son Sarpedon against the Argives as a lion against a herd of horned cattle. Before him he held his shield of hammered bronze, that the smith had beaten so fair and round, and had lined with oxhides which he had made fast with rivets of gold all round the shield. This he held in front of him, and brandishing his two spears came on like some lion of the wilderness, who has been long famished for want of meat and will dare break even into a well-fenced homestead to try and get at the sheep. He may find the shepherds keeping watch over their flocks with dogs and spears, but he is in no mind to be driven from the fold till he has had a try for it; he will either spring on a sheep and carry it off, or be hit by a spear from some strong hand—even so was Sarpedon fain to attack the wall and break down its battlements. Then he said to Glaucus, son of Hippolochus: "Glaucus, why in Lycia do we receive especial honor as regards our place at table? Why are the choicest portions served us and our cups kept brimming, and why do men look up to us as though we were gods? Moreover, we hold a large estate by the banks of the river Xanthus, fair with orchard lawns and wheat-growing land; it becomes us, therefore, to take our stand at the head of all the Lycians and bear the brunt of the fight, that one may say to another, 'Our princes in Lycia eat the fat of the land and drink the best of wine, but they are fine fellows; they fight well and are ever at the front in battle.' My good friend, if, when we were once out of this fight, we could escape old age and death thenceforward and forever, I should neither press forward myself nor bid you do so, but death in ten thousand shapes hangs ever over our heads, and no man can elude him. Therefore, let us go forward and either win glory for ourselves or yield it to another."

Glaucus heeded his saying, and the pair forthwith led on the host of Lycians. Menestheus, son of Peteos, was dismayed when he saw them, for it was against his part of the wall that they came—bringing destruction with them. He looked along the wall for some chieftain to support his comrades and saw the two Ajaxes, men ever eager for the fray, and Teucer, who had just come from his tent, standing near them; but he could not make his voice heard by shouting to them, so great an uproar was there from clashing shields and helmets and the battering of gates with a din which reached the skies. For all the gates had been closed, and the Trojans were hammering at them to try and break their way through them. Menestheus, therefore, sent Thoötes with a message to Ajax. "Run, good Thoötes," said he, "and call Ajax, or better still bid both come, for it will be all over with us here directly; the leaders of the Lycians are upon us, men who have ever fought desperately heretofore. But if the pair have too much on their hands to let them both come, at any rate let Ajax, son of Telamon, do so, and let Teucer, the famous bowman, come with him."

The messenger did as he was told, and set off running along the wall of the Achaeans. When he reached the Ajaxes he said to them: "Sirs, princes of the Argives, the son of noble Peteos bids you come to him for a while and help him. You had better both come if you can, or it will be all over with him directly. The leaders of the Lycians are upon him, men who have ever fought desperately heretofore. If you have too much on your hands to let both come, at any rate let Ajax, son of Telamon, do so, and let Teucer, the famous bowman, come with him."

Great Ajax, son of Telamon, heeded the message, and at once spoke to the son of Oïleus. "Ajax," said he, "do you two, yourself and brave Lycomedes, stay here and keep the Danaans in heart to fight their hardest. I will go over yonder, and bear my part in the fray, but I will come back here at once as soon as I have given them the help they need."

With this, Ajax, son of Telamon, set off, and Teucer, his brother by the same father, went also, with Pandion to carry Teucer's bow. They went along inside the wall, and when they came to the tower where Menestheus was (and hard-pressed indeed did they find him) the brave captains and leaders of the Lycians were storming the battlements as it were a thick dark cloud, fighting in close quarters, and raising the battle cry aloud.

First, Ajax, son of Telamon, killed brave Epicles, a comrade of Sarpedon, hitting him with a jagged stone that lay by the battlements at the very top of the wall. As men now are, even one who is in the bloom of youth could hardly lift it with his two hands, but Ajax raised it high aloft and flung it down, smashing Epicles's four-crested helmet so that the bones of his head were crushed to pieces, and he fell from the high wall as though he were diving, with no more life left in him. Then Teucer wounded Glaucus, the brave son of Hippolochus, as he was coming on to attack the wall. He saw his shoulder bare and aimed an arrow at it, which made Glaucus leave off fighting. Thereon he sprang covertly down for fear some of the Achaeans might see that he was wounded and taunt him. Sarpedon was stung with grief when he saw Glaucus leave him, still he did not leave off fighting, but aimed his spear at Alcmaon, the son of Thestor, and hit him. He drew his spear back again and Alcmaon came down headlong after it with his bronzed armor rattling round him. Then Sarpedon seized the battlement in his strong hands, and tugged at it till it all gave way together, and a breach was made through which many might pass.

Ajax and Teucer then both of them attacked him. Teucer hit him with an arrow on the band that bore the shield which covered his body, but Zeus saved his son from destruction that he might not fall by the ships' sterns. Meanwhile Ajax sprang on him and pierced his shield, but the spear did not go clean through, though it hustled him back that he could come on no further. He therefore retired a little space from the battlement, yet without losing all his ground, for he still thought to cover himself with glory. Then he turned round and shouted to the brave Lycians, saying: "Lycians, why do you thus fail me? For all my prowess I cannot break through the wall and open a way to the ships single-handed. Come close on behind me, for the more there are of us the better."

The Lycians, shamed by his rebuke, pressed closer round him who was their counselor and their king. The Argives on their part got their men in fighting order within the wall, and there was a deadly struggle between them. The Lycians could not break through the wall and force their way to the ships, nor could the Danaans drive the Lycians from the wall now that they had once reached it. As two men, measuring rods in hand, quarrel about their boundaries in a field that they own in common, and stickle for their rights though they be but in a mere strip, even so did the battlements now serve as a bone of contention, and they beat one another's round shields for their possession.

Many a man's body was wounded with the pitiless bronze as he turned round and bared his back to the foe, and many were struck clean through their shields. The wall and battlements were everywhere deluged with the blood alike of Trojans and of Achaeans. But even so the Trojans could not rout the Achaeans, who still held on; and as some honest hard-working woman weighs wool in her balance and sees that the scales be true, for she would gain some pitiful earnings for her little ones, even so was the fight balanced evenly between them till the time came when Zeus gave the greater glory to Hector, son of Priam, who was first to spring toward the walls of the Achaeans. As he did so, he cried aloud to the Trojans, "Up, Trojans, break the wall of the Argives, and fling fire upon their ships!"

Thus did he hound them on, and in one body they rushed straight at the wall as he had bidden them, and scaled the battlements with sharp spears in their hands. Hector laid hold of a stone that lay just outside the gates and was thick at one end but pointed at the other; two of the best men in a town, as men now are, could hardly raise it from the ground and put it on to a wagon, but Hector lifted it quite easily by himself, for the son of scheming Cronus made it light for him. As a shepherd picks up a ram's fleece with one hand and finds it no burden, so easily did Hector lift the great stone and drive it right at the doors that closed the gates so strong and so firmly set. These doors were double and high, and were kept closed by two crossbars to which there was but one key. When he had got close up to them, Hector strode towards them that his blow might gain in force and struck them in the middle, leaning his whole weight against them. He broke both hinges, and the stone fell inside by reason of its great weight. The portals reechoed with the sound, the bars held no longer, and the doors flew open, one one way, and the other the other, through the force of the blow. Then brave Hector leaped inside with a face as dark as that of flying night. The gleaming bronze flashed fiercely about his body and he had two spears in his hand. None but a god could have withstood him as he flung himself into the gateway, and his eyes glared like fire. Then he turned round towards the Trojans and called on them to scale the wall, and they did as he bade them—some of them at once climbing over the wall, while others passed through the gates. The Danaans then fled panic-stricken towards their ships, and all was uproar and confusion.

BOOK XIII

The sea-god Poseidon is angry with Zeus for showing such favor to the Trojans. In a series of disguises, he rallies the Greeks to stand against their onrushing enemies. The Cretan Idomeneus performs valorous deeds on the Greek side. Some Trojans retreat but Hector leads them on again.

Now when Zeus had thus brought Hector and the Trojans to the ships, he left them to their never-ending toil, and turned his keen eyes away, looking elsewhither towards the horse-breeders of Thrace, the Mysians, fighters at close quarters, the noble Hippemolgi, who live on milk, and the Abians, justest of mankind. He no longer turned so much as a glance towards Troy, for he did not think that any of the immortals would go and help either Trojans or Danaans.

But King Poseidon had kept no blind lookout; he had been looking admiringly on the battle from his seat on the topmost crests of wooded Samothrace, whence he could see all Ida, with the city of Priam and the ships of the Achaeans. He had come from under the sea and taken his place here, for he pitied the Achaeans who were being overcome by the Trojans; and he was furiously angry with Zeus.

Presently he came down from his post on the mountain top, and as he strode swiftly onwards the high hills and the forest quaked beneath the tread of his immortal feet. Three strides he took, and with the fourth he reached his goal—Aegae, where is his glittering golden palace, imperishable, in the depths of the sea. When he got there, he yoked his fleet brazen-footed steeds with their manes of gold all flying in the wind. He clothed himself in raiment of gold, grasped his gold whip, and took his stand upon his chariot. As he went his way over the waves the sea-monsters left their lairs, for they knew their lord, and came gamboling round him from every quarter of the deep, while the sea in her gladness opened a path before his chariot. So lightly did the horses fly that the bronze axle of the car was not even wet beneath it; and thus his bounding steeds took him to the ships of the Achaeans.

Now there is a certain huge cavern in the depths of the sea midway between Tenedos and rocky Imbrus. Here Poseidon, lord of the earthquake, stayed his horses, unyoked them, and set before them their ambrosial forage. He hobbled their feet with hobbles of gold which none could either unloose or break, so that they might stay there in that place until their lord should return. This done, he went his way to the host of the Achaeans.

Now the Trojans followed Hector, son of Priam, in close array like a storm cloud or flame of fire, fighting with might and main and raising the cry of battle; for they deemed that they should take the ships of the Achaeans and kill all their chiefest heroes then and there. Meanwhile, earth-encircling Poseidon, lord of the earthquake, cheered on the Argives, for he had come up out of the sea and had assumed the form and voice of Calchas.

First he spoke to the two Ajaxes, who were doing their best already, and said: "Ajaxes, you two can be the saving of the Achaeans if you will put out all your strength and not let yourselves be daunted. I am not afraid that the Trojans, who have got over the wall in force, will be victorious in any other part, for the Achaeans can hold all of them in check, but I much fear that some evil will befall us here where furious Hector, who boasts himself the son of great Zeus himself, is leading them on like a pillar of flame. May some god, then, put it into your hearts to make a firm stand here, and to incite others to do the like. In this case you will drive him from the ships even though he be inspired by Zeus himself."

As he spoke the earth-encircling lord of the earthquake struck both of them with his scepter and filled their hearts with daring. He made their legs light and active, as also their hands and their feet. Then, as the soaring falcon poises on the wing high above some sheer rock, and presently swoops down to chase some bird over the plain, even so did Poseidon, lord of the earthquake, wing his flight into the air and leave them. Of the two, swift Ajax, son of Oïleus, was the first to know who it was that had been speaking with them, and said to Ajax, son of Telamon: "Ajax, this is one of the gods that dwell on Olympus, who in the likeness of the prophet is bidding us fight hard by our ships. It was not Calchas, the seer and diviner of omens; I knew him at once by his feet and knees as he turned away, for the gods are soon recognized. Moreover I feel the lust of battle burn more fiercely within me, while my hands and my feet under me are more eager for the fray."

And Ajax, son of Telamon, answered: "I too feel my hands grasp my spear more firmly; my strength is greater, and my feet more nimble; I long, moreover, to meet furious Hector, son of Priam, even in single combat."

Thus did they converse, exulting in the hunger after battle with which the god had filled them. Meanwhile the earth-encircler roused the Achaeans, who were resting in the rear by the ships overcome at once by hard fighting and by grief at seeing that the Trojans had got over the wall in force. Tears began falling from their eyes as they beheld them, for they made sure that they should not escape destruction; but the lord of the earthquake passed lightly about among them and urged their battalions to the front.

First he went up to Teucer and Leïtus, the hero Peneleos, and Thoas and Deïpyrus; Meriones also and Antilochus, valiant warriors; all these did he exhort. "Shame on you, young Argives!" he cried. "It was on your prowess I relied for the saving of our ships;

if you fight not with might and main, this very day will see us overcome by the Trojans. Of a truth my eyes behold a great and terrible portent which I had never thought to see—the Trojans at our ships—they, who heretofore were like panic-stricken hinds, the prey of jackals and wolves in a forest, with no strength but in flight for they cannot defend themselves. Hitherto the Trojans dared not for one moment face the attack of the Achaeans, but now they have sallied far from their city and are fighting at our very ships through the cowardice of our leader and the disaffection of the people themselves, who in their discontent care not to fight in defense of the ships but are being slaughtered near them. True, King Agamemnon, son of Atreus, is the cause of our disaster by having insulted the son of Peleus, still this is no reason why we should leave off fighting. Let us be quick to heal, for the hearts of the brave heal quickly. You do ill to be thus remiss, you, who are the finest soldiers in our whole army. I blame no man for keeping out of battle if he is a weakling, but I am indignant with such men as you are. My good friends, matters will soon become even worse through this slackness. Think, each one of you, of his own honor and credit, for the hazard of the fight is extreme. Great Hector is now fighting at our ships; he has broken through the gates and the strong bolt that held them."

Thus did the earth-encircler address the Achaeans and urge them on. Thereon round the two Ajaxes there gathered strong bands of men, of whom not even Ares nor Athene, marshaler of hosts, could make light if they went among them, for they were the picked men of all those who were now awaiting the onset of Hector and the Trojans. They made a living fence, spear to spear, shield to shield, buckler to buckler, helmet to helmet, and man to man. The horsehair crests on their gleaming helmets touched one another as they nodded forward, so closely serried were they; the spears they brandished in their strong hands were interlaced, and their hearts were set on battle.

The Trojans advanced in a dense body, with Hector at their head pressing right on as a rock that comes thundering down the side of some mountain from whose brow the winter torrents have torn it; the foundations of the dull thing have been loosened by floods of rain, and as it bounds headlong on its way it sets the whole forest in an uproar. It swerves neither to right nor left till it reaches level ground, but then for all its fury it can go no further—even so easily did Hector for a while seem as though he would career through the tents and ships of the Achaeans till he had reached the sea in his murderous course; but the closely serried battalions stayed him when he reached them, for the sons of the Achaeans thrust at him with swords and spears pointed at both ends, and drove him from them so that he staggered and gave ground. Thereon he shouted to the Trojans: "Trojans, Lycians, and Dardanians, fighters in close combat, stand firm! The Achaeans have set themselves as a wall against me, but they will not check me for long. They will give ground before me if the mightiest of the gods, the thundering spouse of Hera, has indeed inspired my onset."

With these words he put heart and soul into them all. Deïphobus, son of Priam, went about among them intent on deeds of daring with his round shield before him, under cover of which he strode quickly forward. Meriones took aim at him with a spear, nor did he fail to hit the broad orb of oxhide; but he was far from piercing it for the spear broke in two pieces long ere he could do so; moreover, Deïphobus had seen it coming and had held his shield well away from him. Meriones drew back under cover of his comrades, angry alike at having failed to vanquish Deïphobus and having broken his spear. He turned therefore towards the ships and tents to fetch a spear which he had left behind in his tent.

The others continued fighting, and the cry of battle rose up into the heavens. Teucer, son of Telamon, was the first to kill his man, to wit, the warrior Imbrius, son of Mentor, rich in horses. Until the Achaeans came he had lived in Pedaeum, and had married Medesicaste, a bastard daughter of Priam; but on the arrival of the Danaan fleet he had gone back to Ilium, and was a great man among the Trojans, dwelling near Priam himself, who gave him like honor with his own sons. The son of Telamon now struck him under the ear with a spear which he then drew back again, and Imbrius fell headlong as an ash tree when it is felled on the crest of some high mountain beacon, and its delicate green foliage comes toppling down to the ground. Thus did he fall with his bronze-dight armor ringing harshly round him, and Teucer sprang forward with intent to strip him of his armor; but as he was doing so, Hector took aim at him with a spear. Teucer saw the spear coming and swerved aside, whereon it hit Amphimachus, son of Cteatus, son of Actor, in the chest as he was coming into battle, and his armor rang rattling round him as he fell heavily to the ground. Hector sprang forward to take Amphimachus's helmet from off his temples, and in a moment Ajax threw a spear at him, but did not wound him, for he was encased all over in his terrible armor. Nevertheless, the spear struck the boss of his shield with such force as to drive him back from the two corpses, which the Achaeans then drew off. Stichius and Menestheus, captains of the Athenians, bore away Amphimachus to the host of the Achaeans, while the two brave and impetuous Ajaxes did the like by Imbrius. As two lions snatch a goat from the hounds that have it in their fangs, and bear it through thick brushwood high above the ground in their jaws, thus did the Ajaxes bear aloft the body of Imbrius, and strip it of its armor. Then the son of Oïleus severed the head from the neck in revenge for the death of Amphimachus, and sent it whirling over the crowd as though it had been a ball, till it fell in the dust at Hector's feet.

Poseidon was exceedingly angry that his grandson Amphimachus should have fallen. He therefore went to the tents and ships of the Achaeans to urge the Danaans still further, and to devise evil for the Trojans. Idomeneus met him, as he was taking leave of a comrade, who had just come to him from the fight, wounded in the knee. His fellow soldiers bore him off the field, and Idomeneus having given orders to the physicians went on to his tent, for he was still thirsting for battle. Poseidon spoke in the likeness and with the voice of Thoas, son of Andraemon, who ruled the Aetolians of all Pleuron and high Calydon, and was honored among his people as though he were a god. "Idomeneus," said he, "lawgiver to the Cretans, what has now become of the threats with which the sons of the Achaeans used to threaten the Trojans?"

And Idomeneus, chief among the Cretans, answered: "Thoas, no one, so far as I know, is in fault, for we can all fight. None are held back neither by fear nor slackness, but it seems to be the will of almighty Zeus that the Achaeans should perish ingloriously here far from Argos. You, Thoas, have been always staunch, and you keep others in heart if you see any fail in duty. Be not then remiss now, but exhort all to do their utmost."

To this Poseidon, lord of the earthquake, made answer: "Idomeneus, may he never return from Troy, but remain here for dogs to batten upon, who is this day willfully slack in fighting. Get your armor and go; we must make all haste together if we may be of any use, though we are only two. Even cowards gain courage from companionship, and we two can hold our own with the bravest."

Therewith the god went back into the thick of the fight, and Idomeneus when he had reached his tent donned his armor, grasped his two spears, and sallied forth. As the lightning which the son of Cronus brandishes from bright Olympus when he would show a sign to mortals, and its gleam flashes far and wide—even so did his armor gleam about him as he ran. Meriones, his sturdy squire, met him while he was still near his tent (for he was going to fetch his spear) and Idomeneus said:

"Meriones, fleet son of Molus, best of comrades, why have you left the field? Are you wounded, and is the point of the weapon hurting you? or have you been sent to fetch me? I want no fetching; I had far rather fight than stay in my tent."

"Idomeneus," answered Meriones, "I come for a spear, if I can find one in my tent. I have broken the one I had in throwing it at the shield of Deïphobus."

And Idomeneus, captain of the Cretans, answered: "You will find one spear, or twenty if you so please, standing up against the end wall of my tent. I have taken them from Trojans whom I have killed, for I am not one to keep my enemy at arm's length. Therefore I have spears, bossed shields, helmets, and burnished corslets."

Then Meriones said: "I too in my tent and at my ship have spoils taken from the Trojans, but they are not at hand. I have been at all times valorous, and wherever there has been hard fighting have held my own among the foremost. There may be those among the Achaeans who do not know how I fight, but you know it well enough yourself."

Idomeneus answered: "I know you for a brave man—you need not tell me. If the best men at the ships were being chosen to go on an ambush—and there is nothing like this for showing what a man is made of; it comes out then who is cowardly and who brave; the coward will change color at every touch and turn; he is full of fears, and keeps shifting his weight first on one knee and then on the other; his heart beats fast as he thinks of death, and one can hear the chattering of his teeth. Whereas the brave man will not change color nor be frightened on finding himself in ambush, but is all the time longing to go into action—if the best men were being chosen for such a service, no one could make light of your courage nor feats of arms. If you were struck by a dart or smitten in close combat, it would not be from behind, in your neck nor back, but the weapon would hit you in the chest or belly as you were pressing forward to a place in the front ranks. But let us no longer stay here talking like children, lest we be ill spoken of; go, fetch your spear from the tent at once."

On this Meriones, peer of Ares, went to the tent and got himself a spear of bronze. He then followed after Idomeneus, big with great deeds of valor. As when baneful Ares sallies forth to battle, and his son Panic so strong and dauntless goes with him, to strike terror even into the heart of a hero—the pair have gone from Thrace to arm themselves among the Ephyri or the brave Phlegyans, but they will not listen to both the contending hosts, and will give victory to one side or to the other—even so did Meriones and Idomeneus, captains of men, go out to battle clad in their bronze armor. Meriones was first to speak. "Son of Deucalion," said he, "where would you have us begin fighting? On the right wing of the host, in the center, or on the left wing, where I take it the Achaeans will be weakest?"

Idomeneus answered: "There are others to defend the center—the two Ajaxes and Teucer, who is the finest archer of all the Achaeans, and is good also in a hand-to-hand fight. These will give Hector, son of Priam, enough to do; fight as he may, he will find it hard to vanquish their indomitable fury, and fire the ships, unless the son of Cronus fling a firebrand upon them with his own hand. Great Ajax, son of Telamon, will yield to no man who is in mortal mold and eats the grain of Demeter, if bronze and great stones can overthrow him. He would not yield even to Achilles in hand-to-hand fight, and in fleetness of foot there is none to beat him; let us turn therefore towards the left wing, that we may know forthwith whether we are to give glory to some other, or he to us."

Meriones, peer of fleet Ares, then led the way till they came to the part of the host which Idomeneus had named.

Now when the Trojans saw Idomeneus coming on like a flame of fire, him and his squire clad in their richly wrought armor, they shouted and made towards him all in a body, and a furious hand-to-hand fight raged under the ships' sterns. Fierce as the shrill winds that whistle upon a day when dust lies deep on the roads, and the gusts raise it into a thick cloud—even such was the fury of the combat, and might and main did they hack at each other with spear and sword throughout the host. The field bristled with the long and deadly spears which they bore. Dazzling was the sheen of their gleaming helmets, their fresh-burnished breastplates, and glittering shields as they joined battle with one another. Iron indeed must be his courage who could take pleasure in the sight of such a turmoil, and look on it without being dismayed.

Thus did the two mighty sons of Cronus devise evil for mortal heroes. Zeus was minded to give victory to the Trojans and to Hector, so as to do honor to fleet Achilles, nevertheless he did not mean to utterly overthrow the Achaean host before Ilium, and only wanted to glorify Thetis and her valiant son. Poseidon on the other hand went about among the Argives to incite them, having come up from the gray sea in secret, for he was grieved at seeing them vanquished by the Trojans, and was furiously angry with Zeus. Both were of the same race and country, but

Zeus was elder born and knew more, therefore Poseidon feared to defend the Argives openly, but in the likeness of man, he kept on encouraging them throughout their host. Thus, then, did these two devise a knot of war and battle, that none could unloose or break, and set both sides tugging at it, to the failing of men's knees beneath them.

And now Idomeneus, though his hair was already flecked with gray, called loud on the Danaans and spread panic among the Trojans as he leaped in among them. He slew Othryoneus from Cabesus, a sojourner, who had but lately come to take part in the war. He sought Cassandra, the fairest of Priam's daughters in marriage, but offered no gifts of wooing, for he promised a great thing, to wit, that he would drive the sons of the Achaeans willy-nilly from Troy. Old King Priam had given his consent and promised her to him, whereon he fought on the strength of the promises thus made to him. Idomeneus aimed a spear, and hit him as he came striding on. His cuirass of bronze did not protect him, and the spear stuck in his belly, so that he fell heavily to the ground. Then Idomeneus vaunted over him saying: "Othryoneus, there is no one in the world whom I shall admire more than I do you, if you indeed perform what you have promised Priam, son of Dardanus, in return for his daughter. We two will make you an offer; we will give you the loveliest daughter of the son of Atreus, and will bring her from Argos for you to marry, if you will sack the goodly city of Ilium in company with ourselves. So come along with me, that we may make a covenant at the ships about the marriage, and we will not be hard upon you about gifts of wooing."

With this Idomeneus began dragging him by the foot through the thick of the fight, but Asius came up to protect the body, on foot, in front of his horses, which his esquire drove so close behind him that he could feel their breath upon his shoulder. He was longing to strike down Idomeneus, but ere he could do so Idomeneus smote him with his spear in the throat under the chin, and the bronze point went clean through it. He fell as an oak, or poplar, or pine which shipwrights have felled for ship's timber upon the mountains with whetted axes—even thus did he lie full length in front of his chariot and horses, grinding his teeth and clutching at the bloodstained dust. His charioteer was struck with panic and did not dare turn his horses round and escape. Thereupon Antilochus hit him in the middle of his body with a spear; his cuirass of bronze did not protect him, and the spear stuck in his belly. He fell gasping from his chariot and Antilochus, great Nestor's son, drove his horses from the Trojans to the Achaeans.

Deïphobus then came close up to Idomeneus to avenge Asius, and took aim at him with a spear, but Idomeneus was on the lookout and avoided it, for he was covered by the round shield he always wore—a shield of oxhide and bronze with two arm-rods on the inside. He crouched under cover of this, and the spear flew over him, but the shield rang out as the spear grazed it, and the weapon sped not in vain from the strong hand of Deïphobus, for it struck Hypsenor, son of Hippasus, shepherd of his people, in the liver under the midriff, and his limbs failed beneath him. Deïphobus vaunted over him and cried with a loud voice, saying, "Of a truth Asius has not fallen unavenged; he will be glad even while passing into the house of Hades, strong warden of the gate, that I have sent someone to escort him."

Thus did he vaunt, and the Argives were stung by his saying. Noble Antilochus was more angry than anyone, but grief did not make him forget his friend and comrade. He ran up to him, bestrode him, and covered him with his shield. Then two of his staunch comrades, Mecisteus, son of Echius, and Alastor, stooped down and bore him away groaning heavily to the ships. But Idomeneus ceased not his fury. He kept on striving continually either to enshroud some Trojan in the darkness of death, or himself to fall while warding off the evil day from the Achaeans. Then fell Alcathoüs, son of noble Aesyetes; he was son-in-law to Anchises, having married his eldest daughter Hippodameia, who was the darling of her father and mother and excelled all her generation in beauty, accomplishments, and understanding, wherefore the bravest man in all Troy had taken her to wife—him did Poseidon lay low by the hand of Idomeneus, blinding his bright eyes and binding his strong limbs in fetters so that he could neither go back nor to one side, but stood stock still like a pillar or lofty tree when Idomeneus struck him with a spear in the middle of his chest. The coat of mail that had hitherto protected his body was now broken and rang harshly as the spear tore through it. He fell heavily to the ground, and the spear stuck in his heart, which still beat, and made the butt end of the spear quiver till dread Ares put an end to his life. Idomeneus vaunted over him and cried with a loud voice, saying: "Deïphobus, since you are in a mood to vaunt, shall we cry quits now that we have killed three men to your one? Nay, sir, stand in fight with me yourself, that you may learn what manner of Zeus-begotten man am I that have come hither. Zeus first begot Minos chief ruler in Crete, and Minos in his turn begot a son, noble Deucalion. Deucalion begot me to be a ruler over many men in Crete, and my ships have now brought me hither, to be the bane of yourself, your father, and the Trojans."

Thus did he speak, and Deïphobus was in two minds, whether to go back and fetch some other Trojan to help him, or to take up the challenge single-handed. In the end, he deemed it best to go and fetch Aeneas, whom he found standing in the rear, for he had long been aggrieved with Priam because in spite of his brave deeds he did not give him his due share of honor. Deïphobus went up to him and said: "Aeneas, prince among the Trojans, if you know any ties of kinship, help me now to defend the body of your sister's husband. Come with me to the rescue of Alcathoüs, who being husband to your sister brought you up when you were a child in his house, and now Idomeneus has slain him."

With these words he moved the heart of Aeneas, and he went in pursuit of Idomeneus, big with great deeds of valor. But Idomeneus was not to be thus daunted as though he were a mere child. He held his ground as a wild boar at bay upon the mountains, who abides the coming of a great crowd of men in some lonely place—the bristles stand upright on his back, his eyes flash fire, and he whets his tusks in his eagerness to defend himself against hounds and men—even so did famed Idomeneus hold his ground and budge not at the coming of Aeneas. He cried aloud to his comrades, looking towards Ascalaphus, Aphareus, Deïpyrus, Meriones, and Antilochus, all of them brave soldiers. "Hither, my friends," he cried, "and leave me not single-handed—I go in great fear by fleet Aeneas, who is coming against me, and is a redoubtable dispenser of death in battle. Moreover, he is in the flower of youth when a man's strength is greatest. If I was of the same age as he is and in my present mind, either he or I should soon bear away the prize of victory."

On this, all of them as one man stood near him, shield on shoulder. Aeneas on the other side called to his comrades, looking towards Deïphobus, Paris, and Agenor, who were leaders of the Trojans along with himself, and the people followed them as sheep follow the ram when they go down to drink after they have been feeding, and the heart of the shepherd is glad—even so was the heart of Aeneas gladdened when he saw his people follow him.

Then they fought furiously in close combat about the body of Alcathoüs, wielding their long spears; and the bronze armor about their bodies rang fearfully as they took aim at one another in the press of the fight, while the two heroes, Aeneas and Idomeneus, peers of Ares, outvied everyone in their desire to hack at each other with sword and spear. Aeneas took aim first, but Idomeneus was on the lookout and avoided the spear, so that it sped from Aeneas's strong hand in vain and fell quivering in the ground. Idomeneus meanwhile smote Oenomaus in the middle of his belly and broke the plate of his corslet, whereon his bowels came gushing out and he clutched the earth in the palms of his hands as he fell sprawling in the dust. Idomeneus drew his spear out of the body, but could not strip him of the rest of his armor for the rain of darts that were showered upon him. Moreover, his strength was now beginning to fail him so that he could no longer charge, and could neither spring forward to recover his own weapon nor swerve aside to avoid one that was aimed at him. Therefore, though he still defended himself in hand-to-hand fight, his heavy feet could not bear him swiftly out of the battle. Deïphobus aimed a spear at him as he was retreating slowly from the field, for his bitterness against him was as fierce as ever, but again he missed him, and hit Ascalaphus, the son of Ares. The spear went through his shoulder, and he clutched the earth in the palms of his hands as he fell sprawling in the dust.

Grim Ares of awful voice did not yet know that his son had fallen, for he was sitting on the summits of Olympus under the golden clouds, by command of Zeus, where the other gods were also sitting, forbidden to take part in the battle. Meanwhile men fought furiously about the body. Deïphobus tore the helmet from off his head, but Meriones sprang upon him and struck him on the arm with a spear so that the visored helmet fell from his hand and came ringing down upon the ground. Thereon Meriones sprang upon him like a vulture, drew the spear from his shoulder, and fell back under cover of his men. Then Polites, own brother of Deïphobus, passed his arms around his waist, and bore him away from the battle till he got to his horses that were standing in the rear of the fight with the chariot and their driver. These took him towards the city groaning and in great pain, with the blood flowing from his arm.

The others still fought on, and the battle cry rose to heaven without ceasing. Aeneas sprang on Aphareus, son of Caletor, and struck him with a spear in his throat which was turned towards him; his head fell on one side, his helmet and shield came down along with him, and death, life's foe, was shed around him. Antilochus spied his chance, flew forward towards Thoön, and wounded him as he was turning round. He laid open the vein that runs all the way up the back to the neck; he cut this vein clean away throughout its whole course, and Thoön fell in the dust face upwards, stretching out his hands imploringly towards his comrades. Antilochus sprang upon him and stripped the armor from his shoulders, glaring round him fearfully as he did so. The Trojans came about him on every side and struck his broad and gleaming shield, but could not wound his body, for Poseidon stood guard over the son of Nestor, though the darts fell thickly round him. He was never clear of the foe, but was always in the thick of the fight; his spear was never idle; he poised and aimed it in every direction, so eager was he to hit someone from a distance or to fight him hand to hand.

As he was thus aiming among the crowd, he was seen by Adamas, son of Asius, who rushed towards him and struck him with a spear in the middle of his shield, but Poseidon made its point without effect, for he grudged him the life of Antilochus. One half, therefore, of the spear stuck fast like a charred stake in Antilochus's shield, while the other lay on the ground. Adamas then sought shelter under cover of his men, but Meriones followed after and hit him with a spear midway between the private parts and the navel, where a wound is particularly painful to wretched mortals. There did Meriones transfix him, and he writhed convulsively about the spear as some bull whom mountain herdsmen have bound with ropes of withes and are taking away perforce. Even so did he move convulsively for a while, but not for very long, till Meriones came up and drew the spear out of his body, and his eyes were veiled in darkness.

Helenus then struck Deïpyrus with a great Thracian sword, hitting him on the temple in close combat and tearing the helmet from his head. The helmet fell to the ground, and one of those who were fighting on the Achaean side took charge of it as it rolled at his feet, but the eyes of Deïpyrus were closed in the darkness of death.

On this Menelaus was grieved, and made menacingly towards Helenus, brandishing his spear; but Helenus drew his bow, and the two attacked one another at one and the same moment, the one with his spear, and the other with his bow and arrow. The son of Priam hit the breastplate of Menelaus's corslet, but the arrow glanced from off it. As black beans or pulse come pattering down on to a threshing floor from the broad winnowing-shovel, blown by shrill winds and shaken by the shovel—even so did the arrow glance off and recoil from the shield of Menelaus, who in his turn wounded the hand with which Helenus carried his bow. The spear went right through his hand and stuck in the bow itself, so that to save his life he retreated under cover of his men, with his hand dragging by his side—for the spear weighed it down till Agenor drew it out and bound the hand carefully up in a woolen sling which his esquire had with him.

Pisander then made straight at Menelaus—his evil destiny luring him on to his doom, for he was to fall in fight with you, O Menelaus. When the two were hard by one another the spear of the son of Atreus turned aside and he missed his aim. Pisander then struck the shield of brave Menelaus but could not pierce it, for the shield stayed the spear and broke the shaft. Nevertheless, he was glad and made sure of victory. Forthwith, however, the son of Atreus drew his sword and sprang upon him. Pisander then seized the bronze battle-ax with its long and polished handle of olive wood that hung by his side under his shield, and the two made at one another. Pisander struck the peak of Menelaus's crested helmet just under the crest itself, and Menelaus hit Pisander as he was coming towards him, on the forehead, just at the rise of his nose. The bones cracked and his two gore-bedrabbled eyes fell by his feet in the dust. He fell backwards to the ground, and Menelaus set his heel upon him, stripped him of his armor, and vaunted over him, saying:

"Even thus shall you Trojans leave the ships of the Achaeans, proud and insatiate of battle though you be, nor shall you lack any of the disgrace and shame which you have heaped upon myself. Cowardly she-wolves that you are, you feared not the anger of dread Zeus, avenger of violated hospitality, who will one day destroy your city. You stole my wedded wife and wickedly carried off much treasure when you were her guest, and now you would fling fire upon our ships and kill our heroes. A day will come when, rage as you may, you shall be stayed. O father Zeus, you, who they say art above all, both gods and men, in wisdom, and from whom all things that befall us do proceed, how can you thus favor the Trojans—men so proud and overweening that they are never tired of fighting? All things pall after a while—sleep, love, sweet song, and stately dance—still these are things of which a man would surely have his fill rather than of battle, whereas it is of battle that the Trojans are insatiate."

So saying, Menelaus stripped the bloodstained armor from the body of Pisander and handed it over to his men; then he again ranged himself among those who were in the front of the fight.

Harpalion, son of King Pylaemenes, then sprang upon him. He had come to fight at Troy along with his father, but he did not go home again. He struck the middle of Menelaus's shield with his spear but could not pierce it, and to save his life drew back under cover of his men, looking round him on every side lest he should be wounded. But Meriones aimed a bronze-tipped arrow at him as he was leaving the field, and hit him on the right buttock. The arrow pierced the bone through and through, and penetrated the bladder, so he sat down where he was and breathed his last in the arms of his comrades, stretched like a worm upon the ground and watering the earth with the blood that flowed from his wound. The brave Paphlagonians tended him with all due care; they raised him into his chariot, and bore him sadly off to the city of Troy. His father went also with him weeping bitterly, but there was no ransom that could bring his dead son to life again.

Paris was deeply grieved by the death of Harpalion, who was his host when he went among the Paphlagonians; he aimed an arrow, therefore, in order to avenge him. Now there was a certain man named Euchenor, son of Polyidus, the prophet, a brave man and wealthy, whose home was in Corinth. This Euchenor had set sail for Troy well knowing that it would be the death of him, for his good old father Polyidus had often told him that he must either stay at home and die of a terrible disease, or go with the Achaeans and perish at the hands of the Trojans. He chose, therefore, to avoid incurring the heavy fine the Achaeans would have laid upon him, and at the same time to escape the pain and suffering of disease. Paris now smote him on the jaw under his ear, whereon the life went out of him and he was enshrouded in the darkness of death.

Thus then did they fight as it were a flaming fire. But Hector had not yet heard, and did not know that the Argives were making havoc of his men on the left wing of the battle, where the Achaeans ere long would have triumphed over them, so vigorously did Poseidon cheer them on and help them. He therefore held on at the point where he had first forced his way through the gates and the wall, after breaking through the serried ranks of Danaan warriors. It was here that the ships of Ajax and Protesilaus were drawn up by the seashore. Here the wall was at its lowest, and the fight both of man and horse raged most fiercely. The Boeotians and the Ionians with their long tunics, the Locrians, the men of Phthia, and the famous force of the Epeans could hardly stay Hector as he rushed on towards the ships, nor could they drive him from them, for he was as a wall of fire. The chosen men of the Athenians were in the van, led by Menestheus, son of Peteos, with whom were also Pheidas, Stichius, and stalwart Bias; Meges, son of Phyleus, Amphion, and Dracius commanded the Epeans, while Medon and staunch Podarces led the men of Phthia. Of these, Medon was bastard son to Oïleus and brother of Ajax, but he lived in Phylace away from his own country, for he had killed the brother of his stepmother Eriopis, the wife of Oïleus. The other, Podarces, was the son of Iphiclus, son of Phylacus. These two stood in the van of the Phthians, and defended the ships along with the Boeotians.

Ajax, son of Oïleus, never for a moment left the side of Ajax, son of Telamon, but as two swart oxen both strain their utmost at the plow which they are drawing in a fallow field, and the sweat steams upwards from about the roots of their horns—nothing but the yoke divides them as they break up the ground till they reach the end of the field—even so did the two Ajaxes stand shoulder to shoulder by one another. Many and brave comrades followed the son of Telamon, to relieve him of his shield when he was overcome with sweat and toil, but the Locrians did not follow so close after the son of Oïleus, for they could not hold their own in a hand-to-hand fight. They had no bronze helmets with plumes of horsehair, neither had they shields nor ashen spears, but they had come to Troy armed with bows and with slings of twisted wool from which they showered their missiles to break the ranks of the Trojans. The others, therefore, with their heavy armor bore the brunt of the fight with the Trojans and with

Hector, while the Locrians shot from behind, under their cover; and thus the Trojans began to lose heart, for the arrows threw them into confusion.

The Trojans would now have been driven in sorry plight from the ships and tents back to windy Ilium had not Polydamas presently said to Hector: "Hector, there is no persuading you to take advice. Because heaven has so richly endowed you with the arts of war, you think that you must therefore excel others in counsel; but you cannot thus claim preeminence in all things. Heaven has made one man an excellent soldier; of another it has made a dancer or a singer and player on the lyre; while yet in another Zeus has implanted a wise understanding of which men reap fruit to the saving of many, and he himself knows more about it than anyone; therefore I will say what I think will be best. The fight has hemmed you in as with a circle of fire, and even now that the Trojans are within the wall some of them stand aloof in full armor, while others are fighting scattered and outnumbered near the ships. Draw back, therefore, and call your chieftains round you, that we may advise together whether to fall now upon the ships in the hope that heaven may vouchsafe us victory, or to beat a retreat while we can yet safely do so. I greatly fear that the Achaeans will pay us their debt of yesterday in full, for there is one abiding at their ships who is never weary of battle, and who will not hold aloof much longer."

Thus spoke Polydamas, and his words pleased Hector well. He sprang in full armor from his chariot and said, "Polydamas, gather the chieftains here; I will go yonder into the fight, but will return at once when I have given them their orders."

He then sped onward, towering like a snowy mountain, and with a loud cry flew through the ranks of the Trojans and their allies. When they heard his voice they all hastened to gather round Polydamas, the excellent son of Panthoüs, but Hector kept on among the foremost, looking everywhere to find Deïphobus and prince Helenus, Adamas, son of Asius, and Asius, son of Hyrtacus; living, indeed, and scatheless he could no longer find them, for the two last were lying by the sterns of the Achaean ships, slain by the

Argives, while the others had been also stricken and wounded by them; but upon the left wing of the dread battle he found Paris, husband of lovely Helen, cheering his men and urging them on to fight. He went up to him and upbraided him. "Paris," said he, "evil-hearted Paris, fair to see but woman-mad and false of tongue, where are Deïphobus and King Helenus? Where are Adamas, son of Asius, and Asius, son of Hyrtacus? Where too is Othryoneus? Ilium is undone and will now surely fall!"

Paris answered: "Hector, why find fault when there is no one to find fault with? I should hold aloof from battle on any day rather than this, for my mother bore me with nothing of the coward about me. From the moment when you set our men fighting about the ships we have been staying here and doing battle with the Danaans. Our comrades about whom you ask me are dead. Deïphobus and King Helenus alone have left the field, wounded both of them in the hand, but the son of Cronus saved them alive. Now, therefore, lead on where you would have us go, and we will follow with right goodwill. You shall not find us fail you in so far as our strength holds out, but no man can do more than in him lies, no matter how willing he may be."

With these words he satisfied his brother, and the two went towards the part of the battle where the fight was thickest, about Cebriones, brave Polydamas, Phalces, Orthaeus, godlike Polyphetes, Palmys, Ascanius, and Morys, son of Hippotion, who had come from fertile Ascania on the preceding day to relieve other troops. Then Zeus urged them on to fight. They flew forth like the blasts of some fierce wind that strike earth in the van of a thunderstorm—they buffet the salt sea into an uproar. Many and mighty are the great waves that come crashing in one after the other upon the shore with their arching heads all crested with foam—even so did rank behind rank of Trojans arrayed in gleaming armor follow their leaders onward. The way was led by Hector, son of Priam, peer of murderous Ares, with his round shield before him—his shield of oxhides covered with plates of bronze—and his gleaming helmet upon his temples. He kept stepping forward under cover of his shield in every direction, making trial of the ranks to see if they would give way before him, but he could not daunt the courage of the Achaeans. Ajax was the first to stride out and challenge him.

"Sir," he cried, "draw near! Why do you think thus vainly to dismay the Argives? We Achaeans are excellent soldiers, but the scourge of Zeus has fallen heavily upon us. Your heart, forsooth, is set on destroying our ships, but we too have hands that can keep you at bay, and your own fair town shall be sooner taken and sacked by ourselves. The time is near when you shall pray to Zeus and all the gods in your flight that your steeds may be swifter than hawks as they raise the dust on the plain and bear you back to your city."

As he was thus speaking a bird flew by upon his right hand, and the host of the Achaeans shouted, for they took heart at the omen. But Hector answered: "Ajax, braggart and false of tongue, would that I were as sure of being son forevermore to aegis-bearing Zeus, with Queen Hera for my mother, and of being held in like honor with Athene and Apollo, as I am that this day is big with the destruction of the Achaeans; and you shall fall among them if you dare abide my spear. It shall rend your fair body and bid you glut our hounds and birds of prey with your fat and your flesh, as you fall by the ships of the Achaeans."

With these words he led the way and the others followed after with a cry that rent the air, while the host shouted behind them. The Argives on their part raised a shout likewise, nor did they forget their prowess, but stood firm against the onslaught of the Trojan chieftains, and the cry from both the hosts rose up to heaven and to the brightness of Zeus's presence.

BOOK XIV

As the Greeks fall back, Agamemnon is again ready to take to the ships, but Odysseus and Diomed declare that, shattered as their forces are, they will return to the fray. Hera, plotting to distract the attention of Zeus, borrows the magic girdle of Aphrodite, and entices her husband to love and slumber on Mount Ida. While Zeus sleeps, the fortunes of battle change: Hector is wounded by Ajax, and countless Trojans are slaughtered.

NESTOR WAS SITTING OVER HIS WINE, BUT THE CRY OF BATTLE did not escape him, and he said to the son of Asclepius: "What, noble Machaon, is the meaning of all this? The shouts of men fighting by our ships grow stronger and stronger. Stay here, therefore, and sit over your wine, while fair Hecamedé heats you a bath and washes the clotted blood from off you. I will go at once to the lookout station and see what it is all about."

As he spoke he took up the shield of his son Thrasymedes that was lying in his tent, all gleaming with bronze, for Thrasymedes had taken his father's shield. He grasped his redoubtable bronze-shod spear, and as soon as he was outside saw the disastrous rout of the Achaeans who, now that their wall was overthrown, were flying pell-mell before the Trojans. As when there is a heavy swell upon the sea, but the waves are dumb—they keep their eyes on the watch for the quarter whence the fierce winds may spring upon them, but they stay where they are and set neither this way nor that till some particular wind sweeps down from heaven to determine them—even so did the old man ponder whether to make for the crowd of Danaans, or go in search of Agamemnon. In the end he deemed it best to go to the son of Atreus; but meanwhile the hosts were fighting and killing one another, and the hard bronze rattled on the bodies as they thrust at one another with their swords and spears.

The wounded kings, the son of Tydeus, Odysseus, and Agamemnon, son of Atreus, fell in with Nestor as they were coming up from their ships—for theirs were drawn up some way from where the fighting was going on, being on the shore itself, inasmuch as they had been beached first, while the wall had been built behind the hindermost. The stretch of the shore, wide though it was, did not afford room for all the ships, and the host was cramped for space; therefore they had placed the ships in rows one behind the other and had filled the whole opening of the bay between the two points that formed it. The kings, leaning on their spears, were coming out to survey the fight, being in great anxiety, and when old Nestor met them they were filled with dismay. Then King Agamemnon said to him: "Nestor, son of Neleus, honor to the Achaean name, why have you left the battle to come hither? I fear that what dread Hector said will come true, when he vaunted among the Trojans saying that he would not return to Ilium till he had fired our ships and killed us; this is what he said, and now it is all coming true. Alas! others of the Achaeans, like Achilles, are in anger with me that they refuse to fight by the sterns of our ships."

Then Nestor, knight of Gerene, answered: "It is indeed as you say; it is all coming true at this moment, and even Zeus who thunders from on high cannot prevent it. Fallen is the wall on which we relied as an impregnable bulwark both for us and our fleet. The Trojans are fighting stubbornly and without ceasing at the ships. Look where you may you cannot see from what quarter the rout of the Achaeans is coming; they are being killed in a confused mass and the battle cry ascends to heaven. Let us think, if counsel can be of any use, what we had better do; but I do not advise our going into battle ourselves, for a man cannot fight when he is wounded."

And King Agamemnon answered: "Nestor, if the Trojans are indeed fighting at the rear of our ships, and neither the wall nor the trench has served us—over which the Danaans toiled so hard, and which they deemed would be an impregnable bulwark both for us and our fleet—I see it must be the will of Zeus that the Achaeans should perish ingloriously here, far from Argos. I knew when Zeus was willing to defend us, and I know now that he is raising the Trojans to like honor with the gods, while us, on the other hand, he has bound hand and foot. Now, therefore, let us all do as I say. Let us bring down the ships that are on the beach and draw them into the water. Let us make them fast to their mooring-stones a little way out, against the fall of night—if even by night the Trojans will desist from fighting; we may then draw down the rest of the fleet. There is nothing wrong in flying ruin even by night: it is better for a man that he should fly and be saved than be caught and killed."

Odysseus looked fiercely at him and said: "Son of Atreus, what are you talking about? Wretch, you should have commanded some other and baser army, and not been ruler over us to whom Zeus has allotted a life of hard fighting from youth to old age, till we everyone of us perish. Is it thus that you would quit the city of Troy, to win which we have suffered so much hardship? Hold your peace, lest some other of the Achaeans hear you say what no man who knows how to give good counsel, no king over so great a host as that of the Argives should ever have let fall from his lips. I despise your judgment utterly for what you have been saying. Would you, then, have us draw down our ships into the water while the battle is raging and thus play further into the hands of the conquering Trojans? It would be ruin; the Achaeans will not go on fighting when they see the ships being drawn into the water, but will cease attacking and keep turning their eyes towards them; your counsel, therefore, sir captain, would be our destruction."

Agamemnon answered: "Odysseus, your rebuke has stung me to the heart. I am not, however, ordering the Achaeans to draw their ships into the sea whether they will or no. Someone, it may be, old or young, can offer us better counsel which I shall rejoice to hear."

Then said Diomed: "Such a one is at hand; he is not far to seek, if you will listen to me and not resent my speaking though I am younger than any of you. I am by lineage son to a noble sire, Tydeus, who lies buried at Thebes. For Portheus had three noble sons, two of whom, Agrius and Melas, abode in Pleuron and rocky Calydon. The third was the knight Oeneus, my father's father, and he was the most valiant of them all. Oeneus remained in his own country, but my father (as Zeus and the other gods ordained it) migrated to Argos. He married into the family of Adrastus, and his house was one of great abundance, for he had large estates of rich corn-growing land, with much orchard ground as well, and he had many sheep. Moreover, he excelled all the Argives in the use of the spear. You must yourselves have heard whether these things are true or no. Therefore when I say well, despise not my words as though I were a coward or of ignoble birth. I say, then, let us go to the fight as we needs must, wounded though we be. When there, we may keep out of the battle and beyond the range of the spears lest we get fresh wounds in addition to what we have already, but we can spur on others who have been indulging their spleen and holding aloof from battle hitherto."

Thus did he speak. Whereon they did even as he had said and set out, King Agamemnon leading the way.

Meanwhile Poseidon had kept no blind lookout and came up to them in the semblance of an old man. He took Agamemnon's right hand in his own and said: "Son of Atreus, I take it Achilles is glad now that he sees the Achaeans routed and slain, for he is utterly without remorse—may he come to a bad end and heaven confound him. As for yourself, the blessed gods are not yet so bitterly angry with you but that the princes and councilors of the Trojans shall again raise the dust upon the plain, and you shall see them flying from the ships and tents towards their city."

With this he raised a mighty cry of battle and sped forward to the plain. The voice that came from his deep chest was as that of nine or ten thousand men when they are shouting in the thick of a fight, and it put fresh courage into the hearts of the Achaeans to wage war and do battle without ceasing.

Hera of the golden throne looked down as she stood upon a peak of Olympus and her heart was gladdened at the sight of him who was at once her brother and her brother-in-law, hurrying hither and thither amid the fighting. Then she turned her eyes to Zeus as he sat on the topmost crests of many-fountained Ida, and loathed him. She set herself to think how she might hoodwink him, and in the end she deemed that it would be best for her to go to Ida and array herself in rich attire, in the hope that Zeus might become enamored of her, and wish to embrace her. While he was thus engaged a sweet and careless sleep might be made to steal over his eyes and senses.

She went, therefore, to the room which her son Hephaestus had made her, and the doors of which he had cunningly fastened by means of a secret key so that no other god could open them. Here she entered and closed the doors behind her. She cleansed all the dirt from her fair body with ambrosia, then she anointed herself with olive oil, ambrosial, very soft, and scented specially for herself—if it were so much as shaken in the bronze-floored house of Zeus, the scent pervaded the universe of heaven and earth. With this she anointed her delicate skin, and then she plaited the fair ambrosial locks that flowed in a stream of golden tresses from her immortal head. She put on the wondrous robe which Athene had worked for her with consummate art, and had embroidered with manifold devices. She fastened it about her bosom with golden clasps and she girded herself with a girdle that had a hundred tassels; then she fastened her earrings, three brilliant pendants that glistened most beautifully, through the pierced lobes of her ears, and threw a lovely new veil over her head. She bound her sandals on to her feet, and when she had arrayed herself perfectly to her satisfaction, she left her room and called Aphrodite to come aside and speak to her. "My dear child," said she, "will you do what I am going to ask of you, or will you refuse me because you are angry at my being on the Danaan side, while you are on the Trojan?"

Zeus's daughter Aphrodite answered, "Hera, august queen of goddesses, daughter of mighty Cronus, say what you want, and I will do it for you at once, if I can, and if it can be done at all."

Then Hera told her a lying tale and said: "I want you to endow me with some of those fascinating charms, the spells of which bring all things mortal and immortal to your feet. I am going to the world's end to visit Oceanus (from whom all we gods proceed) and mother Tethys: they received me in their house, took care of me, and brought me up, having taken me over from Rhea when Zeus imprisoned great Cronus in the depths that are under earth and sea. I must go and see them that I may make peace between them; they have been quarreling, and are so angry that they have not slept with one another this long while. If I can bring them round and restore them to one another's embraces, they will be grateful to me and love me forever afterwards."

Thereon laughter-loving Aphrodite said, "I cannot and must not refuse you, for you sleep in the arms of Zeus who is our king."

As she spoke she loosed from her bosom the curiously embroidered girdle into which all her charms had been wrought—love, desire, and that sweet flattery which steals the judgment even of the most prudent. She gave the girdle to Hera and said, "Take this girdle wherein all my charms reside and lay it in your bosom. If you will wear it I promise you that your errand, be it what it may, will not be bootless."

When she heard this Hera smiled, and still smiling she laid the girdle in her bosom.

Aphrodite now went back into the house of Zeus, while Hera darted down from the summits of Olympus. She passed over Pieria and fair Emathia, and went on and on till she came to the snowy ranges of the Thracian horsemen, over whose topmost crests she sped without ever setting foot to ground. When she came to Athos she went on over the waves of the sea till she reached Lemnos, the city of noble Thoas. There she met Sleep, own brother to

Death, and caught him by the hand, saying: "Sleep, you who lord it alike over mortals and immortals, if you ever did me a service in times past, do one for me now, and I shall be grateful to you ever after. Close Zeus's keen eyes for me in slumber while I hold him clasped in my embrace, and I will give you a beautiful golden seat, that can never fall to pieces. My club-footed son Hephaestus shall make it for you, and he shall give it a footstool for you to rest your fair feet upon when you are at table."

Then Sleep answered: "Hera, great queen of goddesses, daughter of mighty Cronus, I would lull any other of the gods to sleep without compunction, not even excepting the waters of Oceanus from whom all of them proceed, but I dare not go near Zeus, nor send him to sleep unless he bids me. I have had one lesson already through doing what you asked me, on the day when Zeus's mighty son Heracles set sail from Ilium after having sacked the city of the Trojans. At your bidding I suffused my sweet self over the mind of aegis-bearing Zeus, and laid him to rest; meanwhile you hatched a plot against Heracles, and set the blasts of the angry winds beating upon the sea till you took him to the goodly city of Cos, away from all his friends. Zeus was furious when he awoke and began hurling the gods about all over the house. He was looking more particularly for myself, and would have flung me down through space into the sea where I should never have been heard of any more, had not Night who cows both men and gods protected me. I fled to her and Zeus left off looking for me in spite of his being so angry, for he did not dare do anything to displease Night. And now you are again asking me to do something on which I cannot venture."

And Hera said: "Sleep, why do you take such notions as those into your head? Do you think Zeus will be as anxious to help the Trojans as he was about his own son? Come, I will marry you to one of the youngest of the Graces, and she shall be your own—Pasithea, whom you have always wanted to marry."

Sleep was pleased when he heard this, and answered: "Then swear it to me by the dread waters of the river Styx. Lay one hand on the bounteous earth and the other on the sheen of the sea, so that all the gods who dwell down below with Saturn may be our witnesses, and see that you really do give me one of the youngest of the Graces, Pasithea, whom I have always wanted to marry."

Hera did as he had said. She swore, and invoked all the gods of the nether world, who are called Titans, to witness. When she had completed her oath, the two enshrouded themselves in a thick mist and sped lightly forward, leaving Lemnos and Imbrus behind them. Presently they reached many-fountained Ida, mother of wild beasts, and Lectum, where they left the sea to go on by land, and the tops of the trees of the forest soughed under the going of their feet. Here Sleep halted, and ere Zeus caught sight of him he climbed a lofty pine tree—the tallest that reared its head towards heaven on all Ida. He hid himself behind the branches and sat there in the semblance of the sweet-singing bird that haunts the mountains and is called Chalcis by the gods, but men call it Cymindis. Hera then went to Gargarus, the topmost peak of Ida, and Zeus, driver of the clouds, set eyes upon her. As soon as he did so he became inflamed with the same passionate desire for her that he had felt when they had first enjoyed each other's embraces, and slept with one another without their dear parents knowing anything about it. He went up to her and said, "What do you want that you have come hither from Olympus—and that too with neither chariot nor horses to convey you?"

Then Hera told him a lying tale and said: "I am going to the world's end, to visit Oceanus, from whom all we gods proceed, and mother Tethys; they received me into their house, took care of me, and brought me up. I must go and see them that I may make peace between them: they have been quarreling, and are so angry that they have not slept with one another this long time. The horses that will take me over land and sea are stationed on the lowermost spurs of many-fountained Ida, and I have come here from Olympus on purpose to consult you. I was afraid you might be angry with me later on, if I went to the house of Oceanus without letting you know."

And Zeus said: "Hera, you can choose some other time for paying your visit to Oceanus—for the present let us devote ourselves to love and to the enjoyment of one another. Never yet have I been so overpowered by passion neither for goddess nor mortal woman as I am at this moment for yourself—not even when I was in love with the wife of Ixion who bore me Pirithoüs, peer of gods in counsel, nor yet with Danaë, the daintily ankled daughter of Acrisius, who bore me the famed hero Perseus. Then there was the daughter of Phoenix, who bore me Minos and Rhadamanthus. There was Semele, and Alcmena in Thebes by whom I begot my lion-hearted son Heracles, while Semele became mother to Bacchus, the comforter of mankind. There was queen Demeter again, and lovely Leto, and yourself—but with none of these was I ever so much enamored as I now am with you."

Hera again answered him with a lying tale. "Most dread son of Cronus," she exclaimed, "what are you talking about? Would you have us enjoy one another here on the top of Mount Ida, where everything can be seen? What if one of the ever-living gods should see us sleeping together, and tell the others? It would be such a scandal that when I had risen from your embraces I could never show myself inside your house again; but if you are so minded, there is a room which your son Hephaestus has made me, and he has given it good strong doors; if you would so have it, let us go thither and lie down."

And Zeus answered, "Hera, you need not be afraid that either god or man will see you, for I will enshroud both of us in such a dense golden cloud, that the very sun for all his bright piercing beams shall not see through it."

With this the son of Cronus caught his wife in his embrace; whereon the earth sprouted them a cushion of young grass, with dew-bespangled lotus, crocus, and hyacinth, so soft and thick that it raised them well above the ground. Here they laid themselves down and overhead they were covered by a fair cloud of gold from which there fell glittering dewdrops.

Thus, then, did the sire of all things repose peacefully on the crest of Ida, overcome at once by sleep and love, and he held his spouse in his arms. Meanwhile Sleep made off to the ships of the Achaeans, to tell earth-encircling Poseidon, lord of the earthquake. When he had found him he said, "Now, Poseidon, you can help the Danaans with a will and give them victory, though it be only for a short time while Zeus is still sleeping. I have sent him into a sweet slumber, and Hera has beguiled him into going to bed with her."

Sleep now departed and went his ways to and fro among mankind, leaving Poseidon more eager than ever to help the Danaans. He darted forward among the first ranks and shouted, saying, "Argives, shall we let Hector, son of Priam, have the triumph of taking our ships and covering himself with glory? This is what he says that he shall now do, seeing that Achilles is still in dudgeon at his ships. We shall get on very well without him if we keep each other in heart and stand by one another. Now, therefore, let us all do as I say. Let us each take the best and largest shield we can lay hold of, put on our helmets, and sally forth with our longest spears in our hands. I will lead you on, and Hector, son of Priam, rage as he may, will not dare to hold out against us. If any good staunch soldier has only a small shield, let him hand it over to a worse man, and take a larger one for himself."

Thus did he speak, and they did even as he had said. The son of Tydeus, Odysseus, and Agamemnon, wounded though they were, set the others in array, and went about everywhere effecting the exchanges of armor; the most valiant took the best armor, and gave the worse to the worse man. When they had donned their bronze armor they marched on with Poseidon at their head. In his strong hand he grasped his terrible sword, keen of edge and flashing like lightning. Woe to him who comes across it in the day of battle; all men quake for fear and keep away from it.

Hector on the other side set the Trojans in array. Thereon Poseidon and Hector waged fierce war on one another—Hector on the Trojan and Poseidon on the Argive side. Mighty was the uproar as the two forces met; the sea came rolling in towards the ships and tents of the Achaeans, but waves do not thunder on the shore more loudly when driven before the blast of Boreas, nor do the flames of a forest fire roar more fiercely when it is well alight upon the mountains, nor does the wind bellow with ruder music as it tears on through the tops of the oaks when it is blowing its hardest, than the terrible shout which the Trojans and Achaeans raised as they sprang upon one another.

Hector first aimed his spear at Ajax, who was turned full towards him, nor did he miss his aim. The spear struck him where two bands passed over his chest—the band of his shield and that of his silver-studded sword—and these protected his body. Hector was angry that his spear should have been hurled in vain, and withdrew under cover of his men. As he was thus retreating, Ajax, son of Telamon, struck him with a stone, of which there were many lying about under the men's feet as they fought—brought there to give support to the ship's sides as they lay on the shore. Ajax caught up one of them and struck Hector above the rim of his shield close to his neck; the blow made him spin round like a top and reel in all directions. As an oak falls headlong when uprooted by the lightning flash of father Zeus, and there is a terrible smell of brimstone—no man can help being dismayed if he is standing near it, for a thunderbolt is a very awful thing—even so did Hector fall to earth and bite the dust. His spear fell from his hand, but his shield and helmet were made fast about his body, and his bronze armor rang about him.

The sons of the Achaeans came running with a loud cry towards him, hoping to drag him away, and they showered their darts on the Trojans, but none of them could wound him before he was surrounded and covered by the princes Polydamas, Aeneas, Agenor, Sarpedon, captain of the Lycians, and noble Glaucus. Of the others, too, there was not one who was unmindful of him, and they held their round shields over him to cover him. His comrades then lifted him off the ground and bore him away from the battle to the place where his horses stood waiting for him at the rear of the fight with their driver and the chariot. These then took him towards the city groaning and in great pain. When they reached the ford of the fair stream of Xanthus, begotten of immortal Zeus, they took him from off his chariot and laid him down on the ground. They poured water over him, and as they did so he breathed again and opened his eyes. Then kneeling on his knees he vomited blood, but soon fell back on to the ground, and his eyes were again closed in darkness for he was still stunned by the blow.

When the Argives saw Hector leaving the field, they took heart and set upon the Trojans yet more furiously. Ajax, fleet son of Oïleus, began by springing on Satnius, son of Enops, and wounding him with his spear. A fair naiad nymph had borne him to Enops as he was herding cattle by the banks of the river Satniöeis. The son of Oïleus came up to him and struck him in the flank so that he fell, and a fierce fight between Trojans and Danaans raged round his body. Polydamas, son of Panthoüs, drew near to avenge him, and wounded Prothoënor, son of Areïlycus, on the right shoulder. The terrible spear went right through his shoulder, and he clutched the earth as he fell in the dust. Polydamas vaunted loudly over him, saying: "Again I take it that the spear has not sped in vain from the strong hand of the son of Panthoüs. An Argive has caught it in his body, and it will serve him for a staff as he goes down into the house of Hades."

The Argives were maddened by this boasting. Ajax, son of Telamon, was more angry than any, for the man had fallen close beside him; so he aimed at Polydamas as he was retreating, but Polydamas saved himself by swerving aside and the spear struck Archelochus, son of Antenor, for heaven counseled his destruction. It struck him where the head springs from the neck at the top joint of the spine, and severed both the tendons at the back of the head. His head, mouth, and nostrils reached the ground long before his legs and knees could do so, and Ajax shouted to Polydamas, saying, "Think, Polydamas, and tell me truly whether this man is not as well worth killing as Prothoënor was: he seems rich, and of rich family, a brother, it may be, or son of the knight Antenor, for he is very like him."

But he knew well who it was, and the Trojans were greatly angered. Acamas then bestrode his brother's body and wounded

Promachus the Boeotian with his spear, for he was trying to drag his brother's body away. Acamas vaunted loudly over him, saying: "Argive archers, braggarts that you are, toil and suffering shall not be for us only, but some of you too shall fall here as well as ourselves. See how Promachus now sleeps, vanquished by my spear. Payment for my brother's blood has not been long delayed; a man, therefore, may well be thankful if he leaves a kinsman in his house behind him to avenge his fall."

His taunts infuriated the Argives, and Peneleos was more enraged than any of them. He sprang towards Acamas, but Acamas did not stand his ground, and he killed Ilioneus, son of the rich flock-master Phorbas, whom Mercury had favored and endowed with greater wealth than any other of the Trojans. Ilioneus was his only son, and Peneleos now wounded him in the eye under his eyebrows, tearing the eyeball from its socket. The spear went right through the eye into the nape of the neck, and he fell, stretching out both hands before him. Peneleos then drew his sword and smote him on the neck, so that both head and helmet came tumbling down to the ground with the spear still sticking in the eye. He then held up the head as though it had been a poppy-head, and showed it to the Trojans, vaunting over them as he did so. "Trojans," he cried, "bid the father and mother of noble Ilioneus make moan for him in their house, for the wife also of Promachus, son of Alegenor, will never be gladdened by the coming of her dear husband when we Argives return with our ships from Troy."

As he spoke fear fell upon them, and every man looked round about to see whither he might fly for safety.

Tell me now, O Muses that dwell on Olympus, who was the first of the Argives to bear away bloodstained spoils after Poseidon, lord of the earthquake, had turned the fortune of war? Ajax, son of Telamon, was first to wound Hyrtius, son of Gyrtius, captain of the staunch Mysians. Antilochus killed Phalces and Mermerus, while Meriones slew Morys and Hippotion, Teucer also killed Prothoön and Periphetes. The son of Atreus then wounded Hyperenor, shepherd of his people, in the flank, and the bronze point made his entrails gush out as it tore in among them; on this his life came hurrying out of him at the place where he had been wounded, and his eyes were closed in darkness. Ajax, son of Oïleus, killed more than any other, for there was no man so fleet as he to pursue flying foes when Zeus had spread panic among them.

BOOK XV

When Zeus discovers the guile of Hera, he tells her that the Greeks will conquer Troy, but not until his promise to Thetis has been fulfilled. Whereupon Hera returns sullenly to Olympus. Ares, who starts toward the battlefield, is held back by Athene. Zeus orders Poseidon to stop aiding the Greeks and Apollo to heal Hector's wound. Hector now leads another assault over the Greek wall, calling on his men to set fire to the ships. Patroclus tells Achilles of the Greek plight.

But when their flight had taken them past the trench and the set stakes, and many had fallen by the hands of the Danaans, the Trojans made a halt on reaching their chariots, routed and pale with fear. Zeus now woke on the crests of Ida, where he was lying with golden-throned Hera by his side, and starting to his feet he saw the Trojans and Achaeans, the one thrown into confusion, and the others driving them pell-mell before them with King Poseidon in their midst. He saw Hector lying on the ground with his comrades gathered round him, gasping for breath, wandering in mind and vomiting blood, for it was not the feeblest of the Achaeans who struck him.

The sire of gods and men had pity on him, and looked fiercely on Hera. "I see, Hera," said he, "you mischief-making trickster, that your cunning has stayed Hector from fighting and has caused the rout of his host. I am in half a mind to thrash you, in which case you will be the first to reap the fruits of your scurvy knavery. Do you not remember how once upon a time I had you hanged? I fastened two anvils on to your feet, and bound your hands in a chain of gold which none might break, and you hung in midair among the clouds. All the gods in Olympus were in a fury, but they could not reach you to set you free. When I caught any one of them I gripped him and hurled him from the heavenly threshold till he came fainting down to earth. Yet even this did not relieve my mind from the incessant anxiety which I felt about noble Heracles whom you and Boreas had spitefully conveyed beyond the seas to Cos, after suborning the tempests; but I rescued him, and notwithstanding all his mighty labors I brought him back again to Argos. I would remind you of this that you may learn to leave off being so deceitful and discover how much you are likely to gain by the embraces out of which you have come here to trick me."

Hera trembled as he spoke, and said: "May heaven above and earth below be my witnesses, with the waters of the river Styx—and this is the most solemn oath that a blessed god can take—nay, I swear also by your own almighty head and by our bridal bed—things over which I could never possibly perjure myself—that Poseidon is not punishing Hector and the Trojans and helping the Achaeans through any doing of mine. It is all of his own mere motion because he was sorry to see the Achaeans hard-pressed at their ships: if I were advising him, I should tell him to do as you bid him."

The sire of gods and men smiled and answered: "If you, Hera, were always to support me when we sit in council of the gods, Poseidon, like it or no, would soon come round to your and my way of thinking. If, then, you are speaking the truth and mean what you say, go among the rank and file of the gods, and tell Iris and Apollo, lord of the bow, that I want them—Iris, that she may go to the Achaean host and tell Poseidon to leave off fighting and go home, and Apollo, that he may send Hector again into battle and give him fresh strength. He will thus forget his present sufferings, and drive the Achaeans back in confusion till they fall among the ships of Achilles, son of Peleus. Achilles will then send his comrade Patroclus into battle, and Hector will kill him in front of Ilium after he has slain many warriors, and among them my own noble son Sarpedon. Achilles will kill Hector to avenge Patroclus, and from that time I will bring it about that the Achaeans shall persistently drive the Trojans back till they fulfill the counsels of Athene and take Ilium. But I will not stay my anger, nor permit any god to help the Danaans till I have accomplished the desire of the son of Peleus, according to the promise I made by bowing my head on the day when Thetis touched my knees and besought me to give him honor."

Hera heeded his words and went from the heights of Ida to great Olympus. Swift as the thought of one whose fancy carries him over vast continents, and he says to himself, "Now I will be here, or there," and he would have all manner of things—even so swiftly did Hera wing her way till she came to high Olympus and went in among the gods who were gathered in the house of Zeus. When they saw her they all of them came up to her and held out their cups to her by way of greeting. She let the others be, but took the cup offered her by lovely Themis, who was first to come running up to her. "Hera," said she, "why are you here? And you seem troubled—has your husband, the son of Cronus, been frightening you?"

And Hera answered: "Themis, do not ask me about it. You know what a proud and cruel disposition my husband has. Lead the gods to table, where you and all the immortals can hear the wicked designs which he has avowed. Many a one, mortal and immortal, will be angered by them, however peaceably he may be feasting now."

On this Hera sat down, and the gods were troubled throughout the house of Zeus. Laughter sat on her lips, but her brow was furrowed with care, and she spoke up in a rage. "Fools that we are," she cried, "to be thus madly angry with Zeus. We keep on wanting to go up to him and stay him by force or by persuasion, but he sits aloof and cares for nobody, for he knows that he is much stronger than any other of the immortals. Make the best, therefore, of whatever ills he may choose to send each one of you. Ares, I take it, has had a taste of them already, for his son Ascalaphus has fallen in battle—the man whom of all others he loved most dearly and whose father he owns himself to be."

When he heard this Ares smote his two sturdy thighs with the flat of his hands, and said in anger, "Do not blame me, you gods that dwell in heaven, if I go to the ships of the Achaeans and avenge the death of my son, even though it end in my being struck by Zeus's lightning and lying in blood and dust among the corpses."

As he spoke he gave orders to yoke his horses Panic and Rout, while he put on his armor. On this, Zeus would have been roused to still more fierce and implacable enmity against the other immortals, had not Athene, alarmed for the safety of the gods, sprung from her seat and hurried outside. She tore the helmet from his head and the shield from his shoulders, and she took the bronze spear from his strong hand and set it on one side; then she said to Ares:

"Madman, you are undone; you have ears that hear not, or you have lost all judgment and understanding; have you not heard what Hera has said on coming straight from the presence of Olympian Zeus? Do you wish to go through all kinds of suffering before you are brought back sick and sorry to Olympus, after having caused infinite mischief to all us others? Zeus would instantly leave the Trojans and Achaeans to themselves; he would come to Olympus to punish us, and would grip us up one after another, guilty or not guilty. Therefore lay aside your anger for the death of your son. Better men than he have either been killed already or will fall hereafter, and one cannot protect everyone's whole family."

With these words she took Ares back to his seat. Meanwhile Hera called Apollo outside, with Iris the messenger of the gods. "Zeus," she said to them, "desires you to go to him at once on

Mount Ida; when you have seen him you are to do as he may then bid you."

Thereon Hera left them and resumed her seat inside, while Iris and Apollo made all haste on their way. When they reached many-fountained Ida, mother of wild beasts, they found Zeus seated on topmost Gargarus with a fragrant cloud encircling his head as with a diadem. They stood before his presence, and he was pleased with them for having been so quick in obeying the orders his wife had given them.

He spoke to Iris first. "Go," said he, "fleet Iris, tell King Poseidon what I now bid you—and tell him true. Bid him leave off fighting, and either join the company of the gods, or go down into the sea. If he takes no heed and disobeys me, let him consider well whether he is strong enough to hold his own against me if I attack him. I am older and much stronger than he is; yet he is not afraid to set himself up as on a level with myself, of whom all the other gods stand in awe."

Iris, fleet as the wind, obeyed him, and as the cold hail or snowflakes that fly from out the clouds before the blast of Boreas, even so did she wing her way till she came close up to the great shaker of the earth. Then she said: "I have come, O dark-haired king that holds the world in his embrace, to bring you a message from Zeus. He bids you leave off fighting and either join the company of the gods or go down into the sea. If, however, you take no heed and disobey him, he says he will come down here and fight you. He would have you keep out of his reach, for he is older and much stronger than you are, and yet you are not afraid to set yourself up as on a level with himself, of whom all the other gods stand in awe."

Poseidon was very angry and said: "Great heavens! Strong as Zeus may be, he has said more than he can do if he has threatened violence against me, who am of like honor with himself. We were three brothers whom Rhea bore to Cronus—Zeus, myself, and Hades who rules the world below. Heaven and earth were divided into three parts, and each of us was to have an equal share. When we cast lots, it fell to me to have my dwelling in the sea forevermore. Hades took the darkness of the realms under the earth, while air and sky and clouds were the portion that fell to Zeus; but earth and great Olympus are the common property of all. Therefore I will not walk as Zeus would have me. For all his strength, let him keep to his own third share and be contented without threatening to lay hands upon me as though I were nobody. Let him keep his bragging talk for his own sons and daughters, who must perforce obey him."

Iris, fleet as the wind, then answered: "Am I really, Poseidon, to take this daring and unyielding message to Zeus, or will you reconsider your answer? Sensible people are open to argument, and you know that the Erinyes always range themselves on the side of the older person."

Poseidon answered: "Goddess Iris, your words have been spoken in season. It is well when a messenger shows so much discretion. Nevertheless, it cuts me to the very heart that anyone should rebuke so angrily another who is his own peer, and of like empire with himself. Now, however, I will give way in spite of my displeasure; furthermore let me tell you, and I mean what I say—if contrary to the desire of myself, Athene, driver of the spoil, Hera, Hermes, and King Hephaestus, Zeus spares steep Ilium, and will not let the Achaeans have the great triumph of sacking it, let him understand that he will incur our implacable resentment."

Poseidon now left the field to go down under the sea, and sorely did the Achaeans miss him. Then Zeus said to Apollo: "Go, dear Phoebus, to Hector, for Poseidon who holds the earth in his embrace has now gone down under the sea to avoid the severity of my displeasure. Had he not done so those gods who are below with Cronus would have come to hear of the fight between us. It is better for both of us that he should have curbed his anger and kept out of my reach, for I should have had much trouble with him. Take, then, your tasseled aegis, and shake it furiously, so as to set the Achaean heroes in a panic; take, moreover, brave Hector, O Far-darter, into your own care, and rouse him to deeds of daring, till the Achaeans are sent flying back to their ships and to the Hellespont. From that point I will think it well over, how the Achaeans may have a respite from their troubles."

Apollo obeyed his father's saying, and left the crests of Ida, flying like a falcon, bane of doves and swiftest of all birds. He found Hector no longer lying upon the ground, but sitting up, for he had just come to himself again. He knew those who were about him, and the sweat and hard breathing had left him from the moment when the will of aegis-bearing Zeus had revived him. Apollo stood beside him and said, "Hector, son of Priam, why are you so faint, and why are you here away from the others? Has any mishap befallen you?"

Hector in a weak voice answered: "And which, kind sir, of the gods are you, who now ask me thus? Do you not know that Ajax struck me on the chest with a stone as I was killing his comrades at the ships of the Achaeans, and compelled me to leave off fighting? I made sure that this very day I should breathe my last and go down into the house of Hades."

Then King Apollo said to him: "Take heart; the son of Cronus has sent you a mighty helper from Ida to stand by you and defend you, even me, Phoebus Apollo of the golden sword, who have been guardian hitherto not only of yourself but of your city. Now, therefore, order your horsemen to drive their chariots to the ships in great multitudes. I will go before your horses to smooth the way for them, and will turn the Achaeans in flight."

As he spoke he infused great strength into the shepherd of his people. And as a horse, stabled and full-fed, breaks loose and gallops gloriously over the plain to the place where he is wont to take his bath in the river—he tosses his head, and his mane streams over his shoulders as in all the pride of his strength he flies full speed to the pastures where the mares are feeding—even so Hector, when he heard what the god said, urged his horsemen on, and sped forward as fast as his limbs could take him. As country peasants set their hounds on to a horned stag or wild goat—he has taken shelter under rock or thicket, and they cannot find him, but, lo, a bearded lion whom their shouts have roused stands in their path, and they are in no further humor for the chase—even so the Achaeans were still charging on in a body, using their swords and spears pointed at both ends, but when they saw Hector going about among his men they were afraid, and their hearts fell down into their feet.

Then spoke Thoas, son of Andraemon, leader of the Aetolians, a man who could throw a good throw, and who was staunch also in close fight, while few could surpass him in debate when opinions were divided. He then with all sincerity and goodwill addressed them thus: "What, in heaven's name, do I now see? Is it not Hector come to life again? Everyone made sure he had been killed by Ajax, son of Telamon, but it seems that one of the gods has again rescued him. He has killed many of us Danaans already, and I take it will yet do so, for the hand of Zeus must be with him or he would never dare show himself so masterful in the forefront of the battle. Now, therefore, let us all do as I say; let us order the main body of our forces to fall back upon the ships, but let those of us who profess to be the flower of the army stand firm, and see whether we cannot hold Hector back at the point of our spears as soon as he comes near us. I conceive that he will then think better of it before he tries to charge into the press of the Danaans."

Thus did he speak, and they did even as he had said. Those who were about Ajax and King Idomeneus, the followers moreover of Teucer, Meriones, and Meges, peer of Ares, called all their best men about them and sustained the fight against Hector and the Trojans, but the main body fell back upon the ships of the Achaeans.

The Trojans pressed forward in a dense body, with Hector striding on at their head. Before him went Phoebus Apollo, shrouded in cloud about his shoulders. He bore aloft the terrible aegis with its shaggy fringe, which Hephaestus, the smith, had given Zeus to strike terror into the hearts of men. With this in his hand he led on the Trojans.

The Argives held together and stood their ground. The cry of battle rose high from either side, and the arrows flew from the bowstrings. Many a spear sped from strong hands and fastened in the bodies of many a valiant warrior, while others fell to earth midway, before they could taste of man's fair flesh and glut themselves with blood. So long as Phoebus Apollo held his aegis quietly and without shaking it, the weapons on either side took effect and the people fell, but when he shook it straight in the face of the Danaans and raised his mighty battle cry their hearts fainted within them and they forgot their former prowess. As when two wild beasts spring in the dead of night on a herd of cattle or a large flock of sheep when the herdsman is not there—even so were the Danaans struck helpless, for Apollo filled them with panic and gave victory to Hector and the Trojans.

The fight then became more scattered and they killed one another where they best could. Hector killed Stichius and Arcesilaus, the one, leader of the Boeotians, and the other, friend and comrade of Menestheus. Aeneas killed Medon and Iasus. The first was bastard son to Oïleus, and brother to Ajax, but he lived in Phylace, away from his own country, for he had killed a man, a kinsman of his stepmother Eriopis, whom Oïleus had married. Iasus had become a leader of the Athenians, and was son of Sphelus, the son of Boucolos. Polydamas killed Mecisteus, and Polites Echius, in the front of the battle, while Agenor slew Clonius. Paris struck Deïochus from behind in the lower part of the shoulder as he was flying among the foremost, and the point of the spear went clean through him.

While they were spoiling these heroes of their armor, the Achaeans were flying pell-mell to the trench and the set stakes, and were forced back within their wall. Hector then cried out to the Trojans: "Forward to the ships, and let the spoils be! If I see any man keeping back on the other side of the wall away from the ships I will have him killed. His kinsmen and kinswomen shall not give him his dues of fire, but dogs shall tear him in pieces in front of our city."

As he spoke he laid his whip about his horses' shoulders and called to the Trojans throughout their ranks. The Trojans shouted with a cry that rent the air, and kept their horses neck and neck with his own. Phoebus Apollo went before, and kicked down the banks of the deep trench into its middle so as to make a great broad bridge, as broad as the throw of a spear when a man is trying his strength. The Trojan battalions poured over the bridge, and Apollo with his redoubtable aegis led the way. He kicked down the wall of the Achaeans as easily as a child who, playing on the seashore, has built a house of sand and then kicks it down again and destroys it—even so did you, O Apollo, shed toil and trouble upon the Argives, filling them with panic and confusion.

Thus then were the Achaeans hemmed in at their ships, calling out to one another and raising their hands with loud cries every man to heaven. Nestor of Gerene, tower of strength to the Achaeans, lifted up his hands to the starry firmament of heaven and prayed more fervently than any of them. "Father Zeus," said he, "if ever anyone in wheat-growing Argos burned you fat thigh-bones of sheep or heifer and prayed that he might return safely home, whereon you bowed your head to him in assent, bear it in mind now, and suffer not the Trojans to triumph thus over the Achaeans."

All-counseling Zeus thundered loudly in answer to the prayer of the aged son of Neleus. When the Trojans heard Zeus thunder they flung themselves yet more fiercely on the Achaeans. As a wave breaking over the bulwarks of a ship when the sea runs high before a gale—for it is the force of the wind that makes the waves so great—even so did the Trojans spring over the wall with a shout, and drive their chariots onwards. The two sides fought with their double-pointed spears in hand-to-hand encounter—the Trojans from their chariots, and the Achaeans climbing up into their ships and wielding the long pikes that were lying on the decks ready for use in a sea-fight, jointed and shod with bronze.

Now Patroclus, so long as the Achaeans and Trojans were fighting about the wall, but were not yet within it and at the ships, remained sitting in the tent of good Eurypylus, entertaining him with his conversation and spreading herbs over his wound to ease his pain. When, however, he saw the Trojans swarming through the breach in the wall, while the Achaeans were clamoring and struck with panic, he cried aloud, and smote his two thighs with the flat of his hands. "Eurypylus," said he in his dismay, "I know you want me badly, but I cannot stay with you any longer, for there is hard fighting going on. A servant shall take care of you now, for I must make all speed to Achilles, and induce him to fight if I can; who knows but with heaven's help I may persuade him. A man does well to listen to the advice of a friend."

When he had thus spoken he went his way. The Achaeans stood firm and resisted the attack of the Trojans, yet though these were fewer in number, they could not drive them back from the ships, neither could the Trojans break the Achaean ranks and make their way in among the tents and ships. As a carpenter's line gives a true edge to a piece of ship's timber, in the hand of some skilled workman whom Athene has instructed in all kinds of useful arts—even so level was the issue of the fight between the two sides as they fought, some round one ship and some round another.

Hector made straight for Ajax, and the two fought fiercely about the same ship. Hector could not force Ajax back and fire the ship, nor yet could Ajax drive Hector from the spot to which heaven had brought him.

Then Ajax struck Caletor, son of Clytius, in the chest with a spear as he was bringing fire towards the ship. He fell heavily to the ground and the torch dropped from his hand. When Hector saw his cousin fallen in front of the ship he shouted to the Trojans and Lycians, saying, "Trojans, Lycians, and Dardanians, good in close fight, bate not a jot, but rescue the son of Clytius, lest the Achaeans strip him of his armor now that he has fallen."

He then aimed a spear at Ajax, and missed him, but he hit Lycophron, a follower of Ajax, who came from Cythera, but was living with Ajax, inasmuch as he had killed a man among the Cythereans. Hector's spear struck him on the head below the ear, and he fell headlong from the ship's prow on to the ground with no life left in him. Ajax shook with rage and said to his brother: "Teucer, my good fellow, our trusty comrade, the son of Mastor, has fallen—he who came to live with us from Cythera and whom we honored as much as our own parents. Hector has just killed him; fetch your deadly arrows at once and the bow which Phoebus Apollo gave you."

Teucer heard him and hastened towards him with his bow and quiver in his hands. Forthwith he showered his arrows on the Trojans, and hit Cleitus, the son of Pisenor, comrade of Polydamas, the noble son of Panthoüs, with the reins in his hands as he was attending to his horses. He was in the middle of the very thickest part of the fight, doing good service to Hector and the Trojans, but evil had now come upon him, and not one of those who were fain to do so could avert it, for the arrow struck him on the back of the neck. He fell from his chariot and his horses shook the empty car as they swerved aside. King Polydamas saw what had happened, and was the first to come up to the horses. He gave them in charge to Astynoüs, son of Protiaon, and ordered him to look on, and to keep the horses near at hand. He then went back and took his place in the front ranks.

Teucer then aimed another arrow at Hector, and there would have been no more fighting at the ships if he had hit him and killed him then and there. Zeus, however, who kept watch over Hector, had his eyes on Teucer, and deprived him of his triumph by breaking his bowstring for him just as he was drawing it and about to take his aim; on this the arrow went astray and the bow fell from his hands. Teucer shook with anger and said to his brother, "Alas, see how heaven thwarts us in all we do; it has broken my bowstring and snatched the bow from my hand, though I strung it this selfsame morning that it might serve me for many an arrow."

Ajax, son of Telamon, answered: "My good fellow, let your bow and your arrows be, for Zeus has made them useless in order to spite the Danaans. Take your spear, lay your shield upon your shoulder, and both fight the Trojans yourself and urge others to do so. They may be successful for the moment, but if we fight as we ought they will find it a hard matter to take the ships."

Teucer then took his bow and put it by in his tent. He hung a shield four hides thick about his shoulders and on his comely head he set his helmet well wrought with a crest of horsehair that nodded menacingly above it; he grasped his redoubtable bronze-shod spear and forthwith he was by the side of Ajax.

When Hector saw that Teucer's bow was of no more use to him, he shouted out to the Trojans and Lycians: "Trojans, Lycians, and Dardanians good in close fight, be men, my friends, and show your mettle here at the ships, for I see the weapon of one of their chieftains made useless by the hand of Zeus. It is easy to see when Zeus is helping people and means to help them still further, or again when he is bringing them down and will do nothing for them. He is now on our side and is going against the Argives. Therefore swarm round the ships and fight. If any of you is struck by spear or sword and loses his life, let him die. He dies with honor who dies fighting for his country; and he will leave his wife and children safe behind him, with his house and allotment unplundered if only the Achaeans can be driven back to their own land, they and their ships."

With these words he put heart and soul into them all. Ajax on the other side exhorted his comrades, saying: "Shame on you, Argives, we are now utterly undone unless we can save ourselves by driving the enemy from our ships. Do you think, if Hector takes them, that you will be able to get home by land? Can you not hear him cheering on his whole host to fire our fleet and bidding them remember that they are not at a dance but in battle? Our only course is to fight them with might and main. We had better chance it, life or death, once for all, than fight long and without issue hemmed in at our ships by worse men than ourselves."

With these words he put life and soul into them all. Hector then killed Schedius, son of Perimedes, leader of the Phoceans, and Ajax killed Laodamas, captain of foot soldiers and son to Antenor. Polydamas killed Otus of Cyllene, a comrade of the son of Phyleus and chief of the proud Epeans. When Meges saw this he sprang upon him, but Polydamas crouched down, and he missed him, for Apollo would not suffer the son of Panthoüs to fall in battle; but the spear hit Croesmus in the middle of his chest, whereon he fell heavily to the ground, and Meges stripped him of his armor. At that moment the valiant soldier Dolops, son of Lampus, sprang upon him; Lampus was son of Laomedon and noted for his valor, while his son Dolops was versed in all the ways of war. He then struck the middle of the son of Phyleus's shield with his spear, setting on him at close quarters, but his good corslet made with plates of metal saved him. Phyleus had brought it from Ephyra and the river Selleïs, where his host, King Euphetes, had given it him to wear in battle and protect him. It now served to save the life of his son. Then Meges struck the topmost crest of Dolops's bronze helmet with his spear and tore away its plume of horsehair, so that all newly dyed with scarlet as it was it tumbled down into the dust.

While he was still fighting and confident of victory, Menelaus came up to help Meges, and got by the side of Dolops unperceived. He then speared him in the shoulder from behind, and the point, driven so furiously, went through into his chest, whereon he fell headlong. The two then made towards him to strip him of his armor, but Hector called on all his brothers for help, and he especially upbraided brave Melanippus, son of Hiketaon, who erewhile used to pasture his herds of cattle in Percote before the war broke out; but when the ships of the Danaans came, he went back to Ilium, where he was eminent among the Trojans, and lived near Priam who treated him as one of his own sons. Hector now rebuked him and said: "Why, Melanippus, are we thus remiss? Do you take no note of the death of your kinsman, and do you not see how they are trying to take Dolops's armor? Follow me; there must be no fighting the Argives from a distance now, but we must do so in close combat till either we kill them or they take the high wall of Ilium and slay her people."

He led on as he spoke, and the hero Melanippus followed after. Meanwhile Ajax, son of Telamon, was cheering on the Argives. "My friends," he cried, "be men, and fear dishonor! Quit yourselves in battle so as to win respect from one another. Men who respect each other's good opinion are less likely to be killed than those who do not, but in flight there is neither gain nor glory."

Thus did he exhort men who were already bent upon driving back the Trojans. They laid his words to heart and hedged the ships as with a wall of bronze, while Zeus urged on the Trojans. Menelaus of the loud battle cry urged Antilochus on.

"Antilochus," said he, "you are young and there is none of the Achaeans more fleet of foot or more valiant than you are. See if you cannot spring upon some Trojan and kill him."

He hurried away when he had thus spurred Antilochus, who at once darted out from the front ranks and aimed a spear, after looking carefully round him. The Trojans fell back as he threw, and the dart did not speed from his hand without effect, for it struck Melanippus, the proud son of Hiketaon, in the breast by the nipple as he was coming forward, and his armor rang rattling round him as he fell heavily to the ground. Antilochus sprang upon him as a dog springs on a fawn which a hunter has hit as it was breaking away from its covert, and killed it. Even so, O Melanippus, did stalwart Antilochus spring upon you to strip you of your armor; but noble Hector marked him, and came running up to him through the thick of the battle. Antilochus, brave soldier though he was, would not stay to face him, but fled like some savage creature which knows it has done wrong, and flies, when it has killed a dog or a man who is herding his cattle, before a body of men can be gathered to attack it. Even so did the son of Nestor fly, and the Trojans and Hector, with a cry that rent the air, showered their weapons after him; nor did he turn round and stay his flight till he had reached his comrades.

The Trojans, fierce as lions, were still rushing on towards the ships in fulfillment of the behests of Zeus who kept spurring them on to new deeds of daring, while he deadened the courage of the Argives and defeated them by encouraging the Trojans. For he meant giving glory to Hector, son of Priam, and letting him throw fire upon the ships, till he had fulfilled the unrighteous prayer that Thetis had made him. Zeus, therefore, bided his time till he should see the glare of a blazing ship. From that hour he was about so to order it that the Trojans should be driven back from the ships and to vouchsafe glory to the Achaeans. With this purpose he inspired Hector, son of Priam, who was eager enough already, to assail the ships. His fury was as that of Ares, or as when a fire is raging in the glades of some dense forest upon the mountains. He foamed at the mouth, his eyes glared under his terrible eyebrows, and his helmet quivered on his temples by reason of the fury with which he fought. Zeus from heaven was with him, and though he was but one against many, vouchsafed him victory and glory; for he was doomed to an early death, and already Pallas Athene was hurrying on the hour of his destruction at the hands of the son of Peleus. Now, however, he kept trying to break the ranks of the enemy wherever he could see them thickest, and in the goodliest armor; but do what he might he could not break through them, for they stood as a tower foursquare, or as some high cliff rising from the gray sea that braves the anger of the gale, and of the waves that thunder up against it. He fell upon them like flames of fire from every quarter.

As when a wave, raised mountain high by wind and storm, breaks over a ship and covers it deep in foam, the fierce winds roar against the mast, the hearts of the sailors fail them for fear, and they are saved but by a very little from destruction—even so were the hearts of the Achaeans fainting within them. Or as a savage lion attacking a herd of cows while they are feeding by thousands in the low-lying meadows by some wide-watered shore—the herdsman is at his wits' end how to protect his herd and keeps going about now in the van and now in the rear of his cattle, while the lion springs into the thick of them and fastens on a cow so that they all tremble for fear—even so were the Achaeans utterly panic-stricken by Hector and father Zeus. Nevertheless, Hector only killed Periphetes of Mycenae; he was son of Copreus who was wont to take the orders of King Eurystheus to mighty Heracles, but the son was a far better man than the father in every way; he was fleet of foot, a valiant warrior, and in understanding ranked among the foremost men of Mycenae. He it was who then afforded Hector a triumph, for as he was turning back he stumbled against the rim of his shield which reached his feet, and served to keep the javelins off him. He tripped against this and fell face upward, his helmet ringing loudly about his head as he did so. Hector saw him fall and ran up to him; he then thrust a spear into his chest, and killed him close to his own comrades. These, for all their sorrow, could not help him for they were themselves terribly afraid of Hector.

They had now reached the ships and the prows of those that had been drawn up first were on every side of them, but the Trojans came pouring after them. The Argives were driven back from the first row of ships, but they made a stand by their tents without being broken up and scattered; shame and fear restrained them. They kept shouting incessantly to one another, and Nestor of Gerene, tower of strength to the Achaeans, was loudest in imploring every man by his parents, and beseeching him to stand firm.

"Be men, my friends," he cried, "and respect one another's good opinion! Think, all of you, on your children, your wives, your property, and your parents whether these be alive or dead. On their behalf though they are not here, I implore you to stand firm, and not to turn in flight."

With these words he put heart and soul into them all. Athene lifted the thick veil of darkness from their eyes, and much light fell upon them, alike on the side of the ships and on that where the fight was raging. They could see Hector and all his men, both those in the rear who were taking no part in the battle and those who were fighting by the ships.

Ajax could not bring himself to retreat along with the rest, but strode from deck to deck with a great sea-pike in his hands twelve cubits long and jointed with rings. As a man skilled in feats of horsemanship couples four horses together and comes tearing full speed along the public way from the country into some large town—many both men and women marvel as they see him for he keeps all the time changing his horse, springing from one to another without ever missing his feet while the horses are at a gallop—even so did Ajax go striding from one ship's deck to another, and his voice went up into the heavens. He kept on shouting his orders to the Danaans and exhorting them to defend their ships and tents; neither did Hector remain within the main body of the Trojan warriors, but as a dun eagle swoops down upon a flock of wild fowl feeding near a river—geese, it may be, or cranes, or long-necked swans—even so did Hector make straight for a dark-prowed ship, rushing right towards it; for Zeus with his mighty hand impelled him forward and roused his people to follow him.

And now the battle again raged furiously at the ships. You would have thought the men were coming on fresh and unwearied, so fiercely did they fight; and this was the mind in which they were—the Achaeans did not believe they should escape destruction, but thought themselves doomed, while there was not a Trojan but his heart beat high with the hope of firing the ships and putting the Achaean heroes to the sword.

Thus were the two sides minded. Then Hector seized the stern of the good ship that had brought Protesilaus to Troy, but never bore him back to his native land. Round this ship there raged a close hand-to-hand fight between Danaans and Trojans. They did not fight at a distance with bows and javelins, but with one mind hacked at one another in close combat with their mighty swords and spears pointed at both ends; they fought moreover with keen battle-axes and with hatchets. Many a good stout blade hiked and scabbarded with iron fell from hand or shoulder as they fought, and the earth ran red with blood. Hector, when he had seized the ship, would not loose his hold but held on to its curved stern and shouted to the Trojans: "Bring fire, and raise the battle cry all of you with a single voice. Now has Zeus vouchsafed us a day that will pay us for all the rest; this day we shall take the ships which came hither against heaven's will, and which have caused us such infinite suffering through the cowardice of our councilors, who when I would have done battle at the ships held me back and forbade the host to follow me; if Zeus did then indeed warp our judgments, himself now commands me and cheers me on."

As he spoke thus the Trojans sprang yet more fiercely on the Achaeans, and Ajax no longer held his ground, for he was overcome by the darts that were flung at him, and made sure that he was doomed. Therefore he left the raised deck at the stern, and stepped back on to the seven-foot bench of the oarsmen. Here he stood on the lookout, and with his spear held back any Trojan whom he saw bringing fire to the ships. All the time he kept on shouting at the top of his voice and exhorting the Danaans. "My friends," he cried, "Danaan heroes, servants of Ares, be men, my friends, and fight with might and with main. Can we hope to find helpers hereafter, or a wall to shield us more surely than the one we have? There is no strong city within reach whence we may draw fresh forces to turn the scales in our favor. We are on the plain of the armed Trojans with the sea behind us and far from our own country. Our salvation, therefore, is in the might of our hands and in hard fighting."

As he spoke he wielded his spear with still greater fury, and when any Trojan made towards the ships with fire at Hector's bidding, he would be on the lookout for him, and drive at him with his long spear. Twelve men did he thus kill in hand-to-hand fight before the ships.

BOOK XVI

When Achilles hears that the situation is desperate, he tells Patroclus to put on his armor, take his horses, and lead his Myrmidons into the fight, charging him not to go beyond the Greek wall. The first ship is set afire. At Patroclus's appearance, the Trojans take him for Achilles and flee. Patroclus kills Sarpedon and drives the Trojans beyond the wall, across the plain, and up to the city gates. Disabled by Apollo, the hero falls before Hector's spear.

THUS DID THEY FIGHT ABOUT THE SHIP OF PROTESILAUS. THEN Patroclus drew near to Achilles with tears welling from his eyes, as from some spring whose crystal stream falls over the ledges of a high precipice. When Achilles saw him thus weeping he was sorry for him and said: "Why, Patroclus, do you stand there weeping like some silly child that comes running to her mother, and begs to be taken up and carried—she catches hold of her mother's dress to stay her, though she is in a hurry, and looks tearfully up until her mother carries her—even such tears, Patroclus, are you now shedding. Have you anything to say to the Myrmidons or to myself? Or have you had news from Phthia which you alone know? They tell me Menoetius, son of Actor, is still alive, as also Peleus, son of Aeacus, among the Myrmidons—men whose loss we two should bitterly deplore; or are you grieving about the Argives and the way in which they are being killed at the ships, through their own high-handed doings? Do not hide anything from me, but tell me that both of us may know about it."

Then, O knight Patroclus, with a deep sigh you answered: "Achilles, son of Peleus, foremost champion of the Achaeans, do not be angry, but I weep for the disaster that has now befallen the Argives. All those who have been their champions so far are lying at the ships, wounded by sword or spear. Brave Diomed, son of Tydeus, has been hit with a spear, while famed Odysseus and Agamemnon have received sword wounds; Eurypylus again has been struck with an arrow in the thigh; skilled apothecaries are attending to these heroes, and healing them of their wounds. Are you still, O Achilles, so inexorable? May it never be my lot to nurse such a passion as you have done, to the baning of your own good name. Who in future story will speak well of you unless you now save the Argives from ruin? You know no pity; knight Peleus was not your father nor Thetis your mother, but the gray sea bore you and the sheer cliffs begot you, so cruel and remorseless are you. If, however, you are kept back through knowledge of some oracle, or if your mother Thetis has told you something from the mouth of Zeus, at least send me and the Myrmidons with me, if I may bring deliverance to the Danaans. Let me, moreover, wear your armor. The Trojans may thus mistake me for you and quit the field, so that the hard-pressed sons of the Achaeans may have breathing time—which while they are fighting may hardly be. We who are fresh might soon drive tired men back from our ships and tents to their own city."

He knew not what he was asking, nor that he was suing for his own destruction. Achilles was deeply moved and answered: "What, noble Patroclus, are you saying? I know no prophesyings which I am heeding, nor has my mother told me anything from the mouth of Zeus, but I am cut to the very heart that one of my own rank should dare to rob me because he is more powerful than I am. This, after all that I have gone through, is more than I can endure. The girl whom the sons of the Achaeans chose for me, whom I won as the fruit of my spear on having sacked a city—her has King Agamemnon taken from me as though I were some common vagrant. Still, let bygones be bygones: no man may keep his anger forever. I said I would not relent till battle and the cry of war had reached my own ships. Nevertheless, now gird my armor about your shoulders, and lead the Myrmidons to battle, for the dark cloud of Trojans has burst furiously over our fleet. The Argives are driven back on to the beach, cooped within a narrow space, and the whole people of Troy has taken heart to sally out against them, because they see not the vizor of my helmet gleaming near them. Had they seen this, there would not have been a creek nor grip that had not been filled with their dead as they fled back again. And so it would have been, if only King Agamemnon had dealt fairly by me. As it is, the Trojans have beset our host. Diomed, son of Tydeus, no longer wields his spear to defend the Danaans, neither have I heard the voice of the son of Atreus coming from his hated head, whereas that of murderous Hector rings in my ears as he gives orders to the Trojans, who triumph over the Achaeans and fill the whole plain with their cry of battle. But even so, Patroclus, fall upon them and save the fleet, lest the Trojans fire it and prevent us from being able to return. Do, however, as I now bid you, that you may win me great honor from all the Danaans, and that they may restore the girl to me again and give me rich gifts into the bargain.

"When you have driven the Trojans from the ships, come back again. Though Hera's thundering husband should put triumph within your reach, do not fight the Trojans further in my absence, or you will rob me of glory that should be mine. And do not for lust of battle go on killing the Trojans nor lead the Achaeans on to Ilium, lest one of the ever-living gods from Olympus attack you—for Phoebus Apollo loves them well: return when you have freed the ships from peril, and let others wage war upon the plain. Would, by father Zeus, Athene, and Apollo, that not a single man of all the Trojans might be left alive, nor yet of the Argives, but that we two might be alone left to tear aside the mantle that veils the brow of Troy."

Thus did they converse. But Ajax could no longer hold his ground for the shower of darts that rained upon him. The will of Zeus and the javelins of the Trojans were too much for him; the helmet that gleamed about his temples rang with the continuous clatter of the missiles that kept pouring on to it and on to the cheek-pieces that protected his face. Moreover his left shoulder was tired with having held his shield so long; yet for all this, let fly at him as they would, they could not make him give ground. He could hardly draw his breath, the sweat rained from every pore of his body, he had not a moment's respite, and on all sides he was beset by danger upon danger.

And now, tell me, O Muses that hold your mansions on Olympus, how fire was thrown upon the ships of the Achaeans. Hector came close up and let drive with his great sword at the ashen spear of Ajax. He cut it clean in two just behind where the point was fastened on to the shaft of the spear. Ajax, therefore, had now nothing but a headless spear, while the bronze point flew some way off and came ringing down on to the ground. Ajax knew the hand of heaven in this, and was dismayed at seeing that Zeus had now left him utterly defenseless and was willing victory for the Trojans. Therefore he drew back, and the Trojans flung fire upon the ship which was at once wrapped in flame.

The fire was now flaring about the ship's stern, whereon Achilles smote his two thighs and said to Patroclus: "Up, noble knight, for I see the glare of hostile fire at our fleet; up, lest they destroy our ships, and there be no way by which we may retreat. Gird on your armor at once while I call our people together."

As he spoke Patroclus put on his armor. First he greaved his legs with greaves of good make, and fitted with ankle-clasps of silver; after this he donned the cuirass of the son of Aeacus, richly inlaid and studded. He hung his silver-studded sword of bronze about his shoulders, and then his mighty shield. On his comely head he set his helmet, well-wrought, with a crest of horsehair that nodded menacingly above it. He grasped two redoubtable spears that suited his hands, but he did not take the spear of noble Achilles, so stout and strong, for none other of the Achaeans could wield it, though Achilles could do so easily. This was the ashen spear from Mount Pelion, which Chiron had cut upon a mountain top and had given to Peleus, wherewith to deal out death among heroes. He bade Automedon yoke his horses with all speed, for he was the man whom he held in honor next after Achilles, and on whose support in battle he could rely most firmly. Automedon, therefore, yoked the fleet horses Xanthus and Balius, steeds that could fly like the wind. These were they whom the harpy Podarge bore to the west wind, as she was grazing in a meadow by the waters of the river Oceanus. In the side traces he set the noble horse Pedasus, whom Achilles had brought away with him when he sacked the city of Eëtion, and who, mortal steed though he was, could take his place along with those that were immortal.

Meanwhile Achilles went about everywhere among the tents, and bade his Myrmidons put on their armor. Even as fierce ravening wolves that are feasting upon a horned stag which they have killed upon the mountains, and their jaws are red with blood—they go in a pack to lap water from the clear spring with their long thin tongues, and they reek of blood and slaughter. They know not what fear is, for it is hunger drives them—even so did the leaders and councilors of the Myrmidons gather round the good squire of the fleet descendant of Aeacus, and among them stood Achilles himself cheering on both men and horses.

Fifty ships had noble Achilles brought to Troy, and in each there was a crew of fifty oarsmen. Over these he set five captains whom he could trust, while he was himself commander over them all. Menestheus of the gleaming corslet, son to the river Spercheius that streams from heaven, was captain of the first company. Fair Polydora, daughter of Peleus, bore him to ever-flowing Spercheius—a woman mated with a god—but he was called son of Borus, son of Perieres, with whom his mother was living as his wedded wife, and who gave great wealth to gain her. The second company was led by noble Eudorus, son to an unwedded woman. Polymele, daughter of Phylas, the graceful dancer, bore him. The mighty slayer of Argus was enamored of her as he saw her among the singing women at a dance held in honor of Artemis, the rushing huntress of the golden arrows; he therefore—Hermes, giver of all good—went with her into an upper chamber, and lay with her in secret, whereon she bore him a noble son Eudorus, singularly fleet of foot and in fight valiant. When Ilithuia, goddess of the pains of childbirth, brought him to the light of day, and he saw the face of the sun, mighty Echecles, son of Actor, took the mother to wife, and gave great wealth to gain her, but her father Phylas brought the child up, and took care of him, doting as fondly upon him as though he were his own son. The third company was led by Pisander, son of Maemalus, the finest spearman among all the Myrmidons next to Achilles's own comrade, Patroclus. The old knight Phoenix was captain of the fourth company, and Alcimedon, noble son of Laërceus, of the fifth.

When Achilles had chosen his men and had stationed them all with their captains, he charged them straitly, saying: "Myrmidons, remember your threats against the Trojans while you were at the ships in the time of my anger, and you were all complaining of me. 'Cruel son of Peleus,' you would say, 'your mother must have suckled you on gall, so ruthless are you. You keep us here at the ships against our will; if you are so relentless it were better we went home over the sea.' Often have you gathered and thus chided with me. The hour is now come for those high feats of arms that you have so long been pining for, therefore keep high hearts each one of you to do battle with the Trojans."

With these words he put heart and soul into them all, and they serried their companies yet more closely when they heard the words of their king. As the stones which a builder sets in the wall of some high house which is to give shelter from the winds—even so closely were the helmets and bossed shields set against one another. Shield pressed on shield, helm on helm, and man on man; so close were they that the horsehair plumes on the gleaming ridges of their helmets touched each other as they bent their heads.

In front of them all two men put on their armor—Patroclus and Automedon—two men, with but one mind to lead the Myrmidons. Then Achilles went inside his tent and opened the lid of the strong chest which silver-footed Thetis had given him to take on board ship, and which she had filled with shirts, cloaks to keep out the cold, and good thick rugs. In this chest he had a cup of rare workmanship from which no man but himself might drink, nor would he make offering from it to any other god save only to father Zeus. He took the cup from the chest and cleansed it with sulfur. This done, he rinsed it in clean water, and after he had washed his hands he drew wine. Then he stood in the middle of the court and prayed, looking towards heaven, and making his drink offering of wine; nor was he unseen of Zeus whose joy is in thunder. "King Zeus," he cried, "lord of Dodona, god of the Pelasgi, who dwellest afar, you who hold wintry Dodona in your sway, where your prophets the Selli dwell around you with their feet unwashed and their couches made upon the ground—if you heard me when I prayed to you aforetime, and did me honor while you sent disaster on the Achaeans, vouchsafe me now the fulfillment of yet this further prayer. I shall stay here where my ships are lying, but I shall send my comrade into battle at the head of many Myrmidons. Grant, O all-seeing Zeus, that victory may go with him; put your courage into his heart that Hector may learn whether my squire is man enough to fight alone, or whether his might is only then so indomitable when I myself enter the turmoil of war. Afterwards when he has chased the fight and the cry of battle from the ships, grant that he may return unharmed, with his armor and his comrades, fighters in close combat."

Thus did he pray, and all-counseling Zeus heard his prayer. Part of it he did indeed vouchsafe him—but not the whole. He granted that Patroclus should thrust back war and battle from the ships, but refused to let him come safely out of the fight.

When he had made his drink offering and had thus prayed, Achilles went inside his tent and put back the cup into his chest. Then he again came out, for he still loved to look upon the fierce fight that raged between the Trojans and Achaeans.

Meanwhile the armed band that was about Patroclus marched on till they sprang high in hope upon the Trojans. They came swarming out like wasps whose nests are by the roadside and whom silly children love to tease, whereon anyone who happens to be passing may get stung—or again, if a wayfarer going along the road vexes them by accident, every wasp will come flying out in a fury to defend his little ones—even with such rage and courage did the Myrmidons swarm from their ships, and their cry of battle rose heavenwards. Patroclus called out to his men at the top of his voice: "Myrmidons, followers of Achilles, son of Peleus, be men, my friends, fight with might and with main, that we may win glory for the son of Peleus, who is far the foremost man at the ships of the Argives—he, and his close-fighting followers. The son of Atreus, King Agamemnon, will thus learn his folly in showing no respect to the bravest of the Achaeans."

With these words he put heart and soul into them all, and they fell in a body upon the Trojans. The ships rang again with the cry which the Achaeans raised, and when the Trojans saw the brave son of Menoetius and his squire all gleaming in their armor, they were daunted and their battalions were thrown into confusion, for they thought the fleet son of Peleus must now have put aside his anger, and have been reconciled to Agamemnon. Everyone, therefore, looked round about to see whither he might fly for safety.

Patroclus first aimed a spear into the middle of the press where men were packed most closely by the stern of the ship of Protesilaus. He hit Pyraechmes who had led his Paeonian horsemen from the Amydon and the broad waters of the river Axius. The spear struck him on the right shoulder, and with a groan he fell backwards in the dust. On this his men were thrown into confusion, for by killing their leader, who was the finest soldier among them, Patroclus struck panic into them all. He thus drove them from the ship and quenched the fire that was then blazing—leaving the half-burnt ship to lie where it was. The Trojans were now driven back with a shout that rent the skies, while the Danaans poured after them from their ships, shouting also without ceasing. As when Zeus, gatherer of the thundercloud, spreads a dense canopy on the top of some lofty mountain, and all the peaks, the jutting headlands, and forest glades show out in the great light that flashes from the bursting heavens, even so when the Danaans had now driven back the fire from their ships, they took breath for a little while; but the fury of the fight was not yet over, for the Trojans were not driven back in utter rout, but still gave battle, and were ousted from their ground only by sheer fighting.

The fight then became more scattered, and the chieftains killed one another when and how they could. The valiant son of Menoetius first drove his spear into the thigh of Areïlycus just as he was turning round. The point went clean through and broke the bone so that he fell forward. Meanwhile Menelaus struck Thoas in the chest, where it was exposed near the rim of his shield, and he fell dead. The son of Phyleus saw Amphiclus about to attack him, and ere he could do so took aim at the upper part of his thigh, where the muscles are thicker than in any other part. The spear tore through all the sinews of the leg, and his eyes were closed in darkness. Of the sons of Nestor one, Antilochus, speared Atymnius, driving the point of the spear through his throat, and down he fell. Maris then sprang on Antilochus in hand-to-hand fight to avenge his brother and bestrode the body spear in hand. But valiant Thrasymedes was too quick for him, and in a moment had struck him in the shoulder ere he could deal his blow. His aim was true, and the spear severed all the muscles at the root of his arm, and tore them right down to the bone, so he fell heavily to the ground and his eyes were closed in darkness. Thus did these two noble comrades of Sarpedon go down to Erebus, slain by the two sons of Nestor; they were the warrior sons of Amisodorus, who had reared the invincible Chimaera, to the bane of many. Ajax, son of Oïleus, sprang on Cleobulus and took him alive as he was entangled in the crush; but he killed him then and there by a sword blow on the neck. The sword reeked with his blood, while dark death and the strong hand of fate gripped him and closed his eyes.

Peneleos and Lycon now met in close fight, for they had missed each other with their spears. They had both thrown without effect, so now they drew their swords. Lycon struck the plumed crest of Peneleos's helmet but his sword broke at the hilt, while Peneleos smote Lycon on the neck under the ear. The blade sank so deep that the head was held on by nothing but the skin, and there was no more life left in him. Meriones gave chase to Acamas on foot and caught him up just as he was about to mount his chariot. He drove a spear through his right shoulder so that he fell headlong from the car, and his eyes were closed in darkness. Idomeneus speared Erymas in the mouth. The bronze point of the spear went clean through it beneath the brain, crashing in among the white bones and smashing them up. His teeth were all of them knocked out and the blood came gushing in a stream from both his eyes; it also came gurgling up from his mouth and nostrils, and the darkness of death enfolded him round about.

Thus did these chieftains of the Danaans each of them kill his man. As ravening wolves seize on kids or lambs, fastening on them when they are alone on the hillsides and have strayed from the main flock through the carelessness of the shepherd—and when the wolves see this they pounce upon them at once because they cannot defend themselves—even so did the Danaans now fall on the Trojans, who fled with ill-omened cries in their panic and had no more fight left in them.

Meanwhile great Ajax kept on trying to drive a spear into Hector, but Hector was so skillful that he held his broad shoulders well under cover of his oxhide shield, ever on the lookout for the whizzing of the arrows and the heavy thud of the spears. He well knew that the fortunes of the day had changed, but still stood his ground and tried to protect his comrades.

As when a cloud goes up into heaven from Olympus, rising out of a clear sky when Zeus is brewing a gale—even with such panic-stricken rout did the Trojans now fly, and there was no order in their going. Hector's fleet horses bore him and his armor out of the fight, and he left the Trojan host penned in by the deep trench against their will. Many a yoke of horses snapped the pole of their chariots in the trench and left their master's car behind them. Patroclus gave chase, calling impetuously on the Danaans and full of fury against the Trojans, who, being now no longer in a body, filled all the ways with their cries of panic and rout.

The air was darkened with the clouds of dust they raised, and the horses strained every nerve in their flight from the tents and ships towards the city.

Patroclus kept on heading his horses wherever he saw most men flying in confusion, cheering on his men the while. Chariots were being smashed in all directions, and many a man came tumbling down from his own car to fall beneath the wheels of that of Patroclus whose immortal steeds, given by the gods to Peleus, sprang over the trench at a bound as they sped onward. He was intent on trying to get near Hector, for he had set his heart on spearing him, but Hector's horses were now hurrying him away. As the whole dark earth bows before some tempest on an autumn day when Zeus rains his hardest to punish men for giving crooked judgment in their courts and driving justice therefrom without heed to the decrees of heaven—all the rivers run full and the torrents tear many a new channel as they roar headlong from the mountains to the dark sea, and it fares ill with the works of men—even such was the stress and strain of the Trojan horses in their flight.

Patroclus now cut off the battalions that were nearest to him and drove them back to the ships. They were doing their best to reach the city, but he would not let them, and bore down on them between the river and the ships and wall. Many a fallen comrade did he then avenge. First he hit Pronoüs with a spear on the chest where it was exposed near the rim of his shield, and he fell heavily to the ground. Next he sprang on Thestor, son of Enops, who was sitting all huddled up in his chariot, for he had lost his head and the reins had been torn out of his hands. Patroclus went up to him and drove a spear into his right jaw; he thus hooked him by the teeth and the spear pulled him over the rim of his car, as one who sits at the end of some jutting rock and draws a strong fish out of the sea with a hook and a line—even so with his spear did he pull Thestor all gaping from his chariot; he then threw him down on his face and he died while falling. On this, as Erylaus was coming on to attack him, he struck him full on the head with a stone, and his brains were all battered inside his helmet, whereon he fell headlong to the ground and the pangs of death took hold upon him.

Then he laid low, one after the other, Erymas, Amphoterus, Epaltes, Tlepolemus, Echius, son of Damastor, Pyris, Ipheus, Euippus, and Polymelus, son of Argeas.

Now when saw his comrades, men who wore ungirdled tunics, being overcome by Patroclus, son of Menoetius, he rebuked the Lycians, saying: "Shame on you, where are you flying to? Show your mettle. I will myself meet this man in fight and learn who it is that is so masterful; he has done us much hurt, and has stretched many a brave man upon the ground."

He sprang from his chariot as he spoke, and Patroclus, when he saw this, leaped on to the ground also. The two then rushed at one another with loud cries like eagle-beaked crook-taloned vultures that scream and tear at one another in some high mountain fastness.

The son of scheming Cronus looked down upon them in pity and said to Hera who was his wife and sister: "Alas, that it should be the lot of whom I love so dearly to perish by the hand of Patroclus! I am in two minds whether to catch him up out of the fight and set him down safe and sound in the fertile land of Lycia, or to let him now fall by the hand of the son of Menoetius."

And Hera answered: "Most dread son of Cronus, what is this that you are saying? Would you snatch a mortal man, whose doom has long been fated, out of the jaws of death? Do as you will, but we shall not all of us be of your mind. I say further, and lay my saying to your heart, that if you send safely to his own home, some other of the gods will be also wanting to escort his son out of battle, for there are many sons of gods fighting round the city of Troy, and you will make everyone jealous. If, however, you are fond of him and pity him, let him indeed fall by the hand of Patroclus, but as soon as the life is gone out of him, send Death and sweet Sleep to bear him off the field and take him to the broad lands of Lycia, where his brothers and his kinsmen will bury him with mound and pillar, in due honor to the dead."

The sire of gods and men assented, but he shed a rain of blood upon the earth in honor of his son whom Patroclus was about to kill on the rich plain of Troy far from his home.

When they were now come close to one another, Patroclus struck Thrasydemus, the brave squire of Sarpedon, in the lower part of the belly, and killed him. Sarpedon then aimed a spear at Patroclus and missed him, but he struck the horse Pedasus in the right shoulder, and it screamed aloud as it lay, groaning in the dust until the life went out of it. The other two horses began to plunge; the pole of the chariot cracked, and they got entangled in the reins through the fall of the horse that was yoked along with them. But Automedon knew what to do; without the loss of a moment he drew the keen blade that hung by his sturdy thigh and cut the third horse adrift; whereon the other two righted themselves, and pulling hard at the reins again went together into battle.

Sarpedon now took a second aim at Patroclus, and again missed him; the point of the spear passed over his left shoulder without hitting him. Patroclus then aimed in his turn, and the spear sped not from his hand in vain, for he hit Sarpedon just where the midriff surrounds the ever-beating heart. He fell like some oak or silver poplar or tall pine to which woodmen have laid their axes upon the mountains to make timber for ship-building—even so did he he stretched at full length in front of his chariot and horses, moaning and clutching at the bloodstained dust. As when a lion springs with a bound upon a herd of cattle and fastens on a great black bull which dies bellowing in its clutches—even so did the leader of the Lycian warriors struggle in death as he fell by the hand of Patroclus. He called on his trusty comrade and said: "Glaucus, my brother, hero among heroes, put forth all your strength, fight with might and main, now if ever quit yourself like a valiant soldier. First go about among the Lycian captains and bid them fight for Sarpedon; then yourself also do battle to save my armor from being taken. My name will haunt you henceforth and forever if the Achaeans rob me of my armor, now that I have fallen at their ships. Do your very utmost and call all my people together."

Death closed his eyes as he spoke. Patroclus planted his heel on his breast whereon his senses came out along with it, and he drew out both spear point and Sarpedon's soul at the same time. Hard by the Myrmidons held his snorting steeds, who were wild with panic at finding themselves deserted by their lords.

Glaucus was overcome with grief when he heard what Sarpedon said, for he could not help him. He had to support his arm with his other hand, being in great pain through the wound which Teucer's arrow had given him when Teucer was defending the wall as he, Glaucus, was assailing it. Therefore he prayed to far-darting Apollo, saying: "Hear me, O king, from your seat, maybe in the rich land of Lycia, or maybe in Troy, for in all places you can hear the prayer of one who is in distress, as I now am. I have a grievous wound; my hand is aching with pain, there is no staunching the blood, and my whole arm drags by reason of my hurt, so that I cannot grasp my sword nor go among my foes and fight them, though our prince, Zeus's son Sarpedon, is slain. Zeus defended not his son, do you, therefore, O king, heal me of my wound, ease my pain and grant me strength both to cheer on the Lycians and to fight along with them round the body of him who has fallen."

Thus did he pray, and Apollo heard his prayer. He eased his pain, stanched the black blood from the wound, and gave him new strength. Glaucus perceived this, and was thankful that the mighty god had answered his prayer; forthwith, therefore, he went among the Lycian captains, and bade them come to fight about the body of Sarpedon. From these he strode on among the Trojans to Polydamas, son of Panthoüs, and Agenor; he then went in search of Aeneas and Hector, and when he had found them he said: "Hector, you have utterly forgotten your allies, who languish here for your sake far from friends and home while you do nothing to support them. Sarpedon, leader of the Lycian warriors, has fallen—he who was at once the right and might of Lycia; Ares has laid him low by the spear of Patroclus. Stand by him, my friends, and suffer not the Myrmidons to strip him of his armor, nor to treat his body with contumely in revenge for all the Danaans whom we have speared at the ships."

As he spoke the Trojans were plunged in extreme and ungovernable grief; for Sarpedon, alien though he was, had been one of the mainstays of their city, both as having much people with him, and as himself the foremost among them all. Led by Hector, who was infuriated by the fall of Sarpedon, they made instantly for the Danaans with all their might, while the undaunted spirit of Patroclus, son of Menoetius, cheered on the Achaeans. First he spoke to the two Ajaxes, men who needed no bidding. "Ajaxes," said he, "may it now please you to show yourselves the men you always have been, or even better—Sarpedon is fallen—he who was first to overleap the wall of the Achaeans; let us take the body and outrage it; let us strip the armor from his shoulders, and kill his comrades if they try to rescue his body."

He spoke to men who of themselves were full eager; both sides, therefore, the Trojans and Lycians on the one hand, and the Myrmidons and Achaeans on the other, strengthened their battalions and fought desperately about the body of Sarpedon, shouting fiercely the while. Mighty was the din of their armor as they came together, and Zeus shed a thick darkness over the fight, to increase the fury of the battle over the body of his son.

At first the Trojans made some headway against the Achaeans, for one of the best men among the Myrmidons was killed, Epeigeus, son of noble Agacles who had erewhile been king in the good city of Budeum; but presently, having killed a valiant kinsman of his own, he took refuge with Peleus and Thetis, who sent him to Ilium, the land of noble steeds, to fight the Trojans under Achilles. Hector now struck him on the head with a stone just as he had caught hold of the body, and his brains inside his helmet were all battered in, so that he fell face foremost upon the body of Sarpedon, and there died. Patroclus was enraged by the death of his comrade, and sped through the front ranks as swiftly as a hawk that swoops down on a flock of daws or starlings. Even so swiftly, O noble knight Patroclus, did you make straight for the Lycians and Trojans to avenge your comrade! Forthwith he struck Sthenelaus, the son of Ithaemenes, on the neck with a stone, and broke the tendons that join it to the head and spine. On this Hector and the front rank of his men gave ground. As far as a man can throw a javelin when competing for some prize, or even in battle—so far did the Trojans now retreat before the Achaeans. Glaucus, captain of the Lycians, was the first to rally them, by killing Bathycles, son of Chalcon, who lived in Hellas and was the richest man among the Myrmidons. Glaucus turned round suddenly, just as Bathycles who was pursuing him was about to lay hold of him, and drove his spear right into the middle of his chest, whereon he fell heavily to the ground, and the fall of so good a man filled the Achaeans with dismay, while the Trojans were exultant, and came up in a body round the corpse. Nevertheless the Achaeans, mindful of their prowess, bore straight down upon them.

Meriones then killed a helmed warrior of the Trojans, Laogonus, son of Onetor, who was priest of Zeus of Mount Ida, and was honored by the people as though he were a god. Meriones struck him under the jaw and ear, so that life went out of him and the darkness of death laid hold upon him. Aeneas then aimed a spear at Meriones, hoping to hit him under the shield as he was advancing, but Meriones saw it coming and stooped forward to avoid it, whereon the spear flew past him and the point stuck in the ground, while the butt end went on quivering till Ares robbed it of its force. The spear, therefore, sped from Aeneas's hand in vain and fell quivering to the ground. Aeneas was angry and said, "Meriones, you are a good dancer, but if I had hit you my spear would soon have made an end of you."

And Meriones answered: "Aeneas, for all your bravery, you will not be able to make an end of everyone who comes against you. You are only a mortal like myself, and if I were to hit you in the middle of your shield with my spear, however strong and self-confident you may be, I should soon vanquish you, and you would yield your life to Hades of the noble steeds."

On this the son of Menoetius rebuked him and said: "Meriones, hero though you be, you should not speak thus. Taunting speeches, my good friend, will not make the Trojans draw away from the dead body. Some of them must go under ground first; blows for battle, and words for counsel; fight, therefore, and say nothing."

He led the way as he spoke and the hero went forward with him. As the sound of woodcutters in some forest glade upon the mountains—and the thud of their axes is heard afar—even such a din now rose from earth—clash of bronze armor and of good oxhide shields, as men smote each other with their swords and spears pointed at both ends. A man had need of good eyesight now to know Sarpedon, so covered was he from head to foot with spears and blood and dust. Men swarmed about the body, as flies that buzz round the full milk-pails in spring when they are brimming with milk—even so did they gather round Sarpedon. Nor did Zeus turn his keen eyes away for one moment from the fight, but kept looking at it all the time, for he was settling how best to kill Patroclus, and considering whether Hector should be allowed to end him now in the fight round the body of Sarpedon, and strip him of his armor, or whether he should let him give yet further trouble to the Trojans. In the end, he deemed it best that the brave squire of Achilles, son of Peleus, should drive Hector and the Trojans back towards the city and take the lives of many. First, therefore, he made Hector turn fainthearted, whereon he mounted his chariot and fled, bidding the other Trojans fly also, for he saw that the scales of Zeus had turned against him. Neither would the brave Lycians stand firm: they were dismayed when they saw their king lying struck to the heart amid a heap of corpses—for when the son of Cronus made the fight wax hot many had fallen above him. The Achaeans, therefore, stripped the gleaming armor from his shoulders and the brave son of Menoetius gave it to his men to take to the ships. Then Zeus, lord of the storm cloud, said to Apollo: "Dear Phoebus, go, I pray you, and take Sarpedon out of range of the weapons. Cleanse the black blood from off him, and then bear him a long way off where you may wash him in the river, anoint him with ambrosia, and clothe him in immortal raiment; this done, commit him to the arms of the two fleet messengers, Death and Sleep, who will carry him straightaway to the rich land of Lycia, where his brothers and kinsmen will inter him and will raise both mound and pillar to his memory, in due honor to the dead."

Thus he spoke. Apollo obeyed his father's saying and came down from the heights of Ida into the thick of the fight. Forthwith he took Sarpedon out of range of the weapons, and then bore him a long way off, where he washed him in the river, anointed him with ambrosia, and clothed him in immortal raiment. This done, he committed him to the arms of the two fleet messengers, Death and Sleep, who presently set him down in the rich land of Lycia.

Meanwhile Patroclus, with many a shout to his horses and to Automedon, pursued the Trojans and Lycians in the pride and foolishness of his heart. Had he but obeyed the bidding of the son of Peleus, he would have escaped death and have been scatheless; but the counsels of Zeus pass man's understanding; he will put even a brave man to flight and snatch victory from his grasp, or again he will set him on to fight, as he now did when he put a high spirit into the heart of Patroclus.

Who then first, and who last, was slain by you, O Patroclus, when the gods had now called you to meet your doom? First Adrestus, Autonoüs, Echeclus, Perimus, the son of Megas, Epistor and Melanippus; after these he killed Elasus, Mulius, and Pylartes. These he slew, but the rest saved themselves by flight.

The sons of the Achaeans would now have taken Troy by the hands of Patroclus, for his spear flew in all directions, had not Phoebus Apollo taken his stand upon the wall to defeat his purpose and to aid the Trojans. Thrice did Patroclus charge at an angle of the high wall, and thrice did Apollo beat him back, striking his shield with his own immortal hands. When Patroclus was coming on like a god for yet a fourth time, Apollo shouted to him with an awful voice and said: "Draw back, noble Patroclus, it is not your lot to sack the city of the Trojan chieftains, nor yet will it be that of Achilles who is a far better man than you are." On hearing this, Patroclus withdrew to some distance and avoided the anger of Apollo.

Meanwhile Hector was waiting with his horses inside the Scaean gates, in doubt whether to drive out again and go on fighting, or to call the army inside the gates. As he was thus doubting,

Phoebus Apollo drew near him in the likeness of a young and lusty warrior Asius, who was Hector's uncle, being own brother to Hecuba and son of Dymas who lived in Phrygia by the waters of the river Sangarius. In his likeness Zeus's son Apollo now spoke to Hector, saying: "Hector, why have you left off fighting? It is ill done of you. If I were as much better a man than you, as I am worse, you should soon rue your slackness. Drive straight towards Patroclus, if so be that Apollo may grant you a triumph over him, and you may kill him."

With this the god went back into the hurly-burly, and Hector bade Cebriones drive again into the fight. Apollo passed in among them, and struck panic into the Argives, while he gave triumph to Hector and the Trojans. Hector let the other Danaans alone and killed no man, but drove straight at Patroclus. Patroclus then sprang from his chariot to the ground, with a spear in his left hand, and in his right a jagged stone as large as his hand could hold. He stood still and threw it, nor did it go far without hitting someone. The cast was not in vain, for the stone struck Cebriones, Hector's charioteer, a bastard son of Priam, as he held the reins in his hands. The stone hit him on the forehead and drove his brows into his head, for the bone was smashed, and his eyes fell to the ground at his feet. He dropped dead from his chariot as though he were diving, and there was no more life left in him. Over him did you then vaunt, O knight Patroclus, saying: "Bless my heart, how active he is, and how well he dives. If we had been at sea this fellow would have dived from the ship's side and brought up as many oysters as the whole crew could stomach, even in rough water, for he has dived beautifully off his chariot on to the ground. It seems, then, that there are divers also among the Trojans."

As he spoke, he flung himself on Cebriones with the spring, as it were, of a lion that while attacking a stockyard is himself struck in the chest, and his courage is his own bane—even so furiously, O Patroclus, did you then spring upon Cebriones. Hector sprang also from his chariot to the ground. The pair then fought over the body of Cebriones. As two famished lions fight fiercely on some high mountain over the body of a stag that they have killed, even so did these two mighty warriors, Patroclus, son of Menoetius, and brave Hector, hack and hew at one another over the corpse of Cebriones. Hector would not let him go when he had once got him by the head, while Patroclus kept fast hold of his feet, and a fierce fight raged between the other Danaans and Trojans. As the east and south wind buffet one another when they beat upon some dense forest on the mountains—there is beech and ash and spreading cornel; the tops of the trees roar as they beat on one another, and one can hear the boughs cracking and breaking—even so did the Trojans and Achaeans spring upon one another and lay about each other, and neither side would give way. Many a pointed spear fell to ground and many a winged arrow sped from its bowstring about the body of Cebriones. Many a great stone, moreover, beat on many a shield as they fought around his body, but there he lay in the whirling clouds of dust, all huge and hugely, heedless of his driving now.

So long as the sun was still high in midheaven the weapons of either side were alike deadly, and the people fell; but when he went down towards the time when men loose their oxen, the Achaeans proved to be beyond all forecast stronger, so that they drew Cebriones out of range of the darts and tumult of the Trojans, and stripped the armor from his shoulders. Then Patroclus sprang like Ares with fierce intent and a terrific shout upon the Trojans, and thrice did he kill nine men; but as he was coming on like a god for a fourth time, then, O Patroclus, was the hour of your end approaching, for Phoebus fought you in fell earnest. Patroclus did not see him as he moved about in the crush, for he was enshrouded in thick darkness, and the god struck him from behind on his back and his broad shoulders with the flat of his hand, so that his eyes turned dizzy. Phoebus Apollo beat the helmet from off his head, and it rolled rattling off under the horses' feet, where its horsehair plumes were all begrimed with dust and blood. Never indeed had that helmet fared so before, for it had served to protect the head and comely forehead of the godlike hero Achilles. Now, however, Zeus delivered it over to be worn by Hector. Nevertheless, the end of Hector also was near. The bronze-shod spear, so great and so strong, was broken in the hand of Patroclus, while his shield that covered him from head to foot fell to the ground as did also the band that held it, and Apollo undid the fastenings of his corslet.

On this his mind became clouded; his limbs failed him, and he stood as one dazed; whereon Euphorbus, son of Panthoüs, a Dardanian, the best spearman of his time, as also the finest horseman and fleetest runner, came behind him and struck him in the back with a spear, midway between the shoulders. This man as soon as ever he had come up with his chariot had dismounted twenty men, so proficient was he in all the arts of war—he it was, O knight Patroclus, that first drove a weapon into you, but he did not quite overpower you. Euphorbus then ran back into the crowd, after drawing his ashen spear out of the wound; he would not stand firm and wait for Patroclus, unarmed though he now was, to attack him; but Patroclus, unnerved, alike by the blow the god had given him and by the spear wound, drew back under cover of his men in fear for his life. Hector on this, seeing him to be wounded and giving ground, forced his way through the ranks, and when close up with him struck him in the lower part of the belly with a spear, driving the bronze point right through it, so that he fell heavily to the ground to the great grief of the Achaeans. As when a lion has fought some fierce wild boar and worsted him—the two fight furiously upon the mountains over some little fountain at which they would both drink, and the lion has beaten the boar till he can hardly breathe—even so did Hector, son of Priam, take the life of the brave son of Menoetius, who had killed so many, striking him from close at hand and vaunting over him the while. "Patroclus," said he, "you deemed that you should sack our city, rob our Trojan women of their freedom, and carry them off in your ships to your own country. Fool! Hector and his fleet horses were ever straining their utmost to defend them. I am foremost of all the Trojan warriors to stave the day of bondage from off them. As for you, vultures shall devour you here. Poor wretch, Achilles with all his bravery availed you nothing; and yet I ween when you left him he charged you straitly, saying, 'Come not back to the ships, knight Patroclus, till you have rent the bloodstained shirt of murderous Hector about his body.' Thus I ween did he charge you, and your fool's heart answered him 'yea' within you."

Then, as the life ebbed out of you, you answered, O knight Patroclus: "Hector, vaunt as you will, for Zeus, the son of Cronus, and Apollo have vouchsafed you victory; it is they who have vanquished me so easily, and they who have stripped the armor from my shoulders; had twenty such men as you attacked me, all of them would have fallen before my spear. Fate and the son of Leto have overpowered me, and among mortal men Euphorbus; you are yourself third only in the killing of me. I say further, and lay my saying to your heart, you too shall live but for a little season. Death and the day of your doom are close upon you, and they will lay you low by the hand of Achilles, son of Aeacus."

When he had thus spoken his eyes were closed in death, his soul left his body and flitted down to the house of Hades, mourning its sad fate and bidding farewell to the youth and vigor of its manhood. Dead though he was, Hector still spoke to him, saying, "Patroclus, why should you thus foretell my doom? Who knows but Achilles, son of lovely Thetis, may be smitten by my spear and die before me?"

As he spoke he drew the bronze spear from the wound, planting his foot upon the body, which he thrust off and let lie on its back. He then went spear in hand after Automedon, squire of the fleet descendant of Aeacus, for he longed to lay him low, but the immortal steeds which the gods had given as a rich gift to Peleus bore him swiftly from the field.

BOOK XVII

A struggle rages over the body of Patroclus, which Hector strips of its armor. Menelaus, assisted by Ajax, tries to rescue the body. Apollo aids the Trojans, Athene the Greeks. Achilles's horses stand mourning their driver's death. Menelaus sends word to Achilles of what has happened, and the Greeks, bearing Patroclus's body, push slowly toward the ships.

BRAVE MENELAUS, SON OF ATREUS, NOW CAME TO KNOW THAT Patroclus had fallen, and made his way through the front ranks clad in full armor to bestride him. As a cow stands lowing over her first calf, even so did yellow-haired Menelaus bestride Patroclus. He held his round shield and his spear in front of him, resolute to kill any who should dare face him. But the son of Panthoüs had also noted the body, and came up to Menelaus, saying: "Menelaus, son of Atreus, draw back, leave the body, and let the bloodstained spoils be. I was first of the Trojans and their brave allies to drive my spear into Patroclus, let me, therefore, have my full glory among the Trojans, or I will take aim and kill you."

To this Menelaus answered in great anger: "By father Zeus, boasting is an ill thing. The pard is not more bold, nor the lion nor savage wild boar, which is fiercest and most dauntless of all creatures, than are the proud sons of Panthoüs. Yet Hyperenor did not see out the days of his youth when he made light of me and withstood me, deeming me the meanest soldier among the Danaans. His own feet never bore him back to gladden his wife and parents. Even so shall I make an end of you too, if you withstand me. Get you back into the crowd and do not face me, or it shall be worse for you. Even a fool may be wise after the event."

Euphorbus would not listen and said: "Now indeed, Menelaus, shall you pay for the death of my brother over whom you vaunted, and whose wife you widowed in her bridal chamber while you brought grief unspeakable on his parents. I shall comfort these poor people if I bring your head and armor and place them in the hands of Panthoüs and noble Phrontis. The time is come when this matter shall be fought out and settled, for me or against me."

As he spoke he struck Menelaus full on the shield, but the spear did not go through, for the shield turned its point. Menelaus then took aim, praying to father Zeus as he did so. Euphorbus was drawing back, and Menelaus struck him about the roots of his throat, leaning his whole weight on the spear, so as to drive it home. The point went clean through his neck, and his armor rang rattling round him as he fell heavily to the ground. His hair, which was like that of the Graces, and his locks so deftly bound in bands of silver and gold were all bedrabbled with blood. As one who has grown a fine young olive tree in a clear space where there is abundance of water—the plant is full of promise, and though the winds beat upon it from every quarter it puts forth its white blossoms till the blasts of some fierce hurricane sweep down upon it and level it with the ground—even so did Menelaus strip the fair youth Euphorbus of his armor after he had slain him. Or as some fierce lion upon the mountains in the pride of his strength fastens on the finest heifer in a herd as it is feeding—first he breaks her neck with his strong jaws and then gorges on her blood and entrails. Dogs and shepherds raise a hue and cry against him, but they stand aloof and will not come close to him, for they are pale with fear—even so no one had the courage to face valiant Menelaus. The son of Atreus would have then carried off the armor of the son of Panthoüs with ease had not Phoebus

Apollo been angry and in the guise of Mentes, chief of the Cicons, incited Hector to attack him. "Hector," said he, "you are now going after the horses of the noble son of Aeacus, but you will not take them. They cannot be kept in hand and driven by mortal man, save only by Achilles, who is son to an immortal mother. Meanwhile, Menelaus, son of Atreus, has bestridden the body of Patroclus and killed the noblest of the Trojans, Euphorbus, son of Panthoüs, so that he can fight no more."

The god then went back into the toil and turmoil, but the soul of Hector was darkened with a cloud of grief; he looked along the ranks and saw Euphorbus lying on the ground with the blood still flowing from his wound, and Menelaus stripping him of his armor. On this he made his way to the front like a flame of fire, clad in his gleaming armor, and crying with a loud voice. When the son of Atreus heard him, he said to himself in his dismay: "Alas! what shall I do? I may not let the Trojans take the armor of Patroclus who has fallen fighting on my behalf, lest some Danaan who sees me should cry shame upon me. Still if for my honor's sake I fight Hector and the Trojans single-handed, they will prove too many for me, for Hector is bringing them up in force. Why, however, should I thus hesitate? When a man fights in despite of heaven with one whom a god befriends, he will soon rue it. Let no Danaan think ill of me if I give place to Hector, for the hand of heaven is with him. Yet, if I could find Ajax, the two of us would fight Hector and heaven too, if we might only save the body of Patroclus for Achilles, son of Peleus. This, of many evils, would be the least."

While he was thus in two minds, the Trojans came up to him with Hector at their head; he therefore drew back and left the body, turning about like some bearded lion who is being chased by dogs and men from a stockyard with spears and hue and cry, whereon he is daunted and slinks sulkily off—even so did Menelaus, son of Atreus, turn and leave the body of Patroclus. When among the body of his men, he looked around for mighty Ajax, son of Telamon, and presently saw him on the extreme left of the fight, cheering on his men and exhorting them to keep on fighting, for Phoebus Apollo had spread a great panic among them. He ran up to him and said, "Ajax, my good friend, come with me at once to dead Patroclus, if so be that we may take the body to Achilles—as for his armor, Hector already has it."

These words stirred the heart of Ajax, and he made his way among the front ranks, Menelaus going with him. Hector had stripped Patroclus of his armor, and was dragging him away to cut off his head and take the body to fling before the dogs of Troy. But Ajax came up with his shield like a wall before him, on which Hector withdrew under shelter of his men, and sprang on to his chariot, giving the armor over to the Trojans to take to the city, as a great trophy for himself. Ajax, therefore, covered the body of Patroclus with his broad shield and bestrode him; as a lion stands over his whelps if hunters have come upon him in a forest when he is with his little ones—in the pride and fierceness of his strength he draws his knit brows down till they cover his eyes—even so did Ajax bestride the body of Patroclus, and by his side stood Menelaus, son of Atreus, nursing great sorrow in his heart.

Then Glaucus, son of Hippolochus, looked fiercely at Hector and rebuked him sternly. "Hector," said he, "you make a brave show, but in fight you are sadly wanting. A runaway like yourself has no claim to so great a reputation. Think how you may now save your town and citadel by the hands of your own people born in Ilium; for you will get no Lycians to fight for you, seeing what thanks they have had for their incessant hardships. Are you likely, sir, to do anything to help a man of less note, after leaving Sarpedon, who was at once your guest and comrade in arms, to be the spoil and prey of the Danaans? So long as he lived he did good service both to your city and yourself. Yet you had no stomach to save his body from the dogs. If the Lycians will listen to me, they will go home and leave Troy to its fate. If the Trojans had any of that daring fearless spirit which lays hold of men who are fighting for their country and harassing those who would attack it, we should soon bear off Patroclus into Ilium. Could we get this dead man away and bring him into the city of Priam, the Argives would readily give up the armor of Sarpedon, and we should get his body to boot. For he whose squire has been now killed is the foremost man at the ships of the Achaeans—he and his close-fighting followers. Nevertheless, you dared not make a stand against Ajax, nor face him, eye to eye, with battle all round you, for he is a braver man than you are."

Hector scowled at him and answered: "Glaucus, you should know better. I have held you so far as a man of more understanding than any in all Lycia, but now I despise you for saying that I am afraid of Ajax. I fear neither battle nor the din of chariots, but Zeus's will is stronger than ours. Zeus at one time makes even a strong man draw back and snatches victory from his grasp, while at another he will set him on to fight. Come hither then, my friend, stand by me and see indeed whether I shall play the coward the whole day through as you say, or whether I shall not stay some even of the boldest Danaans from fighting round the body of Patroclus."

As he spoke he called loudly on the Trojans, saying, "Trojans, Lycians, and Dardanians, fighters in close combat, be men, my friends, and fight might and main, while I put on the goodly armor of Achilles, which I took when I killed Patroclus."

With this Hector left the fight, and ran full speed after his men who were taking the armor of Achilles to Troy, but had not yet got far. Standing for a while apart from the woeful fight, he changed his armor. His own he sent to the strong city of Ilium and to the Trojans, while he put on the immortal armor of the son of Peleus, which the gods had given to Peleus, who in his age gave it to his son; but the son did not grow old in his father's armor.

When Zeus, lord of the storm cloud, saw Hector standing aloof and arming himself in the armor of the son of Peleus, he wagged his head and muttered to himself, saying: "Alas! poor wretch, you arm in the armor of a hero before whom many another trembles, and you reck nothing of the doom that is already close upon you. You have killed his comrade so brave and strong, but it was not well that you should strip the armor from his head and shoulders. I do indeed endow you with great might now, but as against this you shall not return from battle to lay the armor of the son of Peleus before Andromache."

The son of Cronus bowed his portentous brows, and Hector fitted the armor to his body, while terrible Ares entered into him and filled his whole body with might and valor. With a shout he strode in among the allies, and his armor flashed about him so that he seemed to all of them like the great son of Peleus himself. He went about among them and cheered them on—Mesthles, Glaucus, Medon, Thersilochus, Asteropaeus, Deisenor, Hippothoüs, Phorcys, Chromius, and Ennomus, the augur. All these did he exhort, saying: "Hear me, allies from other cities who are here in your thousands, it was not in order to have a crowd about me that I called you hither each from his several city, but that with heart and soul you might defend the wives and little ones of the Trojans from the fierce Achaeans. For this do I oppress my people with your food and the presents that make you rich. Therefore turn, and charge at the foe, to stand or fall as is the game of war. Whoever shall bring Patroclus, dead though he be, into the hands of the Trojans, and shall make Ajax give way before him, I will give him one half of the spoils while I keep the other. He will thus share like honor with myself."

When he had thus spoken they charged full weight upon the Danaans with their spears held out before them, and the hopes of each ran high that he should force Ajax, son of Telamon, to yield up the body—fools that they were, for he was about to take the lives of many. Then Ajax said to Menelaus: "My good friend Menelaus, you and I shall hardly come out of this fight alive. I am less concerned for the body of Patroclus, who will shortly become meat for the dogs and vultures of Troy, than for the safety of my own head and yours. Hector has wrapped us round in a storm of battle from every quarter, and our destruction seems now certain. Call then upon the princes of the Danaans if there is any who can hear us."

Menelaus did as he said, and shouted to the Danaans for help at the top of his voice. "My friends," he cried, "princes and counselors of the Argives, all you who with Agamemnon and Menelaus drink at the public cost, and give orders each to his own people as Zeus vouchsafes him power and glory, the fight is so thick about me that I cannot distinguish you severally. Come on, therefore, every man unbidden, and think it shame that Patroclus should become meat and morsel for Trojan hounds."

Fleet Ajax, son of Oïleus, heard him and was first to force his way through the fight and run to help him. Next came Idomeneus and Meriones, his esquire, peer of murderous Ares. As for the others that came into the fight after these, who of his own self could name them?

The Trojans with Hector at their head charged in a body. As a great wave that comes thundering in at the mouth of some heaven-born river, and the rocks that jut into the sea ring with the roar of the breakers that beat and buffet them—even with such a roar did the Trojans come on; but the Achaeans in singleness of heart stood firm about the son of Menoetius and fenced him with their bronze shields. Zeus, moreover, hid the brightness of their helmets in a thick cloud, for he had borne no grudge against the son of Menoetius while he was still alive and squire to the descendant of Aeacus. Therefore he was loath to let him fall a prey to the dogs of his foes, the Trojans, and urged his comrades on to defend him.

At first the Trojans drove the Achaeans back, and they withdrew from the dead man daunted. The Trojans did not succeed in killing anyone, nevertheless they drew the body away. But the Achaeans did not lose it long, for Ajax, foremost of all the Danaans after the son of Peleus alike in stature and prowess, quickly rallied them and made towards the front like a wild boar upon the mountains when he stands at bay in the forest glades and routs the hounds and lusty youths that have attacked him—even so did Ajax, son of Telamon, passing easily in among the phalanxes of the Trojans, disperse those who had bestridden Patroclus and were most bent on winning glory by dragging him off to their city. At this moment Hippothoüs, brave son of the Pelasgian Lethus, in his zeal for Hector and the Trojans, was dragging the body off by the foot through the press of the fight, having bound a strap round the sinews near the ankle; but a mischief scon befell him from which none of those could save him who would have gladly done so, for the son of Telamon sprang forward and smote him on his bronze-cheeked helmet. The plumed headpiece broke about the point of the weapon, struck at once by the spear and by the strong hand of Ajax, so that the bloody brain came oozing out through the crest-socket. His strength then failed him and he let Patroclus's foot drop from his hand, as he fell full length dead upon the body. Thus he died far from the fertile land of Larisa and never repaid his parents the cost of bringing him up, for his life was cut short early by the spear of mighty Ajax. Hector then took aim at Ajax with a spear, but he saw it coming and just managed to avoid it. The spear passed on and struck Schedius, son of noble Iphitus, captain of the Phoceans, who dwelt in famed Panopeus and reigned over much people. It struck him under the middle of the collarbone; the bronze point went right through him, coming out at the bottom of his shoulder blade, and his armor rang rattling round him as he fell heavily to the ground. Ajax in his turn struck noble Phorcys, son of Phaenops, in the middle of the belly as he was bestriding Hippothoüs, and broke the plate of his cuirass; whereon the spear tore out his entrails and he clutched the ground in his palm as he fell to earth. Hector and those who were in the front rank then gave ground, while the Argives raised a loud cry of triumph and drew off the bodies of Phorcys and Hippothoüs, which they stripped presently of their armor.

The Trojans would now have been worsted by the brave Achaeans and driven back to Ilium through their own cowardice, while the Argives, so great was their courage and endurance, would have achieved a triumph even against the will of Zeus, if Apollo had not roused Aeneas, in the likeness of Periphas, son of Epytus, an attendant who had grown old in the service of Aeneas's aged father and was at all times devoted to him. In his likeness, then, Apollo said: "Aeneas, can you not manage, even though heaven be against us, to save high Ilium? I have known men, whose numbers, courage, and self-reliance have saved their people in spite of Zeus, whereas in this case he would much rather give victory to us than to the Danaans, if you would only fight instead of being so terribly afraid."

Aeneas knew Apollo when he looked straight at him, and shouted to Hector, saying: "Hector and all other Trojans and allies, shame on us if we are beaten by the Achaeans and driven back to Ilium through our own cowardice. A god has just come up to me and told me that Zeus the supreme disposer will be with us. Therefore, let us make for the Danaans, that it may go hard with them ere they bear away dead Patroclus to the ships."

As he spoke he sprang out far in front of the others, who then rallied and again faced the Achaeans. Aeneas speared Leiocritus, son of Arisbas, a valiant follower of Lycomedes, and Lycomedes was moved with pity as he saw him fall. He therefore went close up, and speared Apisaon, son of Hippasus, shepherd of his people, in the liver under the midriff, so that he died. He had come from fertile Paeonia and was the best man of them all after Asteropaeus. Asteropaeus flew forward to avenge him and attack the Danaans, but this might no longer be, inasmuch as those about Patroclus were well-covered by their shields, and held their spears in front of them, for Ajax had given them strict orders that no man was either to give ground, or to stand out before the others, but all were to hold well together about the body and fight hand to hand. Thus did huge Ajax bid them, and the earth ran red with blood as the corpses fell thick on one another alike on the side of the Trojans and allies, and on that of the Danaans; for these last, too, fought no bloodless fight though many fewer of them perished, through the care they took to defend and stand by one another.

Thus did they fight as it were a flaming fire. It seemed as though it had gone hard even with the sun and moon, for they were hidden over all that part where the bravest heroes were fighting about the dead son of Menoetius, whereas the other Danaans and Achaeans fought at their ease in full daylight with brilliant sunshine all round them, and there was not a cloud to be seen, neither on plain nor mountain. These last, moreover, would rest for a while and leave off fighting, for they were some distance apart and beyond the range of one another's weapons, whereas those who were in the thick of the fray suffered both from battle and darkness. All the best of them were being worn out by the great weight of their armor, but the two valiant heroes, Thrasymedes and Antilochus, had not yet heard of the death of Patroclus, and believed him to be still alive and leading the van against the Trojans. They were keeping themselves in reserve against the death or rout of their own comrades, for so Nestor had ordered when he sent them from the ships into battle.

Thus through the livelong day did they wage fierce war, and the sweat of their toil rained ever on their legs under them, and on their hands and eyes, as they fought over the squire of the fleet son of Peleus. It was as when a man gives a great oxhide all drenched in fat to his men, and bids them stretch it; whereon they stand round it in a ring and tug till the moisture leaves it, and the fat soaks in for the many that pull at it, and it is well-stretched—even so did the two sides tug the dead body hither and thither within the compass of but a little space—the Trojans steadfastly set on dragging it into Ilium, while the Achaeans were no less so on taking it to their ships; and fierce was the fight between them. Not Ares, himself, the lord of hosts, nor yet Athene, even in their fullest fury could make light of such a battle.

Such fearful turmoil of men and horses did Zeus on that day ordain round the body of Patroclus. Meanwhile Achilles did not know that he had fallen, for the fight was under the wall of Troy, a long way off the ships. He had no idea, therefore, that Patroclus was dead, and deemed that he would return alive as soon as he had gone close up to the gates. He knew that he was not to sack the city neither with nor without himself, for his mother had often told him this when he had sat alone with her, and she had informed him of the counsels of great Zeus. Now, however, she had not told him how great a disaster had befallen him in the death of the one who was far dearest to him of all his comrades.

The others still kept on charging one another round the body with their pointed spears and killing each other. Then would one say, "My friends, we can never again show our faces at the ships—better, and greatly better, that earth should open and swallow us here in this place, than that we should let the Trojans have the triumph of bearing off Patroclus to their city." The Trojans also on their part spoke to one another, saying: "Friends, though we fall to a man beside this body, let none shrink from fighting." With such words did they exhort each other. They fought and fought, and an iron clank rose through the void air to the brazen vault of heaven.

The horses of the descendant of Aeacus stood out of the fight and wept when they heard that their driver had been laid low by the hand of murderous Hector. Automedon, valiant son of Diores, lashed them again and again. Many a time did he speak kindly to them, and many a time did he upbraid them, but they would neither go back to the ships by the waters of the broad Hellespont, nor yet into battle among the Achaeans. They stood with their chariot stock still, as a pillar set over the tomb of some dead man or woman, and bowed their heads to the ground. Hot tears fell from their eyes as they mourned the loss of their charioteer, and their noble manes drooped all wet from under the yoke-straps on either side the yoke.

The son of Cronus saw them and took pity upon their sorrow. He wagged his head and muttered to himself, saying: "Poor things, why did we give you to King Peleus who is a mortal, while you are yourselves ageless and immortal? Was it that you might share the sorrows that befall mankind? For of all creatures that live and move upon the earth there is none so pitiable as he is—still, Hector, son of Priam, shall drive neither you nor your chariot. I will not have it. It is enough that he should have the armor over which he vaunts so vainly. Furthermore, I will give you strength of heart and limb to bear Automedon safely to the ships from battle, for I shall let the Trojans triumph still further and go on killing till they reach the ships; whereon night shall fall and darkness overshadow the land."

As he spoke he breathed heart and strength into the horses so that they shook the dust from out of their manes and bore their chariot swiftly into the fight that raged between Trojans and

Achaeans. Behind them fought Automedon, full of sorrow for his comrade, as a vulture amid a flock of geese. In and out and here and there, full speed he dashed amid the throng of the Trojans, but for all the fury of his pursuit he killed no man, for he could not wield his spear and keep his horses in hand when alone in the chariot. At last, however, a comrade, Alcimedon, son of Laerces, son of Haemon, caught sight of him and came up behind his chariot. "Automedon," said he, "what god has put this folly into your heart and robbed you of your right mind, that you fight the Trojans in the front rank single-handed? He who was your comrade is slain, and Hector plumes himself on being armed in the armor of the descendant of Aeacus."

Automedon, son of Diores, answered: "Alcimedon, there is no one else who can control and guide the immortal steeds so well as you can, save only Patroclus—while he was alive—peer of gods in counsel. Take then the whip and reins, while I go down from the car and fight."

Alcimedon sprang on to the chariot and caught up the whip and reins, while Automedon leaped from off the car. When Hector saw him he said to Aeneas, who was near him: "Aeneas, counselor of the mail-clad Trojans, I see the steeds of the fleet son of Aeacus come into battle with weak hands to drive them. I am sure, if you think well, that we might take them; they will not dare face us if we both attack them."

The valiant son of Anchises was of the same mind, and the pair went right on, with their shoulders covered under shields of tough dry oxhide, overlaid with much bronze. Chromius and Arenas went also with them, and their hearts beat high with hope that they might kill the men and capture the horses—fools that they were, for they were not to return scatheless from their meeting with Automedon, who prayed to father Zeus and was forthwith filled with courage and strength abounding. He turned to his trusty comrade Alcimedon and said: "Alcimedon, keep your horses so close up that I may feel their breath upon my back. I doubt that we shall not stay Hector, son of Priam, till he has killed us and mounted behind the horses; he will then either spread panic among the ranks of the Achaeans, or himself be killed among the foremost."

On this he cried out to the two Ajaxes and Menelaus: "Ajaxes, captains of the Argives, and Menelaus, give the dead body over to them that are best able to defend it, and come to the rescue of us living; for Hector and Aeneas, who are the two best men among the Trojans, are pressing us hard in the full tide of war. Nevertheless, the issue lies on the lap of heaven. I will therefore hurl my spear and leave the rest to Zeus."

He poised and hurled as he spoke, whereon the spear struck the round shield of Aretus, and went right through it for the shield stayed it not, so that it was driven through his belt into the lower part of his belly. As when some sturdy youth, ax in hand, deals his blow behind the horns of an ox and severs the tendons at the back of its neck so that it springs forward and then drops, even so did Aretus give one bound and then fall on his back—the spear quivering in his body till it made an end of him. Hector then aimed a spear at Automedon but he saw it coming and stooped forward to avoid it, so that it flew past him and the point stuck in the ground, while the butt end went on quivering till Ares robbed it of its force. They would then have fought hand to hand with swords had not the two Ajaxes forced their way through the crowd when they heard their comrade calling, and parted them for all their fury—for Hector, Aeneas, and Chromius were afraid and drew back, leaving Aretus to lie there struck to the heart. Automedon, peer of fleet Ares, then stripped him of his armor and vaunted over him, saying: "I have done little to assuage my sorrow for the son of Menoetius, for the man I have killed is not so good as he was."

As he spoke he took the bloodstained spoils and laid them upon his chariot; then he mounted the car with his hands and feet all steeped in gore as a lion that has been gorging upon a bull.

And now the fierce groanful fight again raged about Patroclus, for Athene came down from heaven and roused its fury by the command of far-seeing Zeus, who had changed his mind and sent her to encourage the Danaans. As when Zeus bends his bright bow in heaven in token to mankind either of war or of the chill storms that stay men from their labor and plague the flocks—even so, wrapped in such radiant raiment, did Athene go in among the host and speak man by man to each. First she took the form and voice of Phoenix and spoke to Menelaus, son of Atreus, who was standing near her. "Menelaus," said she, "it will be shame and dishonor to you if dogs tear the noble comrade of Achilles under the walls of Troy. Therefore be staunch and urge your men to be so also."

Menelaus answered: "Phoenix, my good old friend, may Athene vouchsafe me strength and keep the darts from off me, for so shall I stand by Patroclus and defend him. His death has gone to my heart, but Hector is as a raging fire and deals his blows without ceasing, for Zeus is now granting him a time of triumph."

Athene was pleased at his having named herself before any of the other gods. Therefore she put strength into his knees and shoulders and made him as bold as a fly, which, though driven off will yet come again and bite if it can, so dearly does it love man's blood—even so bold as this did she make him as he stood over Patroclus and threw his spear. Now there was among the Trojans a man named Podes, son of Eëtion, who was both rich and valiant. Hector held him in the highest honor for he was his comrade and boon companion. The spear of Menelaus struck this man in the girdle just as he had turned in flight, and went right through him. Whereon he fell heavily forward, and Menelaus, son of Atreus, drew off his body from the Trojans into the ranks of his own people.

Apollo then went up to Hector and spurred him on to fight, in the likeness of Phaenops, son of Asius, who lived in Abydos and was the most favored of all Hector's guests. In his likeness Apollo said: "Hector, who of the Achaeans will fear you henceforward now that you have quailed before Menelaus, who has ever been rated poorly as a soldier? Yet he has now got a corpse away from the Trojans single-handed, and has slain your own true comrade, a man brave among the foremost, Podes, son of Eëtion."

A dark cloud of grief fell upon Hector as he heard, and he made his way to the front clad in full armor. Thereon the son of Cronus seized his bright-tasseled aegis and veiled Ida in cloud. He sent forth his lightnings and his thunders, and as he shook his aegis he gave victory to the Trojans and routed the Achaeans.

The panic was begun by Peneleos, the Boeotian, for while keeping his face turned ever towards the foe he had been hit with a spear on the upper part of the shoulder. A spear thrown by Polydamas had grazed the top of the bone, for Polydamas had come up to him and struck him from close at hand. Then Hector in close combat struck Leïtus, son of noble Alectryon, in the hand by the wrist, and disabled him from fighting further. He looked about him in dismay, knowing that never again should he wield spear in battle with the Trojans. While Hector was in pursuit of Leïtus, Idomeneus struck him on the breastplate over his chest near the nipple, but the spear broke in the shaft, and the Trojans cheered aloud. Hector then aimed at Idomeneus, son of Deucalion, as he was standing on his chariot, and very narrowly missed him, but the spear hit Coiranus, a follower and charioteer of Meriones who had come with him from Lyctus. Idomeneus had left the ships on foot and would have afforded a great triumph to the Trojans if Coiranus had not driven quickly up to him; he therefore brought life and rescue to Idomeneus, but himself fell by the hand of murderous Hector. For Hector hit him on the jaw under the ear; the end of the spear drove out his teeth and cut his tongue in two pieces, so that he fell from his chariot and let the reins fall to the ground. Meriones gathered them up from the ground and took them into his own hands, then he said to Idomeneus, "Lay on, till you get back to the ships, for you must see that the day is no longer ours." On this Idomeneus lashed the horses to the ships, for fear had taken hold upon him.

Ajax and Menelaus noted how Zeus had turned the scale in favor of the Trojans, and Ajax was first to speak. "Alas," said he, "even a fool may see that father Zeus is helping the Trojans. All their weapons strike home; no matter whether it be a brave man or a coward that hurls them, Zeus speeds all alike, whereas ours fall each one of them without effect. What, then, will be best both as regards rescuing the body, and our return to the joy of our friends who will be grieving as they look hitherwards? For they will make sure that nothing can now check the terrible hands of Hector, and that he will fling himself upon our ships. I wish that someone would go and tell the son of Peleus at once, for I do not think he can have yet heard the sad news that the dearest of his friends has fallen. But I can see not a man among the Achaeans to send, for they and their chariots are alike hidden in darkness. O father Zeus, lift this cloud from over the sons of the Achaeans! Make heaven serene, and let us see; if you will that we perish, let us fall, at any rate, by daylight."

Father Zeus heard him and had compassion upon his tears. Forthwith he chased away the cloud of darkness, so that the sun shone out and all the fighting was revealed. Ajax then said to Menelaus, "Look, Menelaus, and if Antilochus, son of Nestor, be still living, send him at once to tell Achilles that by far the dearest to him of all his comrades has fallen."

Menelaus heeded his words and went his way as a lion from a stockyard—the lion is tired of attacking the men and hounds, who keep watch the whole night through and will not let him feast on the fat of their herd. In his lust of meat he makes straight at them but in vain, for darts from strong hands assail him, and burning brands which daunt him for all his hunger, so in the morning he slinks sulkily away—even so did Menelaus sorely against his will leave Patroclus, in great fear lest the Achaeans should be driven back in rout and let him fall into the hands of the foe. He charged Meriones and the two Ajaxes straitly, saying, "Ajaxes and Meriones, leaders of the Argives, now indeed remember how good Patroclus was; he was ever courteous while alive, bear it in mind now that he is dead."

With this Menelaus left them, looking round him as keenly as an eagle, whose sight they say is keener than that of any other bird—however high he may be in the heavens, not a hare that runs can escape him by crouching under bush or thicket, for he will swoop down upon it and make an end of it—even so,

O Menelaus, did your keen eyes range round the mighty host of your followers to see if you could find the son of Nestor still alive? Presently Menelaus saw him on the extreme left of the battle, cheering on his men and exhorting them to fight boldly. Menelaus went up to him and said: "Antilochus, come here and listen to sad news, which I would indeed were untrue. You must see with your own eyes that heaven is heaping calamity upon the Danaans, and giving victory to the Trojans. Patroclus has fallen, who was the bravest of the Achaeans, and sorely will the Danaans miss him. Run instantly to the ships and tell Achilles, that he may come to rescue the body and bear it to the ships. As for the armor, Hector already has it."

Antilochus was struck with horror. For a long time he was speechless. His eyes filled with tears and he could find no utterance, but he did as Menelaus had said, and set off running as soon as he had given his armor to a comrade, Laodocus, who was wheeling his horses round, close beside him.

Thus, then, did he run weeping from the field, to carry the bad news to Achilles, son of Peleus. Nor were you, O Menelaus, minded to succor his harassed comrades, when Antilochus had left the Pylians—and greatly did they miss him—but he sent them noble Thrasymedes, and himself went back to Patroclus. He came running up to the two Ajaxes and said: "I have sent Antilochus to the ships to tell Achilles, but rage against Hector as he may, he cannot come, for he cannot fight without armor. What then will be our best plan both as regards rescuing the dead and our own escape from death amid the battle cries of the Trojans?"

Ajax answered: "Menelaus, you have said well: do you, then, and Meriones stoop down, raise the body, and bear it out of the fray, while we two behind you keep off Hector and the Trojans, one in heart as in name, and long used to fighting side by side with one another."

On this Menelaus and Meriones took the dead man in their arms and lifted him high aloft with a great effort. The Trojan host raised a hue and cry behind them when they saw the Achaeans bearing the body away, and flew after them like hounds attacking a wounded boar at the loo of a band of young huntsmen. For a while the hounds fly at him as though they would tear him in pieces, but now and again he turns on them in a fury, scaring and scattering them in all directions—even so did the Trojans for a while charge in a body, striking with sword and with spears pointed at both the ends, but when the two Ajaxes faced them and stood at bay, they would turn pale and no man dared press on to fight further about the dead.

In this wise did the two heroes strain every nerve to bear the body to the ships out of the fight. The battle raged round them like fierce flames that when once kindled spread like wildfire over a city and the houses fall in the glare of its burning—even such was the roar and tramp of men and horses that pursued them as they bore Patroclus from the field. Or as mules that put forth all their strength to draw some beam or great piece of ship's timber down a rough mountain track, and they pant and sweat as they go—even so did Menelaus and Meriones pant and sweat as they bore the body of Patroclus. Behind them the two Ajaxes held stoutly out. As some wooded mountain spur that stretches across a plain will turn water and check the flow even of a great river, nor is there any stream strong enough to break through it—even so did the two Ajaxes face the Trojans and stem the tide of their fighting though they kept pouring on towards them—and foremost among them all was Aeneas, son of Anchises, with valiant Hector. As a flock of daws or starlings fall to screaming and chattering when they see a falcon, foe to all small birds, come soaring near them, even so did the Achaean youth raise a babel of cries as they fled before Aeneas and Hector, unmindful of their former prowess. In the rout of the Danaans much goodly armor fell round about the trench, and of fighting there was no end.

BOOK XVIII

Thetis promises Achilles, grief-stricken at Patroclus's death, to get him new armor. Achilles shows himself on the wall, shouting encouragement, and the Trojans fall back in terror. Patroclus's body is borne into the camp. In view of Achilles's reappearance, Polydamas advises Hector to draw the Trojans back to the shelter of the city walls. Hector refuses. The god Hephaestus forges magnificent new armor for Achilles.

THUS THEN DID THEY FIGHT AS IT WERE A FLAMING FIRE. Meanwhile, the fleet runner Antilochus, who had been sent as messenger, reached Achilles, and found him sitting by his tall ships and boding that which was indeed too surely true. "Alas," said he to himself in the heaviness of his heart, "why are the Achaeans again scouring the plain and flocking towards the ships? Heaven grant the gods be not now bringing that sorrow upon me of which my mother Thetis spoke, saying that while I was yet alive the bravest of the Myrmidons should fall before the Trojans and see the light of the sun no longer. I fear the brave son of Menoetius has fallen through his own daring—and yet I bade him return to the ships as soon as he had driven back those that were bringing fire against them, and not join battle with Hector."

As he was thus pondering, the son of Nestor came up to him and told his sad tale, weeping bitterly the while. "Alas," he cried, "son of noble Peleus, I bring you bad tidings! Would indeed that they were untrue. Patroclus has fallen, and a fight is raging about his naked body—for Hector holds his armor."

A dark cloud of grief fell upon Achilles as he listened. He filled both hands with dust from off the ground and poured it over his head, disfiguring his comely face and letting the refuse settle over his shirt so fair and new. He flung himself down all huge and hugely at full length and tore his hair with his hands. The bondswomen whom Achilles and Patroclus had taken captive screamed aloud for grief, beating their breasts, and with their limbs failing them for sorrow. Antilochus bent over him the while, weeping and holding both his hands as he lay groaning, for he feared that he might plunge a knife into his own throat.

Then Achilles gave a loud cry and his mother heard him as she was sitting in the depths of the sea by the old man her father, whereon she screamed, and all the goddesses, daughters of Nereus that dwelt at the bottom of the sea, came gathering round her. There were Glauce, Thalia and Cymodoce, Nesaia, Speo, Thoë and dark-eyed Halië, Cymothoë, Actaea and Limnorea, Melite, Iaera, Amphithoë and Agave, Doto and Proto, Pherusa and Dynamene, Dexamene, Amphinome and Callianeira, Doris, Panope, and the famous sea nymph Galatea, Nemertes, Apseudes, and Callianassa. There were also Clymene, Ianeira and Ianassa, Maera, Oreithuia and Amatheia of the lovely locks, with other Nereids who dwell in the depths of the sea. The crystal cave was filled with their multitude and they all beat their breasts while Thetis led them in their lament.

"Listen," she cried, "sisters, daughters of Nereus, that you may hear the burden of my sorrows! Alas, woe is me, woe in that I have borne the most glorious of offspring. I bore him fair and strong, hero among heroes, and he shot up as a sapling. I tended him as a plant in a goodly garden, and sent him with his ships to Ilium to fight the Trojans, but never shall I welcome him back to the house of Peleus. So long as he lives to look upon the light of the sun he is in heaviness, and though I go to him I cannot help him. Nevertheless, I will go, that I may see my dear son and learn what sorrow has befallen him though he is still holding aloof from battle."

She left the cave as she spoke, while the others followed weeping after, and the waves opened a path before them. When they reached the rich plain of Troy, they came up out of the sea in a long line on to the sands, at the place where the ships of the Myrmidons were drawn up in close order round the tents of Achilles. His mother went up to him as he lay groaning; she laid her hand upon his head and spoke piteously, saying: "My son, why are you thus weeping? What sorrow has now befallen you? Tell me; hide it not from me. Surely Zeus has granted you the prayer you made him, when you lifted up your hands and besought him that the Achaeans might all of them be pent up at their ships, and rue it bitterly in that you were no longer with them."

Achilles groaned and answered: "Mother, Olympian Zeus has indeed vouchsafed me the fulfillment of my prayer, but what boots it to me, seeing that my dear comrade Patroclus has fallen—he whom I valued more than all others and loved as dearly as my own life? I have lost him; aye, and Hector when he had killed him stripped him of the wondrous armor, so glorious to behold, which the gods gave to Peleus when they laid you in the couch of a mortal man. Would that you were still dwelling among the immortal sea nymphs, and that Peleus had taken to himself some mortal bride. For now you shall have grief infinite by reason of the death of that son whom you can never welcome home—nay, I will not live nor go about among mankind unless Hector fall by my spear, and thus pay me for having slain Patroclus, son of Menoetius."

Thetis wept and answered, "Then, my son, is your end near at hand—for your own death awaits you full soon after that of Hector."

Then said Achilles in his great grief: "I would die here and now, in that I could not save my comrade. He has fallen far from home, and in his hour of need my hand was not there to help him. What is there for me? Return to my own land I shall not, and I have brought no saving neither to Patroclus nor to my other comrades of whom so many have been slain by mighty Hector. I stay here by my ships a bootless burden upon the earth, I, who in fight have no peer among the Achaeans, though in counsel there are better than I. Therefore, perish strife both from among gods and men, and anger, wherein even a righteous man will harden his heart—which rises up in the soul of a man like smoke, and the taste thereof is sweeter than drops of honey. Even so has Agamemnon angered me. And yet—so be it, for it is over; I will force my soul into subjection as I needs must; I will go; I will pursue Hector, who has slain him whom I loved so dearly, and will then abide my doom when it may please Zeus and the other gods to send it. Even Heracles, the best loved of Zeus—even he could not escape the hand of death, but fate and Hera's fierce anger laid him low, as I too shall lie when I am dead if a like doom awaits me. Till then I will win fame and will bid Trojan and Dardanian women wring tears from their tender cheeks with both their hands in the grievousness of their great sorrow; thus shall they know that he who has held aloof so long will hold aloof no longer. Hold me not back, therefore, in the love you bear me, for you shall not move me."

Then silver-footed Thetis answered: "My son, what you have said is true. It is well to save your comrades from destruction, but your armor is in the hands of the Trojans. Hector bears it in triumph upon his own shoulders. Full well I know that his vaunt shall not be lasting, for his end is close at hand. Go not, however, into the press of battle till you see me return hither; tomorrow at break of day I shall be here, and will bring you goodly armor from King Hephaestus."

On this she left her brave son, and as she turned away she said to the sea nymphs, her sisters: "Dive into the bosom of the sea and go to the house of the old sea-god, my father. Tell him everything; as for me, I will go to the cunning workman Hephaestus on high Olympus, and ask him to provide my son with a suit of splendid armor."

When she had so said, they dived forthwith beneath the waves, while silver-footed Thetis went her way that she might bring the armor for her son.

Thus, then, did her feet bear the goddess to Olympus, and meanwhile the Achaeans were flying with loud cries before murderous Hector till they reached the ships and the Hellespont, and they could not draw the body of Ares's servant Patroclus out of reach of the weapons that were showered upon him, for Hector, son of Priam, with his host and horsemen had again caught up to him like the flame of a fiery furnace; thrice did brave Hector seize him by the feet, striving with might and main to draw him away and calling loudly on the Trojans, and thrice did the two Ajaxes, clothed in valor as with a garment, beat him from off the body; but all undaunted he would now charge into the thick of the fight, and now again he would stand still and cry aloud, but he would give no ground. As upland shepherds that cannot chase some famished lion from a carcass, even so could not the two Ajaxes scare Hector, son of Priam, from the body of Patroclus.

And now he would even have dragged it off and have won imperishable glory had not Iris, fleet as the wind, winged her way as messenger from Olympus to the son of Peleus and bidden him arm. She came secretly without the knowledge of Zeus and of the other gods, for Hera sent her, and when she had got close to him she said: "Up, son of Peleus, mightiest of all mankind! Rescue Patroclus about whom this fearful fight is now raging by the ships. Men are killing one another, the Danaans in defense of the dead body, while the Trojans are trying to hale it away, and take it to windy Ilium; Hector is the most furious of them all; he is for cutting the head from the body and fixing it on the stakes of the wall. Up, then, and bide here no longer; shrink from the thought that Patroclus may become meat for the dogs of Troy. Shame on you, should his body suffer any kind of outrage."

And Achilles said, "Iris, which of the gods was it that sent you to me?"

Iris answered, "It was Hera, the royal spouse of Zeus, but the son of Cronus does not know of my coming, nor yet does any other of the immortals who dwell on the snowy summits of Olympus."

Then fleet Achilles answered her, saying: "How can I go up into the battle? They have my armor. My mother forbade me to arm till I should see her come, for she promised to bring me goodly armor from Hephaestus; I know no man whose arms I can put on, save only the shield of Ajax, son of Telamon, and he surely must be fighting in the front rank and wielding his spear about the body of dead Patroclus."

Iris said: "We know that your armor has been taken, but go as you are; go to the deep trench and show yourself before the Trojans, that they may fear you and cease fighting. Thus will the fainting sons of the Achaeans gain some brief breathing time, which in battle may hardly be."

Iris left him when she had so spoken. But Achilles, dear to Zeus, arose, and Athene flung her tasseled aegis round his strong shoulders; she crowned his head with a halo of golden cloud from which she kindled a glow of gleaming fire. As the smoke that goes up into heaven from some city that is being beleaguered on an island far out at sea—all day long do men sally from the city and fight their hardest, and at the going down of the sun the line of beacon fires blazes forth, flaring high for those that dwell near them to behold, if so be that they may come with their ships and succor them—even so did the light flare from the head of Achilles, as he stood by the trench, going beyond the wall—but he did not join the Achaeans, for he heeded the charge which his mother laid upon him.

There did he stand and shout aloud. Athene also raised her voice from afar and spread terror unspeakable among the Trojans. Ringing as the note of a trumpet that sounds alarm when the foe is at the gates of a city, even so brazen was the voice of the son of Aeacus, and when the Trojans heard its clarion tones they were dismayed. The horses turned back with their chariots for they boded mischief, and their drivers were awestruck by the steady flame which the gray-eyed goddess had kindled above the head of the great son of Peleus.

Thrice did Achilles raise his loud cry as he stood by the trench, and thrice were the Trojans and their brave allies thrown into confusion; whereon twelve of their noblest champions fell beneath the wheels of their chariots and perished by their own spears. The Achaeans to their great joy then drew Patroclus out of reach of the weapons and laid him on a litter. His comrades stood mourning round him, and among them fleet Achilles who wept bitterly as he saw his true comrade lying dead upon his bier. He had sent him out with horses and chariots into battle, but his return he was not to welcome.

Then Hera sent the busy sun, loath though he was, into the waters of Oceanus; so he set, and the Achaeans had rest from the tug and turmoil of war.

Now the Trojans, when they had come out of the fight, unyoked their horses and gathered in assembly before preparing their supper. They kept their feet, nor would any dare to sit down, for fear had fallen upon them all because Achilles had shown himself after having held aloof so long from battle. Polydamas, son of Panthoüs, was first to speak, a man of judgment, who alone among them could look both before and after. He was comrade to Hector, and they had been born upon the same night. With all sincerity and goodwill, therefore, he addressed them thus:

"Look to it well, my friends; I would urge you to go back now to your city and not wait here by the ships till morning, for we are far from our walls. So long as this man was at enmity with Agamemnon the Achaeans were easier to deal with, and I would have gladly camped by the ships in the hope of taking them. But now I go in great fear of the fleet son of Peleus. He is so daring that he will never bide here on the plain whereon the Trojans and Achaeans fight with equal valor, but he will try to storm our city and carry off our women. Do then as I say, and let us retreat. For this is what will happen. The darkness of night will for a time stay the son of Peleus, but if he find us here in the morning when he sallies forth in full armor, we shall have knowledge of him in good earnest. Glad indeed will he be who can escape and get back to Ilium, and many a Trojan will become meat for dogs and vultures—may I never live to hear it. If we do as I say, little though we may like it, we shall have strength in counsel during the night, and the great gates with the doors that close them will protect the city. At dawn we can arm and take our stand on the walls. He will then rue it if he sallies from the ships to fight us. He will go back when he has given his horses their fill of being driven all whithers under our walls, and will be in no mind to try and force his way into the city. Neither will he ever sack it; dogs shall devour him ere he do so."

Hector looked fiercely at him and answered: "Polydamas, your words are not to my liking in that you bid us go back and be pent within the city. Have you not had enough of being cooped up behind walls? In the old days the city of Priam was famous the whole world over for its wealth of gold and bronze, but our treasures are wasted out of our houses, and much goods have been sold away to Phrygia and fair Meonia, for the hand of Zeus has been laid heavily upon us. Now, therefore, that the son of scheming Cronus has vouchsafed me to win glory here and to hem the Achaeans in at their ships, prate no more in this fool's wise among the people. You will have no man with you; it shall not be; do all of you as I now say; take your suppers in your companies throughout the host, and keep your watches and be wakeful every man of you. If any Trojan is uneasy about his possessions, let him gather them and give them out among the people. Better let these, rather than the Achaeans, have them. At daybreak we will arm and fight about the ships. Granted that Achilles has again come forward to defend them, let it be as he will, but it shall go hard with him. I shall not shun him, but will fight him, to fall or conquer. The god of war deals out like measure to all, and the slayer may yet be slain."

Thus spoke Hector, and the Trojans, fools that they were, shouted in applause, for Pallas Athene had robbed them of their understanding. They gave ear to Hector with his evil counsel, but the wise words of Polydamas no man would heed. They took their supper throughout the host, and meanwhile through the whole night the Achaeans mourned Patroclus, and the son of Peleus led them in their lament. He laid his murderous hands upon the breast of his comrade, groaning again and again as a bearded lion when a man who was chasing deer has robbed him of his young in some dense forest. When the lion comes back he is furious, and searches dingle and dell to track the hunter if he can find him, for he is mad with rage—even so with many a sigh did Achilles speak among the Myrmidons, saying: "Alas! vain were the words with which I cheered the hero Menoetius in his own house; I said that I would bring his brave son back again to Opöeis after he had sacked Ilium and taken his share of the spoils—but Zeus does not give all men their heart's desire. The same soil shall be reddened here at Troy by the blood of us both, for I too shall never be welcomed home by the old knight Peleus, nor by my mother Thetis, but even in this place shall the earth cover me. Nevertheless, O Patroclus, now that I am left behind you, I will not bury you till I have brought hither the head and armor of mighty Hector who has slain you. Twelve noble sons of Trojans will I behead before your bier to avenge you; till I have done so you shall lie as you are by the ships, and fair women of Troy and Dardanus, whom we have taken with spear and strength of arm when we sacked men's goodly cities, shall weep over you both night and day."

Then Achilles told his men to set a large tripod upon the fire that they might wash the clotted gore from off Patroclus. Thereon they set a tripod full of bath water on to a clear fire; they threw sticks on to it to make a blaze, and the water became hot as the flame played about the belly of the tripod. When the water in the cauldron was boiling they washed the body, anointed it with oil, and closed its wounds with ointment that had been kept nine years. Then they laid it on a bier and covered it with a linen cloth from head to foot, and over this they laid a fair white robe. Thus all night long did the Myrmidons gather round Achilles to mourn Patroclus.

Then Zeus said to Hera, his sister-wife: "So, Queen Hera, you have gained your end, and have roused fleet Achilles. One would think that the Achaeans were of your own flesh and blood."

And Hera answered: "Dread son of Cronus, why should you say this thing? May not a man though he be only mortal and knows less than we do, do what he can for another person? And shall not I—foremost of all goddesses both by descent and as wife to you who reign in heaven—devise evil for the Trojans if I am angry with them?"

Thus did they converse. Meanwhile Thetis came to the house of Hephaestus, imperishable, star-bespangled, fairest of the abodes in heaven, a house of bronze wrought by the lame god's own hands. She found him busy with his bellows, sweating and hard at work, for he was making twenty tripods that were to stand by the wall of his house, and he set wheels of gold under them all that they might go of their own selves to the assemblies of the gods, and come back again—marvels indeed to see. They were finished all but the ears of cunning workmanship which yet remained to be fixed to them; these he was now fixing, and he was hammering at the rivets. While he was thus at work, silver-footed Thetis came to the house. Charis, of graceful headdress, wife to the far-famed lame god, came towards her as soon as she saw her and took her hand in her own, saying: "Why have you come to our house, Thetis, honored and ever welcomed? for you do not visit us often. Come inside and let me set refreshment before you."

The goddess led the way as she spoke and bade Thetis sit on a richly decorated seat inlaid with silver; there was a footstool also under her feet. Then she called Hephaestus and said, "Hephaestus, come here, Thetis wants you"; and the far-famed lame god answered: "Then it is indeed an august and honored goddess who has come here; she it was that took care of me when I was suffering from the heavy fall which I had through my cruel mother's anger—for she would have got rid of me because I was lame. It would have gone hardly with me had not Eurynome, daughter of the ever-encircling waters of Oceanus, and Thetis taken me to their bosom. Nine years did I stay with them, and many beautiful works in bronze, brooches, spiral armlets, cups, and chains did I make for them in their cave, with the roaring waters of Oceanus foaming as they rushed ever past it; and no one knew, neither of gods nor men, save only Thetis and Eurynome who took care of me. If, then, Thetis has come to my house I must make her due requital for having saved me. Entertain her, therefore, with all hospitality, while I put by my bellows and all my tools."

On this the mighty monster hobbled off from his anvil, his thin legs plying lustily under him. He set the bellows away from the fire and gathered his tools into a silver chest. Then he took a sponge and washed his face and hands, his shaggy chest and brawny neck; he donned his shirt, grasped his strong staff, and limped towards the door. There were golden handmaids also who worked for him and were like real young women, with sense and reason, voice also and strength, and all the learning of the immortals. These busied themselves as the king bade them, while he drew near to Thetis, seated her upon a goodly seat, and took her hand in his own, saying: "Why have you come to our house, Thetis honored and ever welcome?—for you do not visit us often. Say what you want, and I will do it for you at once if I can, and if it can be done at all."

Thetis wept and answered: "Hephaestus, is there another goddess in Olympus whom the son of Cronus has been pleased to try with so much affliction as he has me? Me alone of the marine goddesses did he make subject to a mortal husband, Peleus, son of Aeacus, and sorely against my will did I submit to the embraces of one who was but mortal, and who now stays at home worn out with age. Neither is this all. Heaven vouchsafed me a son, hero among heroes, and he shot up as a sapling. I tended him as a plant in a goodly garden and sent him with his ships to Ilium to fight the Trojans, but never shall I welcome him back to the house of Peleus. So long as he lives to look upon the light of the sun, he is in heaviness, and though I go to him I cannot help him. King Agamemnon has made him give up the maiden whom the sons of the Achaeans had awarded him, and he wastes with sorrow for her sake.

"Then the Trojans hemmed the Achaeans in at their ships' sterns and would not let them come forth. The elders, therefore, of the Argives besought Achilles and offered him great treasure, whereon he refused to bring deliverance to them himself, but put his own armor on Patroclus and sent him into the fight with much people after him. All day long they fought by the Scaean gates and would have taken the city there and then had not Apollo vouchsafed glory to Hector and slain the valiant son of Menoetius after he had done the Trojans much evil. Therefore I am suppliant at your knees if haply you may be pleased to provide my son, whose end is near at hand, with helmet and shield, with goodly greaves fitted with ankle-clasps, and with a breastplate, for he lost his own when his true comrade fell at the hands of the Trojans, and he now lies stretched on earth in the bitterness of his soul."

And Hephaestus answered: "Take heart, and be no more disquieted about this matter. Would that I could hide him from death's sight when his hour is come, so surely as I can find him armor that shall amaze the eyes of all who behold it."

When he had so said he left her and went to his bellows, turning them towards the fire and bidding them do their office. Twenty bellows blew upon the melting pots, and they blew blasts of every kind, some fierce to help him when he had need of them, and others less strong as Hephaestus willed it in the course of his work. He threw tough copper into the fire, and tin, with silver and gold. He set his great anvil on its block, and with one hand grasped his mighty hammer while he took the tongs in the other.

First he shaped the shield so great and strong, adorning it all over and binding it round with a gleaming circuit in three layers; and the baldric was made of silver. He made the shield in five thicknesses, and with many a wonder did his cunning hand enrich it.

He wrought the earth, the heavens, and the sea; the moon also at her full and the untiring sun, with all the signs that glorify the face of heaven—the Pleiades, the Hyades, huge Orion, and the Bear, which men also call the Wain and which turns round ever in one place, facing Orion, and alone never dips into the stream of Oceanus.

He wrought also two cities, fair to see and busy with the hum of men. In the one were weddings and wedding feasts, and they were going about the city with brides whom they were escorting by torchlight from their chambers. Loud rose the cry of Hymen, and the youths danced to the music of flute and lyre, while the women stood each at her house door to see them.

Meanwhile the people were gathered in assembly, for there was a quarrel, and two men were wrangling about the blood money for a man who had been killed, the one saying before the people that he had paid damages in full and the other that he had not been paid. Each was trying to make his own case good, and the people took sides, each man backing the side that he had taken; but the heralds kept them back, and the elders sate on their seats of stone in a solemn circle, holding the staves which the heralds had put into their hands. Then they rose and each in his turn gave judgment, and there were two talents laid down, to be given to him whose judgment should be deemed the fairest.

About the other city there lay encamped two hosts in gleaming armor, and they were divided whether to sack it, or to spare it and accept the half of what it contained. But the men of the city would not yet consent, and armed themselves for a surprise; their wives and little children kept guard upon the walls, and with them were the men who were past fighting through age; but the others sallied forth with Ares and Pallas Athene at their head—both of them wrought in gold and clad in golden raiment, great and fair with their armor as befitting gods, while they that followed were smaller. When they reached the place where they would lay their ambush, it was on a riverbed to which livestock of all kinds would come from far and near to water. Here, then, they lay concealed, clad in full armor. Some way off them there were two scouts who were on the lookout for the coming of sheep or cattle, which presently came, followed by two shepherds who were playing on their pipes, and had not so much as a thought of danger. When those who were in ambush saw this, they cut off the flocks and herds and killed the shepherds.

Meanwhile the besiegers, when they heard much noise among the cattle as they sat in council, sprang to their horses, and made with all speed towards them. When they reached them they set battle in array by the banks of the river, and the hosts aimed their bronze-shod spears at one another. With them were Strife and Riot, and fell Fate who was dragging three men after her, one with a fresh wound, and the other unwounded, while the third was dead, and she was dragging him along by his heel: and her robe was bedrabbled in men's blood. They went in and out with one another and fought as though they were living people haling away one another's dead.

He wrought also a fair fallow field, large and thrice ploughed already. Many men were working at the plough within it, turning their oxen to and fro, furrow after furrow. Each time that they turned on reaching the headland a man would come up to them and give them a cup of wine, and they would go back to their furrows looking forward to the time when they should again reach the headland. The part that they had ploughed was dark behind them, so that the field, though it was of gold, still looked as if it were being ploughed—very curious to behold.

He wrought also a field of harvest corn, and the reapers were reaping with sharp sickles in their hands. Swathe after swathe fell to the ground in a straight line behind them, and the binders bound them in bands of twisted straw. There were three binders, and behind them there were boys who gathered the cut corn in armfuls and kept on bringing them to be bound. Among them all the owner of the land stood by in silence and was glad. The servants were getting a meal ready under an oak, for they had sacrificed a great ox and were busy cutting him up while the women were making a porridge of much white barley for the laborers' dinner.

He wrought also a vineyard, golden and fair to see, and the vines were loaded with grapes. The bunches overhead were black, but the vines were trained on poles of silver. He ran a ditch of dark metal all round it and fenced it with a fence of tin; there was only one path to it, and by this the vintagers went when they would gather the vintage. Youths and maidens all blithe and full of glee carried the luscious fruit in plaited baskets, and with them there went a boy who made sweet music with his lyre and sang the Linus-song with his clear boyish voice.

He wrought also a herd of horned cattle. He made the cows of gold and tin, and they lowed as they came full speed out of the yards to go and feed among the waving reeds that grow by the banks of the river. Along with the cattle there went four shepherds, all of them in gold, and their nine fleet dogs went with them. Two terrible lions had fastened on a bellowing bull that was with the foremost cows, and bellow as he might they haled him, while the dogs and men gave chase. The lions tore through the bull's thick hide and were gorging on his blood and bowels, but the herdsmen were afraid to do anything, and only hounded on their dogs; the dogs dared not fasten on the lions but stood by barking and keeping out of harm's way.

The god wrought also a pasture in a fair mountain dell, and a large flock of sheep, with a homestead and huts, and sheltered sheepfolds.

Furthermore, he wrought a green, like that which Daedalus once made in Cnossus for lovely Ariadne. Hereon there danced youths and maidens whom all would woo, with their hands on one another's wrists. The maidens wore robes of light linen, and the youths well-woven shirts that were slightly oiled. The girls were crowned with garlands, while the young men had daggers of gold that hung by silver baldrics. Sometimes they would dance deftly in a ring with merry twinkling feet, as it were a potter sitting at his work and making trial of his wheel to see whether it will run, and sometimes they would go all in line with one another, and much people were gathered joyously about the green. There was a bard also to sing to them and play his lyre, while two tumblers went about performing in the midst of them when the man struck up with his tune.

All round the outermost rim of the shield he set the mighty stream of the river Oceanus.

Then when he had fashioned the shield so great and strong, he made a breastplate also that shone brighter than fire. He made a helmet, close fitting to the brow, and richly worked, with a golden plume overhanging it; and he made greaves also of beaten tin.

Lastly, when the famed lame god had made all the armor, he took it and set it before the mother of Achilles; whereon she darted like a falcon from the snowy summits of Olympus and bore away the gleaming armor from the house of Hephaestus.

BOOK XIX

With the morning Thetis brings new armor to Achilles, who calls all the Greeks to an assembly on the beach and is reconciled to Agamemnon. Agamemnon expresses regret for his folly, and sends the girl Briseis with rich gifts back to Achilles's tent. The Greek army eats and prepares for battle. As Achilles dons his armor and springs into his chariot, his horse Xanthus warns him of his own approaching death.

NOW WHEN DAWN IN ROBE OF SAFFRON WAS HASTING FROM the streams of Oceanus, to bring light to mortals and immortals, Thetis reached the ships with the armor that the god had given her. She found her son fallen about the body of Patroclus and weeping bitterly. Many also of his followers were weeping round him, but when the goddess came among them she clasped his hand in her own, saying, "My son, grieve as we may we must let this man lie, for it is by heaven's will that he has fallen; now, therefore, accept from Hephaestus this rich and goodly armor, which no man has ever yet borne upon his shoulders."

As she spoke she set the armor before Achilles, and it rang out bravely as she did so. The Myrmidons were struck with awe, and none dared look full at it, for they were afraid; but Achilles was roused to still greater fury, and his eyes gleamed with a fierce light, for he was glad when he handled the splendid present which the god had made him. Then, as soon as he had satisfied himself with looking at it, he said to his mother: "Mother, the god has given me armor, meet handiwork for an immortal and such as no man living could have fashioned. I will now arm, but I much fear that flies will settle upon the son of Menoetius and breed worms about his wounds, so that his body, now he is dead, will be disfigured and the flesh will rot."

Silver-footed Thetis answered: "My son, be not disquieted about this matter. I will find means to protect him from the swarms of noisome flies that prey on the bodies of men who have been killed in battle. He may lie for a whole year, and his flesh shall still be as sound as ever, or even sounder. Call, therefore, the Achaean heroes in assembly. Unsay your anger against Agamemnon. Arm at once, and fight with might and main."

As she spoke she put strength and courage into his heart, and she then dropped ambrosia and red nectar into the wounds of Patroclus, that his body might suffer no change.

Then Achilles went out upon the seashore, and with a loud cry called on the Achaean heroes. On this even those who as yet had stayed always at the ships, the pilots and helmsmen, and even the stewards who were about the ships and served out rations, all came to the place of assembly because Achilles had shown himself after having held aloof so long from fighting. Two sons of Ares, Odysseus and the son of Tydeus, came limping, for their wounds still pained them; nevertheless they came, and took their seats in the front row of the assembly. Last of all came Agamemnon, king of men, he too wounded, for Coön, son of Antenor, had struck him with a spear in battle.

When the Achaeans were got together Achilles rose and said: "Son of Atreus, surely it would have been better alike for both you and me, when we two were in such high anger about Briseis, surely it would have been better had Artemis's arrow slain her at the ships on the day when I took her after having sacked Lyrnessus. For so, many an Achaean the less would have bitten dust before the foe in the days of my anger. It has been well for Hector and the Trojans, but the Achaeans will long indeed remember our quarrel. Now, however, let it be, for it is over. If we have been angry, necessity has schooled our anger. I put it from me: I dare not nurse it forever. Therefore, bid the Achaeans arm forthwith that I may go out against the Trojans, and learn whether they will be in a mind to sleep by the ships or no. Glad, I ween, will he be to rest his knees who may fly my spear when I wield it."

Thus did he speak, and the Achaeans rejoiced in that he had put away his anger.

Then Agamemnon spoke, rising in his place, and not going into the middle of the assembly. "Danaan heroes," said he, "servants of Ares, it is well to listen when a man stands up to speak, and it is not seemly to interrupt him, or it will go hard even with a practiced speaker. Who can either hear or speak in an uproar? Even the finest orator will be disconcerted by it. I will expound to the son of Peleus, and do you other Achaeans heed me and mark me well. Often have the Achaeans spoken to me of this matter and upbraided me, but it was not I that did it: Zeus, and Fate, and Erinys that walks in darkness struck me mad when we were assembled on the day that I took from Achilles the meed that had been awarded to him. What could I do? All things are in the hand of heaven, and Folly, eldest of Zeus's daughters, shuts men's eyes to their destruction. She walks delicately, not on the solid earth, but hovers over the heads of men to make them stumble or to ensnare them.

"Time was when she fooled Zeus himself, who, they say, is greatest whether of gods or men; for Hera, woman though she was, beguiled him on the day when Alcmena was to bring forth mighty Heracles in the fair city of Thebes. He told it out among the gods, saying, 'Hear me all gods and goddesses, that I may speak even as I am minded; this day shall an Ilithuia, helper of women who are in labor, bring a man-child into the world who shall be lord over all that dwell about him who are of my blood and lineage.' Then said Hera, all crafty and full of guile, 'You will play false, and will not hold to your word. Swear me, O Olympian, swear me a great oath that he who shall this day fall between the feet of a woman shall be lord over all that dwell about him who are of your blood and lineage.'

"Thus she spoke, and Zeus suspected her not, but swore the great oath, to his much ruing thereafter. For Hera darted down from the high summit of Olympus and went in haste to Achaean Argos where she knew that the noble wife of Sthenelus, son of Perseus, then was. She being with child and in her seventh month, Hera brought the child to birth though there was a month still wanting, but she stayed the offspring of Alcmena and kept back the Ilithuiae. Then she went to tell Zeus, the son of Cronus, and said, 'Father Zeus, lord of the lightning—I have a word for your ear. There is a fine child born this day, Eurystheus, son to Sthenelus, the son of Perseus. He is of your lineage; it is well, therefore, that he should reign over the Argives.'

"On this Zeus was stung to the very quick, and in his rage he caught Folly by the hair, and swore a great oath that never should she again invade starry heaven and Olympus, for she was the bane of all. Then he whirled her round with a twist of his hand and flung her down from heaven so that she fell on to the fields of mortal men; and he was ever angry with her when he saw his son groaning under the cruel labors that Eurystheus laid upon him. Even so did I grieve when mighty Hector was killing the Argives at their ships, and all the time I kept thinking of Folly who had so baned me. I was blind, and Zeus robbed me of my reason. I will now make atonement, and will add much treasure by way of amends. Go, therefore, into battle, you and your people with you. I will give you all that Odysseus offered you yesterday in your tents; or, if it so please you, wait, though you would fain fight at once, and my squires shall bring the gifts from my ship, that you may see whether what I give you is enough."

And Achilles answered: "Son of Atreus, king of men, Agamemnon, you can give such gifts as you think proper, or you can withhold them: it is in your own hands. Let us now set battle in array.

It is not well to tarry talking about trifles, for there is a deed which is as yet to do. Achilles shall again be seen fighting among the foremost, and laying low the ranks of the Trojans: bear this in mind each one of you when he is fighting."

Then Odysseus said: "Achilles, godlike and brave, send not the Achaeans thus against Ilium to fight the Trojans fasting, for the battle will be no brief one, when it is once begun, and heaven has filled both sides with fury; bid them first take food, both bread and wine, by the ships, for in this there is strength and stay. No man can do battle the livelong day to the going down of the sun if he is without food. However much he may want to fight his strength will fail him before he knows it; hunger and thirst will find him out, and his limbs will grow weary under him. But a man can fight all day if he is full fed with meat and wine; his heart beats high, and his strength will stay till he has routed all his foes. Therefore, send the people away and bid them prepare their meal. King Agamemnon will bring out the gifts in presence of the assembly, that all may see them and you may be satisfied. Moreover, let him swear an oath before the Argives that he has never gone up into the couch of Briseis, nor been with her after the manner of men and women; and do you, too, show yourself of a gracious mind. Let Agamemnon entertain you in his tents with a feast of reconciliation, that so you may have had your dues in full. As for you, son of Atreus, treat people more righteously in future. It is no disgrace even to a king that he should make amends if he was wrong in the first instance."

And King Agamemnon answered: "Son of Laertes, your words please me well, for throughout you have spoken wisely. I will swear as you would have me do; I do so of my own free will, neither shall I take the name of heaven in vain. Let, then, Achilles wait, though he would fain fight at once, and do you others wait also, till the gifts come from my tent and we ratify the oath with sacrifice. Thus, then, do I charge you: take some noble young Achaeans with you, and bring from my tents the gifts that I promised yesterday to Achilles, and bring the women also. Furthermore, let

Talthybius find me a boar from those that are with the host, and make it ready for sacrifice to Zeus and to the sun."

Then said Achilles: "Son of Atreus, king of men, Agamemnon, see to these matters at some other season, when there is breathing time and when I am calmer. Would you have men eat while the bodies of those whom Hector, son of Priam, slew are still lying mangled upon the plain? Let the sons of the Achaeans, say I, fight fasting and without food, till we have avenged them; afterwards at the going down of the sun let them eat their fill. As for me, Patroclus is lying dead in my tent, all hacked and hewn, with his feet to the door, and his comrades are mourning round him. Therefore I can take thought of nothing save only slaughter and blood and the rattle in the throat of the dying."

Odysseus answered: "Achilles, son of Peleus, mightiest of all the Achaeans, in battle you are better than I, and that more than a little, but in counsel I am much before you, for I am older and of greater knowledge. Therefore be patient under my words. Fighting is a thing of which men soon surfeit, and when Zeus, who is war's steward, weighs the upshot, it may well prove that the straw which our sickles have reaped is far heavier than the grain. It may not be that the Achaeans should mourn the dead with their bellies; day by day men fall thick and threefold continually. When should we have respite from our sorrow? Let us mourn our dead for a day and bury them out of sight and mind, but let those of us who are left eat and drink that we may arm and fight our foes more fiercely. In that hour let no man hold back, waiting for a second summons; such summons shall bode ill for him who is found lagging behind at our ships. Let us rather sally as one man and loose the fury of war upon the Trojans."

When he had thus spoken he took with him the sons of Nestor, with Meges, son of Phyleus, Thoas, Meriones, Lycomedes, son of Creontes, and Melanippus, and went to the tent of Agamemnon, son of Atreus. The word was not sooner said than the deed was done. They brought out the seven tripods which Agamemnon had promised, with the twenty metal cauldrons and the twelve horses; they also brought the women skilled in useful arts, seven in number, with Briseis, which made eight. Odysseus weighed out the ten talents of gold and then led the way back, while the young Achaeans brought the rest of the gifts and laid them in the middle of the assembly.

Agamemnon then rose, and Talthybius, whose voice was like that of a god, came up to him with the boar. The son of Atreus drew the knife which he wore by the scabbard of his mighty sword, and began by cutting off some bristles from the boar, lifting up his hands in prayer as he did so. The other Achaeans sat where they were all silent and orderly to hear the king, and Agamemnon looked into the vault of heaven and prayed, saying: "I call Zeus, the first and mightiest of all gods, to witness, I call also Earth and Sun and the Erinyes who dwell below and take vengeance on him who shall swear falsely, that I have laid no hand upon the girl Briseis, neither to take her to my bed nor otherwise, but that she has remained in my tents inviolate. If I swear falsely may heaven visit me with all the penalties which it metes out to those who perjure themselves."

He cut the boar's throat as he spoke, whereon Talthybius whirled it round his head, and flung it into the wide sea to feed the fishes. Then Achilles also rose and said to the Argives: "Father Zeus, of a truth you blind men's eyes and bane them. The son of Atreus had not else stirred me to so fierce an anger, nor so stubbornly taken Briseis from me against my will. Surely Zeus must have counseled the destruction of many an Argive. Go, now, and take your food that we may begin fighting."

On this he broke up the assembly, and every man went back to his own ship. The Myrmidons attended to the presents and took them away to the ship of Achilles. They placed them in his tents, while the stablemen drove the horses in among the others.

Briseis, fair as Aphrodite, when she saw the mangled body of Patroclus, flung herself upon it and cried aloud, tearing her breast, her neck, and her lovely face with both her hands. Beautiful as a goddess she wept and said: "Patroclus, dearest friend, when I went hence I left you living; I return, O prince, to find you dead; thus do fresh sorrows multiply upon me one after the other.

I saw him to whom my father and mother married me cut down before our city, and my three own dear brothers perished with him on the selfsame day; but you, Patroclus, even when Achilles slew my husband and sacked the city of noble Mynes, told me that I was not to weep, for you said you would make Achilles marry me, and take me back with him to Phthia, where we should have a wedding feast among the Myrmidons. You were always kind to me and I shall never cease to grieve for you."

She wept as she spoke, and the women joined in her lament—making as though their tears were for Patroclus, but in truth each was weeping for her own sorrows. The elders of the Achaeans gathered round Achilles and prayed him to take food, but he groaned and would not do so. "I pray you," said he, "if any comrade will hear me, bid me neither eat nor drink, for I am in great heaviness, and will stay fasting even to the going down of the sun."

On this he sent the other princes away, save only the two sons of Atreus, Odysseus, Nestor, Idomeneus, and the old knight Phoenix, who stayed behind and tried to comfort him in the bitterness of his sorrow; but he would not be comforted till he should have flung himself into the jaws of battle, and he fetched sigh on sigh, thinking ever of Patroclus. Then he said:

"Hapless and dearest comrade, you it was who would get a good dinner ready for me at once and without delay when the Achaeans were hasting to fight the Trojans; now, therefore, though I have meat and drink in my tents, yet will I fast for sorrow. Grief greater than this I could not know, not even though I were to hear of the death of my father, who is now in Phthia weeping for the loss of me his son, who am here fighting the Trojans in a strange land for the accursed sake of Helen, nor yet though I should hear that my son is no more—he who is being brought up in Scyros—if indeed Neoptolemus is still living. Till now I made sure that I alone was to fall here at Troy away from Argos, while you were to return to Phthia, bring back my son with you in your own ship, and show him all my property, my bondsmen, and the greatness of my house—for Peleus must surely be either dead, or what little life remains to him is oppressed alike with the infirmities of age and ever-present fear lest he should hear the sad tidings of my death."

He wept as he spoke, and the elders sighed in concert as each thought on what he had left at home behind him. The son of Cronus looked down with pity upon them, and said presently to Athene: "My child, you have quite deserted your hero. Is he then gone so clean out of your recollection? There he sits by the ships all desolate for the loss of his dear comrade, and though the others are gone to their dinner he will neither eat nor drink. Go then and drop nectar and ambrosia into his breast, that he may know no hunger."

With these words he urged Athene, who was already of the same mind. She darted down from heaven into the air like some falcon sailing on his broad wings and screaming. Meanwhile the Achaeans were arming throughout the host, and when Athene had dropped nectar and ambrosia into Achilles so that no cruel hunger should cause his limbs to fail him, she went back to the house of her mighty father. Thick as the chill snowflakes shed from the hand of Zeus and borne on the keen blasts of the north wind, even so thick did the gleaming helmets, the bossed shields, the strongly plated breastplates, and the ashen spears stream from the ships. The sheen pierced the sky, the whole land was radiant with their flashing armor, and the sound of the tramp of their treading rose from under their feet. In the midst of them all Achilles put on his armor. He gnashed his teeth, his eyes gleamed like fire, for his grief was greater than he could bear. Thus, then, full of fury against the Trojans, did he don the gift of the god, the armor that Hephaestus had made him.

First he put on the goodly greaves fitted with ankle-clasps, and next he did on the breastplate about his chest. He slung the silver-studded sword of bronze about his shoulders, and then took up the shield so great and strong that shone afar with a splendor as of the moon. As the light seen by sailors from out at sea, when men have lit a fire in their homestead high up among the mountains, but the sailors are carried out to sea by wind and storm far from the haven where they would be—even so did the gleam of

Achilles's wondrous shield strike up into the heavens. He lifted the redoubtable helmet, and set it upon his head, from whence it shone like a star, and the golden plumes which Hephaestus had set thick about the ridge of the helmet waved all around it. Then Achilles made trial of himself in his armor to see whether it fitted him, so that his limbs could play freely under it, and it seemed to buoy him up as though it had been wings.

He also drew his father's spear out of the spear stand, a spear so great and heavy and strong that none of the Achaeans save only Achilles had strength to wield it. This was the spear of Pelian ash from the topmost ridges of Mount Pelion, which Chiron had once given to Peleus, fraught with the death of heroes. Automedon and Alcimus busied themselves with the harnessing of his horses; they made the bands fast about them, and put the bit in their mouths, drawing the reins back towards the chariot. Automedon, whip in hand, sprang up behind the horses, and after him Achilles mounted in full armor, resplendent as the sun-god Hyperion. Then with a loud voice he chided with his father's horses, saying, "Xanthus and Balius, famed offspring of Podarge—this time when we have done fighting be sure and bring your driver safely back to the host of the Achaeans, and do not leave him dead on the plain as you did Patroclus."

Then fleet Xanthus answered from under the yoke—for white-armed Hera had endowed him with human speech—and he bowed his head till his mane touched the ground as it hung down from under the yoke-band. "Dread Achilles," said he, "we will indeed save you now, but the day of your death is near, and the blame will not be ours, for it will be heaven and stern fate that will destroy you. Neither was it through any sloth or slackness on our part that the Trojans stripped Patroclus of his armor. It was the mighty god whom lovely Leto bore that slew him as he fought among the foremost, and vouchsafed a triumph to Hector. We two can fly as swiftly as Zephyrus who they say is fleetest of all winds; nevertheless it is your doom to fall by the hand of a man and of a god."

When he had thus said the Erinyes stayed his speech, and Achilles answered him in great sadness, saying, "Why, O Xanthus, do you thus foretell my death? You need not do so, for I well know that I am to fall here, far from my dear father and mother; none the more, however, shall I stay my hand till I have given the Trojans their fill of fighting."

So saying, with a loud cry he drove his horses to the front.

BOOK XX

Zeus informs the gods that they are now free to take what part they please in the conflict. Apollo incites Aeneas to attack Achilles, but Poseidon intervenes and carries Aeneas off to safety. Apollo delivers Hector from quick death at Achilles's hands. Achilles rages over the field and kills many Trojans.

Thus, then, did the Achaeans arm by their ships round you, O son of Peleus, who were hungering for battle; while the Trojans over against them armed upon the rise of the plain.

Meanwhile Zeus, from the top of many-delled Olympus, bade Themis gather the gods in council, whereon she went about and called them to the house of Zeus. There was not a river absent except Oceanus, nor a single one of the nymphs that haunt fair groves, or springs of rivers and meadows of green grass. When they reached the house of cloud-compelling Zeus, they took their seats in the arcades of polished marble which Hephaestus with his consummate skill had made for father Zeus.

In such wise, therefore, did they gather in the house of Zeus. Poseidon also, lord of the earthquake, obeyed the call of the goddess, and came up out of the sea to join them. There, sitting in the midst of them, he asked what Zeus's purpose might be. "Why," said he, "wielder of the lightning, have you called the gods in council? Are you considering some matter that concerns the Trojans and Achaeans—for the blaze of battle is on the point of being kindled between them?"

And Zeus answered: "You know my purpose, shaker of earth, and wherefore I have called you hither. I take thought for them even in their destruction. For my own part I shall stay here seated on Mount Olympus and look on in peace, but do you others go about among Trojans and Achaeans and help either side as you may be severally disposed. If Achilles fights the Trojans without hindrance they will make no stand against him. They have ever trembled at the sight of him, and now that he is roused to such fury about his comrade, he will override fate itself and storm their city."

Thus spoke Zeus and gave the word for war, whereon the gods took their several sides and went into battle. Hera, Pallas Athene, earth-encircling Poseidon, Hermes, bringer of good luck and excellent in all cunning—all these joined the host that came from the ships; with them also came Hephaestus in all his glory, limping, but yet with his thin legs plying lustily under him. Ares of gleaming helmet joined the Trojans, and with him Apollo of locks unshorn, and the archer-goddess Artemis, Leto, Xanthus, and laughter-loving Aphrodite.

So long as the gods held themselves aloof from mortal warriors the Achaeans were triumphant, for Achilles who had long refused to fight was now with them. There was not a Trojan but his limbs failed him for fear as he beheld the fleet son of Peleus all glorious in his armor, and looking like Ares himself. When, however, the Olympians came to take their part among men, forthwith uprose strong Strife, rouser of hosts, and Athene raised her loud voice, now standing by the deep trench that ran outside the wall and now shouting with all her might upon the shore of the sounding sea. Ares also bellowed out upon the other side, dark as some black thundercloud, and called on the Trojans at the top of his voice, now from the acropolis and now speeding up the side of the river Simois, till he came to the hill Callicolone.

Thus did the gods spur on both hosts to fight, and rouse fierce contention also among themselves. The sire of gods and men thundered from heaven above, while from beneath Poseidon shook the vast earth, and bade the high hills tremble. The spurs and crests of many-fountained Ida quaked, as also the city of the Trojans and the ships of the Achaeans. Hades, king of the realms below, was struck with fear; he sprang panic-stricken from his throne and cried aloud in terror lest Poseidon, lord of the earthquake, should crack the ground over his head, and lay bare his moldy mansions to the sight of mortals and immortals—mansions so ghastly grim that even the gods shudder to think of them. Such was the uproar as the gods came together in battle. Apollo with his arrows took his stand to face King Poseidon, while Athene took hers against the god of war; the archer goddess Artemis with her golden arrows, sister of far-darting Apollo, stood to face Hera; Hermes, the lusty bringer of good luck, faced Leto, while the mighty eddying river whom men call Scamander, but gods Xanthus, matched himself against Hephaestus.

The gods, then, were thus ranged against one another. But the heart of Achilles was set on meeting Hector, son of Priam, for it was with his blood that he longed above all things else to glut the stubborn lord of battle. Meanwhile, Apollo set Aeneas on to attack the son of Peleus, and put courage into his heart, speaking with the voice of Lycaon, son of Priam. In his likeness, therefore, he said to Aeneas, "Aeneas, counselor of the Trojans, where are now the brave words with which you vaunted over your wine before the Trojan princes, saying that you would fight Achilles, son of Peleus, in single combat?"

And Aeneas answered: "Why do you thus bid me fight the proud son of Peleus, when I am in no mind to do so? Were I to face him now, it would not be for the first time. His spear has already put me to flight from Ida, when he attacked our cattle and sacked Lyrnessus and Pedasus. Zeus indeed saved me in that he vouchsafed me strength to fly, else had I fallen by the hands of Achilles and Athene, who went before him to protect him and urged him to fall upon the Lelegae and Trojans. No man may fight Achilles, for one of the gods is always with him as his guardian angel, and even were it not so, his weapon flies ever straight, and fails not to pierce the flesh of him who is against him. If heaven would let me fight him on even terms he should not soon overcome me, though he boasts that he is made of bronze."

Then said King Apollo, son to Zeus: "Nay, hero, pray to the ever-living gods, for men say that you were born of Zeus's daughter Aphrodite, whereas Achilles is son to a goddess of inferior rank. Aphrodite is child to Zeus, while Thetis is but daughter to the old man of the sea. Bring, therefore, your spear to bear upon him, and let him not scare you with his taunts and menaces."

As he spoke he put courage into the heart of the shepherd of his people, and he strode in full armor among the ranks of the foremost fighters. Nor did the son of Anchises escape the notice of white-armed Hera, as he went forth into the throng to meet Achilles. She called the gods about her, and said: "Look to it, you two, Poseidon and Athene, and consider how this shall be; Phoebus Apollo has been sending Aeneas clad in full armor to fight Achilles. Shall we turn him back at once, or shall one of us stand by Achilles and endow him with strength so that his heart fail not, and he may learn that the chiefs of the immortals are on his side, while the others who have all along been defending the Trojans are but vain helpers? Let us all come down from Olympus and join in the fight, that this day he may take no hurt at the hands of the Trojans. Hereafter let him suffer whatever fate may have spun out for him when he was begotten and his mother bore him. If Achilles be not thus assured by the voice of a god, he may come to fear presently when one of us meets him in battle, for the gods are terrible if they are seen face to face."

Poseidon, lord of the earthquake, answered her, saying: "Hera, restrain your fury; it is not well. I am not in favor of forcing the other gods to fight us, for the advantage is too greatly on our own side. Let us take our places on some hill out of the beaten track, and let mortals fight it out among themselves. If Ares or Phoebus Apollo begin fighting, or keep Achilles in check so that he cannot fight, we, too, will at once raise the cry of battle, and in that case they will soon leave the field and go back vanquished to Olympus among the other gods."

With these words the dark-haired god led the way to the high earth-barrow of Heracles, built round solid masonry, and made by the Trojans and Pallas Athene for him to fly to when the sea-monster was chasing him from the shore on to the plain. Here Poseidon and those that were with him took their seats, wrapped in a thick cloud of darkness; but the other gods seated themselves on the brow of Callicolone round you, O Phoebus, and Ares, the waster of cities.

Thus did the gods sit apart and form their plans, but neither side was willing to begin battle with the other, and Zeus from his seat on high was in command over them all. Meanwhile the whole plain was alive with men and horses, and blazing with the gleam of armor. The earth rang again under the tramp of their feet as they rushed towards each other, and two champions, by far the foremost of them all, met between the hosts to fight—to wit, Aeneas, son of Anchises, and noble Achilles.

Aeneas was first to stride forward in attack, his doughty helmet tossing defiance as he came on. He held his strong shield before his breast, and brandished his bronze spear. The son of Peleus from the other side sprang forth to meet him, like some fierce lion that the whole countryside has met to hunt and kill—at first he bodes no ill, but when some daring youth has struck him with a spear, he crouches open-mouthed, his jaws foam, he roars with fury, he lashes his tail from side to side about his ribs and loins, and glares as he springs straight before him, to find out whether he is to slay, or be slain among the foremost of his foes—even with such fury did Achilles burn to spring upon Aeneas.

When they were now close up with one another Achilles was first to speak. "Aeneas," said he, "why do you stand thus out before the host to fight me? Is it that you hope to reign over the Trojans in the seat of Priam? Nay, though you kill me Priam will not hand his kingdom over to you. He is a man of sound judgment, and he has sons of his own. Or have the Trojans been allotting you a demesne of passing richness, fair with orchard lawns and corn lands, if you should slay me? This you shall hardly do. I have discomfited you once already. Have you forgotten how when you were alone I chased you from your herds helter-skelter down the slopes of Ida? You did not turn round to look behind you; you took refuge in Lyrnessus, but I attacked the city, and with the help of Athene and father Zeus I sacked it and carried its women into captivity, though Zeus and the other gods rescued you. You think they will protect you now, but they will not do so. Therefore, I say go back into the host, and do not face me, or you will rue it. Even a fool may be wise after the event."

Then Aeneas answered: "Son of Peleus, think not that your words can scare me as though I were a child. I too, if I will, can brag and talk unseemly. We know one another's race and parentage as matters of common fame, though neither have you ever seen my parents nor I yours. Men say that you are son to noble Peleus, and that your mother is Thetis, fair-haired daughter of the sea. I have noble Anchises for my father, and Aphrodite for my mother. The parents of one or other of us shall this day mourn a son, for it will be more than silly talk that shall part us when the fight is over. Learn, then, my lineage if you will—and it is known to many.

"In the beginning Dardanus was the son of Zeus, and founded Dardania, for Ilium was not yet established on the plain for men to dwell in, and her people still abode on the spurs of many-fountained Ida. Dardanus had a son, King Erichthonius, who was wealthiest of all men living. He had three thousand mares that fed by the water meadows, they and their foals with them. Boreas was enamored of them as they were feeding, and covered them in the semblance of a dark-maned stallion. Twelve filly foals did they conceive and bear him, and these, as they sped over the rich plain, would go bounding on over the ripe ears of corn and not break them; or again when they would disport themselves on the broad back of Ocean they could gallop on the crest of a breaker. Erichthonius begat Tros, king of the Trojans, and Tros had three noble sons, Ilus, Assaracus, and Ganymede who was comeliest of mortal men. Wherefore the gods carried him off to be Zeus's cupbearer, for his beauty's sake, that he might dwell among the immortals. Ilus begat Laomedon, and Laomedon begat Tithonus, Priam, Lampus, Clytius, and Hiketaon of the stock of Ares. But Assaracus was father to Capys, and Capys to Anchises, who was my father, while Hector is son to Priam.

"Such do I declare my blood and lineage, but as for valor, Zeus gives it or takes it as he will, for he is lord of all. And now let there be no more of this prating in midbattle as though we were children. We could fling taunts without end at one another; a hundred-oared galley would not hold them. The tongue can run all whithers and talk all wise. It can go here and there, and as a man says, so shall he be gainsaid. What is the use of our bandying hard words, like women who when they fall foul of one another go out and wrangle in the streets, one half true and the other lies, as rage inspires them? No words of yours shall turn me now that I am fain to fight—therefore let us make trial of one another with our spears."

As he spoke he drove his spear at the great and terrible shield of Achilles, which rang out as the point struck it. The son of Peleus held the shield before him with his strong hand and he was afraid, for he deemed that Aeneas's spear would go through it quite easily, not reflecting that the god's glorious gifts were little likely to yield before the blows of mortal men; and indeed Aeneas's spear did not pierce the shield, for the layer of gold, gift of the god, stayed the point. It went through two layers, but the god had made the shield in five, two of bronze, the two innermost ones of tin, and one of gold; it was in this that the spear was stayed.

Achilles in his turn threw, and struck the round shield of Aeneas at the very edge, where the bronze was thinnest. The spear of Pelian ash went clean through, and the shield rang under the blow. Aeneas was afraid, and crouched backwards, holding the shield away from him; the spear, however, flew over his back, and stuck quivering in the ground, after having gone through both circles of the sheltering shield. Aeneas, though he had avoided the spear, stood still, blinded with fear and grief because the weapon had gone so near him; then Achilles sprang furiously upon him, with a cry as of death and with his keen blade drawn, and Aeneas seized a great stone, so huge that two men, as men now are, would be unable to lift it, but Aeneas wielded it quite easily.

Aeneas would then have struck Achilles as he was springing towards him, either on the helmet or on the shield that covered him, and Achilles would have closed with him and despatched him with his sword had not Poseidon, lord of the earthquake, been quick to mark, and said forthwith to the immortals: "Alas, I am sorry for great Aeneas, who will now go down to the house of Hades, vanquished by the son of Peleus. Fool that he was to give ear to the counsel of Apollo. Apollo will never save him from destruction. Why should this man suffer when he is guiltless, to no purpose, and in another's quarrel? Has he not at all times offered acceptable sacrifice to the gods that dwell in heaven? Let us then snatch him from death's jaws, lest the son of Cronus be angry should Achilles slay him. It is fated, moreover, that he should escape and that the race of Dardanus, whom Zeus loved above all the sons born to him of mortal women, shall not perish utterly without seed or sign. For now indeed has Zeus hated the blood of Priam, while Aeneas shall reign over the Trojans, he and his children's children that shall be born hereafter."

Then answered Hera: "Earth-shaker, look to this matter yourself, and consider concerning Aeneas, whether you will save him, or suffer him, brave though he be, to fall by the hand of Achilles, son of Peleus. For of a truth we two, I and Pallas Athene, have sworn full many a time before all the immortals, that never would we shield Trojans from destruction, not even when all Troy is burning in the flames that the Achaeans shall kindle."

When earth-encircling Poseidon heard this he went into the battle amid the clash of spears and came to the place where Achilles and Aeneas were. Forthwith he shed a darkness before the eyes of the son of Peleus, drew the bronze-headed ashen spear from the shield of Aeneas, and laid it at the feet of Achilles. Then he lifted Aeneas on high from off the earth and hurried him away. Over the heads of many a band of warriors both horse and foot did he soar as the god's hand sped him, till he came to the very fringe of the battle where the Cauconians were arming themselves for fight. Poseidon, shaker of the earth, then came near to him and said: "Aeneas, what god has egged you on to this folly in fighting the son of Peleus, who is both a mightier man of valor and more beloved of heaven than you are? Give way before him whensoever you meet him, lest you go down to the house of Hades even though fate would have it otherwise. When Achilles is dead you may then fight among the foremost undaunted, for none other of the Achaeans shall slay you."

The god left him when he had given him these instructions, and at once removed the darkness from before the eyes of Achilles, who opened them wide indeed and said in great anger: "Alas! what marvel am I now beholding? Here is my spear upon the ground, but I see not him whom I meant to kill when I hurled it. Of a truth Aeneas also must be under heaven's protection, although I had thought his boasting was idle. Let him go hang. He will be in no mood to fight me further, seeing how narrowly he has missed being killed. I will now give my orders to the Danaans and attack some other of the Trojans."

He sprang forward along the line and cheered his men on as he did so. "Let not the Trojans," he cried, "keep you at arm's length, Achaeans, but go for them and fight them man for man. However valiant I may be, I cannot give chase to so many and fight all of them. Even Ares, who is an immortal, or Athene, would shrink from flinging himself into the jaws of such a fight and laying about him. Nevertheless, so far as in me lies I will show no slackness of hand or foot nor want of endurance, not even for a moment. I will utterly break their ranks, and woe to the Trojan who shall venture within reach of my spear."

Thus did he exhort them. Meanwhile Hector called upon the Trojans and declared that he would fight Achilles. "Be not afraid, proud Trojans," said he, "to face the son of Peleus. I could fight gods myself if the battle were one of words only, but they would be more than a match for me, if we had to use our spears. Even so, the deed of Achilles will fall somewhat short of his word; he will do in part, and the other part he will clip short. I will go up against him though his hands be as fire—though his hands be fire and his strength iron."

Thus urged, the Trojans lifted up their spears against the Achaeans and raised the cry of battle as they flung themselves into the midst of their ranks. But Phoebus Apollo came up to Hector and said, "Hector, on no account must you challenge Achilles to single combat. Keep a lookout for him while you are under cover of the others and away from the thick of the fight; otherwise he will either hit you with a spear or cut you down at close quarters."

Thus he spoke, and Hector drew back within the crowd, for he was afraid when he heard what the god had said to him. Achilles then sprang upon the Trojans with a terrible cry, clothed in valor as with a garment. First he killed Iphition, son of Otrynteus, a leader of much people whom a naiad nymph had borne to Otrynteus, waster of cities, in the land of Hyde under the snowy heights of Mount Tmolus. Achilles struck him full on the head as he was coming on towards him, and split it clean in two. Whereon he fell heavily to the ground, and Achilles vaunted over him, saying, "You lie low, son of Otrynteus, mighty hero; your death is here, but your lineage is on the Gygaean lake where your father's estate lies, by Hyllus, rich in fish, and the eddying waters of Hermus."

Thus did he vaunt, but darkness closed the eyes of the other. The chariots of the Achaeans cut him up as their wheels passed over him in the front of the battle, and after him Achilles killed Demoleon, a valiant man of war and son to Antenor. He struck him on the temple through his bronze-cheeked helmet. The helmet did not stay the spear, but it went right on, crushing the bone so that the brain inside was shed in all directions, and his lust of fighting was ended. Then he struck Hippodamas in the midriff as he was springing down from his chariot in front of him, and trying to escape. He breathed his last, bellowing like a bull bellows when young men are dragging him to offer him in sacrifice to the King of Helice, and the heart of the earth-shaker is glad: even so did he bellow as he lay dying. Achilles then went in pursuit of Polydorus, son of Priam, whom his father had always forbidden to fight because he was the youngest of his sons, the one he loved best, and the fastest runner. He, in his folly and showing off the fleetness of his feet, was rushing about among the front ranks until he lost his life, for Achilles struck him in the middle of the back as he was darting past him—he struck him just at the golden fastenings of his belt and where the two pieces of the double breastplate overlapped. The point of the spear pierced him through and came out by the navel, whereon he fell groaning on to his knees and a cloud of darkness overshadowed him as he sank, holding his entrails in his hands.

When Hector saw his brother Polydorus with his entrails in his hands and sinking down upon the ground, a mist came over his eyes, and he could not bear to keep longer at a distance. He therefore poised his spear and darted towards Achilles like a flame of fire. When Achilles saw him he bounded forward and vaunted, saying: "This is he that has wounded my heart most deeply and has slain my beloved comrade. Not for long shall we two quail before one another on the highways of war."

He looked fiercely on Hector and said, "Draw near, that you may meet your doom the sooner." Hector feared him not and answered: "Son of Peleus, think not that your words can scare me as though I were a child; I too if I will can brag and talk unseemly. I know that you are a mighty warrior, mightier by far than I. Nevertheless, the issue lies in the lap of heaven whether I, worse man though I be, may not slay you with my spear, for this too has been found keen ere now."

He hurled his spear as he spoke, but Athene breathed upon it, and though she breathed but very lightly she turned it back from going towards Achilles, so that it returned to Hector and lay at his feet in front of him. Achilles then sprang furiously on him with a loud cry, bent on killing him, but Apollo caught him up easily as a god can, and hid him in a thick darkness. Thrice did Achilles spring towards him spear in hand, and thrice did he waste his blow upon the air. When he rushed forward for the fourth time as though he were a god, he shouted aloud, saying: "Hound, this time too you have escaped death—but of a truth it came exceedingly near you. Phoebus Apollo, to whom it seems you pray before you go into battle, has again saved you; but if I too have any friend among the gods I will surely make an end of you when I come across you at some other time. Now, however, I will pursue and overtake other Trojans."

On this he struck Dryops with his spear, about the middle of his neck, and he fell headlong at his feet. There he let him lie and stayed Demouchus, son of Philetor, a man both brave and of great stature, by hitting him on the knee with a spear. Then he smote him with his sword and killed him. After this, he sprang on Laogonus and Dardanus, sons of Bias, and threw them from their chariot, the one with a blow from a thrown spear, while the other he cut down in hand-to-hand fight. There was also Tros, the son of Alastor—he came up to Achilles and clasped his knees in the hope that he would spare him and not kill him but let him go, because they were both of the same age. Fool, he might have known that he should not prevail with him, for the man was in no mood for pity or forbearance but was in grim earnest. Therefore when Tros laid hold of his knees and sought a hearing for his prayers, Achilles drove his sword into his liver, and the liver came rolling out, while his bosom was all covered with the black blood that welled from the wound. Thus did death close his eyes as he lay lifeless.

Achilles then went up to Mulius and struck him on the ear with a spear, and the bronze spearhead came right out at the other ear. He also struck Echeclus, son of Agenor, on the head with his sword, which became warm with the blood, while death and stern fate closed the eyes of Echeclus. Next in order the bronze point of his spear wounded Deucalion in the forearm where the sinews of the elbow are united, whereon he waited Achilles's onset with his arm hanging down and death staring him in the face. Achilles cut his head off with a blow from his sword and flung it helmet and all away from him, and the marrow came oozing out of his backbone as he lay. He then went in pursuit of Rhigmus, noble son of Peires, who had come from fertile Thrace, and struck him through the middle with a spear which fixed itself in his belly, so that he fell headlong from his chariot. He also speared Areïthoüs, squire to Rhigmus, in the back as he was turning his horses in flight, and thrust him from his chariot, while the horses were struck with panic.

As a fire raging in some mountain glen after long drought—and the dense forest is in a blaze, while the wind carries great tongues of fire in every direction—even so furiously did Achilles rage, wielding his spear as though he were a god and giving chase to those whom he would slay, till the dark earth ran with blood. Or as one who yokes broad-browed oxen that they may tread barley in a threshing floor—and it is soon bruised small under the feet of the lowing cattle—even so did the horses of Achilles trample on the shields and bodies of the slain. The axle underneath and the railing that ran round the car were bespattered with clots of blood thrown up by the horses' hoofs and from the tires of the wheels; but the son of Peleus pressed on to win still further glory, and his hands were bedrabbled with gore.

BOOK XXI

Achilles, storming forward, cuts the Trojan army in two. At the river Scamander, he kills until the stream runs red. The river god, angry at this carnage, rises to overwhelm Achilles, but Hera calls on Hephaestus to scorch the river with his fiery blasts. On the plain, Athene and Hera fight Ares, Aphrodite, and Artemis. Meanwhile, the routed Trojans take refuge within the city walls.

Now when they came to the ford of the full-flowing river Xanthus, begotten of immortal Zeus, Achilles cut their forces in two: one half he chased over the plain towards the city by the same way that the Achaeans had taken when flying panic-stricken on the preceding day with Hector in full triumph. This way did they fly pell-mell, and Hera sent down a thick mist in front of them to stay them. The other half were hemmed in by the deep silver-eddying stream, and fell into it with a great uproar. The waters resounded, and the banks rang again, as they swam hither and thither with loud cries amid the whirling eddies. As locusts flying to a river before the blast of a grass fire—the flame comes on and on till at last it overtakes them and they huddle into the water—even so was the eddying stream of Xanthus filled with the uproar of men and horses, all struggling in confusion before Achilles.

Forthwith the hero left his spear upon the bank, leaning it against a tamarisk bush, and plunged into the river like a god, armed with his sword only. Fell was his purpose as he hewed the Trojans down on every side. Their dying groans rose hideous as the sword smote them, and the river ran red with blood. As when fish fly scared before a huge dolphin, and fill every nook and corner of some fair haven—for he is sure to eat all he can catch—even so did the Trojans cower under the banks of the mighty river, and when Achilles's arms grew weary with killing them, he drew twelve youths alive out of the water, to sacrifice in revenge for Patroclus, son of Menoetius. He drew them out like dazed fawns, bound their hands behind them with the girdles of their own shirts, and gave them over to his men to take back to the ships. Then he sprang into the river, thirsting for still further blood.

There he found Lycaon, son of Priam, seed of Dardanus, as he was escaping out of the water. He it was whom he had once taken prisoner when he was in his father's vineyard, having set upon him by night, as he was cutting young shoots from a wild fig tree to make the wicker sides of a chariot. Achilles then caught him to his sorrow unawares, and sent him by sea to Lemnos, where the son of Jason bought him. But a guest-friend, Eëtion of Imbros, freed him with a great sum, and sent him to Arisbe, whence he had escaped and returned to his father's house. He had spent eleven days happily with his friends after he had come from Lemnos, but on the twelfth heaven again delivered him into the hands of Achilles, who was to send him to the house of Hades sorely against his will. He was unarmed when Achilles caught sight of him, and had neither helmet nor shield; nor yet had he any spear, for he had thrown all his armor from him on to the bank, and was sweating with his struggles to get out of the river, so that his strength was now failing him.

Then Achilles said to himself in his surprise: "What marvel do I see here? If this man can come back alive after having been sold over into Lemnos, I shall have the Trojans also whom I have slain rising from the world below. Could not even the waters of the gray sea imprison him, as they do many another whether he will or no? This time let him taste my spear, that I may know for certain whether mother earth, who can keep even a strong man down, will be able to hold him, or whether thence too he will return."

Thus did he pause and ponder. But Lycaon came up to him dazed and trying hard to embrace his knees, for he would fain live, not die. Achilles thrust at him with his spear, meaning to kill him, but Lycaon ran crouching up to him and caught his knees, whereby the spear passed over his back and stuck in the ground, hungering though it was for blood. With one hand he caught Achilles's knees as he besought him and with the other he clutched the spear and would not let it go. Then he said: "Achilles, have mercy upon me and spare me, for I am your suppliant. It was in your tents that I first broke bread on the day when you took me prisoner in the vineyard; after which you sold me away to Lemnos far from my father and my friends, and I brought you the price of a hundred oxen. I have paid three times as much to gain my freedom. It is but twelve days that I have come to Ilium after much suffering, and now cruel fate has again thrown me into your hands. Surely father Zeus must hate me, that he has given me over to you a second time. Short of life indeed did my mother Laothoë bear me, daughter of aged Altes—of Altes who reigns over the warlike Lelegae and holds steep Pedasus on the river Satniöeis. Priam married his daughter along with many other women and two sons were born of her, both of whom you will have slain. Your spear slew noble Polydorus as he was fighting in the front ranks, and now evil will here befall me, for I fear that I shall not escape you since heaven has delivered me over to you. Furthermore I say, and lay my saying to your heart, spare me, for I am not of the same womb as Hector who slew your brave and noble comrade."

With such words did the princely son of Priam beseech Achilles, but Achilles answered him sternly. "Idiot," said he, "talk not to me of ransom. Until Patroclus fell I preferred to give the Trojans quarter, and sold beyond the sea many of those whom I had taken alive; but now not a man shall live of those whom heaven delivers into my hands before the city of Ilium—and of all Trojans it shall fare hardest with the sons of Priam. Therefore, my friend, you too shall die. Why should you whine in this way? Patroclus fell, and he was a better man than you are. I too—see you not how I am great and goodly? I am son to a noble father and have a goddess for my mother, but the hands of doom and death overshadow me all as surely. The day will come, either at dawn or dark, or at the noontide, when one shall take my life also in battle, either with his spear, or with an arrow sped from his bow."

Thus did he speak, and Lycaon's heart sank within him. He loosed his hold of the spear and held out both hands before him, but Achilles drew his keen blade and struck him by the collar-bone on his neck. He plunged his two-edged sword into him to the very hilt, whereon he lay at full length on the ground with the dark blood welling from him till the earth was soaked. Then Achilles caught him by the foot and flung him into the river to go downstream, vaunting over him the while and saying:

"Lie there among the fishes, who will lick the blood from your wound and gloat over it. Your mother shall not lay you on any bier to mourn you, but the eddies of Scamander shall bear you into the broad bosom of the sea. There shall the fishes feed on the fat of Lycaon as they dart under the dark ripple of the waters—so perish all of you till we reach the citadel of strong Ilium—you in flight, and I following after to destroy you. The river with its broad silver stream shall serve you in no stead, for all the bulls you offered him and all the horses that you flung living into his waters. None the less miserably shall you perish till there is not a man of you but has paid in full for the death of Patroclus and the havoc you wrought among the Achaeans whom you have slain while I held aloof from battle."

So spoke Achilles, but the river grew more and more angry, and pondered within himself how he should stay the hand of Achilles and save the Trojans from disaster. Meanwhile the son of Peleus, spear in hand, sprang upon Asteropaeus, son of Pelegon, to kill him. He was son to the broad river Axius and Periboea, eldest daughter of Acessamenus; for the river had lain with her. Asteropaeus stood up out of the water to face him with a spear in either hand, and Xanthus filled him with courage, being angry for the death of the youths whom Achilles was slaying ruthlessly within his waters. When they were close up with one another, Achilles was first to speak. "Who and whence are you," said he, "who dare to face me? Woe to the parents whose son stands up against me." And the son of Pelegon answered: "Great son of Peleus, why should you ask my lineage? I am from the fertile land of far Paeonia, captain of the Paeonians, and it is now eleven days that I am at Ilium. I am of the blood of the river Axius—of Axius that is the fairest of all rivers that run. He begot the famed warrior Pelegon, whose son men call me. Let us now fight, Achilles."

Thus did he defy him, and Achilles raised his spear of Pelian ash. Asteropaeus failed with both his spears, for he could use both hands alike. With the one spear he struck Achilles's shield, but did not pierce it, for the layer of gold, gift of the god, stayed the point; with the other spear he grazed the elbow of Achilles's right arm, drawing dark blood, but the spear itself went by him and fixed itself in the ground, foiled of its bloody banquet. Then Achilles, fain to kill him, hurled his spear at Asteropaeus, but failed to hit him and struck the steep bank of the river, driving the spear half its length into the earth. The son of Peleus then drew his sword and sprang furiously upon him. Asteropaeus vainly tried to draw Achilles's spear out of the bank by main force. Thrice did he tug at it, trying with all his might to draw it out, and thrice he had to leave off trying; the fourth time he tried to bend and break it, but ere he could do so Achilles smote him with his sword and killed him. He struck him in the belly near the navel, so that all his bowels came gushing out on to the ground, and the darkness of death came over him as he lay gasping. Then Achilles set his foot on his chest and spoiled him of his armor, vaunting over him and saying:

"Lie there—begotten of a river though you be, it is hard for you to strive with the offspring of Cronus's son. You declare yourself sprung from the blood of a broad river, but I am of the seed of mighty Zeus. My father is Peleus, son of Aeacus, ruler over the many Myrmidons, and Aeacus was the son of Zeus. Therefore as

Zeus is mightier than any river that flows into the sea, so are his children stronger than those of any river whatsoever. Moreover, you have a great river hard by if he can be of any use to you, but there is no fighting against Zeus, the son of Cronus, with whom not even King Achelous can compare, nor the mighty stream of deep-flowing Oceanus, from whom all rivers and seas with all springs and deep wells proceed. Even Oceanus fears the lightnings of great Zeus and his thunder that comes crashing out of heaven."

With this he drew his bronze spear out of the bank, and now that he had killed Asteropaeus, he let him lie where he was on the sand with the dark water flowing over him and the eels and fishes busy nibbling and gnawing the fat that was about his kidneys. Then he went in chase of the Paeonians, who were flying along the bank of the river in panic when they saw their leader slain by the hands of the son of Peleus. Therein he slew Thersilochus, Mydon, Astypylus, Mnesus, Thrasius, Oeneus, and Ophelestes, and he would have slain yet others, had not the river in anger taken human form, and spoken to him from out the deep waters, saying: "Achilles, if you excel all in strength, so do you also in wickedness, for the gods are ever with you to protect you. If, then, the son of Cronus has vouchsafed it to you to destroy all the Trojans, at any rate drive them out of my stream, and do your grim work on land. My fair waters are now filled with corpses, nor can I find any channel by which I may pour myself into the sea for I am choked with dead, and yet you go on mercilessly slaying. I am in despair; therefore, O captain of your host, trouble me no further."

Achilles answered: "So be it, Scamander, Zeus-descended; but I will never cease dealing out death among the Trojans till I have pent them up in their city and made trial of Hector face to face, that I may learn whether he is to vanquish me, or I him."

As he spoke he set upon the Trojans with a fury like that of the gods. But the river said to Apollo: "Surely, son of Zeus, lord of the silver bow, you are not obeying the commands of Zeus who charged you straitly that you should stand by the Trojans and defend them till twilight fades and darkness is over all the earth."

Meanwhile Achilles sprang from the bank into midstream, whereon the river raised a high wave and attacked him. He swelled his stream into a torrent and swept away the many dead whom Achilles had slain and left within his waters. These he cast out on to the land, bellowing like a bull the while, but the living he saved alive, hiding them in his mighty eddies. The great and terrible wave gathered about Achilles, falling upon him and beating on his shield, so that he could not keep his feet. He caught hold of a great elm tree, but it came up by the roots and tore away the bank, damming the stream with its thick branches and bridging it all across; whereby Achilles struggled out of the stream and fled full speed over the plain, for he was afraid.

But the mighty god ceased not in his pursuit and sprang upon him with a dark-crested wave, to stay his hands and save the Trojans from destruction. The son of Peleus darted away a spear's throw from him; swift as the swoop of a black hunter-eagle which is the strongest and fleetest of all birds, even so did he spring forward, and the armor rang loudly about his breast. He fled on in front, but the river with a loud roar came tearing after. As one who would water his garden leads a stream from some fountain over his plants, and all his ground—spade in hand he clears away the dams to free the channels, and the little stones run rolling round and round with the water as it goes merrily down the bank faster than the man can follow—even so did the river keep catching up with Achilles albeit he was a fleet runner, for the gods are stronger than men. As often as he would strive to stand his ground, and see whether or no all the gods in heaven were in league against him, so often would the mighty wave come beating down upon his shoulders, and he would have to keep flying on and on in great dismay; for the angry flood was tiring him out as it flowed past him and ate the ground from under his feet.

Then the son of Peleus lifted up his voice to heaven, saying: "Father Zeus, is there none of the gods who will take pity upon me, and save me from the river? I do not care what may happen to me afterwards. I blame none of the other dwellers on Olympus so severely as I do my dear mother, who has beguiled and tricked me. She told me I was to fall under the walls of Troy by the flying arrows of Apollo. Would that Hector, the best man among the Trojans, might there slay me; then should I fall a hero by the hand of a hero. Whereas now it seems that I shall come to a most pitiable end, trapped in this river as though I were some swineherd's boy, who gets carried down a torrent while trying to cross it during a storm."

As soon as he had spoken thus, Poseidon and Athene came up to him in the likeness of two men and took him by the hand to reassure him. Poseidon spoke first. "Son of Peleus," said he, "be not so exceeding fearful; we are two gods, come with Zeus's sanction to assist you, I, and Pallas Athene. It is not your fate to perish in this river. He will abate presently as you will see. Moreover, we strongly advise you, if you will be guided by us, not to stay your hand from fighting till you have pent the Trojan host within the famed walls of Ilium—as many of them as may escape. Then kill Hector and go back to the ships, for we will vouchsafe you a triumph over him."

When they had so said they went back to the other immortals, but Achilles strove onward over the plain, encouraged by the charge the gods had laid upon him. All was now covered with the flood of waters, and much goodly armor of the youths that had been slain was drifting about, as also many corpses, but he forced his way against the stream, speeding right onwards, nor could the broad waters stay him, for Athene had endowed him with great strength. Nevertheless Scamander did not slacken in his pursuit, but was still more furious with the son of Peleus. He lifted his waters into a high crest and cried aloud to Simois, saying:

"Dear brother, let the two of us unite to stay this man, or he will sack the mighty city of King Priam, and the Trojans will not hold out against him. Help me at once. Fill your streams with water from their sources, rouse all your torrents to a fury; raise your wave on high and let snags and stones come thundering down you that we may make an end of this savage creature who is now lording it as though he were a god. Nothing shall serve him longer, not strength nor comeliness, nor his fine armor, which forsooth shall soon be lying low in the deep waters covered over with mud. I will wrap him in sand, and pour tons of shingle round him, so that the Achaeans shall not know how to gather his bones for the silt in which I shall have hidden him, and when they celebrate his funeral they need build no barrow."

On this he upraised his tumultuous flood high against Achilles, seething as it was with foam and blood and the bodies of the dead. The dark waters of the river stood upright and would have overwhelmed the son of Peleus, but Hera, trembling lest Achilles should be swept away in the mighty torrent, lifted her voice on high and called out to Hephaestus, her son. "Crook-foot," she cried, "my child, be up and doing, for I deem it is with you that Xanthus is fain to fight. Help us at once; kindle a fierce fire. I will then bring up the west and the white south wind in a mighty hurricane from the sea that shall bear the flames against the heads and armor of the Trojans and consume them, while you go along the banks of Xanthus burning his trees and wrapping him round with fire. Let him not turn you back neither by fair words nor foul and slacken not till I shout and tell you. Then you may stay your flames."

On this Hephaestus kindled a fierce fire, which broke out first upon the plain and burned the many dead whom Achilles had killed and whose bodies were lying about in great numbers; by this means the plain was dried and the flood stayed. As the north wind, blowing on an orchard that has been sodden with autumn rain, soon dries it, and the heart of the owner is glad—even so the whole plain was dried and the dead bodies were consumed. Then he turned tongues of fire on to the river. He burned the elms, the willows, and the tamarisks, the lotus also, with the rushes and marshy herbage that grew abundantly by the banks of the river. The eels and fishes that go darting about everywhere in the water, these, too, were sorely harassed by the flames that cunning Hephaestus had kindled, and the river himself was scalded, so that he spoke, saying: "Hephaestus, there is no god can hold his own against you. I cannot fight you when you flare out your flames in this way; strive with me no longer. Let Achilles drive the Trojans out of their city immediately. What have I to do with quarreling and helping people?"

He was boiling as he spoke, and all his waters were seething. As a cauldron upon a large fire boils when it is melting the lard of some fatted hog, and the lard keeps bubbling up all over when the dry faggots blaze under it—even so were the goodly waters of Xanthus heated with the fire till they were boiling. He could flow no longer but stayed his stream, so afflicted was he by the blasts of fire which cunning Hephaestus had raised. Then he prayed to Hera and besought her, saying, "Hera, why should your son vex my stream with such especial fury? I am not so much to blame as all the others are who have been helping the Trojans. I will leave off, since you so desire it, and let your son leave off also. Furthermore I swear that never again will I do anything to save the Trojans from destruction, not even when all Troy is burning in the flames which the Achaeans will kindle."

As soon as Hera heard this she said to her son Hephaestus: "Son Hephaestus, hold now your flames; we ought not to use such violence against a god for the sake of mortals."

When she had thus spoken Hephaestus quenched his flames, and the river went back once more into his own fair bed.

Xanthus was now beaten, so these two left off fighting, for Hera stayed them though she was still angry; but a furious quarrel broke out among the other gods, for they were of divided counsels. They fell on one another with a mighty uproar—earth groaned, and the spacious firmament rang out as with a blare of trumpets. Zeus heard as he was sitting on Olympus and laughed for joy when he saw the gods coming to blows among themselves. They were not long about beginning, and Ares, piercer of shields, opened the battle. Sword in hand, he sprang at once upon Athene and reviled her. "Why, vixen," said he, "have you again set the gods by the ears in the pride and haughtiness of your heart? Have you forgotten how you set Diomed, son of Tydeus, on to wound me, and yourself took visible spear and drove it into me to the hurt of my fair body? You shall now suffer for what you then did to me."

As he spoke he struck her on the terrible tasseled aegis—so terrible that not even can Zeus's lightning pierce it. Here did murderous Ares strike her with his great spear. She drew back and with her strong hand seized a stone that was lying on the plain—great and rugged and black—which men of old had set for the boundary of a field. With this she struck Ares on the neck and brought him down. Nine roods did he cover in his fall, and his hair was all soiled in the dust, while his armor rang rattling round him. But Athene laughed and vaunted over him, saying: "Idiot, have you not learned how far stronger I am than you, but you must still match yourself against me? Thus do your mother's curses now roost upon you, for she is angry and would do you mischief because you have deserted the Achaeans and are helping the Trojans."

She then turned her two piercing eyes elsewhere, whereon Zeus's daughter Aphrodite took Ares by the hand and led him away, groaning all the time, for it was only with great difficulty that he had come to himself again. When Queen Hera saw her, she said to Athene, "Look, daughter of aegis-bearing Zeus, unweariable, that vixen Aphrodite is again taking Ares through the crowd out of the battle; go after her at once."

Thus she spoke. Athene sped after Aphrodite with a will, and made at her, striking her on the bosom with her strong hand so that she fell fainting to the ground, and there they both lay stretched at full length. Then Athene vaunted over her, saying: "May all who help the Trojans against the Argives prove just as redoubtable and stalwart as Aphrodite did when she came across me while she was helping Ares. Had this been so, we should long since have ended the war by sacking the strong city of Ilium."

Hera smiled as she listened. Meanwhile King Poseidon turned to Apollo, saying: "Phoebus, why should we keep each other at arm's length? It is not well, now that the others have begun fighting; it will be disgraceful to us if we return to Zeus's bronze-floored mansion on Olympus without having fought each other. Therefore come on, you are the younger of the two, and I ought not to attack you, for I am older and have had more experience. Idiot, you have no sense, and forget how we two alone of all the gods fared hardly round about Ilium when we came from Zeus's house and worked for Laomedon a whole year at a stated wage and he gave us his orders. I built the Trojans the wall about their city, so wide and fair that it might be impregnable, while you, Phoebus, herded cattle for him in the dales of many-valleyed Ida. When, however, the glad hours brought round the time of payment, mighty Laomedon robbed us of all our hire and sent us off with nothing but abuse. He threatened to bind us hand and foot and sell us over into some distant island. He tried, moreover, to cut off the ears of both of us, so we went away in a rage, furious about the payment he had promised us, and yet withheld. In spite of all this, you are now showing favor to his people and will not join us in compassing the utter ruin of the proud Trojans with their wives and children."

And King Apollo answered: "Lord of the earthquake, you would have no respect for me if I were to fight you about a pack of miserable mortals, who come out like leaves in summer and eat the fruit of the field and presently fall lifeless to the ground. Let us stay this fighting at once and let them settle it among themselves."

He turned away as he spoke, for he would lay no hand on the brother of his own father. But his sister, the huntress Artemis, patroness of wild beasts, was very angry with him and said: "So you would fly, Far-darter, and hand victory over to Poseidon with a cheap vaunt to boot. Baby, why keep your bow thus idle? Never let me again hear you bragging in my father's house, as you often have done in the presence of the immortals, that you would stand up and fight with Poseidon."

Apollo made her no answer, but Zeus's august queen was angry and upbraided her bitterly. "Bold vixen," she cried, "how dare you cross me thus? For all your bow you will find it hard to hold your own against me. Zeus made you as a lion among women, and lets you kill them whenever you choose. You will find it better to chase wild beasts and deer upon the mountains than to fight those who are stronger than you are. If you would try war, do so, and find out by pitting yourself against me how far stronger I am than you are."

She caught both Artemis's wrists with her left hand as she spoke and with her right she took the bow from her shoulders, and laughed as she beat her with it about the ears while Artemis wriggled and writhed under her blows. Her swift arrows were shed upon the ground, and she fled weeping from under Hera's hand as a dove that flies before a falcon to the cleft of some hollow rock, when it is her good fortune to escape. Even so did she fly weeping away, leaving her bow and arrows behind her.

Then the slayer of Argus, guide and guardian, said to Leto: "Leto, I shall not fight you; it is ill to come to blows with any of Zeus's wives. Therefore, boast as you will among the immortals that you worsted me in fair fight."

Leto then gathered up Artemis's bow and arrows that had fallen about amid the whirling dust, and when she had got them she made all haste after her daughter. Artemis had now reached Zeus's bronze-floored mansion on Olympus and sat herself down with many tears on the knees of her father, while her ambrosial raiment was quivering all about her. The son of Cronus drew her towards him, and laughing pleasantly the while began to question her, saying: "Which of the heavenly beings, my dear child, has been treating you in this cruel manner, as though you had been misconducting yourself in the face of everybody?" And the fair-crowned goddess of the chase answered: "It was your wife Hera, father, who has been beating me; it is always her doing when there is any quarreling among the immortals."

Thus did they converse, and meanwhile Phoebus Apollo entered the strong city of Ilium, for he was uneasy lest the wall should not hold out and the Danaans should take the city then and there, before its hour had come; but the rest of the ever-living gods went back, some angry and some triumphant, to Olympus, where they took their seats beside Zeus, lord of the storm cloud, while Achilles still kept on dealing out death alike on the Trojans and on their horses. As when the smoke from some burning city ascends to heaven when the anger of the gods has kindled it—there is then toil for all, and sorrow for not a few—even so did Achilles bring toil and sorrow on the Trojans.

Old King Priam stood on a high tower of the wall looking down on huge Achilles as the Trojans fled panic-stricken before him, and there was none to help them. Presently he came down from off the tower and with many a groan went along the wall to give orders to the brave warders of the gate. "Keep the gates," said he, "wide open till the people come flying into the city, for Achilles is hard by and is driving them in rout before him. I see we are in great peril. As soon as our people are inside and in safety, close the strong gates, for I fear lest that terrible man should come bounding inside along with the others."

As he spoke they drew back the bolts and opened the gates, and when these were opened there was a haven of refuge for the Trojans. Apollo then came full speed out of the city to meet them and protect them. Right for the city and the high wall, parched with thirst and grimy with dust, still they fled on, with Achilles wielding his spear furiously behind them. For he was as one possessed and was thirsting after glory.

Then had the sons of the Achaeans taken the lofty gates of Troy if Apollo had not spurred on Agenor, valiant and noble son to Antenor. He put courage into his heart and stood by his side to guard him, leaning against a beech tree and shrouded in thick darkness. When Agenor saw Achilles he stood still and his heart was clouded with care. "Alas," said he to himself in his dismay, "if I fly before mighty Achilles and go where all the others are being driven in rout, he will nonetheless catch me and kill me for a coward. How would it be were I to let Achilles drive the others before him, and then fly from the wall to the plain that is behind Ilium till I reach the spurs of Ida and can hide in the underwood that is thereon? I could then wash the sweat from off me in the river and in the evening return to Ilium. But why commune with myself in this way? Like enough he would see me as I am hurrying from the city over the plain and would speed after me till he had caught me—I should stand no chance against him, for he is mightiest of all mankind. What, then, if I go out and meet him in front of the city? His flesh too, I take it, can be pierced by pointed bronze. Life is the same in one and all, and men say that he is but mortal despite the triumph that Zeus, son of Cronus, vouchsafes him."

So saying he stood on his guard and awaited Achilles, for he was now fain to fight him. As a leopardess that bounds from out a thick covert to attack a hunter—she knows no fear and is not dismayed by the baying of the hounds; even though the man be too quick for her and wound her either with thrust or spear, still, though the spear has pierced her she will not give in till she has either caught him in her grip or been killed outright—even so did noble Agenor, son of Antenor, refuse to fly till he had made trial of Achilles, and took aim at him with his spear, holding his round shield before him and crying with a loud voice. "Of a truth," said he, "noble Achilles, you deem that you shall this day sack the city of the proud Trojans. Fool, there will be trouble enough yet before it, for there is many a brave man of us still inside who will stand in front of our dear parents with our wives and children, to defend Ilium. Here, therefore, huge and mighty warrior though you be, here shall you die."

As he spoke his strong hand hurled his javelin from him, and the spear struck Achilles on the leg beneath the knee. The greave of newly wrought tin rang loudly, but the spear recoiled from the body of him whom it had struck, and did not pierce it, for the god's gift stayed it. Achilles in his turn attacked noble Agenor, but Apollo would not vouchsafe him glory, for he snatched Agenor away and hid him in a thick mist, sending him out of the battle unmolested. Then he craftily drew the son of Peleus away from going after the host, for he put on the semblance of Agenor and stood in front of Achilles, who ran towards him to give him chase and pursued him over the corn lands of the plain, turning him towards the deep waters of the river Scamander. Apollo ran but a little way before him and beguiled Achilles by making him think all the time that he was on the point of overtaking him. Meanwhile the rabble of routed Trojans was thankful to crowd within the city till their numbers thronged it. No longer did they dare wait for one another outside the city walls to learn who had escaped and who were fallen in fight, but all whose feet and knees could still carry them poured pell-mell into the town.

BOOK XXII

Outside the gates of Troy, Hector stands alone to face the oncoming Achilles, deaf to the entreaties of his parents on the wall above him. As Achilles draws near, Hector's courage gives way. He turns and runs, Achilles after him, three times around the city. At length, tricked by Athene, he turns, fights, and is slain. Achilles lashes his body to his chariot, and drags it away, trailing in the dust. Priam, Hecuba, and Andromache bewail Hector's end.

THUS THE TROJANS IN THE CITY, SCARED LIKE FAWNS, WIPED the sweat from off them and drank to quench their thirst, leaning against the goodly battlements, while the Achaeans with their shields laid upon their shoulders drew close up to the walls. But stern fate bade Hector stay where he was before Ilium and the Scaean gates. Then Phoebus Apollo spoke to the son of Peleus, saying: "Why, son of Peleus, do you, who are but man, give chase to me who am immortal? Have you not yet found out that it is a god whom you pursue so furiously? You did not harass the Trojans whom you had routed, and now they are within their walls, while you have been decoyed hither away from them. Me you cannot kill, for death can take no hold upon me."

Achilles was greatly angered and said: "You have balked me, Far-darter, most malicious of all gods, and have drawn me away from the wall, where many another man would have bitten the dust ere he got within Ilium. You have robbed me of great glory and have saved the Trojans at no risk to yourself, for you have nothing to fear, but I would indeed have my revenge if it were in my power to do so."

On this, with fell intent he made towards the city, and as the winning horse in a chariot race strains every nerve when he is flying over the plain, even so fast and furiously did the limbs of Achilles bear him onwards. King Priam was first to note him as he scoured the plain, all radiant as the star which men call Orion's Hound, and whose beams blaze forth in time of harvest more brilliantly than those of any other that shines by night; brightest of them all though he be, he yet bodes ill for mortals, for he brings fire and fever in his train—even so did Achilles's armor gleam on his breast as he sped onwards. Priam raised a cry and beat his head with his hands as he lifted them up and shouted out to his dear son, imploring him to return; but Hector still stayed before the gates, for his heart was set upon doing battle with Achilles.

The old man reached out his arms towards him and bade him for pity's sake come within the walls. "Hector," he cried, "my son, stay not to face this man alone and unsupported, or you will meet death at the hands of the son of Peleus, for he is mightier than you. Monster that he is; would indeed that the gods loved him no better than I do, for so, dogs and vultures would soon devour him as he lay stretched on earth, and a load of grief would be lifted from my heart, for many a brave son has he reft from me, either by killing them or selling them away in the islands that are beyond the sea. Even now I miss two sons from among the Trojans who have thronged within the city, Lycaon and Polydorus, whom Laothoë, peeress among women, bore me. Should they be still alive and in the hands of the Achaeans, we will ransom them with gold and bronze, of which we have store, for the old man Altes endowed his daughter richly; but if they are already dead and in the house of Hades, sorrow will it be to us two who were their parents; albeit the grief of others will be more short-lived unless you too perish at the hands of Achilles. Come, then, my son, within the city, to be the guardian of Trojan men and Trojan women, or you will both lose your own life and afford a mighty triumph to the son of Peleus. Have pity also on your unhappy father while life yet remains to him—on me, whom the son of Cronus will destroy by a terrible doom on the threshold of old age, after I have seen my sons slain and my daughters haled away as captives, my bridal chambers pillaged, little children dashed to earth amid the rage of battle, and my sons' wives dragged away by the cruel hands of the Achaeans. In the end fierce hounds will tear me in pieces at my own gates after someone has beaten the life out of my body with sword or spear—hounds that I myself reared and fed at my own table to guard my gates, but who will yet lap my blood and then lie all distraught at my doors. When a young man falls by the sword in battle, he may lie where he is and there is nothing unseemly; let what will be seen, all is honorable in death, but when an old man is slain there is nothing in this world more pitiable than that dogs should defile his gray hair and beard and all that men hide for shame."

The old man tore his gray hair as he spoke, but he moved not the heart of Hector. His mother hard by wept and moaned aloud as she bared her bosom and pointed to the breast which had suckled him. "Hector," she cried, weeping bitterly the while, "Hector, my son, spurn not this breast, but have pity upon me too! If I have ever given you comfort from my own bosom, think on it now, dear son, and come within the wall to protect us from this man; stand not without to meet him. Should the wretch kill you, neither I nor your richly dowered wife shall ever weep, dear offshoot of myself, over the bed on which you lie, for dogs will devour you at the ships of the Achaeans."

Thus did the two with many tears implore their son, but they moved not the heart of Hector, and he stood his ground awaiting huge Achilles as he drew nearer towards him. As a serpent in its den upon the mountains, full-fed with deadly poisons, waits for the approach of man—he is filled with fury and his eyes glare terribly as he goes writhing round his den—even so Hector leaned his shield against a tower that jutted out from the wall and stood where he was, undaunted.

"Alas," said he to himself in the heaviness of his heart, "if I go within the gates, Polydamas will be the first to heap reproach upon me, for it was he that urged me to lead the Trojans back to the city on that awful night when Achilles again came forth against us. I would not listen, but it would have been indeed better if I had done so. Now that my folly has destroyed the host, I dare not look Trojan men and Trojan women in the face, lest a worse man should say, 'Hector has ruined us by his self-confidence.' Surely it would be better for me to return after having fought Achilles and slain him, or to die gloriously here before the city. What, again, if I were to lay down my shield and helmet, lean my spear against the wall and go straight up to noble Achilles? What if I were to promise to give up Helen, who was the fountainhead of all this war, and all the treasure that Paris brought with him in his ships to Troy, aye, and to let the Achaeans divide the half of everything that the city contains among themselves? I might make the Trojans, by the mouths of their princes, take a solemn oath that they would hide nothing, but would divide into two shares all that is within the city—but why argue with myself in this way? Were I to go up to him he would show me no kind of mercy; he would kill me then and there as easily as though I were a woman, when I had put off my armor. There is no parleying with him from some rock or oak tree as young men and maidens prattle with one another. Better fight him at once, and learn to which of us Zeus will vouchsafe victory."

Thus did he stand and ponder, but Achilles came up to him as it were Ares himself, plumed lord of battle. From his right shoulder he brandished his terrible spear of Pelian ash, and the bronze gleamed around him like flashing fire or the rays of the rising sun. Fear fell upon Hector as he beheld him and he dared not stay longer where he was, but fled in dismay from before the gates, while Achilles darted after him at his utmost speed. As a mountain falcon, swiftest of all birds, swoops down upon some cowering dove—the dove flies before him but the falcon with a shrill scream follows close after, resolved to have her—even so did Achilles make straight for Hector with all his might, while Hector fled under the Trojan wall as fast as his limbs could take him.

On they flew along the wagon-road that ran hard by under the wall, past the lookout station, and past the weather-beaten wild fig tree, till they came to two fair springs which feed the river Scamander. One of these two springs is warm, and steam rises from it as smoke from a burning fire, but the other even in summer is as cold as hail or snow, or the ice that forms on water. Here, hard by the springs, are the goodly washing troughs of stone, where in the time of peace before the coming of the Achaeans the wives and fair daughters of the Trojans used to wash their clothes. Past these did they fly, the one in front and the other giving chase behind him: good was the man that fled, but better far was he that followed after, and swiftly indeed did they run, for the prize was no mere beast for sacrifice or bullock's hide, as it might be for a common foot race, but they ran for the life of Hector. As horses in a chariot race speed round the turning posts when they are running for some great prize—a tripod or a woman—at the games in honor of some dead hero, so did these two run full speed three times round the city of Priam. All the gods watched them, and the sire of gods and men was the first to speak.

"Alas," said he, "my eyes behold a man who is dear to me being pursued round the walls of Troy. My heart is full of pity for Hector, who has burned the thighbones of many a heifer in my honor, at one while on the crests of many-valleyed Ida, and again on the citadel of Troy; and now I see noble Achilles in full pursuit of him round the city of Priam. What say you? Consider among yourselves and decide whether we shall now save him or let him fall, valiant though he be, before Achilles, son of Peleus."

Then Athene said, "Father, wielder of the lightning, lord of cloud and storm, what mean you? Would you pluck this mortal whose doom has long been decreed out of the jaws of death? Do as you will, but we others shall not be of a mind with you."

And Zeus answered, "My child, Trito-born, take heart. I did not speak in full earnest, and I will let you have your way. Do without let or hindrance as you are minded."

Thus did he urge Athene who was already eager, and down she darted from the topmost summits of Olympus.

Achilles was still in full pursuit of Hector, as a hound chasing a fawn which he has started from its covert on the mountains, and hunts through glade and thicket. The fawn may try to elude him by crouching under cover of a bush, but he will scent her out and follow her up until he gets her—even so there was no escape for Hector from the fleet son of Peleus. Whenever he made a set to get near the Dardanian gates and under the walls, that his people might help him by showering down weapons from above, Achilles would gain on him and head him back towards the plain, keeping himself always on the city side. As a man in a dream who fails to lay hands upon another whom he is pursuing—the one cannot escape nor the other overtake—even so neither could Achilles come up with Hector, nor Hector break away from Achilles. Nevertheless, he might even yet have escaped death had not the time come when Apollo, who thus far had sustained his strength and nerved his running, was now no longer to stay by him. Achilles made signs to the Achaean host and shook his head to show that no man was to aim a dart at Hector, lest another might win the glory of having hit him and he might himself come in second. Then, at last, as they were nearing the fountains for the fourth time, the father of all balanced his golden scales and placed a doom in each of them, one for Achilles and the other for Hector. As he held the scales by the middle, the doom of Hector fell down deep into the house of Hades—and then Phoebus Apollo left him. Thereon Athene went close up to the son of Peleus and said: "Noble Achilles, favored of heaven, we two shall surely take back to the ships a triumph for the Achaeans by slaying Hector, for all his lust of battle. Do what Apollo may as he lies groveling before his father, aegis-bearing Zeus, Hector cannot escape us longer. Stay here and take breath, while I go up to him and persuade him to make a stand and fight you."

Thus spoke Athene. Achilles obeyed her gladly and stood still, leaning on his bronze-pointed ashen spear, while Athene left him and went after Hector in the form and with the voice of Deïphobus. She came close up to him and said, "Dear brother, I see you are hard-pressed by Achilles who is chasing you at full speed round the city of Priam; let us await his onset and stand on our defense."

And Hector answered, "Deïphobus, you have always been dearest to me of all my brothers, children of Hecuba and Priam, but henceforth I shall rate you yet more highly, inasmuch as you have ventured outside the wall for my sake when all the others remain inside."

Then Athene said: "Dear brother, my father and mother went down on their knees and implored me, as did all my comrades, to remain inside, so great a fear has fallen upon them all; but I was in an agony of grief when I beheld you. Now, therefore, let us two make a stand and fight, and let there be no keeping our spears in reserve, that we may learn whether Achilles shall kill us and bear off our spoils to the ships, or whether he shall fall before you."

Thus did Athene inveigle him by her cunning, and when the two were now close to one another great Hector was first to speak. "I will no longer fly you, son of Peleus," said he, "as I have been doing hitherto. Three times have I fled round the mighty city of Priam, without daring to withstand you, but now, let me either slay or be slain, for I am in the mind to face you. Let us, then, give pledges to one another by our gods, who are the fittest witnesses and guardians of all covenants; let it be agreed between us that if Zeus vouchsafes me the longer stay and I take your life, I am not to treat your dead body in any unseemly fashion, but when I have stripped you of your armor, I am to give up your body to the Achaeans. And do you likewise."

Achilles glared at him and answered: "Fool, prate not to me about covenants. There can be no covenants between men and lions; wolves and lambs can never be of one mind, but hate each other out and out all through. Therefore there can be no understanding between you and me, nor may there be any covenants between us, till one or other shall fall and glut grim Ares with his life's blood. Put forth all your strength; you have need now to prove yourself indeed a bold soldier and man of war. You have no more chance, and Pallas Athene will forthwith vanquish you by my spear: you shall now pay me in full for the grief you have caused me on account of my comrades whom you have killed in battle."

He poised his spear as he spoke and hurled it. Hector saw it coming and avoided it; he watched it and crouched down so that it flew over his head and stuck in the ground beyond; Athene then snatched it up and gave it back to Achilles without Hector's seeing her; Hector thereon said to the son of Peleus: "You have missed your aim, Achilles, peer of the gods, and Zeus has not yet revealed to you the hour of my doom, though you made sure that he had done so. You were a false-tongued liar when you deemed that I should forget my valor and quail before you. You shall not drive your spear into the back of a runaway—drive it, should heaven so grant you power, drive it into me as I make straight towards you; and now for your own part avoid my spear if you can—would that you might receive the whole of it into your body. If you were once dead the Trojans would find the war an easier matter, for it is you who have harmed them most."

He poised his spear as he spoke and hurled it. His aim was true for he hit the middle of Achilles's shield, but the spear rebounded from it, and did not pierce it. Hector was angry when he saw that the weapon had sped from his hand in vain, and stood there in dismay for he had no second spear. With a loud cry he called Deïphobus and asked him for one, but there was no man; then he saw the truth and said to himself, "Alas! the gods have lured me on to my destruction. I deemed that the hero Deïphobus was by my side, but he is within the wall, and Athene has inveigled me; death is now indeed exceedingly near at hand and there is no way out of it—for so Zeus and his son Apollo, the far-darter, have willed it, though heretofore they have been ever ready to protect me. My doom has come upon me; let me not then die ingloriously and without a struggle, but let me first do some great thing that shall be told among men hereafter."

As he spoke he drew the keen blade that hung so great and strong by his side, and gathering himself together he sprang on Achilles like a soaring eagle which swoops down from the clouds on to some lamb or timid hare—even so did Hector brandish his sword and spring upon Achilles. Achilles, mad with rage, darted towards him, with his wondrous shield before his breast, and his gleaming helmet, made with four layers of metal, nodding fiercely forward. The thick tresses of gold with which Hephaestus had crested the helmet floated round it, and as the evening star that shines brighter than all others through the stillness of night, even such was the gleam of the spear which Achilles poised in his right hand, fraught with the death of noble Hector. He eyed his fair flesh over and over to see where he could best wound it, but all was protected by the goodly armor of which Hector had spoiled Patroclus after he had slain him, save only the throat where the collarbones divide the neck from the shoulders, and this is a most deadly place. Here then did Achilles strike him as he was coming on towards him, and the point of his spear went right through the fleshy part of the neck, but it did not sever his windpipe so that he could still speak.

Hector fell headlong, and Achilles vaunted over him, saying: "Hector, you deemed that you should come off scatheless when you were spoiling Patroclus, and recked not of myself who was not with him. Fool that you were: for I, his comrade, mightier far than he, was still left behind him at the ships, and now I have laid you low. The Achaeans shall give him all due funeral rites, while dogs and vultures shall work their will upon yourself."

Then Hector said, as the life ebbed out of him, "I pray you by your life and knees, and by your parents, let not dogs devour me at the ships of the Achaeans, but accept the rich treasure of gold and bronze which my father and mother will offer you, and send my body home, that the Trojans and their wives may give me my dues of fire when I am dead."

Achilles glared at him and answered: "Dog, talk not to me neither of knees nor parents; would that I could be as sure of being able to cut your flesh into pieces and eat it raw, for the ill you have done me, as I am that nothing shall save you from the dogs—it shall not be, though they bring ten or twenty-fold ransom and weigh it out for me on the spot, with promise of yet more hereafter. Though Priam, son of Dardanus, should bid them offer me your weight in gold, even so your mother shall never lay you out and make lament over the son she bore, but dogs and vultures shall eat you utterly up."

Hector with his dying breath then said: "I know you what you are, and was sure that I should not move you, for your heart is hard as iron; look to it that I bring not heaven's anger upon you on the day when Paris and Phoebus Apollo, valiant though you be, shall slay you at the Scaean gates."

When he had thus said the shrouds of death enfolded him, whereon his soul went out of him and flew down to the house of Hades, lamenting its sad fate that it should enjoy youth and strength no longer. But Achilles said, speaking to the dead body, "Die; for my part I will accept my fate whensoever Zeus and the other gods see fit to send it."

As he spoke he drew his spear from the body and set it on one side; then he stripped the bloodstained armor from Hector's shoulders while the other Achaeans came running up to view his wondrous strength and beauty; and no one came near him without giving him a fresh wound. Then would one turn to his neighbor and say, "It is easier to handle Hector now than when he was flinging fire on to our ships"—and as he spoke he would thrust his spear into him anew.

When Achilles had done spoiling Hector of his armor, he stood among the Argives and said: "My friends, princes and counselors of the Argives, now that heaven has vouchsafed us to overcome this man, who has done us more hurt than all the others together, consider whether we should not attack the city in force, and discover in what mind the Trojans may be. We should thus learn whether they will desert their city now that Hector has fallen, or will still hold out even though he is no longer living. But why argue with myself in this way, while Patroclus is still lying at the ships unburied, and unmourned—he whom I can never forget so long as I am alive and my strength fails not? Though men forget their dead when once they are within the house of Hades, yet not even there will I forget the comrade whom I have lost. Now, therefore, Achaean youths, let us raise the song of victory and go back to the ships taking this man along with us; for we have achieved a mighty triumph and have slain noble Hector to whom the Trojans prayed throughout their city as though he were a god."

On this he treated the body of Hector with contumely: he pierced the sinews at the back of both his feet from heel to ankle and passed thongs of oxhide through the slits he had made: thus he made the body fast to his chariot, letting the head trail upon the ground. Then when he had put the goodly armor on the chariot and had himself mounted, he lashed his horses on and they flew forward nothing loath. The dust rose from Hector as he was being dragged along, his dark hair flew all abroad, and his head once so comely was laid low on earth, for Zeus had now delivered him into the hands of his foes to do him outrage in his own land.

Thus was the head of Hector being dishonored in the dust. His mother tore her hair, and flung her veil from her with a loud cry as she looked upon her son. His father made piteous moan, and throughout the city the people fell to weeping and wailing. It was as though the whole of frowning Ilium was being smirched with fire. Hardly could the people hold Priam back in his hot haste to rush without the gates of the city. He groveled in the mire and besought them, calling each one of them by his name. "Let be, my friends," he cried, "and for all your sorrow, suffer me to go single-handed to the ships of the Achaeans. Let me beseech this cruel and terrible man, if maybe he will respect the feeling of his fellow men, and have compassion on my old age. His own father is even such another as myself—Peleus, who bred him and reared him to be the bane of us Trojans, and of myself more than of all others. Many a son of mine has he slain in the flower of his youth, and yet, grieve for these as I may, I do so for one—Hector—more than for them all, and the bitterness of my sorrow will bring me down to the house of Hades. Would that he had died in my arms, for so both his ill-starred mother who bore him and myself should have had the comfort of weeping and mourning over him."

Thus did he speak with many tears, and all the people of the city joined in his lament. Hecuba then raised the cry of wailing among the Trojans. "Alas, my son," she cried, "what have I left to live for now that you are no more? Night and day did I glory in you throughout the city, for you were a tower of strength to all in Troy, and both men and women alike hailed you as a god. So long as you lived you were their pride, but now death and destruction have fallen upon you."

Hector's wife had as yet heard nothing, for no one had come to tell her that her husband had remained without the gates. She was at her loom in an inner part of the house, weaving a double purple web, and embroidering it with many flowers. She told her maids to set a large tripod on the fire, so as to have a warm bath ready for Hector when he came out of battle; poor woman, she knew not that he was now beyond the reach of baths, and that Athene had laid him low by the hands of Achilles. She heard the cry coming as from the wall, and trembled in every limb. The shuttle fell from her hands, and again she spoke to her waiting-women. "Two of you," she said, "come with me that I may learn what it is that has befallen. I heard the voice of my husband's honored mother. My own heart beats as though it would come into my mouth and my limbs refuse to carry me; some great misfortune for Priam's children must be at hand. May I never live to hear it, but I greatly fear that Achilles has cut off the retreat of brave Hector and has chased him on to the plain where he was single-handed; I fear he may have put an end to the reckless daring which possessed my husband, who would never remain with the body of his men, but would dash on far in front, foremost of them all in valor."

Her heart beat fast, and as she spoke she flew from the house like a maniac, with her waiting-women following after. When she reached the battlements and the crowd of people, she stood looking out upon the wall, and saw Hector being bome away in front of the city—the horses dragging him without heed or care over the ground towards the ships of the Achaeans. Her eyes were then shrouded as with the darkness of night and she fell fainting backwards. She tore the tiring from her head and flung it from her, the frontlet and net with its plaited band, and the veil which golden Aphrodite had given her on the day when Hector took her with him from the house of Eëtion, after having given countless gifts of wooing for her sake. Her husband's sisters and the wives of his brothers crowded round her and supported her, for she was fain to die in her distraction. When she again presently breathed and came to herself, she sobbed and made lament among the Trojans, saying:

"Woe is me, O Hector! Woe, indeed, that to share a common lot we were born, you at Troy in the house of Priam, and I at Thebes under the wooded mountain of Placus in the house of Eëtion who brought me up when I was a child—ill-starred sire of an ill-starred daughter—would that he had never begotten me. You are now going into the house of Hades under the secret places of the earth, and you leave me a sorrowing widow in your house. The child of whom you and I are the unhappy parents is as yet a mere infant. Now that you are gone, O Hector, you can do nothing for him nor he for you. Even though he escape the horrors of this woeful war with the Achaeans, yet shall his life henceforth be one of labor and sorrow, for others will seize his lands. The day that robs a child of his parents severs him from his own kind. His head is bowed, his cheeks are wet with tears, and he will go about destitute among the friends of his father, plucking one by the cloak and another by the shirt. Some one or other of these may so far pity him as to hold the cup for a moment towards him and let him moisten his lips, but he must not drink enough to wet the roof of his mouth; then one whose parents are alive will drive him from the table with blows and angry words. 'Out with you,' he will say, 'you have no father here,' and the child will go crying back to his widowed mother—he, Astyanax, who erewhile would sit upon his father's knees, and have none but the daintiest and choicest morsels set before him. When he had played till he was tired and went to sleep, he would lie in a bed, in the arms of his nurse, on a soft couch, knowing neither want nor care, whereas now that he has lost his father his lot will be full of hardship—he, whom the Trojans name Astyanax, because you, O Hector, were the only defense of their gates and battlements. The wriggling writhing worms will now eat you at the ships, far from your parents, when the dogs have glutted themselves upon you. You will lie naked, although in your house you have fine and goodly raiment made by the hands of women. This will I now burn; it is of no use to you, for you can never again wear it, and thus you will have respect shown you by the Trojans both men and women."

In such wise did she cry aloud amid her tears, and the women joined in her lament.

BOOK XXIII

Achilles brings Hector's corpse into the Greek camp and gives orders for the funeral of Patroclus, whose spirit visits him in the night. In the morning the funeral pyre is built and all day sacrifices are offered and the rites of honor celebrated to comfort the hero's spirit. The following day Patroclus's ashes are laid in a tomb, and Achilles presides over splendid funeral games.

THUS DID THEY MAKE THEIR MOAN THROUGHOUT THE CITY, while the Achaeans when they reached the Hellespont went back every man to his own ship. But Achilles would not let the Myrmidons go, and spoke to his brave comrades, saying: "Myrmidons, famed horsemen and my own trusted friends, not yet, forsooth, let us unyoke, but with horse and chariot draw near to the body and mourn Patroclus, in due honor to the dead. When we have had full comfort of lamentation we will unyoke our horses and take supper all of us here."

On this they all joined in a cry of wailing and Achilles led them in their lament. Thrice did they drive their chariots all sorrowing round the body, and Thetis stirred within them a still deeper yearning. The sands of the seashore and the men's armor were wet with their weeping, so great a minister of fear was he whom they had lost. Chief in all their mourning was the son of

Peleus: he laid his bloodstained hand on the breast of his friend. "Farewell," he cried, "Patroclus, even in the house of Hades. I will now do all that I erewhile promised you; I will drag Hector hither and let dogs devour him raw; twelve noble sons of Trojans will I also slay before your pyre to avenge you."

As he spoke he treated the body of noble Hector with contumely, laying it at full length in the dust beside the bier of Patroclus. The others then put off every man his armor, took the horses from their chariots, and seated themselves in great multitude by the ship of the fleet descendant of Aeacus, who thereon feasted them with an abundant funeral banquet. Many a goodly ox, with many a sheep and bleating goat, did they butcher and cut up; many a tusked boar, moreover, fat and well-fed, did they singe and set to roast in the flames of Hephaestus; and rivulets of blood flowed all round the place where the body was lying.

Then the princes of the Achaeans took the son of Peleus to Agamemnon, but hardly could they persuade him to come with them, so wroth was he for the death of his comrade. As soon as they reached Agamemnon's tent they told the servingmen to set a large tripod over the fire, in case they might persuade the son of Peleus to wash the clotted gore from his body, but he denied them sternly, and swore it with a solemn oath, saying, "Nay, by King Zeus, first and mightiest of all gods, it is not meet that water should touch my body, till I have laid Patroclus on the flames, have built him a barrow, and shaved my head—for so long as I live no such second sorrow shall ever draw nigh me. Now, therefore, let us do all that this sad festival demands, but at break of day, King Agamemnon, bid your men bring wood, and provide all else that the dead may duly take into the realm of darkness; the fire shall thus burn him out of our sight the sooner, and the people shall turn again to their own labors."

Thus did he speak, and they did even as he had said. They made haste to prepare the meal, they ate, and every man had his full share so that all were satisfied. As soon as they had had enough to eat and drink, the others went to their rest each in his own tent, but the son of Peleus lay grieving among his Myrmidons by the shore of the sounding sea, in an open place where the waves came surging in one after another. Here a very deep slumber took hold upon him and eased the burden of his sorrows, for his limbs were weary with chasing Hector round windy Ilium. Presently the sad spirit of Patroclus drew near him, like what he had been in stature, voice, and the light of his beaming eyes, clad, too, as he had been clad in life. The spirit hovered over his head and said:

"You sleep, Achilles, and have forgotten me. You loved me living, but now that I am dead you think for me no further. Bury me with all speed that I may pass the gates of Hades. The ghosts, vain shadows of men that can labor no more, drive me away from them. They will not yet suffer me to join those that are beyond the river, and I wander all desolate by the wide gates of the house of Hades. Give me now your hand I pray you, for when you have once given me my dues of fire, never shall I again come forth out of the house of Hades. Nevermore shall we sit apart and take sweet counsel among the living; the cruel fate which was my birthright has yawned its wide jaws around me—nay, you too Achilles, peer of gods, are doomed to die beneath the wall of the noble Trojans.

"One prayer more will I make you, if you will grant it. Let not my bones be laid apart from yours, Achilles, but with them. Even as we were brought up together in your own home, what time Menoetius brought me to you as a child from Opöeis because by a sad spite I had killed the son of Amphidamas—not of set purpose, but in childish quarrel over the dice. The knight Peleus took me into his house, entreated me kindly, and named me to be your squire. Therefore let our bones lie in but a single urn, the two-handled golden vase given to you by your mother."

And Achilles answered: "Why, true heart, are you come hither to lay these charges upon me? I will of my own self do all as you have bidden me. Draw closer to me, let us once more throw our arms around one another, and find sad comfort in the sharing of our sorrows."

He opened his arms towards him as he spoke and would have clasped him in them, but there was nothing, and the spirit vanished as a vapor, gibbering and whining into the earth. Achilles sprang to his feet, smote his two hands, and made lamentation, saying: "Of a truth, even in the house of Hades there are ghosts and phantoms that have no life in them. All night long the sad spirit of Patroclus has hovered over my head making piteous moan, telling me what I am to do for him, and looking wondrously like himself."

Thus did he speak and his words set them all weeping and mourning about the poor dumb dead, till rosy-fingered morn appeared. Then King Agamemnon sent men and mules from all parts of the camp to bring wood, and Meriones, squire to Idomeneus, was in charge over them. They went out with woodmen's axes and strong ropes in their hands, and before them went the mules. Up hill and down dale did they go, by straight ways and crooked, and when they reached the heights of many-fountained Ida, they laid their axes to the roots of many a tall branching oak that came thundering down as they felled it. They split the trees and bound them behind the mules, which then wended their way as they best could through the thick brushwood on to the plain. All who had been cutting wood bore logs, for so Meriones, squire to Idomeneus, had bidden them, and they threw them down in a line upon the seashore at the place where Achilles would make a mighty monument for Patroclus and for himself.

When they had thrown down their great logs of wood over the whole ground, they stayed all of them where they were, but Achilles ordered his brave Myrmidons to gird on their armor, and to yoke each man his horses; they therefore rose, girded on their armor, and mounted each his chariot—they and their charioteers with them. The chariots went before, and they that were on foot followed as a cloud in their tens of thousands after. In the midst of them his comrades bore Patroclus and covered him with the locks of their hair which they cut off and threw upon his body. Last came Achilles with his head bowed for sorrow, so noble a comrade was he taking to the house of Hades.

When they came to the place of which Achilles had told them, they laid the body down and built up the wood. Achilles then bethought him of another matter. He went a space away from the pyre, and cut off the yellow lock which he had let grow for the river Spercheius. He looked all sorrowfully out upon the dark sea and said, "Spercheius, in vain did my father Peleus vow to you that when I returned home to my loved native land I should cut off this lock and offer you a holy hecatomb; fifty he-goats was I to sacrifice to you there at your springs, where is your grove and your altar fragrant with burnt offerings. Thus did my father vow, but you have not fulfilled his prayer; now, therefore, that I shall see my home no more, I give this lock as a keepsake to the hero Patroclus."

As he spoke he placed the lock in the hands of his dear comrade, and all who stood by were filled with yearning and lamentation. The sun would have gone down upon their mourning had not Achilles presently said to Agamemnon: "Son of Atreus, for it is to you that the people will give ear; there is a time to mourn and a time to cease from mourning; bid the people now leave the pyre and set about getting their dinners. We, to whom the dead is dearest, will see to what is wanted here, and let the other princes also stay by me."

When King Agamemnon heard this he dismissed the people to their ships, but those who were about the dead heaped up wood and built a pyre a hundred feet this way and that; then they laid the dead all sorrowfully upon the top of it. They flayed and dressed many fat sheep and oxen before the pyre, and Achilles took fat from all of them and wrapped the body therein from head to foot, heaping the flayed carcasses all round it. Against the bier he leaned two-handled jars of honey and unguents; four proud horses did he then cast upon the pyre, groaning the while he did so. The dead hero had had nine house dogs; two of them did Achilles slay and throw upon the pyre; he also put twelve brave sons of noble Trojans to the sword and laid them with the rest, for he was full of bitterness and fury. Then he committed all to the resistless and devouring might of the fire. He groaned aloud and called on his dead comrade by name. "Farewell," he cried, "Patroclus, even in the house of Hades. I am now doing all that I have promised you. Twelve brave sons of noble Trojans shall the flames consume along with yourself, but dogs, not fire, shall devour the flesh of Hector, son of Priam."

Thus did he vaunt, but the dogs came not about the body of Hector, for Zeus's daughter Aphrodite kept them off him night and day, and anointed him with ambrosial oil of roses that his flesh might not be torn when Achilles was dragging him about. Phoebus Apollo moreover sent a dark cloud from heaven to earth, which gave shade to the whole place where Hector lay, that the heat of the sun might not parch his body.

Now the pyre about dead Patroclus would not kindle. Achilles therefore bethought him of another matter; he went apart and prayed to the two winds Boreas and Zephyrus, vowing them goodly offerings. He made them many drink offerings from his golden cup, and besought them to come and help him that the wood might make haste to kindle and the dead bodies be consumed. Fleet Iris heard him praying and started off to fetch the winds. They were holding high feast in the house of boisterous Zephyrus when Iris came running up to the stone threshold of the house and stood there, but as soon as they set eyes on her they all came towards her and each of them called her to him, but Iris would not sit down. "I cannot stay," she said, "I must go back to the streams of Oceanus and the land of the Ethiopians who are offering hecatombs to the immortals, and I would have my share; but Achilles prays that Boreas and shrill Zephyrus will come to him, and he vows them goodly offerings; he would have you blow upon the pyre of Patroclus for whom all the Achaeans are lamenting."

With this she left them, and the two winds rose with a cry that rent the air and swept the clouds before them. They blew on and on until they came to the sea, and the waves rose high beneath them, but when they reached Troy they fell upon the pyre till the mighty flames roared under the blast that they blew. All night long did they blow hard and beat upon the fire, and all night long did Achilles grasp his double cup, drawing wine from a mixing bowl of gold, and calling upon the spirit of dead Patroclus as he poured it upon the ground until the earth was drenched. As a father mourns when he is burning the bones of his bridegroom son whose death has wrung the hearts of his parents, even so did Achilles mourn while burning the body of his comrade, pacing round the bier with piteous groaning and lamentation.

At length as the morning star was beginning to herald the light which saffron-mantled Dawn was soon to suffuse over the sea, the flames fell and the fire began to die. The winds then went home beyond the Thracian sea, which roared and boiled as they swept over it. The son of Peleus now turned away from the pyre and lay down, overcome with toil, till he fell into a sweet slumber. Presently they who were about the son of Atreus drew near in a body, and roused him with the noise and tramp of their coming. He sate upright and said: "Son of Atreus, and all other princes of the Achaeans, first pour red wine everywhere upon the fire and quench it. Let us then gather the bones of Patroclus, son of Menoetius, singling them out with care; they are easily found, for they lie in the middle of the pyre, while all else, both men and horses, has been thrown in a heap and burned at the outer edge. We will lay the bones in a golden urn, in two layers of fat, against the time when I shall myself go down into the house of Hades. As for the barrow, labor not to raise a great one now, but such as is reasonable. Afterwards, let those Achaeans who may be left at the ships when I am gone build it both broad and high."

Thus he spoke and they obeyed the word of the son of Peleus. First they poured red wine upon the thick layer of ashes and quenched the fire. With many tears they singled out the whitened bones of their loved comrade and laid them within a golden urn in two layers of fat: they then covered the urn with a linen cloth and took it inside the tent. They marked off the circle where the barrow should be, made a foundation for it about the pyre, and forthwith heaped up the earth. When they had thus raised a mound they were going away, but Achilles stayed the people and made them sit in assembly. He brought prizes from the ships—cauldrons, tripods, horses and mules, noble oxen, women with fair girdles, and swart iron.

The first prize he offered was for the chariot races—a woman skilled in all useful arts, and a three-legged cauldron that had ears for handles, and would hold twenty-two measures. This was for the man who came in first. For the second there was a six-year-old mare, unbroken, and in foal to a he-ass. The third was to have a goodly cauldron that had never yet been on the fire; it was still bright as when it left the maker, and would hold four measures. The fourth prize was two talents of gold, and the fifth a two-handled urn as yet unsoiled by smoke. Then he stood up and spoke among the Argives, saying:

"Son of Atreus, and all other Achaeans, these are the prizes that lie waiting the winners of the chariot races. At any other time I should carry off the first prize and take it to my own tent. You know how far my steeds excel all others—for they are immortal. Poseidon gave them to my father Peleus, who in his turn gave them to myself; but I shall hold aloof, I and my steeds that have lost their brave and kind driver, who many a time has washed them in clear water and anointed their manes with oil. See how they stand weeping here, with their manes trailing on the ground in the extremity of their sorrow. But do you others set yourselves in order throughout the host, whosoever has confidence in his horses and in the strength of his chariot."

Thus spoke the son of Peleus and the drivers of chariots bestirred themselves. First among them all uprose Eumelus, king of men, son of Admetus, a man excellent in horsemanship. Next to him rose mighty Diomed, son of Tydeus; he yoked the Trojan horses which he had taken from Aeneas, when Apollo bore him out of the fight. Next to him, yellow-haired Menelaus, son of Atreus, rose and yoked his fleet horses, Agamemnon's mare Aethe, and his own horse Podargus. The mare had been given to Agamemnon by Echepolus, son of Anchises, that he might not have to follow him to Ilium, but might stay at home and take his ease; for Zeus had endowed him with great wealth and he lived in spacious Sicyon. This mare, all eager for the race, did Menelaus put under the yoke.

Fourth in order, Antilochus, son to noble Nestor, son of Neleus, made ready his horses. These were bred in Pylos, and his father came up to him to give him good advice of which, however, he stood in but little need. "Antilochus," said Nestor, "you are young, but Zeus and Poseidon have loved you well, and have made you an excellent horseman. I need not therefore say much by way of instruction. You are skillful at wheeling your horses round the post, but the horses themselves are very slow, and it is this that will, I fear, mar your chances. The other drivers know less than you do, but their horses are fleeter; therefore, my dear son, see if you cannot hit upon some artifice whereby you may ensure that the prize shall not slip through your fingers. The woodman does more by skill than by brute force; by skill the pilot guides his storm-tossed bark over the sea, and so by skill one driver can beat another. If a man leaves all to his horses, they will go wide in rounding the posts at either end of the course. He has no command over them and cannot keep them from swerving this way and that, whereas a man who knows what he is doing may have worse horses, but he will keep them well in hand when he sees the doubling-post. He knows the precise moment at which to pull the rein and keeps his eye well on the man in front of him. I will give you this certain token which cannot escape your notice. There is a stump of a dead tree—oak or pine as it may be—some six feet above the ground, and not yet rotted away by rain; it stands at the fork of the road; it has two white stones set one on each side, and there is a clear course all round it. It may have been a monument to someone long since dead, or it may have been used as a doubling-post in days gone by. Now, however, it has been fixed on by Achilles as the mark round which the chariots shall turn; hug it as close as you can, but as you stand in your chariot lean over a little to the left; urge on your right-hand horse with voice and lash, and give him a loose rein, but let the left-hand horse keep so close in, that the nave of your wheel shall almost graze the post; but mind the stone, or you will wound your horses and break your chariot in pieces, which would be sport for others but confusion for yourself. Therefore, my dear son, mind well what you are about, for if you can be first to round the post there is no chance of anyone giving you the go-by later, not even though you had Adrestus's horse Arion behind you—a horse which is of divine race—or those of Laomedon, which are the noblest in this country."

When Nestor had made an end of counseling his son he sat down in his place, and fifth in order, Meriones got ready his horses. They then all mounted their chariots and cast lots. Achilles shook the helmet, and the lot of Antilochus, son of Nestor, fell out first; next came that of King Eumelus, and after his, those of Menelaus, son of Atreus, and of Meriones. The last place fell to the lot of Diomed, son of Tydeus, who was the best man of them all. They took their places in line. Achilles showed them the doubling-post round which they were to turn, some way off upon the plain. Here he stationed his father's follower Phoenix as umpire, to note the running and report truly.

At the same instant they all of them lashed their horses, struck them with the reins, and shouted at them with all their might. They flew full speed over the plain away from the ships, the dust rose from under them as it were a cloud or whirlwind, and their manes were all flying in the wind. At one moment the chariots seemed to touch the ground, and then again they bounded into the air. The drivers stood erect, and their hearts beat fast and furious in their lust of victory. Each kept calling on his horses, and the horses scoured the plain amid the clouds of dust that they raised.

It was when they were doing the last part of the course on their way back towards the sea that their pace was strained to the utmost and it was seen what each could do. The horses of the descendant of Pheres now took the lead, and close behind them came the Trojan stallions of Diomed. They seemed as if about to mount Eumelus's chariot, and he could feel their warm breath on his back and on his broad shoulders, for their heads were close to him as they flew over the course. Diomed would have now passed him, or there would have been a dead heat, but Phoebus Apollo to spite him made him drop his whip. Tears of anger fell from his eyes as he saw the mares going on faster than ever, while his own horses lost ground through his having no whip. Athene saw the trick which Apollo had played the son of Tydeus, so she brought him his whip and put spirit into his horses. Moreover, she went after the son of Admetus in a rage and broke his yoke for him. The mares went one to one side the course, and the other to the other, and the pole was broken against the ground. Eumelus was thrown from his chariot close to the wheel, his elbows, mouth, and nostrils were all torn, and his forehead was bruised above his eyebrows. His eyes filled with tears and he could find no utterance. But the son of Tydeus turned his horses aside and shot far ahead, for Athene put fresh strength into them and covered Diomed himself with glory.

Menelaus, son of Atreus, came next behind him, but Antilochus called to his father's horses. "On with you both," he cried, "and do your very utmost. I do not bid you try to beat the steeds of the son of Tydeus, for Athene has put running into them and has covered Diomed with glory; but you must overtake the horses of the son of Atreus and not be left behind, or Aethe who is so fleet will taunt you. Why, my good fellows, are you lagging? I tell you, and it shall surely be—Nestor will keep neither of you, but will put both of you to the sword, if we win any the worse a prize through your carelessness. Hie after them at your utmost speed; I will hit on a plan for passing them in a narrow part of the way, and it shall not fail me."

They feared the rebuke of their master, and for a short space went quicker. Presently Antilochus saw a narrow place where the road had sunk. The ground was broken, for the winter's rain had gathered and had worn the road so that the whole place was deepened. Menelaus was making towards it so as to get there first, for fear of a foul, but Antilochus turned his horses out of the way, and followed him a little on one side. The son of Atreus was afraid and shouted out: "Antilochus, you are driving recklessly; rein in your horses; the road is too narrow here, it will be wider soon, and you can pass me then; if you foul my chariot you may bring both of us to a mischief."

But Antilochus plied his whip, and drove faster, as though he had not heard him. They went side by side for about as far as a young man can hurl a disc from his shoulder when he is trying his strength, and then Menelaus's mares drew behind, for he left off driving for fear the horses should foul one another and upset the chariots; thus, while pressing on in quest of victory, they might both come headlong to the ground. Menelaus then upbraided Antilochus and said: "There is no greater trickster living than you are. Go, and bad luck go with you. The Achaeans say not well that you have understanding, and come what may you shall not bear away the prize without sworn protest on my part."

Then he called on his horses and said to them: "Keep your pace, and slacken not. The limbs of the other horses will weary sooner than yours, for they are neither of them young."

The horses feared the rebuke of their master and went faster, so that they were soon nearly up with the others.

Meanwhile the Achaeans from their seats were watching how the horses went, as they scoured the plain amid clouds of their own dust. Idomeneus, captain of the Cretans, was first to make out the running, for he was not in the thick of the crowd, but stood on the most commanding part of the ground. The driver was a long way off, but Idomeneus could hear him shouting, and could see the foremost horse quite plainly—a chestnut with a round white star, like the moon, on its forehead. He stood up and said among the Argives: "My friends, princes and counselors of the Argives, can you see the running as well as I can? There seems to be another pair in front now, and another driver. Those that led off at the start must have been disabled out on the plain. I saw them at first making their way round the doubling-post, but now, though I search the plain of Troy, I cannot find them. Perhaps the reins fell from the driver's hand so that he lost command of his horses at the doubling-post, and could not turn it. I suppose he must have been thrown out there, and broken his chariot, while his mares have left the course and gone off wildly in a panic. Come up and see for yourselves, I cannot make out for certain, but the driver seems an Aetolian by descent, ruler over the Argives, brave Diomed, the son of Tydeus."

Ajax, the son of Oïleus, took him up rudely and said: "Idomeneus, why should you be in such a hurry to tell us all about it, when the mares are still so far out upon the plain? You are none of the youngest, nor your eyes none of the sharpest, but you are always laying down the law. You have no right to do so, for there are better men here than you are. Eumelus's horses are in front now, as they always have been, and he is on the chariot holding the reins."

The captain of the Cretans was angry, and answered, "Ajax, you are an excellent railer, but you have no judgment, and are wanting in much else as well, for you have a vile temper. I will wager you a tripod or cauldron, and Agamemnon, son of Atreus, shall decide whose horses are first. You will then know to your cost."

Ajax, son of Oïleus, was for making him an angry answer, and there would have been yet further brawling between them had not Achilles risen in his place and said: "Cease your railing, Ajax and Idomeneus. It is not seemly; you would be scandalized if you saw anyone else do the like: sit down and keep your eyes on the horses. They are speeding towards the winning post and will be here directly. You will then both of you know whose horses are first, and whose come after."

As he was speaking, the son of Tydeus came driving in, plying his whip lustily from his shoulder, and his horses stepping high as they flew over the course. The sand and grit rained thick on the driver, and the chariot inlaid with gold and tin ran close behind his fleet horses. There was little trace of wheel marks in the fine dust, and the horses came flying in at their utmost speed. Diomed stayed them in the middle of the crowd, and the sweat from their manes and chests fell in streams on to the ground. Forthwith he sprang from his goodly chariot, and leaned his whip against his horses' yoke. Brave Sthenelus now lost no time, but at once brought on the prize, and gave the woman and the ear-handled cauldron to his comrades to take away. Then he unyoked the horses.

Next after him came in Antilochus of the race of Neleus, who had passed Menelaus by a trick and not by the fleetness of his horses; but even so Menelaus came in as close behind him as the wheel is to the horse that draws both the chariot and its master. The end hairs of a horse's tail touch the tire of the wheel, and there is never much space between wheel and horse when the chariot is going. Menelaus was no further than this behind Antilochus, though at first he had been a full disc's throw behind him. He had soon caught him up again, for Agamemnon's mare Aethe kept pulling stronger and stronger, so that if the course had been longer he would have passed him, and there would not even have been a dead heat. Idomeneus's brave squire Meriones was about a spear's cast behind Menelaus. His horses were slowest of all, and he was the worst driver. Last of them all came the son of Admetus, dragging his chariot and driving his horses on in front. When Achilles saw him he was sorry, and stood up among the Argives, saying, "The best man is coming in last. Let us give him a prize for it is reasonable. He shall have the second, but the first must go to the son of Tydeus."

Thus did he speak and the others all of them applauded his saying, and were for doing as he had said, but Nestor's son Antilochus stood up and claimed his rights from the son of Peleus. "Achilles," said he, "I shall take it much amiss if you do this thing. You would rob me of my prize because you think Eumelus's chariot and horses were thrown out, and himself too, good man that he is. He should have prayed duly to the immortals: he would not have come in last if he had done so. If you are sorry for him and so choose, you have much gold in your tents, with bronze, sheep, cattle, and horses. Take something from this store if you would have the Achaeans speak well of you, and give him a better prize even than that which you have now offered; but I will not give up the mare, and he that will fight me for her, let him come on."

Achilles smiled as he heard this and was pleased with Antilochus, who was one of his dearest comrades. So he said:

"Antilochus, if you would have me find Eumelus another prize, I will give him the bronze breastplate with a rim of tin running all round it which I took from Asteropaeus. It will be worth much money to him."

He bade his comrade Automedon bring the breastplate from his tent, and he did so. Achilles then gave it over to Eumelus, who received it gladly. But Menelaus got up in a rage, furiously angry with Antilochus. An attendant placed his staff in his hands and bade the Argives keep silence. The hero then addressed them. "Antilochus," said he, "what is this—from you who have been so far blameless? You have made me cut a poor figure and balked my horses by flinging your own in front of them, though yours are much worse than mine are. Therefore, O princes and counselors of the Argives, judge between us and show no favor, lest one of the Achaeans say, 'Menelaus has got the mare through lying and corruption; his horses were far inferior to Antilochus's, but he has greater weight and influence.' Nay, I will determine the matter myself, and no man will blame me, for I shall do what is just. Come here, Antilochus, and stand, as our custom is, whip in hand before your chariot and horses. Lay your hand on your steeds, and swear by earth-encircling Poseidon that you did not purposely and guilefully get in the way of my horses."

And Antilochus answered: "Forgive me; I am much younger, King Menelaus, than you are. You stand higher than I do and are the better man of the two. You know how easily young men are betrayed into indiscretion; their tempers are more hasty and they have less judgment. Make due allowances, therefore, and bear with me. I will of my own accord give up the mare that I have won, and if you claim any further chattel from my own possessions, I would rather yield it to you at once than fall from your good graces henceforth, and do wrong in the sight of heaven."

The son of Nestor then took the mare and gave her over to Menelaus, whose anger was thus appeased; as when dew falls upon a field of ripening corn, and the lands are bristling with the harvest—even so, O Menelaus, was your heart made glad within you. He turned to Antilochus and said: "Now, Antilochus, angry though I have been, I can give way to you of my own free will; you have never been headstrong nor ill-disposed hitherto, but this time your youth has got the better of your judgment. Be careful how you outwit your betters in future. No one else could have brought me round so easily, but your good father, your brother, and yourself have all of you had infinite trouble on my behalf. I therefore yield to your entreaty, and will give up the mare to you, mine though it indeed be; the people will thus see that I am neither harsh nor vindictive."

With this he gave the mare over to Antilochus's comrade Noëmon and then took the cauldron. Meriones, who had come in fourth, carried off the two talents of gold, and the fifth prize, the two-handled urn, being unawarded, Achilles gave it to Nestor, going up to him among the assembled Argives and saying: "Take this, my good old friend, as an heirloom and memorial of the funeral of Patroclus—for you shall see him no more among the Argives. I give you this prize though you cannot win one. You can now neither wrestle nor fight, and cannot enter for the javelin match nor foot races, for the hand of age has been laid heavily upon you."

So saying he gave the urn over to Nestor, who received it gladly and answered: "My son, all that you have said is true. There is no strength now in my legs and feet, nor can I hit out with my hands from either shoulder. Would that I were still young and strong as when the Epeans were burying King Amarynceus in Buprasium, and his sons offered prizes in his honor. There was then none that could vie with me, neither of the Epeans nor the Pylians themselves nor the Aetolians. In boxing I overcame Clytomedes, son of Enops, and in wrestling, Ancaeus of Pleuron who had come forward against me. Iphiclus was a good runner, but I beat him, and threw further with my spear than either Phyleus or Polydorus. In chariot racing alone did the two sons of Actor surpass me by crowding their horses in front of me, for they were angry at the way victory had gone, and at the greater part of the prizes remaining in the place in which they had been offered. They were twins, and the one kept on holding the reins, and holding the reins, while the other plied the whip. Such was I then, but now I must leave these matters to younger men. I must bow before the weight of years, but in those days I was eminent among heroes. And now, sir, go on with the funeral contests in honor of your comrade. Gladly do I accept this urn, and my heart rejoices that you do not forget me but are ever mindful of my goodwill towards you and of the respect due to me from the Achaeans. For all which may the grace of heaven be vouchsafed you in great abundance."

Thereon the son of Peleus, when he had listened to all the thanks of Nestor, went about among the concourse of the Achaeans, and presently offered prizes for skill in the painful art of boxing. He brought out a strong mule and made it fast in the middle of the crowd—a she-mule never yet broken, but six years old—when it is hardest of all to break them: this was for the victor, and for the vanquished he offered a double cup. Then he stood up and said among the Argives: "Son of Atreus, and all other Achaeans, I invite our two champion boxers to lay about them lustily and compete for these prizes. He to whom Apollo vouchsafes the greater endurance, and whom the Achaeans acknowledge as victor, shall take the mule back with him to his own tent, while he that is vanquished shall have the double cup."

As he spoke there stood up a champion both brave and of great stature, a skillful boxer, Epeüs, son of Panopeus. He laid his hand on the mule and said, "Let the man who is to have the cup come hither, for none but myself will take the mule. I am the best boxer of all here present, and none can beat me. Is it not enough that I should fall short of you in actual fighting? Still, no man can be good at everything. I tell you plainly, and it shall come true, if any man will box with me I will bruise his body and break his bones. Therefore let his friends stay here in a body and be at hand to take him away when I have done with him."

They all held their peace, and no man rose save Euryalus, son of Mecisteus, who was son of Talaüs. Mecisteus went once to Thebes after the fall of Oedipus, to attend his funeral, and he beat all the people of Cadmus. The son of Tydeus was Euryalus's second, cheering him on and hoping heartily that he would win. First he put a waistband round him and then he gave him some well-cut thongs of oxhide. The two men being now girt went into the middle of the ring and immediately fell to. Heavily indeed did they punish one another and lay about them with their brawny fists. One could hear the horrid crashing of their jaws, and they sweated from every pore of their skin. Presently Epeüs came on and gave Euryalus a blow on the jaw as he was looking round. Euryalus could not keep his legs; they gave way under him in a moment and he sprang up with a bound, as a fish leaps into the air near some shore that is all bestrewn with sea-wrack, when Boreas furs the top of the waves, and then falls back into deep water. But noble Epeüs caught hold of him and raised him up; his comrades also came round him and led him from the ring, unsteady in his gait, his head hanging on one side, and spitting great clots of gore. They set him down in a swoon and then went to fetch the double cup.

The son of Peleus now brought out the prizes for the third contest and showed them to the Argives. These were for the painful art of wrestling. For the winner there was a great tripod ready for setting upon the fire, and the Achaeans valued it among themselves at twelve oxen. For the loser he brought out a woman skilled in all manner of arts, and they valued her at four oxen. He rose and said among the Argives, "Stand forward, you who will essay this contest."

Forthwith uprose great Ajax, the son of Telamon, and crafty Odysseus, full of wiles, rose also. The two girded themselves and went into the middle of the ring. They gripped each other in their strong hands like the rafters which some master builder frames for the roof of a high house to keep the wind out. Their backbones cracked as they tugged at one another with their mighty arms—and sweat rained from them in torrents. Many a bloody weal sprang up on their sides and shoulders, but they kept on striving with might and main for victory and to win the tripod. Odysseus could not throw Ajax, nor Ajax him. Odysseus was too strong for him, but when the Achaeans began to tire of watching them, Ajax said to Odysseus, "Odysseus, noble son of Laertes, you shall either lift me, or I you, and let Zeus settle it between us."

He lifted him from the ground as he spoke, but Odysseus did not forget his cunning. He hit Ajax in the hollow at the back of his knee, so that he could not keep his feet, but fell on his back with Odysseus lying upon his chest, and all who saw it marveled. Then Odysseus in turn lifted Ajax and stirred him a little from the ground but could not lift him right off it, his knee sank under him, and the two fell side by side on the ground and were all begrimed with dust. They now sprang towards one another and were for wrestling yet a third time, but Achilles rose and stayed them. "Put not each other further," said he, "to such cruel suffering. The victory is with both alike, take each of you an equal prize, and let the other Achaeans now compete."

Thus did he speak and they did even as he had said, and put on their shirts again after wiping the dust from off their bodies.

The son of Peleus then offered prizes for speed in running—a mixing bowl beautifully wrought, of pure silver. It would hold six measures, and far exceeded all others in the whole world for beauty. It was the work of cunning artificers in Sidon and had been brought into port by Phoenicians from beyond the sea, who had made a present of it to Thoas. Eueneus, son of Jason, had given it to Patroclus in ransom of Priam's son Lycaon, and Achilles now offered it as a prize in honor of his comrade to him who should be the swiftest runner. For the second prize he offered a large ox, well-fattened, while for the last there was to be half a talent of gold. He then rose and said among the Argives, "Stand forward, you who will essay this contest."

Forthwith uprose fleet Ajax, son of Oïleus, with cunning Odysseus, and Nestor's son Antilochus, the fastest runner among all the youth of his time. They stood side by side and Achilles showed them the goal. The course was set out for them from the starting post, and the son of Oïleus took the lead at once, with Odysseus as close behind him as the shuttle is to a woman's bosom when she throws the woof across the warp and holds it close up to her; even so close behind him was Odysseus—treading in his footprints before the dust could settle there, and Ajax could feel his breath on the back of his head as he ran swiftly on. The Achaeans all shouted applause as they saw him straining his utmost, and cheered him as he shot past them; but when they were now nearing the end of the course Odysseus prayed inwardly to Athene. "Hear me," he cried, "and help my feet, O goddess!"

Thus did he pray, and Pallas Athene heard his prayer. She made his hands and his feet feel light, and when the runners were at the point of pouncing upon the prize, Ajax, through Athene's spite slipped upon some offal that was lying there from the cattle which Achilles had slaughtered in honor of Patroclus, and his mouth and nostrils were all filled with cow dung. Odysseus therefore carried off the mixing bowl, for he got before Ajax and came in first. But Ajax took the ox and stood with his hand on one of its horns, spitting the dung out of his mouth. Then he said to the Argives: "Alas, the goddess has spoiled my running; she watches over Odysseus and stands by him as though she were his own mother." Thus did he speak and they all of them laughed heartily.

Antilochus carried off the last prize and smiled as he said to the bystanders: "You all see, my friends, that now too the gods have shown their respect for seniority. Ajax is somewhat older than I am, and as for Odysseus, he belongs to an earlier generation, but he is hale in spite of his years, and no man of the Achaeans can run against him save only Achilles."

He said this to pay a compliment to the son of Peleus, and Achilles answered, "Antilochus, you shall not have praised me to no purpose; I shall give you an additional half talent of gold." He then gave the half talent to Antilochus, who received it gladly.

Then the son of Peleus brought out the spear, helmet, and shield that had been borne by Sarpedon, and were taken from him by Patroclus. He stood up and said among the Argives: "We bid two champions put on their armor, take their keen blades, and make trial of one another in the presence of the multitude. Whichever of them can first wound the flesh of the other, cut through his armor, and draw blood, to him will I give this goodly Thracian sword inlaid with silver, which I took from Asteropaeus, but the armor let both hold in partnership, and I will give each of them a hearty meal in my own tent."

Forthwith uprose great Ajax, the son of Telamon, as also mighty Diomed, son of Tydeus. When they had put on their armor each on his own side of the ring, they both went into the middle eager to engage, and with fire flashing from their eyes. The Achaeans marveled as they beheld them, and when the two were now close up with one another, thrice did they spring forward and thrice try to strike each other in close combat. Ajax pierced Diomed's round shield, but did not draw blood, for the cuirass beneath the shield protected him. Thereon the son of Tydeus from over his huge shield kept aiming continually at Ajax's neck with the point of his spear, and the Achaeans alarmed for his safety bade them leave off fighting and divide the prize between them. Achilles then gave the great sword to the son of Tydeus, with its scabbard and the leathern belt with which to hang it.

Achilles next offered the massive iron quoit which mighty Eëtion had erewhile been used to hurl, until Achilles had slain him and carried it off in his ships along with other spoils. He stood up and said among the Argives: "Stand forward, you who would essay this contest. He who wins it will have a store of iron that will last him five years as they go rolling round, and if his fair fields lie far from a town his shepherd or plowman will not have to make a journey to buy iron, for he will have a stock of it on his own premises."

Then uprose the two mighty men, Polypoetes and Leonteus, with Ajax, son of Telamon, and noble Epeus. They stood up one after the other and Epeus took the quoit, whirled it, and flung it from him, which set all the Achaeans laughing. After him threw Leonteus of the race of Ares. Ajax, son of Telamon, threw third, sending the quoit beyond any mark that had been made yet, but when mighty Polypoetes took the quoit he hurled it as though it had been a stockman's stick which he sends flying about among his cattle when he is driving them, so far did his throw outdistance those of the others. All who saw it roared applause, and his comrades carried the prize for him and set it on board his ship.

Achilles next offered a prize of iron for archery—ten double-edged axes and ten with single edges. He set up a ship's mast, some way off upon the sands, and with a fine string tied a pigeon to it by the foot: this was what they were to aim at. "Whoever," he said, "can hit the pigeon shall have all the axes and take them away with him; he who hits the string without hitting the bird will have taken a worse aim and shall have the single-edged axes."

Then uprose King Teucer, and Meriones, the stalwart squire of Idomeneus, rose also. They cast lots in a bronze helmet and the lot of Teucer fell first. He let fly with his arrow forthwith, but he did not promise hecatombs of firstling lambs to King Apollo, and missed his bird, for Apollo foiled his aim, but he hit the string with which the bird was tied, near its foot. The arrow cut the string clean through so that it hung down towards the ground, while the bird flew up into the sky, and the Achaeans shouted applause. Meriones, who had his arrow ready while Teucer was aiming, snatched the bow out of his hand, and at once promised that he would sacrifice a hecatomb of firstling lambs to Apollo, lord of the bow. Then espying the pigeon high up under the clouds, he hit her in the middle of the wing as she was circling upwards; the arrow went clean through the wing and fixed itself in the ground at Meriones's feet, but the bird perched on the ship's mast hanging her head and with all her feathers drooping; the life went out of her, and she fell heavily from the mast. Meriones, therefore, took all ten double-edged axes, while Teucer bore off the single-edged ones to his ships.

Then the son of Peleus brought in a spear and a cauldron that had never been on the fire. It was worth an ox, and was chased with a pattern of flowers. And those that would throw the javelin stood up—to wit, the son of Atreus, king of men, Agamemnon, and Meriones, stalwart squire of Idomeneus. But Achilles spoke, saying: "Son of Atreus, we know how far you excel all others both in power and in throwing the javelin. Take the cauldron back with you to your ships, but if it so please you, let us give the spear to Meriones. This at least is what I should myself wish."

King Agamemnon assented. So he gave the bronze spear to Meriones, and handed the goodly cauldron to Talthybius, his esquire.

BOOK XXIV

Achilles drags Hector's body around Patroclus's tomb. At Apollo's protests, Thetis is sent to tell her son to allow Priam to ransom Hector's body. Guided by Hermes, Priam goes to Achilles, who is moved to pity and restores Hector's body, promising an eleven days' truce. Hermes conducts Priam back to Troy. Andromache, Hecuba, and Helen raise the dirge for Hector. His funeral is celebrated fittingly.

THE ASSEMBLY NOW BROKE UP AND THE PEOPLE WENT THEIR ways each to his own ship. There they made ready their supper, and then bethought them of the blessed boon of sleep; but Achilles still wept for thinking of his dear comrade, and sleep, before whom all things bow, could take no hold upon him. This way and that did he turn as he yearned after the might and manfulness of Patroclus; he thought of all they had done together, and all they had gone through both on the field of battle and on the waves of the weary sea. As he dwelt on these things he wept bitterly and lay now on his side, now on his back, and now face downwards, till at last he rose and went out as one distraught to wander upon the seashore. Then, when he saw dawn breaking over beach and sea, he yoked his horses to his chariot, and bound the body of Hector behind it that he might drag it about. Thrice did he drag it round the tomb of the son of Menoetius, and then went back into his tent, leaving the body on the ground full length and with its face downwards. But Apollo would not suffer it to be disfigured, for he pitied the man, dead though he now was. Therefore, he shielded him with his golden aegis continually, that he might take no hurt while Achilles was dragging him.

Thus shamefully did Achilles in his fury dishonor Hector; but the blessed gods looked down in pity from heaven, and urged Hermes, slayer of Argus, to steal the body. All were of this mind save only Hera, Poseidon, and Zeus's gray-eyed daughter, who persisted in the hate which they had ever borne towards Ilium with Priam and his people; for they forgave not the wrong done them by Paris in disdaining the goddesses who came to him when he was in his sheepyards, and preferring her who had offered him a wanton to his ruin.

When, therefore, the morning of the twelfth day had now come, Phoebus Apollo spoke among the immortals, saying: "You gods ought to be ashamed of yourselves; you are cruel and hard-hearted. Did not Hector burn you thighbones of heifers and of unblemished goats? And now dare you not rescue even his dead body, for his wife to look upon, with his mother and child, his father Priam, and his people, who would forthwith commit him to the flames and give him his due funeral rites? So, then, you would all be on the side of mad Achilles, who knows neither right nor ruth? He is like some savage lion that in the pride of his great strength and daring springs upon men's flocks and gorges on them. Even so has Achilles flung aside all pity, and all that conscience which at once so greatly banes yet greatly boons him that will heed it. A man may lose one far dearer than Achilles has lost—a son, it may be, or a brother born from his own mother's womb; yet when he has mourned him and wept over him he will let him bide, for it takes much sorrow to kill a man; whereas Achilles, now that he has slain noble Hector, drags him behind his chariot round the tomb of his comrade. It were better of him, and for him, that he should not do so, for brave though he be we gods may take it ill that he should vent his fury upon dead clay."

Hera spoke up in a rage. "This were well," she cried, "O lord of the silver bow, if you would give like honor to Hector and to Achilles; but Hector was mortal and suckled at a woman's breast, whereas Achilles is the offspring of a goddess whom I myself reared and brought up. I married her to Peleus, who is above measure dear to the immortals. You gods came all of you to her wedding; you feasted along with them yourself and brought your lyre—false, and fond of low company, that you have ever been."

Then said Zeus: "Hera, be not so bitter. Their honor shall not be equal, but of all that dwell in Ilium, Hector was dearest to the gods, as also to myself, for his offerings never failed me. Never was my altar stinted of its dues, nor of the drink offerings and savor of sacrifice which we claim of right. I shall therefore permit the body of mighty Hector to be stolen; and yet this may hardly be without Achilles coming to know it, for his mother keeps night and day beside him. Let some one of you, therefore, send Thetis to me, and I will impart my counsel to her, namely that Achilles is to accept a ransom from Priam and give up the body."

On this Iris, fleet as the wind, went forth to carry his message. Down she plunged into the dark sea midway between Samos and rocky Imbrus. The waters hissed as they closed over her, and she sank into the bottom as the lead at the end of an ox-horn that is sped to carry death to fishes. She found Thetis sitting in a great cave with the other sea-goddesses gathered round her; there she sat in the midst of them weeping for her noble son who was to fall far from his own land, on the rich plains of Troy. Iris went up to her and said, "Rise, Thetis. Zeus, whose counsels fail not, bids you come to him." And Thetis answered: "Why does the mighty god so bid me? I am in great grief, and shrink from going in and out among the immortals. Still, I will go, and the word that he may speak shall not be spoken in vain."

The goddess took her dark veil, than which there can be no robe more somber, and went forth with fleet Iris leading the way before her. The waves of the sea opened them a path, and when they reached the shore they flew up into the heavens, where they found the all-seeing son of Cronus with the blessed gods that live forever assembled near him. Athene gave up her seat to her, and she sat down by the side of father Zeus. Hera then placed a fair golden cup in her hand, and spoke to her in words of comfort, whereon Thetis drank and gave her back the cup; and the sire of gods and men was the first to speak.

"So, goddess," said he, "for all your sorrow, and the grief that I well know reigns ever in your heart, you have come hither to Olympus, and I will tell you why I have sent for you. This nine days past the immortals have been quarreling about Achilles, waster of cities, and the body of Hector. The gods would have Hermes, slayer of Argus, steal the body, but in furtherance of our peace and amity henceforward, I will concede such honor to your son as I will now tell you. Go, then, to the host and lay these commands upon him. Say that the gods are angry with him, and that I am myself more angry than them all, in that he keeps Hector at the ships and will not give him up. He may thus fear me and let the body go. At the same time I will send Iris to great Priam to bid him go to the ships of the Achaeans, and ransom his son, taking with him such gifts for Achilles as may give him satisfaction."

Silver-footed Thetis did as the god had told her, and forthwith down she darted from the topmost summits of Olympus. She went to her son's tents where she found him grieving bitterly, while his trusty comrades round him were busy preparing their morning meal, for which they had killed a great woolly sheep. His mother sat down beside him and caressed him with her hand, saying: "My son, how long will you keep on thus grieving and making moan? You are gnawing at your own heart, and think neither of food nor of woman's embraces; and yet these too were well, for you have no long time to live, and death with the strong hand of fate is already close beside you. Now, therefore, heed what I say, for I come as a messenger from Zeus. He says that the gods are angry with you, and himself more angry than them all, in that you keep Hector at the ships and will not give him up. Therefore let him go, and accept a ransom for his body."

And Achilles answered: "So be it. If Olympian Zeus of his own motion thus commands me, let him that brings the ransom bear the body away."

Thus did mother and son talk together at the ships in long discourse with one another. Meanwhile, the son of Cronus sent Iris to the strong city of Ilium. "Go," said he, "fleet Iris, from the mansions of Olympus, and tell King Priam in Ilium that he is to go to the ships of the Achaeans and free the body of his dear son. He is to take such gifts with him as shall give satisfaction to Achilles, and he is to go alone, with no other Trojan, save only some honored servant who may drive his mules and wagon, and bring back the body of him whom noble Achilles has slain. Let him have no thought nor fear of death in his heart, for we will send the slayer of Argus to escort him, and bring him within the tent of Achilles. Achilles will not kill him nor let another do so, for he will take heed to his ways and sin not, and he will entreat a suppliant with all honorable courtesy."

On this Iris, fleet as the wind, sped forth to deliver her message. She went to Priam's house, and found weeping and lamentation therein. His sons were seated round their father in the outer courtyard, and their raiment was wet with tears. The old man sat in the midst of them with his mantle wrapped close about his body, and his head and neck all covered with the filth which he had clutched as he lay groveling in the mire. His daughters and his sons' wives went wailing about the house, as they thought of the many and brave men who lay dead, slain by the Argives. The messenger of Zeus stood by Priam and spoke softly to him, but fear fell upon him as she did so.

"Take heart," she said, "Priam, offspring of Dardanus, take heart and fear not. I bring no evil tidings, but am minded well towards you. I come as a messenger from Zeus, who though he be not near, takes thought for you and pities you. The lord of Olympus bids you go and ransom noble Hector, and take with you such gifts as shall give satisfaction to Achilles. You are to go alone, with no other Trojan, save only some honored servant who may drive your mules and wagon, and bring back to the city the body of him whom noble Achilles has slain. You are to have no thought, nor fear of death, for Zeus will send the slayer of Argus to escort you. When he has brought you within Achilles's tent, Achilles will not kill you nor let another do so, for he will take heed to his ways and sin not, and he will treat a suppliant with all honorable courtesy."

Iris went her way when she had thus spoken, and Priam told his sons to get a mule-wagon ready, and to make the body of the wagon fast upon the top of its bed. Then he went down into his fragrant storeroom, high-vaulted and made of cedarwood, where his many treasures were kept, and he called Hecuba, his wife. "Wife," said he, "a messenger has come to me from Olympus, and has told me to go to the ships of the Achaeans to ransom my dear son, taking with me such gifts as shall give satisfaction to Achilles. What think you of this matter? For my own part, I am greatly moved to pass through the host of the Achaeans and go to their ships."

His wife cried aloud as she heard him, and said: "Alas, what has become of that judgment for which you have been ever famous both among strangers and your own people? How can you venture alone to the ships of the Achaeans, and look into the face of him who has slain so many of your brave sons? You must have iron courage, for if the cruel savage sees you and lays hold on you, he will know neither respect nor pity. Let us then weep Hector from afar here in our own house, for when I gave him birth the threads of overruling fate were spun for him that dogs should eat his flesh far from his parents, in the house of that terrible man on whose liver I would fain fasten and devour it. Thus would I avenge my son, who showed no cowardice when Achilles slew him, and thought neither of flight nor of avoiding battle as he stood in defense of Trojan men and Trojan women."

Then Priam said: "I would go; do not, therefore, stay me nor be as a bird of ill omen in my house, for you will not move me. Had it been some mortal man who had sent me—some prophet or priest who divines from sacrifice—I should have deemed him false and have given him no heed; but now I have heard the goddess and seen her face to face; therefore I will go and her saying shall not be in vain. If it be my fate to die at the ships of the Achaeans even so would I have it. Let Achilles slay me, if I may but first have taken my son in my arms and mourned him to my heart's comforting."

So saying he lifted the lids of his chests, and took out twelve goodly vestments. He took also twelve cloaks of single fold, twelve rugs, twelve fair mantles, and an equal number of shirts. He weighed out ten talents of gold, and brought moreover two burnished tripods, four cauldrons, and a very beautiful cup which the Thracians had given him when he had gone to them on an embassy. It was very precious, but he grudged not even this, so eager was he to ransom the body of his son. Then he chased all the Trojans from the court and rebuked them with words of anger. "Out," he cried, "shame and disgrace to me that you are! Have you no grief in your own homes that you are come to plague me here? Is it a small thing, think you, that the son of Cronus has sent this sorrow upon me, to lose the bravest of my sons? Nay, you shall prove it in person, for now he is gone the Achaeans will have easier work in killing you. As for me, let me go down within the house of Hades, ere mine eyes behold the sacking and wasting of the city."

He drove the men away with his staff, and they went forth as the old man sped them. Then he called to his sons, upbraiding Helenus, Paris, noble Agathon, Pammon, Antiphonus, Polites of the loud battle cry, Deïphobus, Hippothoüs, and Dius. These nine did the old man call near him. "Come to me at once," he cried, "worthless sons who do me shame! Would that you had all been killed at the ships rather than Hector. Miserable man that I am, I have had the bravest sons in all Troy—noble Mestor, Troïlus, the dauntless charioteer, and Hector who was a god among men, so that one would have thought he was son to an immortal—yet there is not one of them left. Ares has slain them and those of whom I am ashamed are alone left me. Liars, and light of foot, heroes of the dance, robbers of lambs and kids from your own people, why do you not get a wagon ready for me at once, and put all these things upon it that I may set out on my way?"

Thus did he speak, and they feared the rebuke of their father. They brought out a strong mule-wagon, newly made, and set the body of the wagon fast on its bed. They took the mule-yoke from the peg on which it hung, a yoke of boxwood with a knob on the top of it and rings for the reins to go through. Then they brought a yoke-band eleven cubits long, to bind the yoke to the pole. They bound it on at the far end of the pole and put the ring over the upright pin, making it fast with three turns of the band on either side the knob and bending the thong of the yoke beneath it. This done, they brought from the store-chamber the rich ransom that was to purchase the body of Hector, and they set it all orderly on the wagon. Then they yoked the strong harness-mules which the Mysians had on a time given as a goodly present to Priam; but for Priam himself they yoked horses which the old king had bred, and kept for his own use.

Thus heedfully did Priam and his servant see to the yoking of their cars at the palace. Then Hecuba came to them all sorrowful, with a golden goblet of wine in her right hand, that they might make a drink offering before they set out. She stood in front of the horses and said: 'Take this, make a drink offering to father Zeus, and since you are minded to go to the ships in spite of me, pray that you may come safely back from the hands of your enemies. Pray to the son of Cronus, lord of the whirlwind, who sits on Ida and looks down over all Troy, pray him to send his swift messenger on your right hand, the bird of omen which is strongest and most dear to him of all birds, that you may see it with your own eyes and trust it as you go forth to the ships of the Danaans. If all-seeing Zeus will not send you this messenger, however set upon it you may be, I would not have you go to the ships of the Argives."

And Priam answered, "Wife, I will do as you desire me; it is well to lift hands in prayer to Zeus, if so be he may have mercy upon me."

With this the old man bade the servingwoman pour pure water over his hands, and the woman came, bearing the water in a bowl. He washed his hands and took the cup from his wife; then he made the drink offering and prayed, standing in the middle of the courtyard and turning his eyes to heaven. "Father Zeus," he said, "that rulest from Ida, most glorious and most great, grant that I may be received kindly and compassionately in the tents of Achilles; and send your swift messenger upon my right hand, the bird of omen which is strongest and most dear to you of all birds, that I may see it with my own eyes and trust it as I go forth to the ships of the Danaans."

So did he pray, and Zeus, the lord of counsel, heard his prayer. Forthwith he sent an eagle, the most unerring portent of all birds that fly, the dusky hunter that men also call the Black Eagle. His wings were spread abroad on either side as wide as the well-made and well-bolted door of a rich man's chamber. He came to them flying over the city upon their right hands, and when they saw him they were glad and their hearts took comfort within them. The old man made haste to mount his chariot, and drove out through the inner gateway and under the echoing gatehouse of the outer court. Before him went the mules drawing the four-wheeled wagon, and driven by wise Idaeus; behind these were the horses, which the old man lashed with his whip and drove swiftly through the city, while his friends followed after, wailing and lamenting for him as though he were on his road to death. As soon as they had come down from the city and had reached the plain, his sons and sons-in-law who had followed him went back to Ilium.

But Priam and Idaeus as they showed out upon the plain did not escape the ken of all-seeing Zeus, who looked down upon the old man and pitied him; then he spoke to his son Hermes and said, "Hermes, for it is you who are the most disposed to escort men on their way, and to hear those whom you will hear, go, and so conduct Priam to the ships of the Achaeans that no other of the Danaans shall see him nor take note of him until he reach the son of Peleus."

Thus he spoke and Hermes, guide and guardian, slayer of Argus, did as he was told. Forthwith he bound on his glittering golden sandals with which he could fly like the wind over land and sea; he took the wand with which he seals men's eyes in sleep, or wakes them just as he pleases, and flew holding it in his hand till he came to Troy and to the Hellespont. To look at, he was like a young man of noble birth in the heyday of his youth and beauty with the down just coming upon his face.

Now when Priam and Idaeus had driven past the great tomb of Ilus, they stayed their mules and horses that they might drink in the river, for the shades of night were falling; when, therefore, Idaeus saw Hermes standing near them he said to Priam: "Take heed, descendant of Dardanus; here is matter which demands consideration. I see a man who I think will presently fall upon us. Let us fly with our horses, or at least embrace his knees and implore him to take compassion upon us."

When he heard this the old man's heart failed him, and he was in great fear. He stayed where he was as one dazed, and the hair stood on end over his whole body; but the bringer of good luck came up to him and took him by the hand, saying: "Whither, father, are you thus driving your mules and horses in the dead of night when other men are asleep? Are you not afraid of the fierce Achaeans who are hard by you, so cruel and relentless? Should some one of them see you bearing so much treasure through the darkness of the flying night, what would not your state then be? You are no longer young, and he who is with you is too old to protect you from those who would attack you. For myself, I will do you no harm, and I will defend you from anyone else, for you remind me of my own father."

And Priam answered: "It is indeed as you say, my dear son. Nevertheless, some god has held his hand over me, in that he has sent such a wayfarer as yourself to meet me so opportunely; you are so comely in mien and figure, and your judgment is so excellent that you must come of blessed parents."

Then said the slayer of Argus, guide and guardian: "Sir, all that you have said is right; but tell me and tell me true, are you taking this rich treasure to send it to a foreign people where it may be safe, or are you all leaving strong Ilium in dismay now that your son has fallen who was the bravest man among you and was never lacking in battle with the Achaeans?"

And Priam said: "Who are you, my friend, and who are your parents, that you speak so truly about the fate of my unhappy son?"

The slayer of Argus, guide and guardian, answered him: "Sir, you would prove me, that you question me about noble Hector. Many a time have I set eyes upon him in battle when he was driving the Argives to their ships and putting them to the sword. We stood still and marveled, for Achilles in his anger with the son of Atreus suffered us not to fight. I am his squire and came with him in the same ship. I am a Myrmidon, and my father's name is Polyctor; he is a rich man and about as old as you are; he has six sons besides myself, and I am the seventh. We cast lots, and it fell upon me to sail hither with Achilles. I am now come from the ships on to the plain, for with daybreak the Achaeans will set battle in array about the city. They chafe at doing nothing, and are so eager that their princes cannot hold them back."

Then answered Priam: "If you are indeed the squire of Achilles, son of Peleus, tell me now the whole truth. Is my son still at the ships, or has Achilles hewn him limb from limb and given him to his hounds?"

"Sir," replied the slayer of Argus, guide and guardian, "neither hounds nor vultures have yet devoured him. He is still just lying at the tents by the ship of Achilles, and though it is now twelve days that he has lain there, his flesh is not wasted nor have the worms eaten him, although they feed on warriors. At daybreak Achilles drags him cruelly round the sepulcher of his dear comrade, but it does him no hurt. You should come yourself and see how he lies fresh as dew, with the blood all washed away, and his wounds every one of them closed though many pierced him with their spears. Such care have the blessed gods taken of your brave son, for he was dear to them beyond all measure."

The old man was comforted as he heard him and said: "My son, see what a good thing it is to have made due offerings to the immortals; for, as sure as that he was born, my son never forgot the gods that hold Olympus, and now they requite it to him even in death. Accept, therefore, at my hands this goodly chalice. Guard me and with heaven's help guide me till I come to the tent of the son of Peleus."

Then answered the slayer of Argus, guide and guardian: "Sir, you are tempting me and playing upon my youth, but you shall not move me, for you are offering me presents without the knowledge of Achilles whom I fear and hold it great guiltiness to defraud, lest some evil presently befall me; but as your guide I would go with you even to Argos itself, and would guard you so carefully whether by sea or land that no one should attack you through making light of him who was with you."

The bringer of good luck then sprang on to the chariot, and seizing the whip and reins he breathed fresh spirit into the mules and horses. When they reached the trench and the wall that was before the ships, those who were on guard had just been getting their suppers, and the slayer of Argus threw them all into a deep sleep. Then he drew back the bolts to open the gates, and took Priam inside with the treasure he had upon his wagon. Ere long they came to the lofty dwelling of the son of Peleus for which the Myrmidons had cut pine and which they had built for their king. When they had built it they thatched it with coarse tussock-grass which they had mown out on the plain, and all round it they made a large courtyard, which was fenced with stakes set close together. The gate was barred with a single bolt of pine which it took three men to force into its place, and three to draw back so as to open the gate, but Achilles could draw it by himself. Hermes opened the gate for the old man, and brought in the treasure that he was taking with him for the son of Peleus. Then he sprang from the chariot on to the ground and said: "Sir, it is I, immortal Hermes, that am come with you, for my father sent me to escort you. I will now leave you, and will not enter into the presence of Achilles, for it might anger him that a god should befriend mortal men thus openly. Go you within, and embrace the knees of the son of Peleus. Beseech him by his father, his lovely mother, and his son; thus you may move him."

With these words Hermes went back to high Olympus. Priam sprang from his chariot to the ground, leaving Idaeus where he was, in charge of the mules and horses. The old man went straight into the house where Achilles, loved of the gods, was sitting. There he found him with his men seated at a distance from him: only two, the hero Automedon, and Alcimus of the race of Ares, were busy in attendance about his person, for he had but just done eating and drinking, and the table was still there. King Priam entered without their seeing him, and going right up to Achilles he clasped his knees and kissed the dread murderous hands that had slain so many of his sons.

As when some cruel spite has befallen a man that he should have killed someone in his own country, and must fly to a great man's protection in a land of strangers, and all marvel who see him, even so did Achilles marvel as he beheld Priam. The others looked one to another and marveled also, but Priam besought Achilles, saying, "Think of your father, O Achilles like unto the gods, who is such even as I am, on the sad threshold of old age. It may be that those who dwell near him harass him, and there is none to keep war and ruin from him. Yet when he hears of you as being still alive, he is glad, and his days are full of hope that he shall see his dear son come home to him from Troy; but I, wretched man that I am, had the bravest in all Troy for my sons, and there is not one of them left. I had fifty sons when the Achaeans came here; nineteen of them were from a single womb, and the others were borne to me by the women of my household. The greater part of them has fierce Ares laid low, and Hector, him who was alone left, him who was the guardian of our city and ourselves, him have you lately slain. Therefore I am now come to the ships of the Achaeans to ransom his body from you with a great ransom. Fear, O Achilles, the wrath of heaven! Think on your own father and have compassion upon me, who am the more pitiable, for I have steeled myself as no man has ever yet steeled himself before me, and have raised to my lips the hand of him who slew my son."

Thus spoke Priam, and the heart of Achilles yearned as he bethought him of his father. He took the old man's hand and moved him gently away. The two wept bitterly—Priam, as he lay at Achilles's feet, weeping for Hector, and Achilles, now for his father and now for Patroclus, till the house was filled with their lamentation. But when Achilles was now sated with grief and had unburdened the bitterness of his sorrow, he left his seat and raised the old man by the hand, in pity for his white hair and beard. Then he said: "Unhappy man, you have indeed been greatly daring. How could you venture to come alone to the ships of the Achaeans and enter the presence of him who has slain so many of your brave sons? You must have iron courage. Sit now upon this seat, and for all our grief we will hide our sorrows in our hearts, for weeping will not avail us. The immortals know no care, yet the lot they spin for man is full of sorrow. On the floor of Zeus's palace there stand two urns, the one filled with evil gifts, and the other with good ones. He for whom Zeus, the lord of thunder, mixes the gifts he sends, will meet now with good and now with evil fortune; but he to whom Zeus sends none but evil gifts will be pointed at by the finger of scorn, the hand of famine will pursue him to the ends of the world, and he will go up and down the face of the earth, respected neither by gods nor men. Even so did it befall Peleus; the gods endowed him with all good things from his birth upwards, for he reigned over the Myrmidons, excelling all men in prosperity and wealth, and mortal though he was they gave him a goddess for his bride. But even on him too did heaven send misfortune, for there is no race of royal children born to him in his house, save one son who is doomed to die all untimely; nor may I take care of him now that he is growing old, for I must stay here at Troy to be the bane of you and of your children.

"And you too, O Priam, I have heard that you were aforetime happy. They say that in wealth and plenitude of offspring you surpassed all that is in Lesbos, the realm of Makar to the northward, Phrygia that is more inland, and those that dwell upon the great Hellespont; but from the day when the dwellers in heaven sent this evil upon you, war and slaughter have been about your city continually. Bear up against it, and let there be some intervals in your sorrow. Mourn as you may for your brave son, you will take nothing by it. You cannot raise him from the dead; ere you do so yet another sorrow shall befall you."

And Priam answered: "O king, bid me not be seated, while Hector is still lying uncared for in your tents, but accept the great ransom which I have brought you, and give him to me at once that I may look upon him. May you prosper with the ransom and reach your own land in safety, seeing that you have suffered me to live and to look upon the light of the sun."

Achilles looked at him sternly and said: "Vex me, sir, no longer; I am of myself minded to give up the body of Hector. My mother, daughter of the old man of the sea, came to me from Zeus to bid me deliver it to you. Moreover, I know well, O Priam, and you cannot hide it, that some god has brought you to the ships of the Achaeans, for else, no man however strong and in his prime would dare to come to our host. He could neither pass our guard unseen, nor draw the bolt of my gates thus easily. Therefore, provoke me no further, lest I sin against the word of Zeus, and suffer you not, suppliant though you are, within my tents."

The old man feared him and obeyed. Then the son of Peleus sprang like a lion through the door of his house, not alone, but with him went his two squires, Automedon and Alcimus, who were closer to him than any others of his comrades now that Patroclus was no more. These unyoked the horses and mules, and bade Priam's herald and attendant be seated within the house. They lifted the ransom for Hector's body from the wagon, but they left two mantles and a goodly shirt, that Achilles might wrap the body in them when he gave it to be taken home. Then he called to his servants and ordered them to wash the body and anoint it, but he first took it to a place where Priam should not see it, lest if he did so, he should break out in the bitterness of his grief, and enrage Achilles, who might then kill him and sin against the word of Zeus. When the servants had washed the body and anointed it, and had wrapped it in a fair shirt and mantle, Achilles himself lifted it onto a bier, and he and his men then laid it on the wagon. He cried aloud as he did so and called on the name of his dear comrade. "Be not angry with me, Patroclus," he said, "if you hear even in the house of Hades that I have given Hector to his father for a ransom. It has been no unworthy one, and I will share it equitably with you."

Achilles then went back into the tent and took his place on the richly inlaid seat from which he had risen, by the wall that was at right angles to the one against which Priam was sitting. "Sir," he said, "your son is now laid upon his bier and is ransomed according to your desire. You shall look upon him when you take him away at daybreak; for the present let us prepare our supper. Even lovely Niobe had to think about eating, though her twelve children—six daughters and six lusty sons—had been all slain in her house. Apollo killed the sons with arrows from his silver bow, to punish Niobe, and Artemis slew the daughters, because Niobe had vaunted herself against Leto. She said Leto had borne two children only, whereas she had herself borne many—whereon the two killed the many. Nine days did they lie weltering, and there was none to bury them, for the son of Cronus turned the people into stone; but on the tenth day the gods in heaven themselves buried them, and Niobe then took food, being worn out with weeping. They say that somewhere among the rocks on the mountain pastures of Sipylus, where the nymphs live that haunt the river Acheloüs, there, they say, she lives in stone and still nurses the sorrows sent upon her by the hand of heaven. Therefore, noble sir, let us two now take food; you can weep for your dear son hereafter as you are bearing him back to Ilium—and many a tear will he cost you."

With this Achilles sprang from his seat and killed a sheep of silvery whiteness, which his followers skinned and made ready all in due order. They cut the meat carefully up into smaller pieces, spitted them, and drew them off again when they were well-roasted. Automedon brought bread in fair baskets and served it round the table, while Achilles dealt out the meat, and they laid their hands on the good things that were before them. As soon as they had had enough to eat and drink, Priam, descendant of Dardanus, marveled at the strength and beauty of Achilles for he was as a god to see, and Achilles marveled at Priam as he listened to him and looked upon his noble presence. When they had gazed their fill Priam spoke first. "And now, O king," he said, "take me to my couch that we may lie down and enjoy the blessed boon of sleep. Never once have my eyes been closed from the day your hands took the life of my son; I have groveled without ceasing in the mire of my stableyard, making moan and brooding over my countless sorrows. Now, moreover, I have eaten bread and drunk wine; hitherto I have tasted nothing."

As he spoke Achilles told his men and the womenservants to set beds in the room that was in the gatehouse, and make them with good red rugs, and spread coverlets on the top of them with woolen cloaks for Priam and Idaeus to wear. So the maids went out carrying a torch and got the two beds ready in all haste. Then Achilles said laughingly to Priam: "Dear sir, you shall lie outside, lest some counselor of those who in due course keep coming to advise with me should see you here in the darkness of the flying night, and tell it to Agamemnon. This might cause delay in the delivery of the body. And now tell me and tell me true, for how many days would you celebrate the funeral rites of noble Hector? Tell me, that I may hold aloof from war and restrain the host."

And Priam answered: "Since, then, you suffer me to bury my noble son with all due rites, do thus, Achilles, and I shall be grateful. You know how we are pent up within our city. It is far for us to fetch wood from the mountain, and the people live in fear. Nine days, therefore, will we mourn Hector in my house; on the tenth day we will bury him and there shall be a public feast in his honor; on the eleventh we will build a mound over his ashes, and on the twelfth, if there be need, we will fight."

And Achilles answered: "All, King Priam, shall be as you have said. I will stay our fighting for as long a time as you have named."

As he spoke he laid his hand on the old man's right wrist, in token that he should have no fear; thus then did Priam and his attendant sleep there in the fore court, full of thought, while Achilles lay in an inner room of the house, with fair Briseis by his side.

And now both gods and mortals were fast asleep through the livelong night, but upon Hermes alone, the bringer of good luck, sleep could take no hold for he was thinking all the time how to get King Priam away from the ships without his being seen by the strong force of sentinels. He hovered therefore over Priam's head and said: "Sir, now that Achilles has spared your life, you seem to have no fear about sleeping in the thick of your foes. You have paid a great ransom, and have received the body of your son. Were you still alive and a prisoner the sons whom you have left at home would have to give three times as much to free you; and so it would be if Agamemnon and the other Achaeans were to know of your being here."

When he heard this the old man was afraid and roused his servant. Hermes then yoked their horses and mules and drove them quickly through the host so that no man perceived them. When they came to the ford of eddying Xanthus, begotten of immortal Zeus, Hermes went back to high Olympus, and dawn in robe of saffron began to break over all the land. Priam and Idaeus then drove on towards the city lamenting and making moan, and the mules drew the body of Hector. No one neither man nor woman saw them, till Cassandra, fair as golden Aphrodite standing on Pergamus, caught sight of her dear father in his chariot, and his servant that was the city's herald with him. Then she saw him that was lying upon the bier, drawn by the mules, and with a loud cry she went about the city, saying, "Come hither, Trojans, men and women, and look on Hector. If ever you rejoiced to see him coming from battle when he was alive, look now on him that was the glory of our city and all our people."

At this there was not man nor woman left in the city, so great a sorrow had possessed them. Hard by the gates they met Priam as he was bringing in the body. Hector's wife and his mother were the first to mourn him: they flew towards the wagon and laid their hands upon his head, while the crowd stood weeping round them. They would have stayed before the gates, weeping and lamenting the livelong day to the going down of the sun, had not Priam spoken to them from the chariot and said, "Make way for the mules to pass you. Afterwards, when I have taken the body home, you shall have your fill of weeping."

On this the people stood asunder and made a way for the wagon. When they had borne the body within the house they laid it upon a bed and seated minstrels round it to lead the dirge, whereon the women joined in the sad music of their lament. Foremost among them all Andromache led their wailing as she clasped the head of mighty Hector in her embrace. "Husband," she cried, "you have died young, and leave me in your house a widow. He of whom we are the ill-starred parents is still a mere child, and I fear he may not reach manhood. Ere he can do so our city will be razed and overthrown, for you who watched over it are no more—you who were its savior, the guardian of our wives and children. Our women will be carried away captives to the ships, and I among them, while you, my child, who will be with me will be put to some unseemly tasks, working for a cruel master. Or, maybe, some Achaean will hurl you (O miserable death) from our walls to avenge some brother, son, or father whom Hector slew. Many of them have indeed bitten the dust at his hands, for your father's hand in battle was no light one. Therefore do the people mourn him. You have left, O Hector, sorrow unutterable to your parents, and my own grief is greatest of all, for you did not stretch forth your arms and embrace me as you lay dying, nor say to me any words that might have lived with me in my tears night and day forevermore."

Bitterly did she weep the while, and the women joined in her lament. Hecuba in her turn took up the strains of woe. "Hector," she cried, "dearest to me of all my children! So long as you were alive the gods loved you well, and even in death they have not been utterly unmindful of you; for when Achilles took any other of my sons, he would sell him beyond the seas, to Samos Imbrus or rugged Lemnos. And when he had slain you too with his sword, many a time did he drag you round the sepulcher of his comrade—though this could not give him life—yet here you lie all fresh as dew and comely as one whom Apollo has slain with his painless shafts."

Thus did she too speak through her tears with bitter moan, and then Helen for a third time took up the strain of lamentation. "Hector," said she, "dearest of all my brothers-in-law—for I am wife to Paris who brought me hither to Troy—would that I had died ere he did so—twenty years are come and gone since I left my home and came from over the sea, but I have never heard one word of insult or unkindness from you. When another would chide with me, as it might be one of your brothers or sisters or of your brothers' wives, or my mother-in-law—for Priam was as kind to me as though he were my own father—you would rebuke and check them with words of gentleness and goodwill. Therefore my tears flow both for you and for my unhappy self, for there is no one else in Troy who is kind to me, but all shrink and shudder as they go by me."

She wept as she spoke and the vast crowd that was gathered round her joined in her lament. Then King Priam spoke to them, saying, "Bring wood, O Trojans, to the city, and fear no cunning ambush of the Argives, for Achilles when he dismissed me from the ships gave me his word that they should not attack us until the morning of the twelfth day."

Forthwith they yoked their oxen and mules and gathered together before the city. Nine days long did they bring in great heaps of wood, and on the morning of the tenth day with many tears they took brave Hector forth, laid his dead body upon the summit of the pile, and set the fire thereto. Then when the child of morning, rosy-fingered dawn, appeared on the eleventh day, the people again assembled round the pyre of mighty Hector. When they were got together, they first quenched the fire with wine wherever it was burning, and then his brothers and comrades with many a bitter tear gathered his white bones, wrapped them in soft robes of purple, and laid them in a golden urn, which they placed in a grave and covered over with large stones set close together. Then they built a barrow hurriedly over it keeping guard on every side lest the Achaeans should attack them before they had finished. When they had heaped up the barrow they went back again into the city, and being well assembled they held high feast in the house of Priam, their king.

Thus, then, did they celebrate the funeral of Hector, tamer of horses.